WELCOME TO SAINT ANGEL

WILLIAM LUVAAS

ANAPHORA LITERARY PRESS

BROWNSVILLE, TEXAS

ANAPHORA LITERARY PRESS
1898 Athens Street
Brownsville, TX 78520
https://anaphoraliterary.com

Book design by Anna Faktorovich, Ph.D.

Printed in the United States of America, United Kingdom and in Australia on acid-free paper.

Author photo by Lucinda Luvaas.

Published in 2018 by Anaphora Literary Press

Welcome to Saint Angel
William Luvaas—1st edition.

Library of Congress Control Number: 2017937186

Library Cataloging Information
Luvaas, William, 1945-, author.
    Welcome to Saint Angel / William Luvaas
    234 p. ; 9 in.
    ISBN 978-1-68114-320-0 (softcover : alk. paper)
    ISBN 978-1-68114-321-7 (hardcover : alk. paper)
    ISBN 978-1-68114-322-4 (e-book)
1. Fiction—Satire.
2. Fiction—Narrative Theme—Environmental Issues.
3. Political Science—Public Policy—Social Policy.
PN3311-3503: Literature: Prose fiction
813: American fiction in English

WELCOME TO SAINT ANGEL

WILLIAM LUVAAS

ALSO BY WILLIAM LUVAAS

Novels:
The Seductions of Natalie Bach (Little, Brown)
Going Under (Putnam)
Beneath The Coyote Hills (Spuyten Duyvil)

Story Collections:
A Working Man's Apocrypha (Univ. Oklahoma Press)
Ashes Rain Down: a story cycle (Spuyten Duyvil)

1

THE DESERT GREEN LAWN ASSOCIATION

Those of us foolish enough to grow lawns out here meet once a month at Ches and Penny Noonan's place on Two Horse Flats Road. Although I stopped growing mine years ago, I still attend meetings. The Noonan place covers half an air-conditioned acre: cathedral ceilings, walls of glass, long hallways spoking off the entry hub like a casino hotel in Palm Springs. A cactus garden out front is the only desert-friendly touch—along with Penny Noonan's all-season tan—ornamental gravels color-coordinated by the folks who did the Saint Angel Family Mortuary. The Noonan place is like a plantation in Arabia: one and a half acres of green with desert on all sides, like a Hollywood studio laid turf over the sand. Tourists plow tire tracks in molten asphalt as they pass, rubber-necking at the Noonans' McMansion: Olympic pool, palm trees, all that grass. Ireland gone west. What my ex-wife Sondra would call a "conundrum." Out here conundrum is our way of life. Life and death at loggerheads. In March, life pulls a little ahead, vernal pools fill up, and we get the wildflower bloom; death catches up by mid-May when we get our first triple-digit days.

"What we do," Ches explained at our last Christmas party, "we pump water up from deep earth and spray it on the ground. What doesn't evaporate trickles down into the sand. You can hear grass roots sipping for all they're worth."

"What's it sound like?" Esther Johnson asked.

"Why, like a kid slurping with a straw at the bottom of a glass."

Sam Jenson scowled. "Bullsquat! I been here fifty-six years, I never heard no slurping."

"You don't have any grass roots to slurp, Sam."

Sam dug a boot toe into Ches's turf. "Hell no, I don't. I'm water wise and desert smart. You won't catch me spraying no water or evaporating it off my swimming pool neither."

"Some of us have dreams," Esther said primly.

"No damn snowbird is got nothing to teach me."

"You know very well I'm not a snowbird, Sam. I live here the year 'round."

Sam tapped his forehead. "Up here!" He turned on Ches. "I'll tell you something else, Mr. King of God's Creation, they dug a well over to Hungry Man Canyon deep enough they hit peterfied wood. That's a lesson ri'chere: redwoods drank too much water and look where it got us. Waste not, want not, I say. You and your upnorther ideas is a blot on the desert."

"Doesn't seem to stop you from enjoying my pool though," Ches said.

"Our pool!" Sam barked. "You fill her with water belongs as much to me as it does to you."

Ches called to Penny who was entertaining a group of Silk Setters across the pool, snakes of light writhing across its surface. "Sam says we are running a public swimming pool here."

Penny frowned at the lot of us surrounding her husband. "Ah do believe it."

Ches firmed down the divot Sam had taken in his lawn. It's a grass-growing principle out here: entropy makes the slightest inroad and you have gophers, ground squirrels, fire ants, drought, God knows what-all trashing your lawn.

We started out as the DESERT LAWN GROWING ASSOCIA-TION: DLGA. But the Desert Links Golf Association threatened to sue us for appropriating their acronym. So we switched to the DES-ERT GRASS GROWING ASSOCIATION: DGGA, until long-hairs started leaving petitions to legalize marijuana at our county fair booth. So we changed to DESERT GREEN LAWN ASSOCIATION: DGLA. Rob and Daphne Thompson, Sam Jenson, Tinkerspoon, Mona Sahl-strom, the Littlefeather brothers (representing the *La Cienega del Dia-blo* nation), and me are some of the few members whose income is under six figures. Members in good standing, anyway.

I kept a lawn at first. Until grass woke me up mornings, screaming in anticipation of the day's heat. Some can't hear it. Dogs and black birds can. I've seen gophers emerge from their burrows at height of the racket and scamper down the county road, trying to cover their ears. When members chided me for letting my lawn die, I argued that grass remains grass in its dry state. "Half of California has sere grass. It's why we're called 'The Golden State.'" Sage Littlefeather suggested I spray paint my grass green like they do in modular estates over in Hemet.

Along with Rob and Daphne Thompson, I founded the "Honesty Faction" of the DGLA (later known as the "Dirt Faction") and challenged Ches for presidency. "They're a lot of leftover hippies, Indians, and desert rats," I overheard John Sylvester telling Ches one day. Ches stood by the pool in his swimsuit: bull-chested, his feet cod-belly white and huge (size 16 triple D); I know shoes, I worked as a shoe salesman at WalkSmart in Escondido before being excessed and moving out here. Sondra called it "my foot period." I asked Sylvester which category I fit into. "Why, I'd call you our resident-hippie-hanger-on, Sharpe," he said smugly.

"Goodness!" Clover Abernathy clasped a hand to her chest.

I lost the presidency to Ches but won a free lifetime membership for running.

Back then, no one knew what Ches did for a living. Some said dot-com stuff, others real estate development. "He's in shifty money," Sam Jenson said. "What people make without making nothing." Ches sat on the Municipal Water Board and half the boards in the county, including Western Enterprise Bank. He gave up his county supervisor post once developments started going in. Stayed just long enough to give developers the green light to hijack our way of life. Rightly, the Noonans should be over in Palm Desert among the wealthy, but Ches prefers living among "real people" here in Saint Angel.

Sam Jenson is the true item. Regular *rattus aridus*. His yard dead as long as anyone can remember, even his yucca and prickly pear look thirsty. Come winter, he twines Christmas lights in among dried honeysuckle vines on the cyclone fence out front of his place, so it looks like the honeysuckle has returned to life. Sam doesn't believe in lawns, only comes to DGLA meetings to keep us honest. His skin is mahogany brown and rough as lizard hide. He wears the same ragged khaki shorts and long-sleeved shirt year round. Ches reminds him to shower before going in the pool, believing Sam comes to get a bath. "When does the man ever see water?" But I know better. Sam comes for the free beer. He gave up on water years ago. A hardcore realist, Sam.

His vintage Airstream trailer is parked on its lonesome out Yucca Road, surrounded by what Tinkerspoon has dubbed "the finest Chevy junkyard in SoCal." Lit up like Times Square from Thanksgiving to Easter: "nine-hundred-seventy-six bulbs in six colors, half of them blinking," Sam will tell you. Not including icicle sprays dripping from salt pines and rusted car chassis. Half of Sam's Social Security check goes for replacing bulbs. Flying home nights from meetings in L.A., Ches aligns his Cessna Skylane to Sam's place.

If Sam is the self-appointed representative of sand and creosote bush—Death's own representative to the DGLA—Sage Littlefeather is the closest we have to a pure life force in the valley (along with my daughter, Finley). Saint Angel's native son. "Sam's problem is, he's standing upside down," Sage once declared. "Your desert world is all topsy turvy, like an upside-down lake where the top is dry and the bottom wet. Dig down far enough and you find slimy green water, what the Mexicans over here call '*la cienega.*' Dead water percolates up from below. It's gotta be a whole lots of life force down there to push water up through sand."

"What's dead water?" I asked him.

"Water you don't never want to drink."

"Dingblat Indian," Sam snorted.

Sage laughed and slapped his back. "Oncet, this dude here planted hisself a garden. It didn't grow good so he give it up. He's been give up ever since." Silk Set women laughed uncomfortably to hear him talk this way. I believe it worried them that Sage's people would get to admiring their grass and want to reclaim the valley for themselves. The *La Cienega del Diablo* Indians, named for malodorous sloughs hereabouts, like the one on my place.

Sage is right about the water down below: an ocean of it, fed for eons by the snow melt from the mountains. Fossil water. It tastes like time, our water. Mine, one of the few remaining wells in the valley that doesn't belong to the major ranchers and land magnates (which is to say Ches Noonan and Cal Hale and associates) or wells on the rez. "The Big Four," people call us. Sage calls us "The Big Two" and "Little Two."

It's rumored that Penny Noonan never wanted the DGLA to meet at her place. But Ches is lawn-proud and public-spirited. Figuratively speaking, he agrees with Sam: the water belongs to all of us. Used to, anyway. Penny is the type you find over in Palm Springs: a dedicated hedonist with skin dark as buffed leather. I once wandered by accident into Ches and Penny's bedroom in search of a bathroom just as she peeled off her bikini top. I stared dumbly at her silhouetted against mirrored sliding glass doors leading out to the pool, stripping nonchalantly before her unsuspecting guests who lounged about the pool beyond, her lips parted, bemused at my embarrassment.

"Excuse me, Penny. You know, that's got to be the whitest bra I ever saw," I blurted—to say something—though I plainly saw dark nipples high on her small white breasts. Penny didn't smile, skin wrinkled beside her nose. She peeled off her bikini bottom to see what I would say next. I turned and fled, recalling stories about Penny and Rob Thompson, Penny and Cal Hale. Out here, secrets are like tumbleweeds carried on a dry wind.

When I returned to the pool, Ches was saying, "Come now, Sam. What do you have against grass? If it was up to you, there'd be nothing but sand and creosote bush as far as the eye can see. Where would you get your monthly shower?"

Sam was red-faced. "You sonsabitches. We're running out of gawddamned water, we're in the worst drought in California history, we got global warming up the wazoo, and you morons want to build golf courses and artificial lakes in the desert." Winding a finger around his ear. Time to fetch him a cold brew.

"Now that's a load of cow manure." Cal Hale came striding over from the far side of the pool. If there was an argument, he was going to join in, especially when it came to water. "We got more water than we could ever use in ten thousand years. Why, we got water trickling down from the mountains and forming an ocean underfoot. We got a fresh water lake under the Mojave Desert bigger than Lake Baikal in Russia. My people mapped it out. You surprise me, Sam, buying into that global warming crap. I thought you were a realist. Not like Al Sharpe and his lot of climate alarmists." Giving me a dismissive smirk.

Esther said she didn't know what Sam was doing here anyways since he didn't believe in lawns. "We are the Desert Green Lawn Association, not the Dust Bowl from Hell Club."

Sam pointed at the bleached cow's skull mounted to the hood of his '76 Olds Cutlass parked in back—missing back doors, windshield sand-pocked, rusted body baked enamel brown. "I come as a representative of desert truth. I come to let you know you're visiting but you ain't welcome. Any time *she* wants this back—" sweeping a hand to encompass Ches's lawns, Penny in her itsy black bikini, who studied me from across the pool "—she'll open her mouth and swallow."

Who could doubt it, given sand mounded up against the retaining wall around the pool.

It all seemed innocent enough at the time. We didn't imagine what it would grow into. We looked around and thought Saint Angel is a fine and neighborly place. I smiled at Penny, who regarded me contemptuously, as if to say, "You have no claim on my nudity."

#

The desert seems impervious to change in its vast indifference, when in truth it is change's stepchild. Incessant wind and shifting sand, violent shifts in temperature, waterless but the child of water. I should know.

Ches and his partners had been buying up land around town for years under cover of various shell companies, preparing to make their move, with interest rates at their lowest in decades and land values rising. Although Ches hated the thought of change and couldn't imagine Saint Angel becoming the bedroom community he was helping to make it. He preferred Al Sharpe and Sam Jenson to the snowbird Sylvesters and Philadelphias, who, as Sam said, were "just visiting." You never knew but what Sam would come in sweaty, hands stained purple with olive juice, muttering about how cold the Noonans kept their damned house. But no stopping progress. Sam was an endangered species. Signs the DGLA had erected on the highway would have to come down, remnants of a lazy, dolce far niente time the town could no longer afford:

WELCOME TO SAINT ANGEL

9 miles east of San Jacinto
16 miles southwest of Palm Springs
87 miles due desert of L.A.
1/4 mile from Nowhere
You're not there yet, please don't blink!
Proud home of the DESERT GO-CART
INTERNATIONAL

No, the signs wouldn't do. There were fortunes to be made.

At their annual Christmas party that final year of amicability, Ches toasted DGLA members with a glass of homemade eggnog. "We're what America is all about: people of all kinds come together in neighborly good will. God bless America. God bless Saint Angel. God bless the DGLA."

"Hear hear," Esther Johnson cried. "We even have members who oppose growing lawns. We're like a poodle club whose members dislike poodles."

"We're not about green lawns, anyways," Clover Abernathy suggested. "We're about glad hearts. I call us the Desert Glad Living Association." However, Clover was uneasy of late, what with Ches planting another quarter acre of grass after four years of drought, Sam Jenson increasingly cranky, and Al Sharpe troubled about something. The poor man had raised a daughter on his own. "They say her mother was blown up in that plane over Lockerbie, Scotland," she whispered to his girlfriend, Mona Sahlstrom.

"Horse pucky," Mona said. "She didn't die in a plane crash, Sondra left him."

"Goodness."

We were suspended in a dream of amity and peace, believing the evening news was a warped fiction. Saint Angel's police chief, Charlie Haynes, had cut his staff's work hours in half for lack of anything to do. He only patrolled the streets to show off the department's shiny new cruiser. We had concluded a crime-free decade. Parking meters were so full that people had to stack coins beside them on the curb; kids with cash-flow issues borrowed quarters to buy candy bars, conscientiously paying back the loan when their allowance came in. Main Street meters were an interest-free public bank. When, occasionally, an out-of-towner robbed them, townspeople mumbled about the storm that had swept away stacks of quarters on Main Street the night before. "This place here lives in a happy state of liars' harmony," Sage Littlefeather decreed. "You got to be plain mean-spirited not to believe in it."

Al Sharpe was always the first to volunteer and the last to go home. Ches once told his wife, Penny, that, given a little ambition, Al might make something of himself. "Hmmmph," she said, recalling the afternoon Albert stood gawking at her like a clueless schoolboy. They might have balled on the bed while Ches and half the DGLA membership stood around the pool beyond tinted glass doors. Deliciously illicit. She once told Mona Sahlstrom that "Screwin' Ches is like going to a candidate's debate. Mah husband speechifies nonstop about bond issues and such, and his breath... my Lord! The four of us should hook up some time."

Mona wasn't sure she was joking.

Even after Ches and Cal Hale helped elect Tom Hernshaw to county supervisor and Hernshaw stacked the Planning Commission with his pro-development pals, including Mr. Philadelphia and John Sylvester, we were not alarmed. The Commission was long dormant. So when notices were posted about a public hearing to solicit response to **Saint Angel's Blueprint For The Future and SALCO's proposal to build a housing development in Tourmaline**, *we ignored them. Such notices had been posted for years and nothing ever happened. Generally, the Planning Commission ruled on requests to park a trailer out back of a dwelling or renovate a barn. And what was SALCO? We'd never heard of it. What blueprint for the future? Moreover, meetings were held on Tuesday mornings at 6:00 a.m. Clearly, they couldn't be taken seriously. An official notice in the Saint Angel Clarion announced a public hearing on TexHome Development Corporation's request to add 1,300 housing units on Creosote Canyon Road, near Al Sharpe's place. Sheer nonsense. So were "Proposed changes in the long range land use plan for the Saint Angel River Drainage Basin." What river? What drainage? Our river has been dry for ten thousand years. No one imagined they were hatching a plot to hijack our way of life.*

Commissioners looked out at empty bleachers in the Saint Angel High gym. Boys from the varsity basketball team, who'd come for early practice, sat against the walls hugging their knees. "It appears there are no objections," Hernshaw declared. "The motion carries unanimously." We were stunned when we learned what they were planning. Not even Tahquitz and his cruel lieutenants Whirlwind and Dust Devil had ever posed such a threat to our way of life.

Listening to the plaintive hoot of the little burrowing owl back in the canyon on Second Chance Acres, Al Sharpe's daughter Finley said, "I love that sound, it's like an angel hooting." At that moment, Al realized they were living in a dream from which no one wanted to awaken, least of all himself.

2

WHEN BLACK BIRDS RATTLE DICE

Back in their throats from high in pine trees at mouth of the canyon, we know it will be a scorcher. One-hundred-ten degrees every day for weeks now, and the earth is baked adobe hard. Roots of scrappy live oaks and tamarisks ache in its dry clutch. A woodpecker taps at a tree snag, events rattle and chafe around us like dead sycamore leaves in a Santa Ana wind, but we don't hear them. Nothing much thrives on eight inches of rainfall a year—beyond creosote bush and squaw bush and those of us with nowhere else to go.

I moved out from San Diego eleven years ago with my six-year-old daughter Finley after we lost her mother. Immediately dubbed the place "Second Chance Acres." We built Finley a treehouse sprawled across limb crotches of a giant black oak at mouth of our canyon. Maybe the biggest treehouse in California at 800 square feet. Finley and I crawled about on scaffolding like spider monkeys 30 feet up in that oak tree. Tinkerspoon and the Littlefeather brothers, Matt and Sage, and Rob and Daphne Thompson helped us build it. Rob "salvaged" lumber off building sites where he worked. Sage appeared one day with an outhouse strapped to the roof of his Olds, a crescent moon carved into the door above a sign: "Executive Suite." "Gonna look bee-you-ti-ful up there," Matt said. "Dig you a pit down below her." Finley poked Matt's gut hanging in a swollen loaf over his shorts band. "You don't put an outhouse in a tree, jerk." He hugged her head to his belly. "Why not, little girlfriend? Just gotta aim good."

Matt weighed in at maybe three-fifty; it worried me to have him on the treehouse deck. He called himself the "building inspector." "If she holds under me, she's gonna hold under anything, bro." Finley speculated how high he would bounce if he fell off. Matt regarded her stone faced. "Indians don't bounce, man." She poked his belly. "Right! I bet you'd pop."

"Be careful, little sister, you don't want a frog to eat your turd," Sage warned.

They saw my daughter as a community project. It takes a village to raise a child, especially one who has lost her mother. We didn't talk about Sondra much those first years. Occasionally, Finley would ask, "Momma died, didn't she?" as if to make sure it was still true. I always changed the subject.

Finley wanted sliding glass doors leading onto the deck. A tree-house high in tree limbs is every kid's dream. But I wondered if her mother would approve. She wanted a bathtub, but I told her plumbing was out of the question.

One day, Daphne Thompson and Sage got to arguing about Indian gaming. Our local tribe, the *La Cienega del Diablo* Indians, subtribe of the Soboba people, part of the Luiseño and Cahuilla nations, planned to build a casino on rez land west of town: five acres of slot machines. You couldn't blame them for wanting some of their own back. It must have hurt seeing spreads like Ches Noonan's on land that once belonged to your people. Daphne whipped dirty blond hair out of her eyes, bare-breasted like the rest of us. "I'm saying you're going to have an element."

"Gangsters don't worry me none," Sage said. "We been fighting white gangsters for a hundred-fifty years."

"Can't you wear a bra or something?" Matt Littlefeather hoisted his tan, pendulous man breasts and nodded at Daphne's. Daph hoisted hers in reply. "Can't you wear a bra or something?" We nearly fell off the deck, laughing. Rob Thompson shouted and threw his hammer at a writhing ball of snakes that had dropped from a branch above; they came side-winding across the wooden deck towards him, hissing heads and rattling tails lashing out in all directions, seemingly motored by a single brain. Matt threw Tinkerspoon's filthy yellow Purdue sweatshirt over that fangy bundle, remarkably fast for such a big man, tied it up in a neat package, and dropped it off the deck. He slapped Rob's back. "Dude about crapped his shorts over here." The deck quaked with his laughter. Matt climbed down and stood over that writhing bundle, grinning up at us. "Grandfather says, 'Honor the snake and let him go on his way.' I say, 'Banzai the mothers!'" He leapt up and down atop the sweat-shirted bundle until blood leaked through the weave. "Hey, that's my shirt, dude," Tinkerspoon protested.

Sage sprinkled snake blood around the base of that oak tree, claiming it would keep away rats, snakes, and all forms of calamity. But, in truth, calamity has no more respect for rattlers than it has for us.

After Sondra disappeared, I pledged to be both mother and father to my daughter. When she was afraid to sleep alone in the treehouse as a kid, I slept on the rug beside her bed like a loyal dog. Guided her down the ladder in the dark when she had to pee and stood coyote watch—before inventing my "remote control flusher," which permitted her to use the outhouse the Littlefeathers had mounted on the treehouse deck, opening the crapper cover thirty feet below by remote control lever. One of my many inventions which had no practical use beyond Second Chance Acres. To be sure, hers was an eccentric upbringing. I hoped Finley might find some benefit in it since she hoped to be a writer. I often read her stories while sitting inside a huge refrigerator packing box with a window cut in front like a TV screen, which we dubbed "the world's largest cordless television set."

Mona says I blame myself for Sondra's disappearance. "That's ridiculous. It's not like she planned it, you know, dying in a plane crash. I certainly didn't."

She eyed me dubiously. "Skipping off and leaving you to raise a child on your own."

"There's no evidence that Sondra 'skipped off.' Absolutely none."

"That's what you keep telling me."

Nothing subtle about Mona. Plain-spoken and boisterous in lovemaking, her shouts echoing down the canyon. Townsfolk are scandalized by her freethinking. A little intimidated when they come in to talk to her at the bank about arranging a loan. Half the men in Saint Angel want in her pants, the other half want her out of town, afraid her freethinking will infect their wives.

Finley's brow would occlude at mention of her mom, she'd drop into deep brooding, and finally ask, "Did she really die?" Perhaps infected with Mona's skepticism. She was the closest Finley had to a mother. There is some existential truth to Mona's claim that I blame myself. I knew when Sondra got on that plane to Hawaii years ago that I'd never see her again. Knew with stunning certainty. I tried to convince her not to go. But couldn't stop her from leaving us.

#

Saint Angel is not my formal name as you will find it on the map, but I prefer it. In 1864, J. Mayberry Haynes stood up on the mountain with his party of Indian scouts and San Francisco entrepreneurs and declared,

"*What you see below us, boys, is the Valley of Angels.*" *He christened me Santa Rosa de Los Angeles. Indians in the rancho days, watching their horses sicken and die after drinking from my black sloughs, named me "La Cienega del Diablo." Devil's Swamp. Sam Jenson calls me Saint Ain't. By whatever name, I am a high desert town—and the valley wherein it lies—of 12,000 souls (at story's outset), nearly 50,000 (at mid-point), diminished to 8,000 at the end. All within the space of two hectic years.*

Despite my name, I don't believe in angels or the pious sentimentality attendant to them. That gaudy display in the window of Saint Angel Bridals, for instance, featuring a fat-cheeked mannequin in a lacy bridal veil and white gown with six-foot wings sprouting out of her shoulder blades, covered in swan feathers yellowed with age. Winky Hale collects angels: Barbie dolls with dove's wings glued to their backs, a Folksengill she'd purchased in Oslo decked out in teal feathers that look like iridescent fish scales: a Norse flying fish. Winky regularly informs Al Sharpe of her latest encounter with angels. One hovered protectively over her car the last time she drove to L.A. "I believe she saved my life." "From what?" Al asked. "Oh, you know, those people!" She once rubbed Al's shoulder blades through his sweatshirt and stepped abruptly away when they heaved under her fingertips. "Those aren't bones, Albert," she cried, awestruck, "they're wings that haven't sprouted yet." Her husband, Cal, thought she was a little in love—not so much with Albert but some angelic conception of him. She talked nonstop about angels while he watched pro football games; he turned up the volume loud enough so that he couldn't hear her.

Once long ago, Matt and Sage Littlefeather's great-great-grandfather Lubo, who was no angel but eaten up by hatred for white men who had stolen the rich valley and pushed his people into barren hills, sniffed the air after Tahquitz released a pungent grumble from his bowels. "When the mountain farts," Grandfather Lubo said, "the people suffer black dreams." That night he dreamt of square structures unlike the brush kishes his people built, lined up in perfect rows as far as the eye could see, like nothing that had ever existed before on earth, filling the valley below. Shiny beetles scurried over black tracks between them, like the black stink beetles that raise their asses in the air and spray toadstool gas at their assailants. "This is what becomes of people after Takeetz eats their souls." He slapped the side of his head with the palm of a hand to dislodge the vision.

Geologists say I was tortured to birth by faulting and uplifting, the bump and grind of tectonic plates, like some brutal C-section. I remain precariously perched atop the San Jacinto Fault on unstable soil and could be pulled to pieces at any time. We learn to live with our demons. Grumbling old Tahquitz, for instance, god of thundering bowels and bad temper, who watches disconsolately as events unfold in the valley below him, knowing the souls of these newcomers are too thin to nourish him. We have made peace of sorts, my old enemy and I. He shakes his fist at the newcomers and bowls boulders down canyons. Their cannonades echo across the valley. Beware an old man's wrath and a greedy man's scheming.

Ches Noonan's breath has gone foul as swamp gas. He and his allies look west to suburbs spreading inland from the coast and insist, "There's no stopping progress." While Al Sharpe and his allies say progress is what they came here to escape. Looking west to SoCal's vast population centers, Ches and Cal Hale claim, "This is what we will become." Looking east to the desert, Al Sharpe and his lot insist, "This is what we are." They have begun to pull me apart. No more amicable DGLA meetings at the Noonans' place on Two Horse Flats Road, folks getting soused and leaping in the pool buck naked. Sam Jenson shaking his fist at them, "Fools. Life ain't a gawddamn party."

There were ominous signs, if anyone was paying attention: officious notices posted on telephone poles, secret meetings in the high school gym, wells gone brackish. "No one wants to move out here," Daphne Thompson insisted. There were personal signs, too: Penny Noonan, born and raised in Riverside County, adopted a tidewater drawl as if wishing to expand her horizons. Al Sharpe's daughter, Finley, asked her father's permission to move to the coast to live with her friend Patsy K Jones and attend Carlsbad High. "I'll miss you, Dad, but I can't stay here and go to Braindead High." Al was heartbroken but knew she was right. Mona Sahlstrom confessed to Father Flannagan down at Our Lady of the Angels: "I want to be with Albert; I practically raised his daughter." It astonished her to hear herself confessing this since she was quite content living on her own.

"The girl whose mother abandoned her? Is he Catholic, my daughter?"

"What in fuck's name has that got to do with anything?" Seeing the scandalized hole of Father Flannagan's mouth in shadows beyond the screen, Mona marveled that he was still shocked by her vulgarities after all these years. "Albert's a good man and a faithful atheist," she said. "More devout than most."

Rob Thompson, that irreverently devout hell-raiser, suddenly found Jesus, and the weather betrayed its temperate SoCal faith and went berserk. Rain in July! Below zero weather in March! Sure, we were all happy to have the rain, but not the mud slides that came with it. Soon, mysterious men in white vans would begin trailing Al Sharpe, Daphne Thompson, and the others like paparazzi. Ominous white powder would appear around well heads in people's pump houses. Everywhere the rick-et-ty-rat-a-tat-tat staccato artillery of hammers would trespass the valley's quiet, supplanting white-headed wood- peckers whocking at beetle-infested pines. Black sloughs would spring up. "When Grandfather Earth gets angry, everything goes to hell," Sage Littlefeather decreed.

Revolution was in the air. What is more revolutionary in America than opposition to progress, growth, the promise of Fannie Maes? "I can't understand these people," John Sylvester complained. "You announce a fine good thing—prosperity—and they act like they've been mugged." Ches Noonan chuckled. "Oh, don't judge them too harshly, John. They aren't as bullish on growth as we are. It requires a certain vision." Our hero will be tested, of course. We will see what his heart is made of. My heart will be tested, too. My patience. Until, aching and sciatic from the strain of earthmovers laboring over my spine like inept masseurs, I must look to my old enemy Tahquitz for succor. It is never wise to seek help from the forces of destruction. But what choice?

3

SECOND CHANCES

Finley's mother and I disagreed about what to name her, as we did about most everything. I chose Finley from Philip Wylie's novel *Finnley Wren*, inspired by his line about humans being the only animal conscious that we will die.

"So what's the point?" Sondra asked. "You want her to be phobic about dying?"

"No, I want her to be conscious she is alive. Few people are. We can't keep calling her Poopy Pie, you know, or 'Baby Doe Sharpe,' like on her birth certificate."

"I was thinking 'Dickinson Sharpe.'" A corner of her mouth curling up in apostrophe.

"Sounds like an unemployed private eye."

"But now," she said crisply, "I'm leaning toward 'Paisley.'"

"How about 'Paisley Dickinson Sharpe?' Or 'Paisely Dickinson Sharpe-Finley?'"

"This is no joke, Albert. Names have to wear for a lifetime." It had become her mantra, *It's no joke, Al*, as if she considered my life a comedy: bumping from job to job—truck driver, shoe salesman, burger flipper, postal temp, a stint peddling textbooks—trying my damndest to be adaptable in the new economy. Sondra couldn't decide whether I had a greater genius for finding jobs or for losing them. She was the success in the family. Assistant Professor of Sociology at UCSD. I couldn't hold down a job. Seemed to me it was bad enough having to go to a job every day of your life; having to go to the same job every day would be unbearable.

Sondra only accepted "Finley" when I refused to call her anything else. Maybe unconsciously I was already claiming our daughter for myself. That final year, my wife began calling me evenings to say she would be home late, she had a grad student conference or department meeting. "At ten p.m.?" I suspected she had a lover. Early one morning, I woke up to an empty bed. I found my wife kneeling beside

Finley's bed whispering over her. Looking hard up at me. She'd begun wearing her hair in a spiky brush cut: punk rock professor. Her features seemingly chiseled from travertine. I couldn't recall when we'd last had sex.

"What is it, Al?"

"I never know where you are anymore. Like last night."

"I told you I'd be late."

"Late? It's five a.m., Sondra."

"Early then! Give it a rest, Al, would you please?"

I picked up the peach blouse she'd tossed casually over a chair when she went in to shower and brought it to my nose. Wife-snoop. Sad-husband. An overpowering odor of perspiration rose from it. The thing is, Sondra didn't perspire. Sondra perspiring would be like Nancy Reagan reading *Ulysses*. In her briefcase, I found a tiny blue teddy bear atop a stack of student papers, and a note: "To my huggy bear. Love yah, Charlie." I knew right then I'd lost her.

Finley breathed evenly, features puddled in sleep. Her nose twitched at the touch of my lips. She giggled, a hand stirring as if to shoo away a pesky mouse. My heart swelled. "Mommy isn't mommy anymore," I whispered over her, "but it's going to be all right. I promise." I walked in on Sondra without knocking and threw the blouse at her. She stood naked on the bath mat, her hair dripping from the shower. "What's all this?" she asked, holding up the blouse.

"You tell me. Smells like you used it to wipe down a basketball team."

"You are way out of line, Al."

"Me? I'm out of line?" I turned and put my fist through the wall.

Sondra slept on the couch from then on. Fists clenched to her chest when I placed a second blanket over her and tucked it under her chin. I stood over her, trying to recall how she took her coffee or answered the phone. Could remember nothing, as though I'd been living alone all these years. Or had begun erasing her from consciousness.

She was in the kitchen making coffee. Her eyes hit mine and bounced away.

"Maybe I've disappointed you," I said. "Disappointed myself, too. Maybe *he* has more self-esteem. I can understand the attraction. Gainfully employed, no doubt. Your Charlie hasn't made a career of being excessed. Likely he has a bigger dick." Laughing caustically.

"Oh for piss sake, Albert, Charlie doesn't have a dick."

"Charlie's a woman?"

I was losing my wife to a woman. Some revelation. No real threat to our marriage, anyway, so I thought. No devoted mother would abandon her family for a spiky-haired, baggy-overalled gal Charlie. It was an illicit fantasy. A hair-up-the-ass fling. I could forgive her that. Sondra was a professor, after all; we expect eccentric behavior from professors.

She smiled at Finley who'd come in dressed for Montessori, a single straight line across her brow. "Are you arguing again? I hate it when you argue."

"Nothing serious." Sondra knelt to hug her, and I realized she would take Finley with her when she left. We'd fight for custody. It was just a matter of time. Strangely, I felt numb. Couldn't reach my anger at all in the days that followed. My wife balling a gal, so what? "You haven't gotten there yet," Sondra insisted, her sociologist's wary blue eyes sidling at me. "It's no good, Al. I've never seen you so mild and agreeable."

"You want me to start breaking things?"

"You should hear yourself laugh. Everything is breaking to pieces in your laugh."

#

Early on, after her mother disappeared, Finley refused to eat. Sitting in a Wendy's Restaurant in town, I'd urge, "C'mon, baby, just one bite of your burger, then we can go." "No!" she'd shout, bringing up alarmed eyes around us. My daughter had regressed to age three, had forgotten how to wash her face or tie her shoes. It scared me. I put her on my lap and tickled her, as I had years before. We played "smallest bite": I took a tiny bite, she took a smaller, until we got down to grasshopper nibbles...giggling spasms. It was the only way I could get her to eat at all.

"God bless you," a heavyset woman touched my arm one evening as we left. "I've watched you look after your little girl. It's a blessing to see."

"Thank you!" I said, surprised.

The woman smiled at Finley, who would smile at no one. "You'll be just fine." The woman patted her head. Finley stared rudely at her.

We were part of the great excessing that brought folks out to Saint Angel, Kingdom of the Excessed. Some by Vietnam or Desert Storm or Afghanistan, others by corporate America or unfaithful mates, by age, pov-

erty, drugs, and niggardly fate. Mona's theory is that anyone not tied down slides out to California; anyone not tied down in California slides out to the desert. We have a preacher who begins each sermon shouting, "I found my angel, praise Jesus!" I once considered each lost job a small murder of the ego. Now I realize those many jobs have served me well: Jack of all trades, master of none. It's our way of life out here.

Finley was six when we moved out, still grieving her dead mama. I bought a fixer-upper and twenty acres off Creosote Canyon Road on my wife's' death-benefit settlement. Our land extended a quarter mile back into a box canyon surrounded three sides by rez land on the mesas above. Silver cottonwood leaves shivered on Santa Ana winds that entered the canyon blistering hot but cooled in its shaded turnings as in a Spanish arcade. Mesquite, live oaks and lazy sycamores four feet in diameter at the canyon's mouth. Farther in, stately Washingtonia Palms reached to the top of canyon walls. A spice of pepperwood, sage, and Ceanothus on the air. Ground-squirrel holes pocked the canyon's floor, amidst sand verbena, trumpet-flowered Datura, and creeping puncture weed, whose tiny cruel thorn balls our pig Wallers considered a delicacy—ultimate fiber food. Nearer the entrance, prickly pear, barrel, and spiked cholla cactuses clung to eroded mudstone walls, and rangy ocotillos took root in crevices. At the canyon's terminus, weather-polished granite and sandstone walls narrowed and rose precipitously, banded with streaks of dark shale. Water leaked out of the walls, and fat-leaved succulents covered the ground. Clover Abernathy, who listed the property, considered me crazy for valuing such a feature. But Finley was delighted: "Our very own Grand Canyon." I thought it the Garden of Eden.

What we called "the black slough," our very own cienega, festered near the county road. We had a sweet water well fed by snowmelt from the mountains. Sage Littlefeather says an artesian spring once flowed out of sandstone at rear of the canyon; his great uncle used to live there.

"You asking for it back, Sage?"

"Not yet. You Anglos spend half your time protecting what don't rightly belong to you. You always want to take my lane on the freeway."

"You Indians can't stick to one lane."

"That isn't greed, brother. That's flat enjoyment."

The original farmhouse up front was tumbledown: floor joists shot through with termites and the roof with dry rot; water trickled out of the taps rust red, and sewage emptied into the crawlspace under the house through a four-inch effluent. It stank to high heaven. No septic tank.

Finley and I slept in a tent those first three months, while I salvaged what I could from the house and redid the roof and interior of an adobe cottage with two-foot-thick walls built by some early mestizo squatter far back off the road. I christened the place "Second Chance Acres."

"Second chance for what, Daddy?"

"For doing it right this time. To be self employed and avoid relationships where I'm considered comic relief, to love you as much as two people combined. What's your second chance?" I asked her.

"For Mommy to be back in the airplane and get a second chance to come home."

I wondered if she'd already had that chance and not taken it. I promised to tell her more about her mama when she turned seventeen. "Why seventeen?" she asked. "Because it's older than sixteen," I said solemnly.

Rob Thompson suggested I grow weed back in the canyon. Tempting, but not how I wanted to begin my second chance. A fine canyon, anyway, from which to launch a homespun revolution.

#

You can't be too past-occupied when the present is brewing around you like some deadly decoction from a child's chemistry set. I went out to the garden one day near the slough and found tomato plants missing. Some damned possum or coon had made off with them. Then, before my eyes, an eggplant laden with laquer-skinned fruit disappeared underground with a small bloop. Sonny, the skinniest old man in California, ran past on the county road just then and waved a toothpick-thin arm at me. His limbs and shoulders covered with faded tattoos from his Navy years. Running along on chicken legs, head craning forward, bald as a grape, he seemed an apparition. Many people didn't notice him. Sonny ran through their reality as if through a dark tunnel.

"Goddamn gophers got my tomato plants, Sonny," I yelled.

"Dynamite works best," he called back. Crazy old coot. Just then a breath of steam rose from that eggplant hole. When I stepped through the gate into the garden, my boot sank in to the ankle. When I tried to extract the foot, my other leg sank in to the knee. I knew that the black soil began steaming when you dug down two feet, releasing a methane odor that smelled like cow shit. "Pure compost," Sage said, "richest soil in the valley. But you gotta watch out! Mud People will swallow you and turn you into swamp shit." They had seized my legs and were slowly sucking me down; I caught a fence post and tugged with all my might, but made no progress against suction which had pulled the boots off my feet. "Help, Sonny!" I cried. Could just make him out running heedlessly on, Walkman headset over his ears, bald head swaying side to side.

"SONNY..."

No use. My sweaty hands lost their grip on the post. I fingernail clawed at rock-hard clay beyond the garden, sunk in now to the crotch. Panicked, I shouted, not from my mouth but inside my head. Sonny's headset popped off; he spun on a heel and headed back for me at a run, skinny arms flailing, eyes wide. "That's one mean-ass gopher." Standing over me in his puffy running trunks like Mahatma Gandhi in a diaper, he spit into his palms. What good could a 98-pound old man do against Mud People who were dragging me under? The swamp contracted around me like I'd been sucked into the gullet of a grouper. It would feast. Sonny spread his feet wide, firmed his toes in the hardpack, and wriggled his bony ass side to side. Then caught my hands in his. Slam! Face, mouth, and eye slits grimacing with effort, he pulled me out of there with a single tug, falling backwards on solid earth. Me atop him. Hungry yellow steam rose from the hole I'd left in the muck.

"How'd you do that?" we both asked at once—me meaning his feat of strength, Sonny meaning the shout I'd accomplished inside his head.

#

Scraping mud off my knees after that near-planting in my garden, I brought fingers to my nose. And retched. Smelled like the putrefied entrails of creatures that had wallowed in the great inland sea covering this region eons ago, which had seeped underground to form the Ancient Salt Sea deep below. Fresh water from the mountains floats atop it in the Saint Angel Aquifer. "Use up too much fresh and the salt will rise again," Sam Jenson warned. Perhaps we'd already done that, watering lawns and brushing our teeth. The Ancient Salt Sea was rising. The greenish-brown sludge on my fingers seemed proof of it.

Not the first sign something was amiss, but I didn't know how to read the others. The reemergence of Pissing Springs at back of the canyon, for instance, burbling out of clefts in the rock. When I took Sage back to show him, he rubbed greasy water between his fingers and brought them to his nose, taking small sampling sniffs like a dog does, forehead wrinkling. "That's old old water. Bad water! That goes way back before the Ancient Ones." Shaking his head. "Dead water!" I rubbed some between my fingers: slimy as the Dead Sea with its mercury and potassium. I touched fingers to my lips, and Sage knocked them away. "That's rotted blood right there, brother, animal blood that trickled into the earth's stomach. That'll make you good and sick."

"Plain old water, you ask me. Maybe a bit greasy but crystal clear."

Sage laughed. "Do you see a man's bones before he dies? That's long time dead, all the color bleached out."

Sure enough, nothing grew around Pissing Springs but black mold. Flies swarmed. It stank like a subway urinal back there.

The housing developments going in down near Tourmaline off the freeway were another sign. Townhouses crowded closely together behind cinder-block walls; people moving out from L.A. suburbs to the new outer ring, commuting two hours to work each way. Surely we were safe. No one in their right mind would drive out another half hour to Saint Angel, so I thought.

"You smelled your water lately?" Sam asked every time I saw him. "Listen up, gringo," Sage insisted. "A man smart as you ought to listen." Listen to what? The gurgling black slough on Second Chance Acres that swallowed everything that trespassed on it? Filling the air with bog breath so foul it obscured the smell of cow shit from dairies out near Mystic Lake.

I wore my white linen jacket to the annual DGLA benefit dinner at the Noonans'. Somewhat yellowed and worn at the elbows, but crisply pressed in the new "pressing closet" I'd invented for Finley's seventeenth birthday. I wanted to try it out. Steam was forced through holes in flexible copper plates that pressed fabric against a heated mannequin-like frame when you pulled a lever. I was delighted with the little hiss it made bearing down on the cloth. But not pleased to see heating coils had scorched the lapels of my jacket. I'd have to tweak that. These things always required tweaking. I wore the jacket anyway. As we walked along the breezeway leading to Ches's front door, Mona seized my elbow and steered me out through an archway behind a palmetto. "You can't wear that tatty thing in there, Albert. It's scorched... unless that's dirt?"

"Nicely pressed though, isn't it?"

"Sometimes I don't know whether you have a screw loose or you're dim-witted, Al Sharpe. Take off that jacket. And the idiot tie."

"I love this tie. Finley made it for me. You encouraged her."

For a time those two were into hand painting neckties with earth pigments from Second Chance Acres, selling them at a shop in Saint Angel. This one was six inches wide at the base; orange monkeys frolicked across a purple background, hanging from each other's tails.

Mona wore a wrap dress, snug at the hips, with a plunging neckline: all that creamy cleavage. A stunningly beautiful woman when she chose to be. But we weren't doing sex. I couldn't say why. She whistled Ches's gardener, Pablo Ortiz, over from parking cars, two fingers in her mouth like a boy at a baseball game. Pablo, with his John Deere lawn tractor and attachments, was architect of all that green lawn. He fretted over the place. A weed could launch him into a temper tantrum. I'd once seen him lying on his belly threading dead vines out of ground ivy with a pair of tweezers.

"*Como esta, Pablo?* Whassup?"

"Naw so good, man. Is my ulcer."

Mona frowned. "You shouldn't be working, Pablo. I'm surprised at Ches. I'll talk to him."

"Naw, naw. Is okay, Mizz Sahlstrom. You don' gotta tell the boss. Okay?"

"I'll give Maria my recipe for goat's milk pudding. That stops an ulcer dead in its tracks. Could you take Al's jacket, please, Pablo. He can't wear it in there."

Pablo put off the dyspeptic face and rolled back his shoulders, appraising my jacket. "Is no so bad. Little bit dirty, mebbe. *Verdad?* This you?" Nodding at me as he tried it on.

"Yeh, it's mine, Pablo. I'd like it back when I leave. Okay?"

"Nah, man, no problem." Pablo worked his shoulders for fit and buttoned it up. "Fiss real good. How you say? *Livanito*...no weigh much."

"Keep it, Pablo," Mona said, "I'll get Al another. You'd better take his tie, too."

Ortiz screwed up his mouth regarding it. "Nawww, I dunno, Mizz—"

"You can't just give away my clothes, for crissake, Mona. I'm fond of that jacket. Sondra gave it to me."

"You'll get over it." Mona steered me away by an elbow. Didn't occur to her she had just given Pablo a hand-me-down insult. Apparently it didn't to him either. But it sure as hell would to his wife, Maria. She'd dump my jacket in the trash. Later, I saw Ortiz doing chores around the pool, wearing my jacket like a fucking butler.

I was halted at the door by the rent-a-butler Ches hired for such occasions. "Sorry, sir, it's a jacket and tie affair."

"I'm a member. Besides, I had a jacket a minute ago."

"Ask Mr. Noonan if he has a loaner." Mona hooked the man's shirt collar aside with a finger and studied a red rash on his neck, clucking her tongue. "You should be doing antioxidants."

Ches appeared, chuckling. The wide, sun-soaked face, a trio of warts on the bulb of his left nostril. "I hear you need a jacket, Albert?" He led me back along a hallway to his dressing room. Two huge walk-in closets lined with mirrors. A lazy Susan rack hung with dozens of suits whispered out on its bearings. Ches selected a powder-blue rig such as a loan shark might wear and held it to my shoulders for fit. All were pieces of a puzzle, I would come to see: Ches's willingness to share what belonged to him, mine to be patronized. We stood back-to-back, front-to-front, side-to-side with ourselves between mirroring wardrobe doors, endlessly reiterated down multiple corridors of reflection, like in some existential fun house. What sort of egomaniac would want to stand bare-assed in the glory of his own infinite reflection? Jesus.

"There's something I have been meaning to discuss with you, Al," he said, gripping my forearm. "I'd like to make you an offer on your property along Creosote Canyon Road. I'd give you a good price." Squeezing imperatively.

"My land? Why would you want it? Just scrappy chaparral."

"You aren't using it, are you?"

"It's not for sale, Ches," I snapped, surprised at myself.

He chuckled. "Everything's for sale, Albert, if you get your price. You could use the cash. I'd prefer we kept this between ourselves." Glancing at the door into the master bedroom. "You think about it." Squeezing my arm indelicately. A slice of bed visible through the open door and the aqua pool through tinted patio doors beyond it; Penny Noonan's black bra was coiled on the lush bedspread. A hand yanked it out of frame. With a little stab of excitement, I recalled Penny standing naked that day I walked in on her. I grabbed the jacket out of Ches's hands and hightailed it out of there, mumbling thanks. All events in this world are foreshadowed, though we often miss their announcement. His offer didn't trouble me at the time. Just another of

Ches's fancies.

Linen cloths were spread on the lawn, with wicker baskets full of fried chicken and potato salad, silver wine coolers, women in summery dresses, men in sports jackets and ties. Penny Noonan had proposed at a recent meeting that we should "dress properly now and again, like we live somewhere." Silk Setters agreed: the Houstons, the Philadelphias, and the Sylvesters. Snowbirds. Sam walked out in disgust. Sage Little-feather grumbled, "Indians don't wear neckties. I got me a western string tie." Fiery wit burned in his eyes, lank black hair hung either side of his pocked face.

We all agreed to do a DGLA benefit. Question was what to benefit. I proposed we sponsor the Saint Angel Desert Go-Cart International. Esther Johnson farted air through her lips. "Come now, Albert, that's pathetic." Mrs. Philadelphia regarded me in alarm.

"We're a lawn grow-in-as-soc-i-a-tion," Cal Hale said syllabically.

"Do you mean parks and such?" Esther asked.

"Hell no, I don't mean parks—damned tree-hugger breeding grounds. No sir."

Penny laughed gaily. "Oh, Cal, you are your own true item."

"I'll tell you another thing: I won't be benefittin' no scout troops neither, unless they throw out the damn queers."

"Goodness me!" Clover Abernathy cried, a hand pinned to her chest.

"So what would *you* benefit, Cal?" Daphne Thompson asked.

"True-blue-dyed-in-the-wool American civic improvement."

"Go-carts are American as it gets."

"Go-carts is fine by me, Al. I'm not high falutin."

Always made me nervous when Cal agreed with me.

Mrs. Philadelphia proposed we benefit a desert center for the arts. Ches regarded her quizzically. "Didn't know we had one."

"I believe my wife is proposing we build one," Mr. Philadelphia said.

"A center is okay by me," Cal said, "but I'm not sure about the artsy part. A lot of puffs in that line of work, too."

Penny let go a shrieking laugh that shattered into tinkling peals. It was rumored that Cal and Penny once had a fling. I didn't much believe it. Winky Hale was studying her nails, cocking her head from side to side, likely thinking about her angels. My heart went out to Winky.

"Desert Center For The Arts." Ches rested the notion on his tongue and nodded. "That would draw a higher class of people out here."

"Higher than who?" Rob Thompson glowered at him. Those two had a history going back to when they'd built houses together and Ches made off with most of the profits.

"Are we talking performance arts or martial arts here?" Cal persisted.

Penny laughed again. "Oh, I do love it."

Imogene Sylvester regarded Cal in alarm. "Why, the fine arts, of course."

So it was settled: we were benefitting a yet to be erected Desert Center for the Arts with yet to be determined content. "We ought to go her five thousand dollars a plate and get it done," Cal proposed. Daphne protested that some of us could barely manage fifty dollars a plate. "I'll go five dollars," Sage volunteered. "Are we still a democracy over here or what?"

"Democracy of the rich." Rob glowered at Ches.

We had once tossed horseshoes together in the pitch beyond Ches's perimeter wall, drank cold beer, and tried to out cuss each other, and someone occasionally tossed a horseshoe in the pool to get Ches's goat—back when Rob worked as Ches's construction foreman and we judged a man by whether he rolled down his pickup windows on triple-digit days or rolled them up and turned on the A.C. Money didn't divide us back then. Now Rob declared the only horseshoes he'd ever pitch with that asshole again was a ringer around Ches's neck. What happened to us? Sage believes it has to do with the rise of salt water under the desert. I don't follow his logic.

"We're all friends here, hearty believers in greening the desert," Ches said. "Except Sam maybe."

"And me!" I cried. "And me!" Rob, Daphne, and Mona chimed in.

"It appears some don't wish to do their part." Mr. Philadelphia regarded me with a simpering smile. He resembled Robert McNamara: thinning, slicked-back hair and ardent glasses, a deep rut etched in his forehead. He wore banker's pinstripes, likely even to bed.

"I'm not sure what some of us are doing here," Imogene Sylvester agreed. "Some of us don't grow lawns, we don't maintain our membership dues—"

"What we're doing here is we live here," Sage said.

"Full time," Daphne added.

Mrs. Sylvester turned lips out at the lot of us, segregated to one side of the huge living room.

"You don't want to judge a book by its cover, Imogene." Ches strolled to the bar. "Al here, for example, is our resident scientist and something of an inventor. He doesn't have a lawn out at Second Chance Acres anymore, but he's our local expert on grass varieties. You want to know what percentage of Zoysia and Bermuda to mix with fescue, ask Al. Sage is our naturalist. I've seen him study a lizard's tail and tell me I need to cover the pool since we're about to get a Santa Ana. He's never been wrong."

Penny Noonan was studying me speculatively, as she had since I'd walked in on her undressing, eyes dark as her heart-shaped pubis. I tried looking elsewhere, tried smiling at Ches. Damn her. *What?* her lips formed a question. *Don't know,* mine formed back. Penny's cheeks hollowed, nostrils flared white. She glared at me.

Mona suggested each member contribute what they could. She might manage $200, while some might contribute $2,000. Cal whistled. "Well ain't that a ripe tomato? From each according to his lazy, low character to each according to what he can get. So that's how it is? Communism pure and simple." Catching my eye, he pumped a fist in the air. "Sonsabitches!" I realized the rumors I'd heard about his plans to sink deep well shafts off Indian Springs Road behind Sam Jenson's place were true.

Penny was up, clapping her hands. "Okay, kids, time for a dip. Last one in's a cow's rear end!" We went out sliding glass doors leading to the pool, swimsuits under our street clothes—except for Silk Setters, who would hang out in the den, watching in sour disavowal while we played raucous water tag, the gals in lingerie that left little to the imagination. Mona always stripped first. "That woman's got the finest jugs in the valley," Rob said, "and you aren't sleeping with her? You gone fruit on us or what, Al?"

Penny Noonan pulled the frock over her head and stood in a tiny black bikini, brown toes hooked over the pool rim, watching me. She seized my arm in the commotion and hurried me along a Spanish tiled hallway to a guest room overlooking the pool at far end of the house, purple nails sunk into the soft belly of my elbow. She hip bumped the guest room door closed behind us.

"Listen, Penny, Mona is right outside—"

"Shuddup, Albert, and get busy." Her tongue a flighty moth in my mouth. She stripped off the bikini, small breasts not creamy white but tan as the rest of her. She pushed me back on the bed and mounted me, clawing my chest with long purple nails that left furrows. "Fucking loser." Her nipples stiff against my chest. "Get to work, Albert." I was alarmed—wildly excited—with half the DGLA frolicking unawares beyond mirrored glass doors: Ches talking to Pablo Ortiz, who was still wearing my jacket, like they were right there in the room with us. Can't say whether it terrified or excited me. Penny squatted over me, bouncing off feet planted either side of my hips on the bed, slamming hard. "Asshole," she moaned, "fuck me." Cried out so loud in orgasm I had to firm a hand over her mouth, her face contorted and feral. She bit the palm of my hand and I cried out. Realized I was staring out at Mona talking to Daphne, wet bra and panties barely concealing her dark pubis. I became, if possible, even harder, ready to burst, like I was balling both Mona and Penny at once. Suddenly, Mona cocked her head as if she had picked up my scent on the wind and looked directly into the sliding glass doors. At us! She had a psychic gift. Live out in the desert as long as she has and you're bound to develop it. Whether she could see me or not, she knew I was there. At that instant, Penny bit my fingers and I came like a horse.

Afterwards, we lay panting side by side, Penny's fury spent. I shrank into the bed covers while she combed fingers through my hair. "My sweet little mascot, I'm going to make you bleed."

What was I getting myself into? Mona? Ches? What was I thinking? Or thinking at all? True, I'd long had a thing for Penny. I would sit at poolside watching her bounce up and down on the diving board as if on a trampoline. Girl-woman in a tiny string bikini. Couldn't have weighed more than 110 pounds. Sage Littlefeather slapped my back. "You eye surfing over there? I got your number."

"Naw, Sage. She's Ches's wife. Just admiring. Can't I admire?"

"What other way you plan to admire?"

"No other way," I snapped. Told myself I had no interest in Penny Noonan.

When Mona suddenly loomed at the sliding glass doors just feet away from us, peering in, I clutched a pillow over my head and coiled into a fetal ball.

"Silly boy! She can't see you. She's checking herself in the mirror. Afraid you'll get caught? Hah!" Penny shrieked laughter. Mona cupped hands against the glass to look inside, I slunk eel-like over the

side of the bed, and Penny waved. "Hi there!" Seeing her lying naked on the bed, Mona leapt away. Doubtless wondering where I was.
Surely not inside with the Silk Set.

"Oh that was fun," Penny cried. "Just loads."

4

IN WHICH AL IS IN THRALL TO
HIS LIBIDO

When asked by a coworker what, exactly, her relationship was with Al Sharpe, Mona said, "We are good friends, exactly. Finley is like a daughter to me."

"But you have children of your own, don't you?"

She looked the woman up and down. "I had children once. What are you getting at?"

"Once?" The woman was baffled, then mortified. "Oh, my goodness, I'm sooo sorry. I didn't know—"

"I'm sorry, too," Mona said.

Al arrived in town five years after Mona, a deeply wounded man. He walked stooped over as if dragging a weight behind him. Mona met him at an AA meeting at the Congregational Church. He stood up and said, "I'm Al, and I'm not an alcoholic." Several people booed, including Little Lester. "Well, I'm not. But I am a bad-luck addict. I'm addicted to failure. I thought you folks might understand that." That got their attention. More so when he told them how he had driven his wife into the arms of a lover, then she and her lover died in a plane crash, flying to a conference in Hawaii. Sondra, he was sure, already planned to leave him and their six-year-old daughter. "Except," he said sotto voce, "I'm not one-hundred percent sure she died in that plane crash. Her name wasn't on the flight manifest and bodies were never recovered. Still, I can't believe she would abandon her daughter without a word or regret. I prefer to believe she lies on the ocean floor off Coronado Island in the arms of her lover, Charlie— who happens to be a woman, by the way. I will let you decide what that says about me as a husband."

"What do you think it says?" Loretta Sims asked him. Loretta owns a dude ranch out near Tourmaline that caters to lesbians.

"I have my own opinion. No one wants to lose their mate to another person, man or woman," he said. "Doesn't matter which."

"It says more about your wife," Mona said. "Maybe you're in denial about that. You prefer to blame yourself."

The notion astonished him; he'd never thought of it. "I'm in denial about most everything," he confessed. "I used to deny that I couldn't keep a job, even washing dishes. I denied that I was disappointed in myself. Now I'm in denial about my inadequacy as a single dad. I really want to believe I can raise my daughter on my own."

"You can," several chorused.

"People tell me I have a genius for inventing things, but I don't believe it."

"You do," several insisted, though they didn't know him. Just something about Albert that made people want to believe in him. If his wife Sondra didn't, shame on her.

Father Flannagan once inquired at confession whether Mona was having sex out of wedlock with her atheist friend. "Albert, is it?"

"We comfort each other now and again," she said.

"So that's what you call it, 'comforting'?" She could see his teeth through the screen clenched in a grim smile, the taut line of his jaw.

"No, I call it 'fucking,' but I thought that might offend you, Father F."

It was their mutual agreement. Both valued their friendship, which in earlier days might have been called "companionship," but they'd been seeing less of each other since Finley went away to high school. Both agreed that to declare themselves lovers could kill their friendship. There's no greater enemy of friendship than marriage, they had convinced themselves, given their lonely marriages. In truth, they had crazy, passionate sex on occasion. Mona sometimes wondered if the intensity of their lovemaking didn't drive them away from it. It would have been so easy to fall into that trap. Like a fat person into a tub of ice cream. They determined to keep it platonic.

They were open about it, discussing how they had been deeply wounded in marriage and didn't wish to risk that again. "I'm not sure I could take it, I'm not sure Finley could." "I'm not sure I could keep from killing the bastard," Mona said. The idea of people binding themselves in mutual ownership was repugnant to them. Conjugal slavery. "Indentured sexitude," she called it. "You don't need a contract to be lovers." What they had was ideal: coming together when they desired it and being alone when they needed to, which was most of the time. Wholly voluntary. She didn't love Finley as a mother might, beleaguered by duties and expectations and the fear of failure; she simply loved her. She and Al talked about how parents wanted their children to be their clones, recycled selves, family retreads.

"You'll hear them say, 'I want my children to do better than I did,'" Al said, "but what if the kids don't want to do better? Or disagree on the meaning of 'better,' as so often happens?" He did his best not to impose expectations on Finley. Mona watched him struggle with it. "It's not easy to avoid. Even encouragement is a kind of expectation," he said.

"You mean her writing?"

"Her writing and her wild fancies and dreams of a better world and enthusiasms. I love them. Remember how she stayed up half the night hunting tarantulas with a flashlight in the canyon?"

"And you let her! So many of them in the treehouse it made my skin crawl. You had to put a stop to it. Everything has its limits."

Through Finley's childhood and adolescence, Mona spent much of her free time at Second Chance Acres, neglecting her own place. She often slept in the treehouse with Finley, and they chatted half the night like friends at a slumber party—about her dad's inventive genius, about sex, about "Braindead High" and Finley's dread of going to school there. More rarely, Mona slept in the cottage with Al. He never came out to her place in the desert. It was her sanctuary, he respected that. When Finley started calling her "Mom," Mona gently protested. "I would be proud to be your mother, but I'm not. We need to be straight about that. Listen, hon, duty never holds people together. Only love and agreement hold them together."

Finley was taken aback. "Who said anything about duty?"

"What I am saying is that as soon as you give something a label it becomes a duty."

Then Finley went off to Carlsbad High School and Mona and Al drifted apart. They no longer had sex. She missed him at times, though was loathe to admit it, and he missed her. But Mona's story must wait for another time. Al is in a bit of a jam.

#

I slipped out a side door of the Noonan house through a colonnade skirting the pool, hoping to avoid Ches and Mona, but nearly collided with her on my way out—wrapped in a towel, her lips pulled into a straight line. Every inch the scrupulous loan officer, expert at sniffing out unreliables. She jammed a finger against my Adam's apple and trailed it down my chest, harrowed with bloody scratches from Penny's nails. "What happened, buster, a cat get at you? I've been looking for you."

"I've been here." Wondering why I owed her an explanation and what I'd gotten myself into, recalling how I'd tried to fasten Penny's bikini top, my clumsy fingers fumbling at the catch, how she'd pushed them away. Mona held me with the unflinching gaze of a predatory bird; she had me. Like my daughter, I am temperamentally incapable of lying.

"What's the trouble?"

"I'm asking you...."

I shrugged. Just then, Penny stepped through sliding glass doors, radiant in black leather string bikini, long black braid glistening in the sun. She walked to the end of the diving board and sprang up and down, all eyes focused on her. "Queen of the hop." Mona sneered.

"You'll break my damned board," Ches barked.

"Oh, ah doubt I could break it, darlin'. Ah might bend it some." Winking at me, she sprang weightlessly in the air, touched her toes, and knifed into the water.

Mona studied the ripples she'd left on the pool's surface and tapped my chest. "You better put something on that before it festers."

"You going in, bro?" Sage called from across the pool. "Or you already been in?"

I felt like a rat in a trap, tongue protruding obscenely from my mouth. Avoiding Chester's eyes. "You can keep the jacket, Pablo," I told Ortiz on my way out.

Some days later, I found the fellows at their regular booth at the diner. Matt Littlefeather saying, "There isn't no fertilizer on earth can make grass that green."

"What he does, Ches uses up half the Colorado River. What's left over, the rest of us might wash our neck oncet a month," Sam Jenson grumbled.

"Grandfather Lubo seen the ground sink over to Dead Creek Canyon after houses went in over there. They pumped water out of the underground lake that holds up the land to fill artificial lakes up top,"

"That's nonsense, Sage, water holding up the land. Physically impossible." I slid into the booth beside him.

"Your white man's science don't know everything. You know how to poison the land, but you don't know how to save it."

"You're right there."

"Damned fool Indian," Sam muttered. Then seemed to agree with Sage. "Let the pressure out...whoosh! Like a flat tire. Put your ear to the ground, you can hear it gurgle."

I mentioned how my slough had nearly swallowed me. "I'd swear it's expanding."

"There you go right there!" Sage opened his hands.

"That isn't all that could swallow you," Rob said knowingly. He winked. How could he know about Penny and me? Unless she told him. He leaned over the table, blue eyes bleached nearly white from roofing under the glaring sun. "I'll tell you another thing, Ches and his buds plan to fill the valley with houses. I've seen their master plan."

"You frying the bacon over there?" Matt bellowed laughter.

"Fuck off, Littlefeather. Once we finish Dead Creek Canyon, we start framing out Jack-o'-Lantern Road. We're gonna have half of Orange County moving in."

"It's you building houses for them." Sage's long black braid and headband made him look like a rental Indian off a Hollywood back lot.

"Damned California snowbirds." Sam slammed the table and stalked off in disgust, stiffing us for his pie and coffee as usual. Little Lester came in as he left, wearing his uniform: black leather biker's pants and vest, tattoos twining psychedelically over his biceps, pony tail caught back in a silver napkin holder. Les did time in Nam, then hard time for cooking meth in Anza. I'd never known him to work. You see that out here: people with no visible means of support, like salt pines.

"Whassup, Cochise?" He traded five with Sage and bumped knuckles with Rob.

"Whazzat? Fuckin' white boy gang sign over here?" Matt Littlefeather howled.

"What you boys plotting this morning?" Lester asked. "Nothing good, I bet."

Rob surveyed the room and spoke low. "What we do, okay, once houses are framed over in Creosote Canyon, we fire bomb them. Send Chester a message, God willing."

"Build 'em, burn 'em, and forget 'em." Matt winked at me.

"Violence begets violence begets shit to pay, people." Les wagged a finger at Rob.

"Creosote Canyon? That's over by me," I said. "I haven't heard anything about it."

"My point exactly. Right over by you, Al."

"Angie Beach owns most of that land, and Tinkerspoon. They

wouldn't sell."

"Angie's been selling," Les said. "Your girlfriend is knee deep in it."

"Mona is? Selling to who? Nothing out there but cactus and black sloughs."

"Ches and Cal Hale and their pals. Who else?"

I thought of Ches's offer to buy my land; it sent a chill down my spine. Seemed preposterous: Ches building houses out by me.

Matt scowled at Rob. "You should know, Hammer Man, you the one building them."

"I'll burn them down, too, God willing." Rob's white teeth a blatant contrast to his all-season tan, sunburnt eyes consumed in a conflagration of light, the irises seemingly burned away. A bumper sticker on his pickup proclaimed, *Not Of This World.*

"Isn't nobody burning down houses," Sage insisted.

"Copy that, chief," Les said. "I done all the burning I plan to do, people."

"You done meth cooking, too." Matt pounded his back.

"I'll tell you what, though, Ches and them filed a law suit claiming half your rez belongs to the original *Rancho La Cienega* Land Grant which they hold title to. They plan to take your tribal lands, Littlefeather." Les had a way of knowing things. He once told me that war teaches you what you can ignore and what you can't.

"Isn't happening," Matt bellowed. "That's protected by treaty over there." He jumped up, nearly upending the table, and stomped toward Jack and Meg Crispley's booth across the room, hitching up his pants with one hand and spearing a finger at Jack. "I got my over/under out in the truck, Crispley. Anybody surveys on rez land is gonna be vulture bait."

Jack and Meg sat open mouthed, watching him come. Rob howled, "Go for it, big man." He had hated Crispley since Jack fired him from a construction site for smoking weed.

Sage gripped Matt's arm and led him outside. Returned shortly and sat down with Jack and Meg, speaking low. Jack went sheet white. Sage returned to our booth and spoke solemnly. "Don't shit where you sleep, there's half your white man's trouble right there."

Just then, Cal Hale came in as if we'd conjured him. "How y'all lazy loafers this morning?" he cried merrily. "Wasting a good day per usual."

"Same as you, Cal." Les grinned.

"The hell I am. Somebody's got to make some money for the damn government."

"There you go," Rob said. "Stealing our water and trashing our land."

Cal sat down in the Crispleys' booth and threw us dark looks. Sage held his nose exiting the diner and hard-eyed Cal back. "Something stinks in here."

So it started. Though we didn't know it yet. Cal's mega-wells, housing developments out Dead Creek Canyon, salt water rising. Our cozy community coming apart.

I visited the men's room on my way out and stood a moment studying myself in the mirror. Hardly recognized the man looking back at me. They say we encompass multiple selves, but I knew nothing of this bawdy libertine who betrayed his friends and was in thrall to uncontrolled appetites, too weak to resist them. I was intoxicated by Penny Noonan, lust-drunk on a friend's wife. I couldn't reconcile myself with that. Yet, seemingly, I had.

Sunday was Ches's golf day and our day to hook up. I would park my pickup at side of the house out of view of the drive. Penny greeted me at the front door in a silk kimono and stuck her tongue in my mouth. I'd open her robe and suck a nipple erect, then drop to my knees and inhale her sex. No preamble, no words spoken. We often got no farther than the Persian rug in the entry hall, fucking like cats on the floor. I think it turned Penny on to imagine Ches walking in on us. However, she instructed me to go out a window over the back wall if Ches did come home. "Daddy would crush you like a grape." Kneading her fingers together with relish. "What kind of man fucks a friend's wife?" Stuffing her drawers in my mouth when I attempted reply. I saw Pablo Ortiz pass by the open front door with a weed whacker. Penny led me back to the guest room and pushed me down on the bed, she seized the collar of my T-shirt and tore it down the front, then lifted her robe and straddled me, moaning in my ear, "You bitch! Gawd, but I loathe you." And came boisterously.

I knew I should feel guilty, but didn't. Half convinced myself that Ches knew of our affair and gave it his tacit blessing for some unfathomable reason. He was palsier than usual at DGLA meetings. While Mona had stopped returning my phone calls. Why? She had no claim on me, we had no claim on each other. Finley emailed me from Carlsbad, asking, "Is something wrong between you and Mona?" The air around me vibrated with violation; others surely picked it up.

Out of respect for Ches, we never balled in the master bedroom. Penny lined up lubricants and a stack of condoms on a silver tray in the guest room. "Daddy never comes in here. He's too busy to be snoopin' about the house. No doubt you know every nook and cranny of your own."

"Well, it's not very big."

She laughed gaily. "Truer words never spoken, Albert. Does Mona agree?"

"What's Mona got to do with it? We're friends is all."

"You don't expect me to believe that. Ah can smell her on you— Sixties patchouli oil. Ugh!"

"I'm telling you, we aren't a number, I hardly see her. Sure, we've had sex, but I'm not cheating on Mona like you are on Ches."

She gripped my jowls as you might a dog's. "If ah'm cheatin' on Daddy, y'r double cheatin'—on Mona and Chester both."

"Friends, I tell you, that's it."

"A man and woman can never be 'friends.' Sex always comes into it. That's how we're programmed."

"I must be poorly programmed then."

"Ah do believe it, Albert." Her whinnying laugh.

When she went into the guest bath to wash up, I slipped down hall to Ches's work room, curious about the development plans Rob mentioned. Floor-to-ceiling clerestories looked out on the blue pool, topical maps covered an entire wall, showing contours of the land: Saint Angel, Tourmaline, Dead Creek Canyon, Purgatory. Tiny red stick pin flags scattered about: local wells, I realized. Mine was there. I shuffled through stacks of plans atop a table, looking for the putative master plan. When I looked up, Penny was standing in the doorway wrapped in a towel, another turbaned around her head.

"What are you doing in Daddy's drawers?"

"Daddy?" I stepped away from the table.

"Mah husband, Chester! Ah won't have you snoopin' about mah house, Albert."

"Sorry, Penny. I was just wondering what he's up to."

"None of your damned business what he is up to, you sneaky little freak."

"Maybe it is. There's talk of developments going in on Creosote Canyon Road—out by me."

"Is that what this is about, using me to spy on mah husband?"

"Maybe he's using you to spy on me. This was your idea, Penny, remember."

Her face flushed with anger. "If there's one thing ah despise, it's a man who won't take responsibility for his actions. You want to screw me and don't give a damn who it hurts." She threw clothes and shoes at me. "Get out of mah house, you lowlife bastard."

Me hopping down the hall pulling on my pants, slipping out a side door. I heard things crash inside the house, Penny shouting, "Trash! White trash!" I went over the retaining wall to my pickup in back. Caught a glimpse of Pablo as I sped past the house, a hand shielding his eyes.

Becoming dangerous, I realized. Maybe that's what it was all about. I was seduced as much by the illicitness as by Penny's hunger. Forbidden fruit is always the most delicious.

#

Penny sat in the guestroom closet where she'd told Al Sharpe to hide if Chester came home while they were making love, squeezing meager flesh of her upper arms until she knew they would bruise, chewing words back in her mouth: "Trash trash trash...." She found Al Sharpe sexy. "Screwin' down," as she put it, got her crazy excited, but that's not all it was. Looking out on her guests playing water polo in the pool that first time, she imagined him as Lady Chatterley's Lover and wanted to take all of him in her mouth at once.

I must admit that adultery makes me nervous, their affair particularly so. No good ever comes of it, especially here in the desert where austerity is survival. No saying how it will pan out. I have known husbands to hunt down their wife's lover and blow his head off with a shotgun, and wives to sneak into bed with a steak knife and castrate an unfaithful husband. As much as I prefer to remain impartial, Al Sharpe's innocence arouses my protective instincts; he hasn't a clue. I know their affair is ill destined, since they aren't the people they take each other to be. Al is anything but the hopeless n'er-do-well Penny considers him. He is master of Second Chance Acres, inventor of the Sharpe Smoke Scrubber and countless other items, proud father of a lovely young woman, valued community member. In Saint Angel, Kingdom of the Excessed, he has found both a home and a use for himself. He is almost content. While Penny is not the fierce sex warrior

she appears to be, lips pulled back from her teeth in a goat's rictus. He be-
lieves their affair is a frivolous lark to her, and she will quickly forget him.
How wrong he is. She hangs Al's T-shirt with the faded Valvoline logo on
a hangar in the guestroom closet, presses it flat with her fingers. She crawls
inside and closes the louvered doors behind her, rubs the shirt over her face
and breasts, cursing softly at the smell of him. Ribs of light trellis her na-
kedness. She threatens to do violence to herself. She waits anxiously for Al's
arrival at DGLA meetings, thinking she will walk up and tongue kiss him
in front of the others, declare herself. But he doesn't show up. Pablo Ortiz
finds her out beyond the perimeter wall one evening, sitting cross-legged be-
side a cholla cactus, drunk and forlorn, her blouse shredded by fierce cactus
spines, bloody gouges down her bare arms.

"Why'd ah have to blow it, Pablo?" she moans.

"C'mon, Mizzus, you gotta go back. I don' tell nobody." He tries to
help her to her feet, but she slaps him across the cheek. "Don't you dare
touch me!"

#

As I fled the Noonan's house that day, Penny's eyes met mine, abashed and fragile; her narrow shoulders spasmed. The Queen of Furies, thorniest of women, cactus heart, had become a vulnerable child, eye liner smeared. My heart went out to her. But ours wasn't love. Lusty helplessness more like. We couldn't get enough of each other, like that drug Finley mentioned, ecstasy, leaked out of our pores. I stayed holed up at home for weeks, carved her name in huge letters in rotting sandstone at back of the canyon where no one would see it:

AL LOVES PENNY

PENNYWISE AND ALFOOLISH

Hieroglyphic murals. I recalled the time Sage had pointed at my slough: "That right there can strip the flesh off a man's bones." So can desire, but you convince yourself you can tiptoe around it.

Ches called an emergency meeting of the DGLA. Daphne Thompson insisted I attend, but I didn't want to; I was not just reluctant about seeing Penny, I had it in my head that Ches intended to call me out. Feared it all the more when Ortiz approached as I parked in the

horseshoe drive out front. "No around back?" He winked. "Don'
gotto worry, I no tell the boss." I was staring back at him as I went in
the house. Was he blackmailing me? Ches greeted me boisterously,
throwing his arms out wide. "Good of you to find time for us, Albert."
Behind him, Penny's eyes smoldered like hot embers in a dying fire.
"No!" I heard her say distinctly in my head. Everyone looked up at
me in alarm. Had I spoken aloud? I tried to avoid Ches's smile. His
venomous camel's breath filled the room like some cacodylic bacteria
thrived in his gut. Mona reasoned it was because Ches ate only red
meat, but Sage insisted, "Naw, that's greed breath." His marksmen's
gray eyes targeted mine. No doubt but what he knew about Penny
and me. I envisioned him stacking my bones like firewood, placing
my skull atop the pile. It was only a matter of time. I tried to communicate to him that it was over, *finito*. I wanted my life back. My
cheek muscles spasmed.

"Go ahead," he said, "spit it out." Suddenly, I was asking him if
there was anything to rumors we'd been hearing about development in
the valley. Chester smiled equably. "You can't believe everything you
hear, Sharpe."

"It doesn't make sense. Who would want to move out here?"

"You did." Ches grinned.

Daphne pulled one of the notices we'd seen posted on telephone
poles out of her purse: *Public Hearing on the Proposed Rezoning of Saint
Angel Valley from Agricultural to Residential.*

"So what's this?"

Cal Hale clinked a fingernail against his glass of Wild Turkey. "I
propose we abandon the Desert Puff Art Museum idea and sponsor a
new well for Saint Angel Municipal Golf Course. We're a lawn growin'
association, for crissake, and they need to water their grass. Who seconds?"

"Absolutely out of the question, Calvin." Imogene Sylvester was
outraged.

"Damn straight," Sam Jenson bellowed. "We don't have water to
spare for any damn golf course."

Cal ignored him. "Sink her deep, rebuild the clubhouse and make
it classy." He winked at Imogene Sylvester—like sunlight blinking off
black water at bottom of a bucket.

Cal wanted to sink a 400-foot-deep well, with our water table already down to 150 feet and sinking fast, well water gone milky with

salts and calcium carbonate, Ancient Salt Sea brack osmosing into swimming pools. Madness. The Saint Angel course had already been reclaimed by the desert, sand drifted over greens, ponds had dried up. We called it "Hell's Holes."

"I second." Ches's eyes swept from the Dirt Faction seated on the floor to the Silk Set in chairs across the room. "A new golf course might attract a better class of people out here."

"Better than who?" Daph Thompson demanded.

"You plan to suck up what little water we have left in the aquifer?"

"No one wants your water, Albert."

"*Our water*, damn it! It don't belong to Al Sharpe no more than anyone else. Or your Soboba socialists neither." Cal glared at Sage Littlefeather, who pounded a fist on the floor.

"Who's the socialists over here, blister head? Your white man socialized every inch as far as the eye can see...*Our land! My people's land!*"

Silk Setters shifted uncomfortably to hear Sage talk like this.

"This is a matter for the board to decide," Ches said imperiously.

"Hear hear!" John Sylvester nodded. "The board should decide."

"What board? We don't have a board," Daphne said.

"It's high time we did." Ches proposed the DGLA board be comprised of two members voted at large, plus John Sylvester as legal counsel, Cal, Penny and himself as founding members.

"We're founding, too." Rob was livid. "Daph, Al Sharpe and myself." Sage Littlefeather ducked his head and raised a hand. "Yo! Sage, too."

Ches chuckled. "Everyone can't sit on the damn board."

"No, Chester, only your pals. I do love it." Penny's caustic laughter. Her dark eyes slid at me, playful and defiant. A mole on Ches's forehead had calcified and crusted over like an alkali flat. No wonder she wouldn't sleep with him. Plus his halitosis.

Daph proposed including Rob, Sage, Mona and me on the board. "Definitely Al." Mrs. Philadelphia leaned over to whisper something to her small-headed friend, impaling Penny and me on ice saber eyes. The small-headed friend looked back and forth between us, scandalized.

"We will accept two of you," Ches declared imperially.

"Who appointed you decider, Mr. Chester? You and them Silk Setters. Because you got the biggest lawns? More of your white man democracy over here." Sage roared laughter and pounded fists on the floor.

"Silk who?" Imogene Sylvester demanded of Sage.

"Bunch of damn snowbirds." Sam Jenson stormed out of the house, volatile and transient as a Santa Ana, suddenly blasting hot wind and sand in your face. Out front, his ancient Olds coughed then caught hold with a thunderous belch of smoke, peeling rubber.

Rob argued that Sage should sit on the board to represent the aboriginal peoples. We might have carried it had that tumbleweed idealist, Sam Jenson, not stormed out on us. My eyes fell to Penny's smooth bare knees which I loved to stroke. My libido dangerously out of control.

Afterwards, Sage was talking about his great uncle who once grew maize and squash and watermelon back in my canyon, irrigating it with water from Pissing Springs. First I'd heard of it. Cal Hale took an interest, wanting to know its rate of flow and where it was exactly. "That's a valuable asset, Sharpe. A natural artesian spring. Once there was dozens in the valley."

"Until white squatters used up all our water," Sage hissed.

Cal threw a dismissive hand.

"Doesn't amount to much," I said. "Pretty well dried up. Lets out a trickle now and again."

"You hear that, Ches," Cal called, "we still have natural artesian springs in the valley. So much for this nonsense about running out of water; we got it flowing out of the rocks."

Maybe a week later, I was hanging clothes on the line when I saw a shadowy figure emerge from the canyon, dressed in dark clothes and wearing a back pack. Occurred to me it might be one of our "visitors," one of the elusive itinerants who wander the high desert like human coyotes, scavengers and petty thieves, occasionally camping back in the canyon. I lack heart to run them off. Seeing me waving a hand, the trespasser froze up, then fled into a mesquite thicket. No itinerant. Something ominous and predatory in the look he gave me. I recalled Cal's avid interest in Pissing Springs. Possibly one of his spies?

5

THE REBIRTH OF SAVWA

Little Lester came highballing down the drive on his bicycle and did his over-the-handlebars dismount, boosting up on his arms and kicking legs through them like a gymnast dismounting a pommel horse. "Get your rear end to town, Sharpe. They're gunning to steal the water from under our feet." Les wore his uniform: black leather pants and vest, a bleeding purple heart tattooed on his bare chest with an arrow through it and "Semper fi" curled around it, his biceps strapped with blue veins. Since being gassed with Agent Orange in Nam, Les made it his business to watchdog the "authorities," attended every supervisor and Planning Commission meeting, put out a newsletter: *Saint Angel's Dirty Underwear: all the filth that's fit to print.*

Squatting on his heels, he sketched a map of the Valley in the dust with a finger: flumes leading down from Saint Angel Lake on the mountain, constructed a century ago by the old SAVWA (Saint Angel Valley Water Authority) in apricot and citrus growing days. SAVWA governed groundwater use for a hundred years, until it lapsed and groundwater was left to anyone who sank a well. "Now it's too valuable to give away," Les said. "They plan to resurrect the Water Authority, but only notified the big landowners and developers about it." Les sketched a big-nosed caricature of Ches in the dust, like Winston Churchill in profile. Stood up and checked out my canyon and the craggy cliffs above it. A red-tailed hawk gyred on air currents high overhead and whistled at us. "You got you a natural citadel here, Sharpe. You could hold off an army."

Might have heard an eye blink when we trooped into the meeting at town hall—the lot of us in jeans and t-shirts, contrasting expensive tweeds of lawyers and reps of the big land-owning consortiums in the "Tri-City Area," which had bought up thousands of acres: Saint Angel Land Company (SALCO), Mile High Investments, The Hanover Brothers Investment Corp., TexHome Development. Mostly out-of-towners. They craned their long necks like turtles and smiled uncomfortably, made me think of Sage's warning: When white men smile, they got some meanness in the works. "I am pleased you folks could make it," John Sylvester simpered. "You fellows here on a cooperative basis?"

"Any reason we shouldn't be?" Little Les straddled a chair.

"I'm here to protect my water rights," I said. "The sign on the door says 'Public Hearing.'"

"No need to be snippy," Sylvester said.

Les eyeballed him. "Put a cap on your gas tank, brother. Nobody's snippy."

Ches Noonan got right to it, proposed reviving the Saint Angel Valley Water Authority to govern groundwater distribution in the Valley—given our growing population and diminishing groundwater reserves. "What we have now is water anarchy. It won't do."

Daphne asked if water authority officials would be elected. Ches's lawyer, Leon DeValoir, a portly dude with a round balding head, opined that neither the electorate nor any seated governmental body had authority to appoint a board, since land overlying the watershed had been ceded in perpetuity by its original owners, the Luiseño Nation, to owners, successors, and heirs of the *Rancho La Cienega del Diablo* Land Grant in 1842.

"We never ceded that to nobody," Sage insisted. "They plain took it."

The lawyer continued, "Ches Noonan and Cal Hale recently bought the remnants of the old *Rancho La Cienega* Land Grant from Angie Beach, giving them exclusive, overlying, and appropriative rights to the valley's groundwater. However—" holding up a finger to allay our protests "—my clients have charitably offered to share a portion of their water with Saint Angelinos."

"Damn straight you will," Les shouted.

Another lawyer opined that groundwater supplies, being a providence of God, aren't in the public domain. "The closest we might come to any usufructuary title would be holders of land lying directly above the aquifer, particularly on Indian lands, according to Winters' Doctrine."

"Yo! How about water I drink out of the tap, who owns that?" Les asked.

"Town water is under the jurisdiction of the Saint Angel Municipal Water district."

"Seems like it belongs to me once I swallow it—given 'user fuck-tory' and all."

"Temporarily perhaps," DeValoir conceded. "More a lease than a title."

"So how about when I piss it down the pot?"

"That will do, Lester. There's ladies present," Ches scolded him.

Les looked around, mock befuddled. "Don't ladies piss, too? Maybe I got it wrong."

"We know you don't mean any harm, Lester, but there's strangers present who don't know you as we do. Lester served two tours of duty in Vietnam," Ches told the developers. "He was wounded twice and received a bronze star for gallantry in battle. We're doggoned proud of him."

"First I heard of it. Yo, it's a point I am trying to make here, people."

"We receive your point," Ches's lawyer said.

"Not yet you didn't." Les folded his arms and sat down. I placed a hand on his smoldering shoulder. Sage remained standing, according to his dictum: *Don't let a white man look down at you when you speak.* "My people—" thumping his chest "—the Soboba people, belong to the land. So if water belongs to the land, like you say, we got to be close-related, right?"

Lawyers held a quick tete-a-tete up front, throwing wary glances at Sage. A white-haired gentleman spoke for them. "We believe you forfeited your rights under the Rancho Grant of 1842 and the Land Law of 1851. Nonetheless, yes, the Soboba might be considered concerned cousins of the groundwater supply, so to speak."

"Your white man's law says you can't fuck your cousin, right?" Sage sat down. There was a bewildered silence. Then Mr. Philadelphia spoke from the front table.

"I believe we are all on the same page. We need a body to regulate our groundwater." He proposed Ches Noonan head the revived Saint Angel Valley Water Authority. "You don't want to leave it up to voters. If I've learned anything as a banker, I've learned you can't trust people with their own resources."

"Hear...hear!" Rob shouted. "Never trust the fucking peons. Whoooweee!"

We exited into the desert night full of dread. Soon learned that the county supervisors had named Ches as head of the revived Saint

Angel Valley Water Authority, which was duly appointed as the czar of groundwater resources in the Santa Rosa de Los Angeles Drainage Basin by the California Water Resources Control Board. "We got Owens Valley Two here, people," Les said, "and Chester is the Municipal Water District, Southern Pacific Railroad, and *L.A. Times* rolled into one. Whoop-i-diddy-do."

#

There is a stillness at midday which is harbinger of death and eternal silence. Get to like it or go mad. If you want to touch eternity, go to the desert, the open sea, or night sky. Stand out front of my place in the dazzling brightness of midday looking down Creosote Canyon Road to where it becomes a ribbon and disappears in the hazy distance, approaching the Ramona mountains. The high desert resonates stability and permanence—except for Andy Sanchez's place across the road from mine, which symbolizes chaos.

Some of the orange trees in Andy's grove still bear fruit, remnants of his parents' day when Saint Angelinos grew citrus, figs, olives, walnuts, and apricots. Otherwise, his place is a tribute to the junkyards surrounding tumbledown shacks and derelict trailers all over the desert. Garbage spills from his trailer over the dirt yard and carport—its fiberglass roof in an advanced state of decay; iridescent shards blow off it and hang in the air like sparkling silicon. The trailer looks like a shipwreck dead center of a garbage dump: three rusted TV antennas atop, windows cardboarded over, side door sprung permanently open, inviting trespassing skunks, possum, rattlers, and coyotes inside. We're talking serious "junk." Ask Andy for an airplane propeller or inner tube for a 1950s Schwinn Black Phantom, and he'll likely find it amidst rotting rubber and eviscerated mattresses. "Powder rot," he calls it, dry and odorless. Though the stench of dog dirt can turn your stomach of a hot day. Scrofulous chihuahuas dash frantically back and forth behind a chain-link fence, raising hell's chorus when anyone passes by, along with a blunt-headed mestizo hound that Andy calls "*El Rapido*," one eye blue, the other green.

Andy Sanchez is a piece of work even for Saint Angel. We call him Tinkerspoon, given his tendency to tinker and his former virtuosity playing spoons in the Righteous Alley Cats jug band. Not a lazy man, just piss-poor organized. The best of good men in a pinch, the worst of loonies drunk.

Rattling about in a pile of junk on his patio as I crossed the road, he tossed aside a window fan which cut down one of the pups. "Sorry, dude," Tinkerspoon cooed at the yowling dog, while his sometime girl-friend, Angie Beach, shouted from inside the trailer, "Would everyone shut the fuck up, I'm trying to pee." Why she required silence to piss I couldn't imagine. Angie just enjoyed being pissed off. She had inher-ited the property behind Tinkerspoon's from old man Beach—fifteen hundred acres of arid land, remnant of the original *Rancho La Cienega del Diablo* Spanish Land Grant.

I can't speak to conditions inside Tinkerspoon's derelict Airstream trailer, beyond the roach-infested kitchen where he occasionally held court. He once hung a rack of venison ribs from a curtain rod above the sink, drying it for jerky; flies formed a rollicking carpet over the carcass, and it smelled so bad it nearly drove us out of home across the road. "I found it dead on the side of the road. Waste not, want not, dude." I once heard Angie shrieking that she'd found a bowl of petri-fied chicken noodle soup in his bed; Tinkerspoon mewling in his soft voice, "I'm trying to get organized, dude." Terminal case, Andy. In a small steel building behind the trailer, he'd built a state-of-the-art com-puter lab in a spotless, air-tight room. Designed the huge mainframe computer himself. Hard to imagine that sterile white room given the compost heap in front. I often saw him emerge in white scrubs, eyes dilated from spending the day online hacking secure government sites, returning to his disheveled world from the digital *sanctus sanctorum*. Tinkerspoon was an anchorite of sorts, a cyberspace holy man who didn't belong in the real world.

He bent over the injured pup, caught it by the nape of the neck in his teeth like a bitch would and carried it to a bench. "How's things, Andy?" I asked. His witless hound *El Rapido* growled low in his throat as I approached the fence, trusting no one who bathed regularly.

"Just fine dandy." Nuzzling the pup with his nose, "This is gonna smart, dude." Poor dog let go a piercing shriek when Tinkerspoon set the bone. "I'll tape that up in a few." Two other dogs hobbled about the place with adhesive-taped limbs. Misty, his smallest, seemed less dog than rat. She ran along the fence nipping at me through the links. Finley once saw her climb a palm tree to nab a lizard.

"Is Angie here?" I asked, knowing she was. "I need to ask her something."

Tinkerspoon leaned conspiratorially over the fence, believing his place bugged (convinced the NSA can read our brain waves). "Did Ches make you an offer, dude? I might sell, keep the front acre and buy me a new trailer. Angie says they plan to build houses out here. It ain't happening, dude. Thirty years down the pipe maybe. I mean, check it out—" opening his hands to indicate arid emptiness around us. "Still, there's no way I can sell, dudeski. My pops would curse me to hell from his grave."

Angie exited the trailer. "Al Sharpe! I been looking for you, a-hole."

"Why am I an a-hole?"

"What you done to Mona is why. You and that skinny whore Penny Noonan."

How could she know about Penny and me? Maybe Penny was claiming bragging rights, metaphorically mounting my head as a trophy on her wall; she was capable of that. "I haven't done a thing to Mona," I managed. "I've hardly seen her lately."

Angie stood, hands a hip, yammering, "*I didn't do nothing.* You're fucking pathetic, Al Sharpe." A thick woman: coarse blond hair and bushy black eyebrows. Reaching over the fence, she thumped my chest with the heel of a hand. "You humiliated her in front of your whole humping lawn-growing club is what you done, a-hole."

"I did? How? You know, it's really none of your business, Angie."

She looked me up and down. "He's more pathetic than you, Tinkerspoon. I'm outta here." Pushing past me out the gate and hopping into the sporty little mini Cooper convertible she was driving lately.

"So it's true," I asked her, "you sold Ches and Cal Hale your land and water rights?"

"None of your business, a-hole. Except I'll tell you what: If I knew I owned all the groundwater in the valley I wouldn't have sold so cheap."

"I thought you were one of us, Angie."

"I can sell to anyone I like, a-hole. You got zip to say about it. I always hated this shithole valley, anyways. I'm outta here." She started the car. "You'll sell, too, Sharpe. Every one of you losers will sell."

"Never!"

She grinned and threw me a kiss. "Wait and see, a-hole."

I got Mona's voicemail when I called her, heard my words spiral down an electronic well and sink in dark depths. "Pick up! I know you're there. We need to talk." Visualizing her sitting outside by the garden drinking a cup of coffee. Why did I owe her an explanation? Penny and I had sex, so what? What business was it of hers? I didn't pry into her affair with our former mayor, RJH, though I half suspected they still fucked occasionally. "From what I hear, Ches and Cal are buying up half the valley, and you're involved in it. Is that true?"

She picked up. "It's really none of your business, Albert. It's confidential."

"Of course it's my business, I live here."

Tinkerspoon called me that evening, whispering so quietly I could barely hear him. "A car is parked in your driveway, dude, just hanging out."

"What car?" I whispered back. Stepping away from the screen door and the crickets chorusing outside, recalling my recent mysterious trespasser.

"Gotta be one of *them*! Who'd you piss off, dude?"

"*Them*?" I asked. I heard something rustle outside the kitchen window. Froze right up. "I gotta go, Andy," I whispered. "Call 9-1-1 if you hear anything strange." I grabbed the golf putter from behind my front door and stepped out the screen door into the night, ducked behind my pickup to listen. Nothing but the ululating cry of the little screech owl back in the canyon, like a soul frozen in time. An intoxicating perfume of bougainvillea hung on the night air. Had Ches come to settle accounts? Maybe the elusive trespasser? He would expect me to be in the house.

Just then, an apparition appeared at my living room window, silhouetted against a rectangle of lamp light: deformed cranium and grotesquely distended snout, half pig, half human. Yellow disc eyes turned toward me. Someone, I realized, wearing a gas mask or night vision goggles, one of Cal's thugs no doubt. How often had the bastard spied on me while I sat reading in the arm chair or jerking off? Snoop snout. Disc eyes fixed resolutely on me. A corona of diaphanous hair framed the porcine countenance. I tightened my grip on the golf club and stood up. All hell broke loose. Wallers crashed through the brush behind the stalker, grunting, one feverish eye aglow in the swatch of lamp light. The stalker cried out in alarm and sidled along the cabin wall while Wallers goosed him with his snout, no doubt mistaking the intruder for a lithesome sow. He stood up on stubby hind legs and pinned the bastard against the wall, one cloven hoof either side of his hips, his raucous love squeals intertwined with his victim's shrieks.

Poor bastard squirreled and squirmed, one hand against Wallers' wrinkled forehead, the other trying to pull off the night scope, sensing it was the problem. Wallers shrilled in frustration. It was all I could do not to laugh.

"Who's there?" I shouted.

"Albert! Do something, for crissake."

"Mona?"

"Damn it to hell, do something! Your pig is trying to rape me."

I crossed the drive and gripped hold of Wallers' ears from behind. He let go a squeal and fled into the brush behind me. Mona was sobbing. "You and your goddamned pig." She looked a mess: snout hanging catawampus by a strap, slacks smeared with slough muck. She shoved me off when I tried to embrace her. "Are you all right, Mona?"

"I hate you, Al Sharpe." Beating my chest with her fists. I held her to me.

"You asked for it, snooping about people's places dead of night in a geddup like that. Are you spying on me?"

"Good Lord! Smell me." Wiping her hands on my shirt. "You think it's funny—your pig molesting me?"

"Yeah, kind of. So it was you the other day back in the canyon?"

"I don't know what you're talking about."

"Listen, Mona, it's over. Finished. Penny and me. Okay! I know it was wrong."

"What's over? What are you talking about?"

#

Al had let the place go dowdy since Finley went away to high school in Carlsbad: stacks of library books, clothes, newspapers, bits and pieces of his latest inventions ("Albert's follies," Mona called them) jumbled higgledy-piggledy over the couch and floor, a coating of dust over everything, the vinyl couch upholstery split in places. It could have been Tinkerspoon's trailer across the road, not at all like meticulous Al. It had once been homey. Finley and Al had painted the kitchen wall with purple monkeys strung together hand to tail, and plaster mermaids graced the archway into the living room, their fish scales glistening with flakes of mica schist. Finley had helped him paint a mural in the bedroom: Creosote Canyon Road wended bucolically past Tinkerspoon's mailbox into the hazy distance. What had prompted him to let the place go, the white-washed adobe walls soiled with grime?

After the Wallers incident, Al and Mona sat on deck chairs on the front porch, listening to the crickets and Wallers' grunts off near the black slough, sounding like some paleolithic throwback. Mona's head moved side to side in the infrared goggles, keeping watch. She looked like an animal-headed Egyptian god in the moonlight, holding Al's putter in a two-handed grip before her like a tennis racket. He confessed that he'd had sex with Penny Noonan after the DGLA dinner. "I've never done anything like that before. Never cheated on my friends. I don't feel good about it. I was intoxicated, nothing else to call it."

Mona laughed. "You and Penny Noonan? Who would guess? It's a riot, really. I'd love to see the look on Chester's face. God knows what he'd do."

"I thought you were Ches earlier."

"Lucky for you I wasn't."

"So the bank has been loaning him money to buy us out? You have?"

"It's my job! Like I said, Al, I'm not going there. Drop it."

He got into the shower with her and soaped her down, then stood behind her hard as a rock. They fell on his bed soaking wet and made raucous love, the bed nearly collapsing beneath them. "Wheewy," she whinnied after they'd tried most every position and came to a whooping mutual climax. "I guess Penny flipped a switch in you."

After she'd gone home, Al sat back in the canyon by Pissing Springs, looking up at an alley of night sky above canyon walls, listening to owls softly hooting to each other; a silent shadow passed just overhead, checking him out. Coyotes yipped on the mesa above. He loved this place, loved us—the valley and town of Saint Angel—couldn't imagine Ches or anyone wanting to destroy us. Wallers joined him, grunting softly, lying beside him like a dog. Al scratched his leathery, bristled back, and trailed a finger along scars left from his battles with coyotes. They were no match for him, though never seemed to learn. Al had often heard Wallers' frantic squeals, the crazed yips of attacking coyotes, then low moans when Wallers caught hold of a paw or genitals in his grinding molars. It was a nasty business. Finley once suggested Al make him a fur coat so he looked like a dog and could stay warm in the winter. Al devised one of deer hide, but Wallers tore it off and ate it.

The sound of trickling water sang him to sleep. Huddled against a sandstone wall that retained some of the day's heat through that short night, he dreamt fitfully of Sondra: shiny black hair clinging to her skull like the *sleek coat of a chinchilla, nose attenuated to a snout, morphing to Penny who pointed an accusatory finger and cursed him for sleeping with Mona, Ches waiting for him outside in the hall, clutching a golf putter in his hands. Al woke to a bitter taste in his mouth and remembered that Sondra was dead. He was shivering in shorts and T-shirt, gripping his elbows. High overhead, a red-tailed hawk whistled and floated across a strip of re-splendent blue sky framed by narrow canyon walls that glowed pastel pink in dawn's light, long purple shadows in declivities. A nearly translucent scorpion tiptoed delicately along a granite outcropping not six inches from his head, its tail raised in warning, reminding Al of Little Lester—the don't-tread-on-me demeanor—who said the canyon would make a fine fortress. Finley once took scorpions to school for show and tell; tomorrow was her birthday. Something dislodged a stone high above. Al watched it ricochet between narrow canyon walls and land with a small detonation of sand not two feet from him. Life is fraught with near misses.*

6

MASTER INVENTOR

It began with Finley's allergy to wood smoke. Many Saint Angelinos heated with wood cut in the mountains and a haze of smoke drifted over Second Chance Acres on winter evenings. Finley suffered raw red eyes, a runny nose and sore throat. So Al Sharpe invented a smoke scrubber to install in flues around town. It injected air into hot gases as they rose up the chimney, causing flash combustion to oxidize the carbon and heavier pollutants in the smoke. Residues passed on through baffles and screen filters that captured smoke particles, which were washed away by mini-jets of water; tiny steel brushes scoured the filters every hour, and soot fell down into a removable tray. The device was compact and ingenious in the way Sharpe's inventions were. Twelve-year-old Finley thought it the coolest thing he'd ever invented and urged her father to secure a patent and sell it. Tinkerspoon agreed. "Really, dude. You've finally undone yourself."

"I think you mean 'outdone,' Andy," Finley corrected him.

"Naw, dudette, 'undone,' cause the dude finally made something that actually works." Mona found a patent attorney and sent letters to wood stove manufacturers. The Connecticut Flue Company bought and modified the Sharpe Smoke Scrubber, producing models to fit all sizes of chimney flues and stove pipes (their deluxe model included a vacuum component for easy soot removal). As part of the deal, Al arranged for Saint Angelinos to buy scrubbers at half price. The Sharpe Smoke Scrubber sold well for a time in places like Vermont and Oregon where air pollution from wood burning was a nuisance. In an Ecosphere interview, Al Sharpe was hailed as "a new breed of eco-inventor." Rob Thompson and Sage called him "Eco Man." When he entered Mimi's Diner, townsfolk nodded, pleased to have "an inventive genius" living among them.

Royalties poured in for several years. Then came complaints of clogged filters and scrub brushes deteriorating under the assault of tannic and acetic acid. Houses filled up with backdrafted smoke. Al had warned Connecticut Flue that his scrubber was high maintenance. When mothers sent irate notes accusing him of trying to asphyxiate their children, Al replied,

"Please accept my humble regrets and apologies. I will personally arrange a refund." Connecticut Flue's lawyers were furious at him for admitting culpability. *"They'll sue our pants off."* But the lawsuits only began after Al stopped writing apologies. *Ecosphere* ran another article accusing him of eco-terrorism.

There were sufficient Smoke Scrubber earnings to pay for Finley's college and provide a modest monthly income from Al's securities portfolio. He gave to The Nature Conservancy and made zero-interest loans to friends. It didn't occur to him until it was too late to buy land to conserve locally. Al continued to live modestly. When Rob Thompson asked if he'd ever heard of "the American dream," Al replied, "I'm living it." He basked for a time in the glow of local success. Finley was proud of him, and *The Saint Angel Clarion* referred to him as "Saint Angel's master inventor."

Then royalties dried up and Connecticut Flue took the Sharpe Smoke Scrubber out of production. Al's solar insulation jacket for young citrus trees didn't find a taker. He was excessed again, fully back in Saint Angel.

Unable to sleep the night before Finley's birthday, obsessing over what to tell his daughter about her mother, as he'd promised to do when she turned seventeen, Al walked out under the moon, looking up at the treehouse for signs of life. Finley was still over on the coast and wouldn't be home until tomorrow, but Mona had gone up to sleep in the treehouse, as she often used to do, staying over to help him with tomorrow's preparations. Wallers fell in beside him, making small, lusty grunts as they strolled, while, overhead, Mona perused photos in a scrapbook Finley had left open on the walnut-burl table her father had carved for her twelfth birthday. There were shots of Al and Finley, several of Mona and Finley cheek to cheek, other Saint Angel friends, folksy portraits of "Al Sharpe Master Inventor" clipped from the Saint Angel Clarion, outlined in gold glitter, and MOM'S MEMO-RIAL PAGE at back of the album.

Sondra was taller than Mona had expected, a good inch taller than Albert, and every inch the forbidding academic, with hair pulled severely back from a lofting forehead and a narrow, beaked nose. She'd envisioned a softer, more attractive wife for Al. In one shot, Sondra sat in a tatty terry-cloth robe at her desk, amber-tinted granny glasses slipped down to the bulb of her nose, looking rebukingly over them at the camera—and Al beyond it. Contrasting this, a beach shot of his wife in a knit string bikini that left little to the imagination, hair sun-bleached, toes of her strong feet splayed in the sand, heavy breasts in the bikini top, a caesarean scar snaking into the suit's bottom. On the facing page a photo captioned "Mom two days before." *Spooky.* *Sondra sat in a darkened kitchen, elbow perched on the table, a hand shading her eyes as she stared into space, one bare leg tucked under her on the chair, her mouth sprung open like a boxer on the ropes, defeated by irreconcilable differences. Did Al intuit, when he snapped that picture, that it would be the last he would take of her? The final image in Finley's scrapbook.*

Mona studied the photos—trying to see what Al had seen when he took them—to learn something of this enigmatic woman. It occurred to her there were no pictures of Sondra about the place. Her memory was subterranean, hidden away in a scrapbook. Neither Finley nor Albert ever talked about her. All memory of her lay buried deep underground in their psyches. Tomorrow that was supposed to end.

It seemed to her a form of self-betrayal that she had so enjoyed making love to Al last night in spite of his damned pig, particularly troubling since she'd made peace with not having him in her life. She found life less complicated without men in it. Men meant hard drinking and psychic encumbrance, although Al Sharpe seemed an exception to the rule. She'd vowed to herself never to backslide into romantic involvement again.

In college, she had fallen in love with her English professor, a hipster who wore frayed jeans and a faded blue work shirt to class, outré even for San Francisco State, where most profs still wore sports jackets. He was into Derrida, Robbe-Grillet, and post-modernism long before most had heard of them. Mona found him fascinating, an anodyne to her parents' stuffiness and the reign of the Reaganite throwbacks. Moreover, they had great sex. Their relationship was built on lust; they hardly spoke in their thrice weekly sex sessions. Chip lived on a strict schedule and vegetarian diet: a conundrum given his fierce avant-garde iconoclasm and predatory intellect. His marriage was failing. Instead of trying to fix it, he hooked up with a student. That should have been a warning. After making love in his tiny book-stuffy apartment, she told him her dreams of bicycle touring with him through France, visiting Java and Machu Picchu, all the wondrous places. She wanted to have his children. He laughed derisively and said between reading and raising kids he knew where his loyalties lay. Another warning sign, but she ignored it.

Much to their surprise, since they used protection, Mona became pregnant with twins. Chip about-faced and asked her to marry him. He was giddy about the prospect of having kids and preserving his lineage, confessing to her it had worried him that his family line would die with him since he was a single child, as were both his parents. "It's surprising what life teaches you about yourself," he told her. Excited about having kids in the abstract, now that it was becoming a reality Mona feared she would become mired in child bearing and domesticity (like her mother), forced to abandon her dream of having a career as a psychotherapist. When the twins were born, she went into post-partum depression. She begged Chip to hire day help so she could pursue her Masters degree. He said she needed to accept her responsibility as a wife and mother and give up this pipe dream of hers until the children were grown. A cool hipster on campus, he was a petty tyrant at home, self-involved, indifferent to others. She began drinking on the sly, hiding bottles of Southern Comfort about the house, always tipsy when she went to bed so she could tolerate his groping.

She tried writing, but couldn't concentrate with the twins demanding her constant attention. There was always something: peanut butter smeared on the couch or the toilet left unflushed or a nose that needed blowing. She wasn't cut out for the inflexible demands of motherhood. Chip kept rebuking her for it. Her youthful joi de vivre and sexual enthusiasm, which had once turned him on, now disgusted him. She let the house go, didn't bathe the kids. Chip would come home and have to do the chores instead of his research and grading. Their relationship went quickly south. One day, drunk and demoralized, she left the twins out back in a cold rain. She'd locked the back door so they couldn't come tramping muddily in and wake her from her nap. Hearing them pound on the door and cry out for her, she convinced herself it was only the rain raising havoc against the windows. The boys came down with strep throat, and Chip demanded she seek psychiatric help. When she refused, he filed for divorce. She didn't contest his demand for full custody of the twins or the judge's decision to deny her regular visiting rights, though her lawyer warned she would regret it some day. "No, I won't," she insisted. "I never wanted children, certainly not his." Still, whenever Mona wished to punish herself, she conjured the judge's stern visage—pinched lips, and scowl lines etched into her face like tribal markings—as she sat on the bench in black robes, saying that Mona wasn't fit to be a mother. "You are a selfish, reckless drunk without regard for your children's well being. You are a disgrace."

Mona moved out to the desert, bought a derelict house and began fixing it up. The desert dried her out and stood her up. She got a business degree at College of the Desert, then a job at Saint Angel Federal Bank. She loved life out under the open sky, loved her isolation, nearly forgot that she had twin boys that she had not seen in years. She met Al Sharpe and Finley. The girl touched something in her, as did Al's vulnerability.

"Life teaches us who we are," she once told them, echoing her ex hus-
band. "I had children and learned I don't want to be a mother. I met you,
Finley, and learned that I do."

They shook their heads in puzzlement. Mona did that to you. The
moment you'd decided she was a dedicated nonbeliever, she would surprise
you with her Catholicism.

#

I awoke half frantic and exhausted at 5 a.m., like I'd been running
all night. Getting nowhere. Finley's birthday present, the pressing
closet, was still scorching fabric as well as pressing it. The bellows ap-
paratus, fashioned from an old accordion, needed redesigning, as did
the heating coils. But I was more anxious about my promise to reveal
the circumstances of her mother's death on her 17th birthday. Doubted
I was up to it.

Working on the pressing closet, I heard someone shouting at the
front gate. Two cadaverous old boys in Shriners' straw boaters and black
suits off a thrift store rack stood at my gate calling, "Anybody home?"
Wallers charged the fence from behind a screen of pampas grass, snort-
ing fury. He took his watch pig duties seriously. "Whooaaa...yeah!"
the man in high water trousers backed away from the gate; the other
squatted and reached through to scratch Wallers' chin. "Cute hog."
"Careful," I warned him, "that pig is known to bite." He stood up,
maybe six-five, hollow cheeked, cadaverous. Looked like a hearse
had dropped them off on Creosote Canyon Road as folks sometimes
dropped cats. The other gestured at balloons hung on the fence.
"Somebody's birthday?"

"How can I help you fellows? I'm short on time today." They didn't
carry Bibles, but you can spot an evangelical: they look right through
you, like a field-goal kicker hoping to put you over the crossbar. One
wore a preacher's collar. His breath worse than Ches Noonan's when he
opened his hollow mouth. Even Wallers backed off a few paces. Blue
stubble stippled his waxen jowls. If Tinkerspoon had been home, he
would have come cursing out of his trailer. His dad was a preacher, and
he hated the lot. *El Rapido* dashed along the fence, leaping and nipping at the air. The old boys had to be out-of-towners; local evangelists
had long since consigned Tinkerspoon and me to hell.

"The land shall scour brown, the sun shall desiccate the harvest, and the floods drown them—"

"Not interested," I said.

"Not interested—" the preacher's head came up "—in your eternal soul?"

"I long since consigned it to sin and damnation, brother."

"You're a devil worshiper," the sidekick decided, "a whoremonger."

"Worse. I don't believe in anything, either heaven or hell. Least-wise in a soul."

They threw me sidelong glances, mumbling together, then ambled away without another word, throwing glances back at me, deciding, no doubt, that I wasn't fully human. Mona approached me with mugs of coffee. "Who are the desperados?"

"Death and Pestilence. They came to warn us about the upcoming apocalypse. I might agree with them there. I just don't think we need God to finish us off; we're doing a fine job of it ourselves. I'm trying to finish Finley's present."

"Your fabric-scorching contraption?" Mona wore a pair of my old running shorts and a frayed work shirt, naked underneath; sprigs of blond hair on her arms glistened in sunlight, turning me on. "I was looking at pictures of your wife last night. She's not what I expected."

"Not what I expected either."

"So what happened between you two exactly?"

"You know what happened. She went down off Coronado Island on infamous flight 452, returning home from Hawaii with her girl-friend."

"I mean earlier. What bollixed up your marriage?"

I looked across the road at Tinkerspoon's domestic disaster, his dogs standing guard at the fence. "The usual complaints: mutual dis-appointments and lack of communication. That's part of it. Maybe she could talk to Charlie. Finley doesn't know her mom fell in love with a woman, you realize."

"Does she need to know?"

It came to me as a revelation. "Maybe not." I put an arm around her. "Do you think?"

Tinkerspoon came pedaling down Creosote Canyon Road for all he was worth, leaping from the bike which wobbled on and smacked into my fence. Tinkerspoon wild eyed, black hair spilling from his Dodger's cap. "They're coming, dude, they're breaking ground on Jack-o'-Lantern Road, Angie's land! She sold it to the bastards like she said she was. Fucking bitch!"

"Houses? On Jack-o'-Lantern Road? You're sure, Andy?"

"I saw it, dude: shitloads of wetbacks and Texas crackers in D8 Cats over there."

"Shame on you, Tinkerspoon," Mona admonished him. "You're half Mexican yourself."

"Bullshit!" Tinkerspoon slapped his chest. "I'm American as it gets, dudeski. My people go way back before the *La Cienega* Land Grant, maybe four hundred years."

"Jack-o'-Lantern? Impossible. I was over there two days ago. You're saying they leapt from Dead Creek Canyon to Jack-o'-Lantern in two days? That's two miles?"

Tinkerspoon didn't answer. He carried the bike across the road and heaved it over the fence onto a heap of busted equipment and disappeared into the trailer. "Now he'll hack into TexHome Development's website and do God knows what mischief," I said. "Angie sold us out. Jesus!"

"She bought a house in Barbados—I shouldn't be telling you this. They promised not to start building for five years, the bastards."

We'd recently watched a FRONTLINE special about computer hackers on Finley's TV. One mysterious hacker left his signature on secret Pentagon and corporate sites and the World Bank's privileged protocols: two spoons clacking together in a corner of the screen. "No harm done," the announcer said. "It would appear the hacker simply wants to say, 'Hello there! I'm out here watching—.'" I leapt up from the couch, shouting, "Tinkerspoon! It's fucking Tinkerspoon."

"Right. And I'm Hillary Clinton," Mona said.

#

Finley worried about her dad. She sensed he needed her in some way he couldn't articulate, or wouldn't. She sensed some change in him, and the last thing she wanted in her one remaining parent was change. She wanted to freeze time, like that Christmas scene frozen inside a glass globe, which her mother had given her as a child (the only physical vestige she had of her), wherein snow drifted down on a miniature alpine village when you shook it. She asked her dad to make a diorama with her mother's picture inside, frozen in time. In truth, she hardly remembered her mom.

On the eve of her birthday, as they lay abed in twin cots in Patsy K's

Carlsbad bedroom doing their nightly talk-out, Patsy K asked if Finley ever missed her mom.

"I used to. Not anymore."

"Schnay, bad answer. I don't believe it."

"It's like the truth. Dad has become totally my mom."

"Now you're totally trashing my Dad fantasies."

"Just shuddup, okay. Hands off, he's my father!"

"Albert is a cutting edge person, ubercool. So who's the weird Mexican hombre across the road? I mean, is he seriously reality-challenged or what? He doesn't even act Mexican."

"What's that supposed to mean? Besides, Tinkerspoon isn't Mexican, he's blue blood Saint Angelino. A native son, like Sage and Matt Little-feather."

"PC check, he kept checking out my boobs last time. Gross city."

"So everybody scans your tits. Even God scans your tits. Anyways, people call him Tinkerspoon."

"Tinkerdrool, more like. I mean, he fucking gawked. Your Dad is circumspect at least."

"Hands off my father," Finley cried. "I mean it...totally. He doesn't ogle your tits."

She could almost hear Patsy K shrug in the dark. "Watch him!"

"You're such a fucking slut."

"PC check, Al's a primo dude, that's all I'm saying. Slightly vintaged, true."

Patsy K's whole purpose in life was to invent some neologism that would become a permanent addition to the English language. She was always try-ing out new ones on Finley. "I mean, can you imagine being the dude who coined 'awesome' or 'dis'? Gawd, I'd love to have given the world 'dis.'"

"How can such a brainiac be such a widget wit?"

"Okay, so I invented 'widget wit.' Have you ever heard one solitary person outside of Carlsbad High use 'widget wit'? I mean, it's terminally pathetic."

Finley shrugged. "My father does sometimes."

"Like I said, Dad is a totally rad, cutting-edge person."

Finley heard Patsy K turn over in the dark. "Okay, you're not a slut," she whispered, "not deep down. But try to act half-way normal tomorrow, would you?"

"D'accord," Patsy K mumbled.

"Tomorrow I learn the ugly truth about my mother, whatever that is."

Her dad and Patsy K had much in common: both were rad unconventional, both brainiacs, both droll widget wits. Most importantly, she liked them both. It occurred to her that in another life they might hook up. She banished the thought. Patsy K Jones as her mother! Schnay, totally bad idea.

When they arrived at Second Chance Acres that morning, a sign on the gate announced: "Finley's Belated Birthday Party."

Finley hugged her father. "So what's 'belated' about it?"

"I expected it would be. I haven't finished your present yet."

"You're a dummy, you know, a total widget wit."

"That's so rad," Patsy K cried, "inventing presents instead of buying them like everybody else. I totally love it." Patsy K hugged him a little too ardently, Finley thought.

"It can be stressful. How are you Patsy K? Are you taking good care of my daughter?"

"Schnay. No way, Albert. She's taking care of me. She's like that, you know."

As it happened, early that morning while Al and Mona were still asleep, ominous doings were already underway in Saint Angel, unbeknownst to most everyone except Sam Jenson, who had seen a flyer stapled to a fence post near his place on Yucca Road announcing a public hearing at five-thirty a.m. Saturday to solicit public input on a proposed commercial development near his place. Up by four, he took a thermos full of acidic black coffee to the meeting, tapping his watch as commissioners and contractors filed in at about six, including Ches and Cal Hale. "You're late," he scolded them. The men laughed curtly and stared in surprised alarm at Sam seated alone at rear of the small auditorium. "Howdy do, Sam," Cal chirped. "Glad you could make it."

"Like hell you are."

On an overhead projector, contractors displayed building plans for the Desert Air Supermall to be constructed out Yucca Road adjacent to Sam's place. Watching, he experienced cognitive dissonance. His was a world of chorusing coyotes and baking mesquite, sunlight glinting off the backs of water beetles midday, a huge vacant sky. Big box outlet stores had no place in it, or thousands of houses in neat rows out in the desert. They would maximize yields, the developers promised, to 10 houses per acre.

"What's Temecula have?" Ches Noonan asked.

"Seven-point-eight," someone said.

Sam was up, having as much of this perverse dream as he could stom-

ach. "*There's only but twelve of us live out Yucca Road, including Juan Batista's six kids. We don't need no gawddamn Mack Donalds or Walmart.*" *He stomped out, pursued by a man in a shiny blue shirt whose tie dangled untied around his neck, calling after him, "Say there, Mr. Jenson. You're Sam Jenson?"*

"*Who's asking?*"

"*Ronald DeMillo, Three Mile High Investments. We'd like to make you an offer on your property, sir.*"

"*I ain't selling. Cal send you, did he?*" *Sam whipped the tie from around the young man's neck and snapped it taut between his hands with a gratifying crack, then stuffed it in his pants pocket to replace the broken belt on his water pump. "I been needing this."*

"*That's my tie. You took my necktie.*" *The man laughed incredulously.*

"*Surcharge for my time,*" *Sam said.*

"*Surcharge?*" *He chuckled and tapped Sam's chest with his finger. "They warned me about you.*" *He stuck his business card under the wiper blade on the intact half of Sam's windshield. "Call me when you change your mind.*"

"*I don't have a telephone.*" *Sam scowled. "Wouldn't call you if I did.*"

Al thought Sam's story about the supermall a tall tale, a product of isolation delirium. "It's all ass-backwards, people," *Les said. "Developers don't go before Planning until they own the property and have their financing and plans in place. They don't seek pre-approval before they buy, that's illegal.*"

"*Who's going to notice in Saint Angel?*" *Rob Thompson asked.*

"*We do,*" *Daphne snapped.*

Sam's early morning daymare was seen as precisely that. Big box outlets aren't built in the desert far from population centers. But some days later, Mona came in to Mimi's Diner and sat down at the boys' booth. "Sit down and join us, pretty lady," *Sage said. A few church-going locals eyed her dubiously.*

"*Sam is right, they're planning something big,*" *Mona confessed, "Ches, Cal, John Sylvester and the rest. They have been buying up land on the q.t. for years, not wanting to alarm people. Ches met with Mr. Robinson for two hours at the bank yesterday. Afterwards, Mr. R. asked me what I thought about underwriting ninety million dollars in construction loans. He was grinning ear to ear. I really shouldn't be telling you this.*"

Matt laughed. "Saint Angel Federal? You frigging kidding me over here?"

"I don't believe it," Al agreed. "Ches wouldn't want to fill the valley with houses; he loves it here as much as we do. It's conspiracy paranoia."

"You're in denial as usual, Al," Mona snapped. "Maybe it's too troubling for you to see it. We're hearing that the Planning Commission is meeting secretly very early in the morning so the public won't attend, not announcing their meetings until they are over."

"That right there is illegal," Les insisted.

"Maybe, but that's what they are doing. They're all in on it. Commissioners merely recuse themselves if they stand to make a profit from a project under discussion. There's speculation that supervisors might seize Sam Jenson's land via eminent domain, claiming it is underutilized. They have done that successfully in Cleveland and Portland, Oregon."

"The rich get richer, people. That's about all you can count on, besides death." Les clapped a hand on the table. "They're way out ahead of the rest of us."

"You see what I mean?" Al scoffed. "Conspiracy theories. Why would Ches and the others want to make Saint Angel a suburban nightmare?"

"Because it's going to make them rich," Rob said.

Al went quiet, recalling Ches's clandestine offer to buy his land and Angie's warning that they would all sell in the end.

"They plan to call it The Singing Springs Tract," Mona said glumly.

7

THE REAL ITEM

Ill fortune never takes a holiday, no matter that it was Finley's birthday. Wallers came up missing shortly after Finley arrived. I whistled for him back in the canyon, edged up on the screen of salt grass and sickly willows around the black slough and saw a depression dead center of that seething dark morass, like a finger poke in chocolate pudding. "Wallers, buddy," I groaned. The slough belched a few fat bubbles in reply. Mona shouted laughter and clapped her hands. "The swamp ate your pig! Serves him right, he's a sex offender."

I was downcast on the drive to Tourmaline to find new parts for my pressing closet. We passed the new construction site on Jack-o'-Lantern Road that Tinkerspoon had mentioned, a huge sign announced: COLD CREEK CANYON ESTATES (where there was neither creek nor canyon). Made me sick: chaparral scraped down to raw red earth, huge cat tractors trolling in wide circles, like trawlers dragging seine nets behind them, orange stud walls going up, workers crawling over rafters. "Unbelievable," I cried. "Out here in the middle of nowhere."

Mona frowned. "Nowhere's the middle of nowhere anymore, don't you realize?"

I recognized Rob Thompson's pickup parked among the others, the *My Boss is a Jewish Carpenter* bumper sticker. "Rob says he doesn't want them filling the valley with houses, but here he is helping them do it."

"It's what he does for a living, Albert. You can't fault a lawyer for practicing law."

"Or you for arranging their loans, I guess. They call it 'progress'—I call it 'trespass.' This is cactus and coyote country."

"You don't understand what's going on here, do you? Worry about something you can change; this is a done deal."

"I refuse to believe that."

"Of course you do."

When we got back, Sage had found Wallers wallowing in the mud back by Pissing Springs. "Too sick he can't move. I heard a water baby in them springs back there, a *pa?akniwat*. You hear it crying like that, it means somebody's going to die."

Wallers grunted plaintively at our approach, lying on his side in the Devil's Punch Bowl below where water spewed out of a cleft in the sandstone in sporadic spurts as if expelled by a weak sphincter muscle. His corkscrew tail flicked when Finley knelt beside him and rested her cheek on his pink belly. She loved that pig. Wallers closed his eyes and grunted softly. Hard as I tried, I couldn't hear Sage's water baby.

Then we got a Santa Ana. Hot desert wind funneled into the canyon, moaning against rock outcroppings like when you blow across the lips of a beer bottle, stirring up dust and lashing the table cloth off the banquet table Mona had laid. Drove us inside. Rob arrived downcast; he'd gotten into it with Jack Crispley again and been fired from the construction site.

"Wha'd you do this time, brother?" Matt asked.

"Jack told me I can't spread the good news to my fellow workers on the job. He fired me and Jesus both."

Mona about to say she didn't blame him, but I put a finger against her lips.

Then Esther Johnson called from Saint Angel General to tell us Sam Jenson had suffered a coronary that morning. I heard a water baby whimper in the phone lines.

The whole crew trooped down a hospital corridor, stopped by a nurse in a squashed toadstool cap standing before room 23B with a hand raised. "You can't all go in there at once. He's a very sick man."

"Lizards don't get sick," Matt Littlefeather told her.

"You won't be going in at all, young man, you're drunk."

"I don't drink, old woman."

Cal Hale emerged from Sam's room. "Howdy do, folks. You come visiting Sam? That's real good of you." He pointed a finger at me and cocked his thumb. "If it ain't Al Sharpe...."

"I didn't realize you were so fond of Sam," Mona said.

"We're all family here." Cal's little jalapeno eyes bumped from one of us to the next.

Finley and Patsy K went in first, while the rest of us waited in the lounge with an elderly woman in orange slacks whose lips pulled away from her teeth each time she looked at us. Sage was shaking his head. "This place ri'chere, this is your Anglo death tavern. First, they take your life, then they steal your spirit. That's where all the trouble began right there—the white man taking what don't belong to him."

I thought of the developments going in out Jack-o'-Lantern Road: people, houses, lawns, schools where they don't belong. Destroying the land and stealing its spirit, trying to make the desert what it isn't. Were we dirtbaggers who came out here to make a fresh start any better? Vietnam vets, bikers, meth cooks, desert rats, the grotty SOB with long greasy gray hair whose bondoed '67 Chevy was always parked down at Hefner Brothers Market, plastered with bumper strips: "Rush is Right," "God, Dogs and Guns Keep America Free." "Sage is right," I said. "We don't belong here, none of us. We always bring our discontent with us."

Mona laughed. "Where did that come from?"

"Speak for yourself, Albert. I belong here," Daphne Thompson said.

"I'm saying your yuppies don't fit out here."

"*My* yuppies?"

"We're bad enough. What's coming is worse. Invasion of the SUV legions, Desert Storm Two, water guzzling, lawn growing, reality-challenged Greeniacs."

"I drive an SUV," Daph said testily.

"We're in the desert here, I'm saying."

"It's chaparral, not desert," she corrected me, playing schoolteacher. I had a sudden vision of her bare-breasted at the Noonan's pool, another Daphne altogether.

"What shit are you two talking now?" Rob asked.

The old gal was watching us blankly, not hearing a word. A nurse and the hospital chaplain came for her. "Goodness, no," she cried. Legs nearly buckled under her as they led her out.

Patsy K took me aside as I was going in to see Sam. "PC check, you didn't forget your birthday promise to Finley, did you, Dad? Her seventeenth, capeesh?"

"Of course I didn't." Actually, I was hoping she wouldn't remember it.

I'd never seen Sam looking cleaner or more chipper. "Pretty good deal." He grinned. "Fresh sheets and all the tapioca pudding I can eat."

"How's your heart, Sam?" Mona asked.

"If you got to die, die happy."

It seemed the heart attack had altered Sam's personality one-hundred-eighty degrees, turned him sweet. IV tubes fed into him from dangling bags full of fluid, a screen on the IV stand winked numbers, and a line led from a round disk taped to his sunken chest to a boxy cardiograph monitor. Sam jabbed it with a thumb. "They put my heart in this box. I told the doc he damn sure better gimme back the right one. I don't want no tamale eater's ticker."

"Glad to see you're back to your old ornery self, Sam. You had us worried," I said.

"That girl come in with y'r daughter, Sharpe, I told her we can have sex anytime she's ready. I never seen a bitch so far into heat."

"God, Sam, you are incorrigible." Mona shook her head.

"Not yet I ain't. I told that old cow nurse, 'Y'r fat, but you still got a good set of yams on you.'"

"What did she say?"

"I told him I would pull the plug if he didn't behave himself," answered the nurse, coming in.

"I ain't dead yet." Sam flashed her a thumbs up. "Same as I told that land-grabbing sumbitch Cal Hale. He won't get my heart or my land neither one."

The nurse shooed us out and followed behind. "He might seem sicker in the head than the body, but I assure you he's one sick calf." I told her not to take what Sam said personally.

"Oh, I've seen worse."

We all crowded into Finley's treehouse to eat cake and open her presents. Worried me to have a dozen people up in the crotch of that tree, but there were no creaks or groans. Tinkerspoon gave Finley a first edition of Walt Whitman's *Leaves of Grass* he'd dug out of his shit heap. Fathom that. Rob and Daph gave her a fifty-dollar Treasury I Bond. "I know it's not much, but it will grow." "That's just too weird," Patsy K decided. Mona gave her a bra and panty set from Victoria's Secret. "A bit precocious, don't you think?" I said. The Littlefeathers whistled and called on her to model it. Then Matt stood solemnly up. "My brother and me didn't buy you nothing or nothing. Next Coyote Moon, we're gonna take you up to Singing Springs on the rez over there and show you The Power." Sage nodded. "That's our present." Finley leapt up and hugged them. "That's just so cool, I love it. That's the coolest present I ever got." As far as I knew, no Anglo had ever been invited up to the Mountain Cahuilla holy site. Early settlers who tried going there met with nasty accidents.

I dragged my pressing closet out from behind the world's largest cordless TV set. "I'm still working out the bugs." Everyone was fascinated when I fired it up and pressing plates came together with a hiss of steam. Finley clapped her hands. "You are amazing, Dad." Patsy K said I had a genius for "utter widgetry." Daph asked if she could use it for a dunce closet in her bonehead English class.

Next day, as I was watering the winter garden, the girls collared me. I pointed out the drooping spinach and a saline crust at garden's edge. "Everything's dying. Well water's gone brackish thanks to Cal's deep wells. He's draining our aquifer."

"*Brackish!* I love it," Patsy K cried. "It can be used as an adjective: *You're a totally brackish person.* Or a noun: *I got brackish to show for it.*" Patsy K reminded me of my wife, Sondra, in her fashion statement: tight blue gym shorts, Cal sweatshirt, and Birkenstocks. All that attitude.

"Don't encourage her," Finley said. "You made me a promise, Dad, remember? My seventeenth birthday, capeesh!" Sounding breathless, as if touched with stage fright.

"Finley has every right to know about her mother," Mona said, approaching behind me.

I felt cornered. "Okay—" clapping my hands "—but we need to do this alone, hon."

We sat on the meditation bench built around the base of Finley's oak, surrounded by our small piece of paradise. I had no idea where to begin or what there was to tell. "Your mother and I didn't have much in common. She was a tea drinker, I drank coffee; she was into wine, I preferred beer; she liked movies, I liked the night sky; she had a good job, I couldn't keep one. God knows what we were doing together in the first place. Do you really want to hear this?"

Finley nodded. As I talked, her fingers traced unconsciously over her mother's face in the picture album lying open on her lap. A shot of Sondra seated at kitchen table on "Mom's Memorial Page," titled "Mom two days before," eyes startled by the flash. She looked haggard, argued out. I had intuited that it would be the last picture I ever took of her. "I wanted to give her her freedom," I said, "but I didn't know how. I was afraid she would try to take you with her; I didn't want to lose you." Finley turned to a shot of the three of us mugging on the beach at Del Mar in happier days, Sondra virtually naked in a see-through string bikini.

"Did you ever love each other?" she asked.

"Yes...I think so, at first. Your mother knocked me out: smart and sexy and headstrong. Mostly, we loved you. You were the best thing in our marriage, the one thing we did right. We were arguing about how to arrange custody when I took that last photo of her."

"So you were getting a divorce, right? She was leaving us to be with someone else, abandoning us? Schnay, I hate that. That totally sucks." Tears welled in her eyes.

"No, hon. Not abandoning you. The plan was to share custody."

"It still sucks. Breaking up a family, killing the tribe." Her fingers caressing a cleft in her mother's chin much like her own, tracing its contours with her fingertips.

"Your mother loved you to pieces, kiddo, but she loved Charlie, too, and Charlie didn't want kids. There's the rub. She didn't plan it, you know. These things happen, it's nobody's fault."

"Shit happens!" Her eyes downcast. "Charlie—" spitting it out. "So was he like a total widget or something?"

Charlie was a woman. I just stopped myself from saying it. She didn't need to know, and what did it matter, really? Finley closed the album and folded hands atop it, her moist cheeks reflected stippled sunlight filtered through foliage. "Anyways, it really doesn't matter. She died in a plane crash before she could leave, didn't she?"

I nodded, my voice gone hoarse. "Flight 452 from Honolulu to San Diego. The plane inexplicably lost power and went down off Coronado Island. They never determined why. Your mom had a sociology conference in Hawaii. I remember how you kept asking me if Hawaii was big enough to land a plane on. You were worried about that—intuiting something, I guess."

"So I remember sitting on your lap and crying," she blurted, "and this huge cold cavern with windows looking out on the landing planes. Spooky. The walls were wet, people were crying, every time a plane passed by I told myself Mom was on it. I made up a game called *Nobody Knows But Me.* When she arrived, they would call you over the loudspeaker." Her head came up. "They did call you, I remember now."

I nodded, feeling suddenly morose. "We waited at the airport for two days with the other families, hoping for word of survivors, sleeping on mats on the floor, eating meals out of plastic trays—hospital food delivered by 'Condolence Reps' in blue blazers. No one slept much. People stood crowded against floor-to-ceiling windows day and night, as if hoping their loved ones would come stumbling out of the fog. Early that third morning, they called me over the intercom. It was minutes before I recognized my own name. They led me to a tiny chapel where I met a gaunt chaplain in a black clergy shirt that looked like it had been slept in, backwards collar, thick black eyebrows, and a younger man with a prominent Adam's apple and sunken cheeks. Like brothers, those two, the Brothers Grimm. I could hardly follow the young one's words, I was hypnotized by his bobbing Adam's apple. He was talking about the number of persons who'd boarded versus the number in the flight manifest, something about how the manifest and gate check in didn't match. There was a discrepancy, he said. 'The manifest shows 398 passengers aboard, but check in shows 396. We show your wife on the Honolulu to San Francisco leg, but she didn't check in at gate in San Francisco, neither she nor her traveling companion.' I was stupefied. 'You're telling me my wife wasn't aboard that flight? You're saying she isn't dead?'"

Finley seized my arm. "I knew it, I knew she wasn't." Her face nearly touching mine. "You never told me, but I knew."

"No, no! He told me there was a lot of confusion at the gate in San Francisco over last minute cancellations and standbys. He said Sondra likely slipped in past gate check. Last minute rush-ons aren't always checked in at departure, it's done in-flight. 'I'm very sorry to tell you this,' he said, 'there is simply no way to account for them, since we don't have access to in-flight records.' 'She missed the flight?' I kept asking. He said they couldn't be certain until the bodies were recovered. They couldn't yet say for certain that anyone was dead, but it could be surmised."

Finley was gripping my shoulders. Hard. "Dad...so are you saying Mom is alive?"

"No...no, now. Few bodies were recovered," I mumbled. "No, of course not. Your mother died in that plane crash, there's no doubt about it. If she'd missed the flight, she would have let us know she was alive, whatever her intentions. But she never called, never contacted us. She wouldn't leave us believing she was dead, would never choose such an ugly way to abandon us."

"Abandon me!"

"No mother would leave her little girl waiting night and day at the living room window for a taxi to pull up and her mom to step out.

Least of all Sondra. She was a straight shooter. She loved you."

Finley's brow knit, she dropped into deep brooding. Surely, it made little difference in the end whether her mother left her to be with someone else or abandoned her in death. Either way it was abandonment. No child can reconcile the loss of her mother.

"Listen," I said softly, "it's a hard thing to accept, the uncertainty. It's taken me years. Sondra bought tickets for that flight. No doubt she rushed on at the last minute...with her friend."

"Some guy or something, this Charlie person?"

"It was a woman friend," I said quietly.

"Mom went to Hawaii with a woman?"

"They both taught at UCSD. Charlie was a linguist and your mother was a social anthropologist. They had a lot in common. She was always over at our place."

"*Charlie*? So Charlie is a woman? Mom left you for a woman?"

I sat staring at her, wondering if I should deny it. "Yes, it so happens that she is...was. Does it matter, really? In any case, she hadn't left me yet."

"Okay, so I'm trying to decide. This Charlie person disappeared, too, without a trace?"

I nodded. I'd never heard Finley talk so boldly—except about books she hated. She didn't seem surprised. Perhaps she'd picked up hints as a girl that had been stashed away in the bank vault of memory, subterranean until now. "So you know what I think, Dad, I think you want to believe she's dead when she may be alive, living with this Charlie person. You prefer to think she's dead."

"Nonsense. She was my wife, for crissake. Your mother. Why would I want her dead? She loved you, kiddo. Maybe not me, but you. Why do you think we stayed together after our marriage died?"

"You didn't look for her, did you? I know you didn't. You didn't even bother looking, you didn't really care."

"That's unfair, Finley. Where would I look? Navy divers couldn't find the bodies."

"I can't believe you'd do that, Dad. I would have looked." She got up and walked away. I called after her, but she kept walking into the canyon.

When I went out to the mailbox later, a man leaned out of the window of a white van parked in front of Tinkerspoon's place across the road and snapped my picture. The van sped off. Who would be snapping my picture? Ches Noonan, insurance fraud investigators who'd discovered Sondra was alive? Ridiculous...after all these years. Still, the thought chilled me. I was out all day next day helping paint Clover Abernathy's house. Returning home near dusk and walking into the cottage, I stopped dead in my tracks. Sondra stared back at me from the wall facing the front door—in caricature—hair a glowing, electrified halo about her head, a Valkyrian afro. Charlie beside her—tall, skinny, wearing a yellow jump suit such as Tinkerspoon might wear, unzipped to the waist. An otherworldly aura hovered about them, exacerbated by the orange glow of sunset. "Remarkable resemblance," I said, "except Sondra's tits are too big." Patsy K Jones squatted on the floor in paint-daubed T-shirt, mixing colors; gym shorts, rolled in tight furls, crawled up white cheeks of her ass. Couldn't she dress more modestly? Finley and Mona were at work on the mural. "PC check, we found Charlie's picture," Patsy K said. My whole life was there: Sondra, Finley and me at the Del Mar beach, me inside the World's Largest Cordless TV Set, Finley up at Singing Springs flanked by the Littlefeather brothers, a Breughelish Wallers gobbling up tiny people in a new suburban development, a B747 spinning groundward in the sky overhead, trailing a plume of white smoke, just the suggestion of a nude woman with stark tan lines standing naked in the window of a sprawling house.

"Who's that?" I cried in alarm.

"I think you know." Mona smirked.

"I suppose that was your idea. And that!" I pointed at a silhouette in profile slinking off the mural to the right, shoulders ominously hunched.

"That's shadow man," Patsy K said. "Every story has one."

"I wish you'd asked me first. I'm not sure I can live with this."

"We thought you'd dig it, Dad," Finley said, first words she'd spoken to me in twenty-four hours. "You're always saying honesty above all else. It may not be a work of art but it's truthful."

"I dig it, baby—at least I'd like to. It's going to take some getting used to."

Later, we watched a TV special on global warming up in the treehouse: recent flooding in England and Madagascar, families on rooftops. "You should build an ark, Daddy," Finley proposed, "just in case." "Brackish idea, Dad." Patsy K wore a night shirt with block letters across her chest: WET DREAMS. Crazy kid. "What would we put in this ark—two Wallers, two Sam Jensons?" I thought of those cadaverous evangelicals, Death & Pestilence, with their doomsday pamphlets, rumors that Singing Springs was no longer singing. "It isn't an ark we need, it's water."

I didn't sleep much between that mural, Sam's heart attack, and van man snapping my picture. I tossed and turned atop my sleeping bag on the screened porch. Got up to walk Creosote Canyon Road under a crescent moon. Yipping coyotes and mawkish owls formed a chorus of lost souls. Boxy outlines of two-story houses took shape out of the void, lining the road either side. Ghost houses. Car lights turned a bend in the road and caught me in their glare. I considered fleeing into chaparral, but headlights held me spellbound, coming slowly on. Night-passing cars were a rarity out here. I recognized Cal Hale's long face, tinted orange in dash lights, his yellow eyes holding mine as the car crept past, reflecting light as a coyote's will. What was he doing out here middle of the night? Maybe he couldn't sleep either. Sondra's phosphorescent eyes startled hell out of me when I stepped in the front door of the cottage. "Did you die in that plane crash?" I asked her.

#

Ches Noonan considered his wife a force of nature you learned to tolerate, like stormy weather. Penny was impetuous, unpredictable, erratic, his opposite. Ches outlined a course of action and didn't stray from it. Penny was Ches's holiday from the stern accountancy of his own ambition. He thought of her as a volatile investment: half the fun of owning them was not knowing whether you would lose your shirt or make a pot of money.

While Cal Hale steered not from his head but his stomach. Given his temper, it was remarkable that he'd succeeded in business. Waking at dawn, he would speed off to a work site and fire the entire construction crew before his first cup of coffee, inspired by a conservative shock jockey's rant about overpaid workers on the radio. He once decked a construction foreman for requesting a coffee break for his men. Cal was like Tahquitz. "Born mean and going to die mean," Sage said. Penny confessed to Cal that Al Sharpe had screwed her in the guest room, "while y'all stood around the pool outside."

"What in hell's name is the matter with your husband?" Cal asked.

"You ought to know," she said.

He hadn't figured Al Sharpe for a womanizer. No, that damned fool woman was feeding him a load of crap. He had serious business to conduct with her husband, and Penny was becoming a nuisance.

It infuriated Penny to think of Al screwing that cow Mona Sahlstrom, though maybe they deserved each other. She doubted he wore Mona's panties on his head while they were screwing like he did hers. She knew it was mad to confess their indiscretions to Cal Hale; no telling how he might use it against them, against Ches. That man was capable of anything. But she needed to tell someone. She left a message for Winky Hale when she knew Cal wasn't at home. The first blood drawn always flows most freely.

Winky thought it was the lady from the Mormon Genealogy Data Bank in Utah when the answering machine picked up. She was busy collecting her genealogy of late. Years ago, she'd collected rag dolls (an entire room devoted to Raggedy Anns, lined up in rows on pine shelves and carefully catalogued), then Grandiflora roses ("Love's Promise" her favorite), then angels. Now she collected ancestors. She considered it an offshoot of her angel collection—earthly angels who had prepared a place for us in the world. She had traced her mother's roots back to Charles I and her father's back to Leif Erikson. It worried her a little that ancestry might be considered an enthusiasm for the elderly.

"That peculiar woman called again," she told Cal after the third message. "Her voice sounds familiar, but I can't place it. She says you slept with her, Calvin. Well, I suppose you collect women as I do angels." It came to her as a revelation. "I suppose you enjoy it. Collecting is such a wonderful pastime. Don't you think?"

A lot of blithering nonsense, Cal thought, immediately suspecting that damned hussy Penny Noonan was making the calls. There was no fathoming a woman's whims. "What in hell's wrong with you," he asked Winky, "every damned one of you?"

Mona Sahlstrom was camping out at Second Chance Acres; she couldn't say why. Maybe, after hearing of Al's unlikely tryst with Penny Noonan, she wanted to stake a more solid claim on him. She'd confessed to Father Flannagan that she and Albert were holding out on each other; she didn't know why. "We both fear commitment, I suppose. I imagine that's why he hooked up with Penny. No danger of commitment there."

"Afraid I don't follow, daughter."

"No, you wouldn't. He insists it was just sex and we have something beyond that. In any case, I think Finley needs me now; she's trying to process all these things she's been learning about her mother. It turns out Sondra was a lesbian."

Mona could hear the priest taking short sips of air beyond the screen, trying to process how a married woman could be a lesbian. It amused her to scandalize the poor man. She told him that she herself once tried lesbian sex. "It's just as pleasurable, you know. I know the church considers it sinful, but the church considers all pleasures sinful, that's what's so quaint and charming about it."

That night, Patsy K Jones sat up in bed to listen. "Is that Dad and Mona?" she whispered in the dark. "Wow, radically brackish! I'm impressed."

Finley experienced a transport of humiliation, covering ears with her hands. "That's disgusting," she whispered, "totally. My dad never does that."

"How'd you get here then, widget wit? They've been at it for hours. Awesome. Dad's really something."

"They should just shuddup!" Seriously, couldn't they stop? They sounded like coyotes nipping at each other. Finley could hear them through her hands. Why is he doing this to me? It's just sex, she told herself. No biggie. Just the plunka-plunka thing. Only brain-zero religious fanatics have a problem with sex. Still, ugh! not her dad and Mona, who was like an older sister to her. She didn't want to hear it. She knew she was being unfair. He'd tolerated Skip Oversby, after all, and waved back at him when Skip stood pissing off the treehouse's deck the morning after their first time, calling, "Hey, Mr. Sharpe, whassup?" While Finley huddled inside, blanket clutched to her chin, not yet sixteen. Didn't they believe in liberation? Age liberation, land liberation, sex liberation? "Sunlight purifies," her dad was always saying. "That's why we moved to the desert."

8

DON'T DRINK THE WATER

Mona called my attention to a story on the back page of *The Saint Angel Clarion:*
COURT TO CONSIDER LAND GRANT CLAIM
About how The Saint Angel Land Company had purchased what remained of the original *Rancho La Cienega del Diablo* Land Grant holdings and was claiming a portion of the Soboba reservation as within the bounds of the *La Cienega* holdings, thus legitimately theirs. It didn't mention Ches, but his foul breath rose off the newsprint. "Why would Ches want that land? It's worthless," I insisted. Mona tapped my forehead. "Don't you see what's going on here? I suppose you don't want to see—the old Al Sharpe ostrich routine."

"I know he wants the land, I just don't know why he wants it."

"Use your nose, Albert."

There was, I suppose, no denying recent warning signs: rattlesnakes that multiplied about the huge live oak supporting Finley's treehouse, emerging from dark cavities at branch crotches, slithering along lower limbs, or lying recumbent, white bellies exposed to the sun. Toad-headed rattlers turned their heads to watch me pass with soulless BB eyes. The girls had to abandon the treehouse. Then the snakes disappeared. I saw the last wriggling tail disappear into Wallers' pink mouth, rattles shaking like furious castanets before being swallowed.

The day of the first DGLA board meeting, I stopped for breakfast at Mimi's. Rob Thompson's pickup parked in the lot, a slogan stenciled across the tinted rear window in huge gothic script:

GO B.I.G.
Believe In God

Rob, most irreverent of men, had met a born-again fellow at work who, he said, "scared the devil straight out of me." Daphne told Mona she hardly recognized her husband anymore. "The last time I asked if he wanted to ball, he said, 'God willing.' Can you believe it, Rob?" But there'd always been something of the true believer about him.

Exiting the restaurant, he caught my arm and asked, "You fucking Penny?"

"Christ, no!" I said. "Are you?"

He punched my shoulder a little too hard. "A man who takes the Lord's name in vain is a living fossil, Sharpe." He averted his face and swiveled abruptly away from me as a man approached across the parking lot towards us: balding, fiftyish, polo shirt and slacks, tufts of red hair sprouting out of his collar, big-ass endomorphic type. "Fucking Trinkley," Rob cursed as he passed, grinding the name back in his molars. "Cal's head surveyor. I meet that SOB face to face and I take him down. Someone should shoot that fat-assed prick. Forgive me, Lord." A hula-skirted tattoo dancer did a bump and grind on Rob's right biceps. Thus, I had my introduction to Tripod Trinkley, Trinkling Dan The Boss's Man.

"Cal fired me. I guess you know," Rob said. "They don't need carpenters. Those fuckers don't do carpentry any more, they do nail and bail."

Driving to the Noonans' later, I thought about Ches's offer to buy my front acres and Tinkerspoon's. Seemingly, he did want the whole valley, as Little Les claimed. Noonan megalomania: Penny balling us and Ches buying our land. Pablo Ortiz took my keys to park the truck. "Is valet parking tonight, everybody all dress up. No you?" Nodding at my khaki shirt and jeans and making a sour face. "No me," I said. Ches greeted me at the door. "Speak of the devil. We were just discussing you, Sharpe."

"Nothing good, I hope."

Looking over his shoulder for signs of Penny, he looked me up and down and motioned for me to follow. Here we go again: Ches fitting me for a jacket in his mirrored wardrobe, Penny moving about in the bedroom next door, humming "Do You Know the Way to San Jose." *Deja vu* Noonan style or *jamais vu*.

"Stop fiddling, Sharpe, for crissake," he barked, checking for sleeve length and holding up a jacket for me to try on, stepping back to nod satisfaction. The scent of male cologne hung on the air, half nauseating, masking his camel breath. He tapped my shoulder for me to turn around, dropped to a knee behind me and tugged at the baggy seat of my jeans. "You want to drop these, Albert?" Definitely not. "Sharpe," he barked, "you think we might do this properly?" The blade of a hand shot up my thigh and clipped my balls, yellow measuring tape snapped taut, I bolted forward, Ches chuckled. "I haberdashed in college. We used to say you can take a man's measure by how much he stiffens when you take his inseam. You're stiff as a board."

Going to the closet, Ches rolled out a Lazy Susan filled with brand new shirts in plastic wrappers, spun it and caught one expertly, yanked off the plastic wrap with his teeth, and snapped out shirt tails. "It's a token of trust in a man to lend him the shirt off your back, Albert." Surely he knew about Penny and me, a man as territorial and predaceous as Ches. Biding his time, no doubt; Ches never acted haphazardly. "A shirt loses its character after a laundering," he said. "Nothing is much good used: clothes, cars, or women." He winked and stepped into the bedroom next door so I could change. I heard him speaking low to Penny, heard my name mentioned.

I hardly recognized myself in multiple mirrors: blue dress shirt, charcoal gray suit, banker's pin stripe, Armani tie. Like an interloper suited out in the bridegroom's clothes. Ches regarded me with a Pygmalion smile when I emerged. "You clean up well, Sharpe." He chuckled. "I'm depending on you today, fellah."

"Depending on me for what?"

He patted my arm. "You'll see, you'll see. All in good time."

The Silk Set made a fuss over me. Mrs. Philadelphia said I looked like Errol Flynn (I'd pulled my hair back in a pony tail); her small-headed friend batted coquettish doll's eyelashes at me. Ches said he'd lent me "a rig." I felt like a museum oddity. Penny ignored me as we moved along a buffet table, filling our plates with California rolls and Ahi. Even from a distance, I smelled the spice of cocoa butter lingering about her. A satiny purple sheath dress clung to her hips and ass. I overheard Cal Hale talking to John Sylvester while we ate: "Damned cheesy ground over there. Out Indian Springs Road, we can go down two thousand feet through solid sandstone." Talking wells in Sam Jenson territory.

"So it's true then," I said loud enough for all to hear, "the county intends to seize Sam's place through eminent domain and sell it to Saint Angel Land Company. That's what we hear. It's legalized theft, you realize."

"Sam's not doing a damn nothing with it; that land is under-utilized. To my way of thinking, that's theft. Or worse, it's plain per-versed," Cal said.

"He lives there is what he's doing with it. Where else could Sam live?"

Ches regarded me coolly. "Saint Angel is changing, and there's not a thing you can do to stop it. That's progress. Sam Jenson doesn't understand it either, none of you do, but you will. Eventually, you'll see reason." Sounded like a threat. His foul, carrion-eating breath.

"Join the winning team," John Sylvester agreed.

"I'd like to propose this master-of-ceremonies thing if Al's not too grumpy in my thousand-dollar suit." Ches told me they had invited five hundred estate agents to town from the biggest outfits in the country. "We want to introduce them to our little piece of heaven in Saint Angel. We'd like you to toastmaster the Saturday evening banquet, Albert. We'd feature you as Saint Angel's favorite son and master inventor."

"That's placing a good measure of faith in you, Albert," Mr. Philadelphia said.

"For the record—" Cal Hale shot up a hand "—I oppose."

"Duly noted."

"Real estate agents?" I was incredulous. Maybe what Rob Thompson and Little Les had been saying was true. "Membership never agreed to this."

"That's why we have a board of directors." Warts had multiplied about the base of Ches's nose, piggy-backing atop each other like rambunctious children.

"You missed our last meeting, so did Daphne Thompson," Imogene Sylvester noted, smoky red hair swept back in a ducktail, eyes the color of wallpaper paste, that wide, intimidating face. "You can't have a say if you don't pay your way."

"Daph was teaching; I had Finley's birthday party."

She turned out her palms. "We have to choose our priorities, don't we?"

"Membership will turn it down flat. We came out here to escape the city, not to build one."

"I'm disappointed in you, Sharpe. As good as Saint Angel has been to you, I'd think you would want to share its blessings." Ches frowned at me. He plunked a lobster roll in his mouth and swallowed it whole, like Wallers did snakes. Something twisted in his logic, but I couldn't put my finger on it.

Mr. Philadelphia said, "Chester is a pragmatic visionary. He envisions two million souls living in the tri-city area by 2030. Marvelous notion."

"No hindering progress." Jake Houston nodded.

"What's visionary about it? It's my idea of hell."

"Now, I don't relish the crowding either, Albert, but I'm willing to make sacrifices for the American Dream. Everyone deserves a little piece of Eden, wouldn't you agree?"

Mrs. Houston nodded solemnly. "Little children need a decent, morally upright environment in which to bloom and blossom, just as your daughter did, Albert." Her simpering smile.

I glared at Ches. "Stealing reservation land, is that your idea of progress?"

"You can't stop progress," Jake Houston parroted.

"Jesus fucking Christ! What is it with you people? Put in a nickel and out comes *progress*."

"That's Jake Houston, all right." Ches chuckled.

"Stealing our precious water," I continued, "to keep your golf courses green during the worst drought in California history, while the rest of us don't have enough to flush the toilet."

"Oh, Albert, you are always so dramatic," Mrs. Philadelphia's small-headed friend cried.

"Someone steals your water, you'll be dramatic, too."

"Our damn water," Cal said. "We'll use it any way we please. There's some of us loves playing golf. Hell, it's why half of us moved out here. This talk about drought is a lot of horse manure shat out by the Sierra Club and their mob of San Francisco queers and eco-lunatics. There ain't no drought, never was, and never will be. That's a scientific myth cooked up by quack professors at Harvard or somewheres back east who don't know a damn thing about the West. Bunch of gawddamned lawn haters, you ask me, golf haters and bellyachers."

Others nodded.

"This is desert, Cal, parched desert. Don't you get that?"

"We're turning it green," Ches said expansively. "I'm mighty proud of that. I thought you were, too. I won't apologize for having a dream."

"What you bitching about anyway, Al? You have your own well, you have all the water you need." Cal turned away from me in disgust and muttered to himself.

"Going dry. What good will a dry well do me?"

Mrs. Philadelphia turned to Penny. "You see what *these people* are like? It's all me, me, me...."

"Screw the board, screw your Realtors' convention, I quit." I leapt to my feet, knocking my chair over.

"Damn it all, Sharpe. We've all chipped in to send your daughter to college."

"I'll send her to college myself."

"You see what I mean? Me, me, me."

"You want to return that suit to my closet on your way out, Albert."

"I'll do you one better." I yanked the jacket and shirt over my head, rolled slacks down my legs, and walked out in my skivvies. Behind me, Penny squealed laughter.

I took the winding back-route home over the Tourmaline Hills. The road was newly paved, hills had greened out in recent rains, dense round clumps of mistletoe hung like Christmas baubles high in oak branches, and spindly ocotillos struck dramatic poses on hillsides like stick-figure modern dancers, arms lifted to the sky. A hawk swooped low, clinging to contours of the land; a spice of pepperwood and sage wafted up from ravines on a cool breeze. Cresting the summit of Big Tourmaline Hill, I was suddenly among new houses, lining the road behind cinder-block walls. Carbon copies of each other, though a sign announced three different models: "Chinook," "Silver," or "Coho," named according to some logic only developers fathom. Salmon in the Mojave! I'd entered not just the wrong neighborhood but the wrong cosmic plan. You wake up one morning to realize this isn't where you live anymore. There'd been no houses here last summer when I last passed through. How had they built them so fast? Spanish-tiled roofs marched down terraced slopes toward a sprawling golf course far below, ugly two-story boxes were crowded chockablock around artificial lakes. Giant earth movers lurked like Jurassic beasts in silhouette atop the opposite ridge, hungry for more carnage. I made out in the rearview two shadowed faces hanging just inches off my bumper in a van behind me.

Entering town in a daze, I passed license plates from Texas, Idaho, Louisiana. Les said they brought framers in from out of state, sold them a house, and created a mini-boom, sucked one place dry then moved on to the next. That was their idea of progress.

#

Al Sharpe possessed little talent for parsing human motivations, least of all his own. He couldn't imagine why he turned off on Two Horse Flats Road on his way to town that day or parked behind the Noonan place, as he had during his trysts with Penny. Surely, if he'd come on a civil errand, say to apologize for his rudeness the other night, he would have parked in front. People seemed to him wondrous, if poorly designed, lacking any readable blueprint. Inspired in concept, flawed in design. Thus, he couldn't have understood what was about to happen any more than he could understand why Finley had become convinced her mother was still alive after he'd spent much of an afternoon chronicling her death.

Vaulting the low block wall in the wrong spot, he landed in a patch of prickly pear cactus. Rubbing a palm over the nearly invisible needles bristling over his arms and cheeks, he flinched in singular and exquisite pain, having become a pincushion for tiny acupuncture needles stuck directly into nerve endings, a delicate, maddening kind of pain. Remarkably, Penny sat out by the pool in a terrycloth robe awaiting him. "How did you know I was coming?" he asked. She clutched his chin in her fingers and led him to the guest room.

"Silly boy! You think you can walk out on me, you little prick?" Cuffing him back onto the bed with open palms, she let the robe drop to her ankles and stood in black leather lingerie with a cut-away crotch and nipple slots. He was waving his hands in warning. Penny pinched his mouth shut and mounted him. "Ah despise men who prattle before sex. Shuddup and screw me, Albert." He tried to alert her about the maddening psora of cactus thorns carpeting his upper torso, their tiny barbed needles readily transplanted. Her leather bra traced angry prickles across his chest. "I'm contagious," he managed. She threw her head back, laughing. Cupping his balls in a hand, she transferred fiery little barbs to his scrotum. "Gawd, I've missed you." Her mouth fastened over his. Mini-thorns spread everywhere, an evil, burning fuzz across his thighs and lips, but miraculously did not invade their mating.

Provoked by the burr of stinging nettles across her breasts, cheeks, and belly, Penny was fascinated by this new side of Albert. His skin assaulted hers, feverishly hot. No doubt he'd rubbed some spicy habanero sex lotion over his body. She rubbed her chest furiously against his, slapped his buttocks, and hissed out curses in their needling intimacy. Just then the front door slammed shut.

"Daddy!" Penny exclaimed.

She pushed Al into the walk-in closet and told him to keep still, she'd distract Chester until the getting was good. He sat in the darkness feeling like a sleazy cocksman out of an old Playboy cartoon, hiding under the bed while the cuckold husband stomped about the house. It was not a role he envisioned for himself. It filled him with self-loathing and humiliation. Quietly, he slipped on pants and shirt, the chafing of clothes against inflamed skin nearly intolerable. His shoes were nowhere to be found. His heart thumped in his ears. He could hear Ches moving about the room, just beyond the door, asking Penny what in the world was going on: buck naked as she was, pool doors wide open, her clothes scattered about. Al hunched in the closet, barely daring to breathe. The odor, in that close space, like some sulfurous hot springs emission from the earth's sore bowels. You had to respect breath that rank. The moment they'd left the room, Al went out a window, limping barefoot over cactus spines to his car. As he was going over the wall, he heard Ches cry, "Well, looky here, the little bastard ran off without his shoes."

More humiliation to come; he must ask Mona to remove cactus needles from his back, feet, and buttocks where he couldn't reach them. She laughed at his predicament, said she could just see him limping through the cactus, fleeing Ches, Penny pin-cushioned with cactus spines. "Serves you both right. You aren't cut out for this, I hope you realize." He nodded, telling her how he'd driven home at 10 MPH, using his left foot since his right was full of needles, not able to lean back against the seat. "I can't see myself as some lowlife hiding in a closet. I don't know why I went over there in the first place."

"Of course you do," she said.

"You're not just a little bit angry at me?"

"Not in the least. I think you deserve each other, and Chester deserves you both."

#

It panicked me to be involved with Penny again—if I was. Madness, deadly madness. "You can't trust that little fucker," Mona once warned me, "it's loyal to nothing but its own pleasuring, and damn the consequences." Much like Penny Noonan. That last time, before her husband arrived home, I asked Penny if Ches still wanted my land. She caught a hand to my mouth. "Shuddup, Al. You know ah don't pry into mah husband's business affairs. You don't want to go there."

"Tell Chester I'll never sell."

She smiled slowly and brushed a cowlick off my forehead. "Clueless Al. You might as well make some money like evrahbody else."

Waking from a nightmare of Ches pursuing me with a baseball bat, I stumbled into the kitchen at dawn, cupped hands under the kitchen spigot and lapped up water; it was brackish and sour. I spit it out. Finding Wallers lying on his side near his water trough, moaning, I rested my head on his belly. "Jesus, we're poisoned here, pal." A scum of alkali floated atop water in his trough.

I banged on Tinkerspoon's trailer door, while rat-mutt Misty nipped at my ankles. He called from inside: "Fuck off, I've got a bomb in here."

"It's me, Andy, relax. Call off your fucking mutt."

"Sharpe?" He opened up, hair sleep-matted to one side, blinking at the rising red sun as if he'd never seen it before and wasn't sure what it was.

"How's your well water, Tinkerspoon?" He filled a glass from the tap in the dark kitchen, sipped and spit it out—brackish and slippery on the tongue, like mine.

"It's Cal's new wells out Indian Springs Road near Sam's," he said. "He stole our water to fill artificial lakes and left us the dregs."

A flight of helicopters passed high overhead, rattling dirty dishes stacked in the sink. "We're preparing to invade the Middle East," he said. "It's all over the web. They plan to make Israel the fifty-first state and claim Saudi Arabia and Kuwait as territories."

"You know what worries me? I'm starting to believe you on this shit."

Standing in the dark rank closeness of his kitchen, Tinkerspoon ran it all down: "It's layers of sand, gravel, silt, and hardpan clay thousands of feet thick below us, dude. Our wells draw off the first aquifer down to about four hundred feet. That's mountain water. Your fresh floating atop your salt, dude. The fresh gets too low and salt and toxic metals percolate up through the sand and contaminate it. Bad news, dudeski." Motioning at his sink. "I been researching it."

"Yeah, bad news. Wallers is sick as a dog."

"That's caustic alkali, boron, and calcium chloride poisoning." He dug through rubble in a drawer and produced a small phial. "Give him two drops of this, dude. Down the hatch. And whooaaaa, stand back!"

"What is it?"

"An emetic. Radical fucker. I give it to the mutts all the time." Leaning forward in the gloom, his voice drooping. "Between us and the four walls, right, I'm thinking of selling and getting out of this shit hole. I had enough of this shit."

"You wouldn't do that to us, Andy."

"Not to worry, dudeski," he sighed, "no way I could. Mom's and Pop's graves are here."

Two minutes after swallowing Tinkerspoon's potion, Wallers heaved up a gallon of foul water, shook himself, and sauntered off, pig happy. But water in the rinse glass smelled of sulfur when I brushed my teeth. What were we going to do for drinking water?

Rumor had it that in addition to the deep wells out Indian Springs Road, Cal was drilling more across Angie Beach's former land, emptying our Saint Angel aquifer to water golf courses and fill artificial lakes—including a dry lake bed known as Infinity Sink in Tourmaline. "It's their water now, people," Little Les said, "Saint Angel Valley Water Authority water. Whoever drills the deepest well wins."

Tinkerspoon surmised that when Cal's well shafts penetrated the clay and shale aquiclude five hundred feet down at the floor of the first aquifer, they stirred up mineral salts, and briny water suffused the saturated zone that supplies our well water. "Hydrostatic suction, reverse osmosis and like that, Dude." Tinkerspoon shrugged. "Cal and them is after the big kahuna aquifer floating atop the Ancient Salt Sea a quarter mile down. What they call 'fossil water' down there. Old water. When his drillers break through shale into the second aquifer, wachout! Fossil water will geyser up the shafts and fuckin' flood the world, dude. It's gotta be under moxie pressure that deep." It made sense: artesian springs once abounded in the valley.

The time had come to build a desalination plant. A shitload of technology to master: Darcy's Law and all. But Finley says I'm never happier than when I'm into some "widget project."

Pulling up to Sam Jenson's place off Indian Springs Road, I heard the whunkety-whunk of well-drilling rigs nearby. Three giant new water tanks stood atop rocky knolls behind his place. Two bedraggled palm trees at top of his drive were generally decorated with Christmas lights by now, as were the chain-link fence and junker cars, and white and blue icicle lights usually outlined the chassis of a '37 Chevy flatbed and his decrepit trailer. Not this year. Generally, the lights summoned gawkers from town, and Sam bitched, "You'd think I was Santy Claus."

After he left the hospital, one or another of us stopped by daily to check on him, brought him casseroles. Sam complained that we were coddling him and threatened to shoot the next person who stepped on his property uninvited. Likely meant it. With Sam, you never knew. I was yelling from the moment I parked in the dusty yard and approached his trailer on foot. "It's me, Sam, don't shoot." No sign of him. Odd. Sam always heard and recognized cars the moment they turned off Yucca Road into his long drive, would be awaiting you on his front porch with your own personalized coffee mug in hand, filled with java boiled at five a.m., black and tarry as used motor oil.

"You hear me, Sam? I'm not here about your heart. As far as I can tell, you don't have one." Approaching the trailer gingerly. "I'm here about your well."

Another thing: curtains were drawn. I heard a frenzied electrical buzzing as I stepped onto the porch and feared Sam had electrocuted himself via the ancient toaster which he regularly washed with other dishes. "You home, Sam?" I called softly. An odor of putrefied flesh chased me off the porch. I feared I'd find Sam covered in a glistening carpet of blow flies. Fucking doctors had sent him home with a bad ticker. But it wasn't Sam I was smelling, rather rotting jack-rabbit carcasses pinned by their veiny ears to a clothesline. Flies roiled over them, flashing silvery blue in turmoiling light. "Crissake, Sam—" I stepped back onto the porch and rapped on the screen door "—you plan to eat those, you old bastard?"

I couldn't make out much in the dark interior, only a bare foot extending stiffly off the sofa, artificial and ghostly, illuminated by a shaft of light in which dust motes danced and spun.

"Sam!" I called imperatively.

No answer. Sam in one of his misanthropic moods.

"I'm here, Jenson, you just as well get used to it." Stepping inside, I let the screen door slam behind me. Sam lay stretched out on the couch in khaki shorts and shirt, one arm thrown across his chest, a foot splayed awkwardly on the floor. I prodded his arm. "You got rabbits rotting on the line and a world of opportunity passing you by." His pale eyes stared past me into space.

Death's feel is as unmistakable as its smell: Sam's arm was cold and wooden. I leapt away. "What did they do to you, old fellah?" Then I remembered his bad ticker and heard Sage's water baby, that whimpering *pa?akniwat*. I couldn't bring myself to close his eyes. I worked a slip of paper out of fingers which clutched it in a death grip. A pen-cilled line: *Don' dring the water.* A nauseating rotten-egg smell lingered about him, protecting Sam's corpse from predatory flies that covered the screen door in a fierce, buzzing pellicle. At the hospital, he'd asked me, "Have you smelled your water lately?" I smoothed that note across his chest. They'd killed the old bastard all right: Cal, Ches, TexHome, one or another of them.

Driving into town to inform Charlie Haynes, I saw a white van trailing me in the rearview, keeping its distance. Though I couldn't see them, I knew there were two faces watching me from beyond the windshield.

9

SAM'S COALITION

We strung up banners in town and along Sam's fence:

DON'T DRINK THE WATER! JOIN SAM'S COALITION NOW.

The coroner said he'd died of natural causes. I didn't believe it. I went back out to Sam's place to poke around, not sure what I was looking for. Sam's Olds Deathmobile was still parked out front of the trailer where he'd left it—vinyl top rotting in the sun, a business card shoved under a wiper: *Three Mile High Investments*. The glove compartment hung open like a sprung jaw. Sulfureous death leaked from the trailer. The outline of Sam's corpse remained like a shadow on the Naugahyde couch: a slick organic film nubbly with fly specks. Drawers stood open in the kitchen, nearly empty but for his birth certificate, which I folded and put in my pocket. Born April 7, 1923, eighty-four years old. Incredible. Someone had rifled through drawers and cupboards, leaving the floor littered with broken glass, crockery, and clipped coupons. Cal Hale, I wondered, looking for Sam's deed of trust. Or Three Mile High Investments? Or Ches? "That sumbitch, Cal Hale, told me I ain't got no choice but sell to him," Sam told me that night at the hospital. "If I don't, the county will condemn my place and sell it out from under me. I sooner sell to the devil." He said a white van was parked at top of his drive every night. "Beaner chrome domes. They don't intimidize me one bit." He sat out by the gate with a shotgun across his knees.

"Tinkerspoon thinks it's FBI," I told him.

I dribbled rusty water into a jar from the kitchen tap: exhibit #1. The smell turned my stomach. I went out the kitchen door, peeking around the trailer to see if I'd been followed. Nothing but Cal's rust-red water tanks watching from atop the butte.

The pump-house door hung open on one hinge. Pipe fittings in plastic Dr. Pepper bins along one wall, ground squirrel holes pocked the dirt floor. I examined pipe fittings and pressure valves on the storage tank, looking for I couldn't say what until I found it: white powder sprinkled around the well head and galvanized storage tank, huge shoe prints tracked in the dust—the same herringbone pattern I'd found in the mud back by Pissing Springs on my place. I was squatting in a crime scene. I backed carefully out the door. First time in my life I wanted a cell phone. As I left the shed, a rifle shot cracked just beyond my left ear. The bullet clanged against sheet metal and punched a hole in the pump house wall. I hit the dust and crawled to my pickup on my belly, drove hell bent across the open desert. Another bullet shattered my rear window.

I called Charlie Haynes from Dead Cow Chevron at the corner of Yucca and Big Springs Canyon Roads. "You better get out to Sam's!" I shouted. "They poisoned him: there's white powder sprinkled all around his water storage tank—ricin or arsenic, I'd guess."

"Listen up, Sharpe. I don't have time or patience for this nonsense. The coroner's report says Sam's heart infarcted all to hell. That's the end of it."

"Some poisons will do that," I insisted. "Anthrax or Ricin."

"That powder is welder's flux. Sam had some welding needed doing. Lon Studenmire was likely the last person who saw him alive. No doubt it's Lon's footprints; Lon is a big man."

"Did a heart attack ransack Sam's trailer? Did it take pot shots at me just now?"

"Who's shooting at you? Damn it, Sharpe, leave the policing to me."

"Gladly, if you'd do your job. I'll drop the water sample by so you can get it tested. I'm telling you, Charlie, Sam wouldn't sell to those bastards, so they killed him."

"Who did? Goddamn it, Albert, watch yourself. That's some mighty hefty allegations you're tossing around."

"It's some mighty ugly things happening around here."

Hanging up, I saw that van waiting for me across the road, as if my call to Charlie had alerted them to my whereabouts. I nearly took out a pump exiting the station.

#

Supervisor Hernshaw called the meeting for three o'clock in the after-

noon, expecting few would show up at that time of day. But Saint Angeli-nos took time off work and packed the high school gymnasium. It was the closest we had ever come to a flash mob, with word of the meeting going out through the social media and the local grapevine. Peering out over us from the lectern, Hernshaw looked shell-shocked, folksy in shirt sleeves, a round-cheeked farm boy's face. He introduced planning commissioners at the front table and representatives from TexHome, Mile High Investments, and the SALCO contingent. Ches Noonan said it was splendid to see such a fine turnout, seeming sincere.

TexHome Rep:	_TexHome is to building homes what McDonalds is to hamburgers. (He projected a map of the Valley on a screen and tapped an area south of town shaded like a dark shadow on a lung.) Our Singing Springs Development will bring thousands of beautiful new homes to Saint Angel Valley._
Daph Thompson:	_(Leaping to her feet) We don't want them. Local people should decide whether we want to live in a city, not Texas corporations._
Timothy Leary O'toole:	_Ri'chon!_
Ches Noonan:	_We're local, SALCO's corporate headquarters are here in town._
Little Lester:	_Tell you what, Chester, you're as bad as the rest of them. You don't give a damn about nothing but making a profit._
Shouts:	_Where's the water going to come from? Who will pay for new schools and sewers?_
Little Lester:	_You will, people. (Murmurs all around) Think about it! Chester and them are building a city squat on top of you, which you don't want but you got to finance out of your own pocket._
Timothy Leary O'toole:	_That right there, we got a right to vote on that._
Al Sharpe:	_Ten thousand new houses, fifty thousand people. An overnight city in our backyard. We didn't come out here for that. (Cheers)_
Ches Noonan:	_(Raising his arms pontifically) They'll pay their way, believe you me. We're looking at prosperity, a broader tax base, better schools—_
Daph Thompson:	_Better than what?_

Ches Noonan:	Good jobs. There's some of you going to make a pot of money.
Mrs. Houston:	It's about the children, about building a safer place for the children. Better homes and neighborhoods.
Anonymous Voice:	Bullshit!
Little Lester:	(Stabbing a finger at Ches) Times they are a changing, people. Ask the Man! Them who don't buy their ticket is gonna miss the gravy train.
Sage Littlefeather:	(Stood and faced the Commissioners with grim dignity) Takeetz is flat pissed off here lately. He's got smog blowing up his nostrils, he can't drink the water, he can't hardly see the stars for the lights down below, he's got a bad case of gas....
Tom Hernshaw:	What is your point, sir?
Sage Littlefeather:	(Pointing at Ches) That man there runs Saint Angel Water Authority, his pals run planning. (Sweeping his hand to encompass the men up front) Not one Indian on neither. What about our property rights? Isn't no one here talking about them.
Many voices:	Tell it, brother.
Tom Hernshaw:	That'll do. I'll have to clear the room, folks.
Daph Thompson:	We won't leave, we live here. (A volley of supporting shouts) We won't let Texas developers trash our precious valley.
Al Sharpe:	I call for a vote. (Devastation Acres folks stomped their feet in unison.) Should local people have local control, aye or nay?
Many voices:	AYE!
Jake Houston:	(From the Commissioner's table) It's a man's right to prosper. That's capitalism, that's our American way of life. Love it or leave it.
Tom Hernshaw:	I'm mighty bullish on property rights, I'll tell you what! Nobody can tell a man he can't build houses on his own land.
Mrs. Houston:	(Pointing at developers) These men are Saint Angel's angels. They believe in the children.
Rob Thompson:	They're fucking locusts.

Al Sharpe:	Let them go somewhere else, we don't want them here.
John Sylvester:	Good jobs, fine new homes, better roads—
Stout Woman:	Nobody's asking for none of that.
Construction Worker:	You damn betcha we are. (Sullen men in grubby jeans and hard hats stood at rear of the gym, arms folded, come directly off the job. No one had noticed them come in. One of the developers had called in the troops on his cell.)
A large man:	(Wearing a Nevada Craps t-shirt and a gold stud in one ear) My livelihood isn't negotiable.
Little Lester:	(Whistling) Here we go, people.
Imogene Sylvester:	Others should have an opportunity to share the American dream. It's the Christian thing to do.
Rob Thompson:	Christian, my ass! Sorry, Jesus.
Daph Thompson:	We're under no moral obligation to provide housing for strangers. That's idiotic.
Imogene Sylvester:	Well then, I choose to be an idiot.
Mona Sahlstrom:	No one ever doubted it.
Surly Latino Worker:	(Strolling down the aisle and hovering menacingly over folks from Sam's Coalition) You don't like it, but you gonna get it.
Ches Noonan:	I'm afraid he's right.

Saint Angelinos looked back and forth between Sam's Crew in front and the Grub Crew in back—what we were and what we were becoming. Hernshaw called the hearing adjourned.

"Nothing's been decided," Al protested.

"All opposed?" Les shouted.

"Nay," most yelled in one voice; the Grub Crew provided the "Yeas."

#

Construction workers formed a gauntlet along the path to the parking lot, jostling us and calling us assholes. Rob got into a shoving match with Trinkley; Daph and I pulled him off. The surly Latino worker spit at us. "Fucking losers." Matt Littlefeather up in his face like a football lineman, all 350 pounds of him. "You talking to me?" _Nevada Craps_ warned us we'd be seeing him again. Mona tapped a finger against his chest. "You better hope not, sonny." I put my arm through hers and steered her to my pickup. "We've got company," I warned as we drove through town. "Don't look back." Of course she did.

"What's this? Is this about Penny? Ches Noonan has men trailing you? Good Lord, it is."

"Penny?" It hadn't occurred to me.

"You're seeing her again, Albert?"

I stared at the rearview and faces scrambled in light reflected off the van's windshield: like a Cubist omelet—eyeballs, cheeks, moustaches jumbled together higgledy-piggledy.

"What it is about that woman I can't imagine. What do you see in her? She's a stick figure with pubic hair."

"That's over." Refusing to look at her.

"You're an awful liar, Al. Your forehead wrinkles, your eyes go dodgy. You shouldn't even try."

"They may be Sam's killers," I said, glancing at the mirror. "They want my acreage along Creosote Canyon Road just like they wanted his."

Mona swiveled about in her seat and flipped them off. "Assholes." They followed us onto Creosote Canyon Road. No telling what they had in mind. I floored it but couldn't lose them. It occurred to me I'd drive right through the front gate and sprint to the cabin for my rifle; I wasn't going to let us end up fly bait like Sam. But the van gunned it past us just before my driveway and high-tailed it on down the road, horn blaring, like he'd been awaiting his chance to pass. Mona slumped against my shoulder, heart pounding. "What is happening to us?"

That night I sat on the bed watching her undress: full-figure cover girl in silky blue panties, furry little pussies peeking out under her arms as she reached back to unfasten the bra, chest inflamed with freckles. Turned me on something crazy. "Just forget it, Albert."

"Just looking. I can sleep on the couch if you want."

"I don't want your bed, Al, I want the truth." She flopped belly down beside me. "I'll come clean about RJH if you do about Penny Noonan. Are you in love with her?"

"In lust, maybe...I was. Like you and RJH."

"I don't even like RJH. He reminds me of your pig: he's anal and oral at the same time. He has a penis obsession, he stands before the mirror talking baby talk to his dick."

"All men do that. Listen, I really don't want to hear about RJH's penis."

"He's born again, besides. Someone like RJH is a moral contradiction. He cheats on his wife, he cheats his customers, he cheats God."

"I'm not like that. You can't even consider it cheating with Penny. I mean, you and I make love now and then, but we're not a couple. That's what you keep telling me, anyway."

Incredibly, she flinched. "I didn't say you were cheating; I said you are emotionally dishonest."

"How am I dishonest?" Trying not to stare at the round loaves of her ass under tight panties: world class ass. Lying there on the bed, taunting and untouchable.

"Oh, for crissake, Al. You're still seeing the woman, admit it."

"I'm trying to tell you, she won't hear 'no.'"

"Oh, poor sexually abused Albert." She laughed out loud. "You're a worse phony than RJH. Penny Noonan, for God's sake. What can you possibly see in her?"

I shrugged. "You won't sleep with me."

Her raucous, shivering laugh. "That's good. So now it's my fault you can't control your dick. I couldn't care less who you fuck, Albert, except to say it's pathologically stupid, especially now. You really believe Ches Noonan doesn't know who his wife is balling—king of control freaks—and doesn't condone it? You think the master builder doesn't have a plan? It isn't Penny who's screwing you, it's Big Daddy Chester."

I flinched. "That's fucking disgusting. 'Daddy,' that's what she calls him."

"Is it really? She's one sly, chirrupy little sex cricket, I'll give her. Ches's skinny shill. You remember when Rob and Ches were haggling over percentages in their business? Penny took Rob to bed, and *voila* he folded. She's good, I'll give her. They make a great team."

"I don't believe you. Penny is her own person, she doesn't do anyone's bidding, not even Ches's."

Mona sat up, smelling vaguely of ginseng; her hand, cupping my bare knee, radiated medicinal affection, like a vet would offer a sick dog. She tapped my forehead with a finger. "Think, Albert. Don't be a simp. This has Chester's fingerprints all over it."

It stunned me: Penny whoring for Ches! Impossible. But I remembered her shooing me out of his workroom—his blueprint drawers. His foul breath binding us together in a fetid ménage- a-trois. A conundrum: Penny acting on impulse and serving as Ches's agent at the same time.

"You really think so?" I said.

"I really do. I wonder if I shouldn't tell the others about your Penny fetish."

"It's none of their business."

"Isn't it?" She slipped out of her bra and panties and under the covers.

"I thought you didn't want my bed."

"I changed my mind."

10

A CHRISTMAS CAROL

At Christmas time, Saint Angel is right out of Walt Disney's Fantasia; "a Jesus-freaking Macy's window display," Mona Sahlstrom calls it. Dripping, blinking, shimmering, multi-colored lights everywhere. From outer space we look like a freak algal bloom in the desert. Gaudy crosses in front yards are lit by spotlights—maltese, Roman, gothic, lowbrow that look like they are covered in tattoos. The usual slogans: "Jesus Saves," "I.N.R.I.," "He Is Risen." There are Lawn dioramas replete with plywood camels and wise men, elaborate creches on front porches: madonnas and baby Christ-childs with fat, cherubic cheeks and huge weepy Keanesque eyes, painted by Winky Hale. The Grant Street GloLighters still place a radiant star atop the tallest fir tree in town, although the Saint Angel Yuletide Display Awards Program was abandoned years ago when the Lincoln Street Flashers constructed an overhead trolley to transport Santa's sleigh and reindeer over Lincoln Street, and Rudolph broke off and plunged through a roof, impaling old Mrs. Sylvestri with a hoof. Her husband stood over her shouting, "You see what I mean! You can't even trust Christmas anymore."

One year shortly after he'd been saved, our former mayor, RJH (Richard John Henry), constructed a 40-foot cross atop his house, which is perched like an eagle's nest atop a butte. His plan was to have animatronic baby Jesuses crawl out of a manger at the cross's base and scale the vertical to perch momentarily atop the horizontal cross bar in blinking blue and red neon epiphany before crawling back down again. RJH got the cross up and one baby Jesus scaling its south face when he ran short of funds. "Now that's an eyesore," Ches Noonan complained to the city council. "It looks like a monkey crawling up a coconut palm." (Still sore at RJH for sleeping with Penny.) Some wanted the city to help RJH finish the job, but city attorney Syd Alpine opined that it could violate separation of church and state, though he'd never heard of a case involving baby Jesuses in Santa Claus caps. (Rumor had it that Mona Sahlstrom was having an affair with RJH that season, even though coupling those two would be like mixing water and oil.) Nothing lost, anyway. We already have a 70-foot cross atop

Wordsley Hill south of town, which looks of a dark night like a cruciform UFO hanging in space.

This year's displays were gaudier than ever and had lost all symmetry: lights on one side of a house would blink while those on the other side didn't, or they blinked in a staccato Cole Porter rhythm. Some displays mysteriously abandoned houses and migrated across the street. People blamed it on the devil or Mideast terrorists or Sam's Coalition, which our tea party conservatives and evangelicals consider socialistic. Crosses captioned with apocalyptic Bible verses proliferated, and the speaker on RJH's butte blared gangsta rap instead of Christmas carols, foreshadowing what was to come.

This year, Sam's Coalition doubled the component of bulbs, transforming Sam's tumbledown Airstream into a twinkling, snow-coated Swiss chalet with icicles dripping from eaves, which gave the effect of light glimmering through walls of an ice cave. They outlined old car chassis with shiver lights, and Tinkerspoon devised a rheostat, so that the coalition's slogan, strung along the chain-link fence out front, shone brighter and brighter before blinking off:

DON'T DRINK THE WATER! JOIN SAM'S COALITION NOW.

www.samscoalition.com

Sam's jolly junkyard was reborn. It looked like Santa's sleigh had crashed there off of Yucca Road. He would have been pleased, anyway. But not by the hundreds of cars making a pilgrimage out to see the place and townsfolk hanging poinsettia blooms and silver tinsel on the fence in a makeshift shrine to Sam, sensing inchoately that with Sam's loss—grisly old bastard that he was—we'd lost a sense of who we are.

Sam's display made the 5 p.m. news on KTLA, and Tinkerspoon got hundreds of hits a day on his site, more volunteers for Sam's Coalition than we could handle, with only a vague notion still of what we were about.

"We're about saving the earth," Daph Thompson declared that first meeting.

Mona nodded. "Ending the rape of Saint Angel."

"Stop the so-called Realty Roundup, that's number one," Al said.

"We got to defend our asses against Ches and his buds," Rob said.

"You gonna make more mess than you already in," Sage declared. "When white men talk about saving something, wachout!" His brother Matt nodded solemnly.

"Would you fuck off with the racist bullshit," Rob moaned.

Daph crossed her arms and hard-eyed them. "Y'r in it, too, guys."

Sage shook his head sadly. "We had the cleanest water anywheres be-fore white coyotes come and polluted it."

"Not me!" Daphne was irate. "Don't you dare blame me."

"NOTTT MEEE!" Matt mocked her, pounding his chest.

"Would you two stop, for god's sake," Mona cried. "We're all in this together." It looked like Matt was about to speak, but she stabbed a finger at him and he shrugged.

Despite the incumbent cheeriness and bright fandango of lights, Al had sunk into depression. It was Christmas, after all, the most depressing time of the year. His daughter had gone skiing with Patsy K Jones's family, Mona was snitty, and Tinkerspoon had gone underground. Even all alone out Creosote Canyon Road, far from the giddy potlatch of gift buy-ing, Al felt the manic pulse of the culture's buying frenzy and felt like an outcast. Nothing is more alienating in America than being an alien to jolly Christmas excess in a culture that takes nothing more seriously than it does shopping. Nor was he given to the baby-Jesus joy frenzy that seized some. He saw them out front of RJH's department store the afternoon he went to buy Mona a pair of kid gloves. "Pray with us for peace on earth," a pink-cheeked girl propositioned him. Death and Pestilence rang Salvation Army bells nearby and glowered at passersby. Inside, grinning elves hammered at tiny work benches, and wise men wandered the aisles. "Howdy do, Al," an elf greeted him in a gruff basso profundo, sounding eerily like Sam Jenson. Al fled without a gift. Sitting in the parking lot with his forehead against the cold steering wheel of his pickup, he battled despair: Sam dead, water poisoned, white vans following him, ugly housing tracts going in, and the Silk Set planning a Realty Roundup to promote even more, Penny back in his life again...or maybe not, Finley spending Christmas with Patsy K Jones's family rather than with him. "You go," he insisted when she called him, "I don't mind spending Christmas alone. It's just another day." Idiot tears coursed down his cheeks when he hung up. It would be their first Christmas apart since her birth. As a girl, she would run excitedly to the tree on Christmas morning to discover his latest nutty device: the automatic page-turner designed to clamp to her bed post; a solar-powered planetarium projector which sprayed stars across the domed ceiling of the treehouse, her favorite gift of all. Finley would throw her arms around him in delight and say how lucky she was to have a dad who invented presents instead of buying them.

He dragged the newly-trimmed Christmas tree outside to the fire pit and burned it, bulbs, lights, and all. He couldn't help but wonder if Finley's absence had anything to do with his revelations about her mom. Subliminally, anyway, she resented them. He recalled how she'd devised comforts once her mother had been missing so long that she must concede she would always be missing: Mummy's picture beside her bed, the memory book, a pair of Mom's slippers placed beside the door. Maybe it was true, as Finley had implied, that he hadn't looked for Sondra because he didn't want to find her. He'd taken her insurance money to buy Second Chance Acres and abandoned all hope of her reappearance. He dragged the charred tree back inside, raw burnt wires, exploded bulbs and all, and set it up in the living room: depression's tree.

"Is this meant to be symbolic?" Mona asked when she came to his place for Christmas dinner. He presented her with a gift wrapped in newsprint: the self-warming socks he'd just devised, knowing she suffered from poor circulation. "That's a starter pair. I don't have all the bugs out yet." Mona tapped his forehead. "You can say that again." That night, when she wore the socks to bed, her toes broiled like sausages. She slit the socks open to find a layer of metal foil sandwiched between thick layers of cotton. The big boob's socks didn't permit her feet to breathe. It was just like Albert to get the small things right but screw up the big ones.

She became furious with him at times for denying troubling truths. His relationship with Penny Noonan, for example, his refusal to accept that Finley wanted a broader life than Saint Angel offered her, or that developers planned to turn his rural home into a suburb. When she told him about the huge construction loans being arranged at the bank and secret Planning Commission meetings, he said they were likely putting in a solar farm. Denial was his security blanket; he wrapped himself tightly in it, refusing to accept that his beloved home was under threat. But recently, given Sam Jenson's death and someone taking potshots at him, he was getting nervous.

What annoyed her most was Al's denial of his own talent. He was an inventive genius. He would hold pistons from a junkyard car in his hands, turn them this way and that making little "mmm-hmmm" noises as he mentally invented some new gadget ("widget" as Patsy K Jones called them). Other than the Sharpe Smoke Scrubber, which made him some real money, Al eschewed anything with true commercial potential. "Money doesn't interest me," he said, "I like fiddling with things." Clever oddities mostly: the "pressing closet," a back scratcher he'd invented for Wallers, his "self-peddling bicycle," the "fly zapper" he'd made for Tinkerspoon, which flicked out an electric arc, like a tongue, to zap flies midair. When she encouraged him to take his talent seriously, Al insisted he was nothing but a tinkerer, then designed a self-sufficient, off-the-grid home for the Abernathys, which was built into the side of a hill for passive cooling (so the indoor temperature remained a constant 76 degrees winter and summer). Solar panels on the roof generated electricity and heated water; water vapor condensed on huge glass windows on cool nights and trickled through drip tubing to water lush indoor gardens that produced both oxygen and water vapor, which condensed on the glass panes in a self-perpetuating cycle; sewage was compacted and composted, gray water recycled. "Do you realize," she told him, "that you could patent that house, sell the plans, and make a fortune. We have customers at the bank who would buy your plans."

"I don't need a fortune."

"At least you could build one for yourself here on Second Chance Acres."

"I prefer my adobe cottage and Finley's treehouse."

"Do you realize how out of touch you are? You don't even own a cell phone."

"I don't need one. Who would I call? I prefer being out of touch."

"You know what I think, I think you can't face things as they are. You're an idealist, Al Sharpe, you prefer to see the world as you want it to be rather than as it is. You didn't believe your wife could leave you and her own daughter; you couldn't accept that a mother would do that. Many do. You think iPhones are addictive, so you avoid them. That's a poor example; you may be right there. Still, you are like Winky Hale—except she believes we are protected by God's angels and you believe we are protected by the angels of our better nature."

"Aren't we, most of the time? There is more good in this world than evil or we wouldn't have made it this far. I know there is ugliness. Sam's murder, for example. I don't deny that. I'm doing my damndest to get Charlie Haynes to see it."

She patted his shoulder. "It's all right, Al. I suppose you are only partially blind. It's why people love you." He was the only man she'd ever known who wasn't so full of himself that he didn't collapse in self-satisfied sleep the moment he'd blown his bitsy wad, but wanted to know if it was good for her, too.

#

One night soon after Christmas, I was driving home from town, when the local NPR station began speaking French, then resolved to English with a thick Québecois accent. The announcer said, "You're listening to WBJH, your Northern Portal Station, gateway to Nova Scotia." He was reporting on the small Canadian town of Watersford where half a dozen people had died of *E. coli* poisoning from contaminated wells. The signal had magically made its way five thousand miles to my car radio to deliver insight into Sam's murder. That was it: the white powder I'd found sprinkled around his water storage tank was *E. coli*. I squealed onto the shoulder. RJH's house sat up on its knoll, bright and blinking; I imagined Mona standing nude on RJH's deck looking down at me. I thumped the radio, and it began babbling Arabic. It blinked back on all by itself when I shut it off.

The coroner said Sam died of a heart attack, but I'd concluded that high concentrations of boron, caustic alkali and selenium from the Ancient Salt Sea killed him. Maybe hydrogen sulfide, a product of primal organic decay. The rotten-egg smell that filled Sam's trailer the day I found him smelled like it could kill you. Our water had begun to taste like crude oil. Sage Littlefeather said the white man gave the earth cancer and its bowels were rotting. "Ours is level-one water," Tinkerspoon said, "Sam's was level-three death water from the Ancient Salt Sea a mile and a half down. Cal drilled too deep, dude, and his shaft cracked the rock aquiclude confining it, death water seeped up through fissures and faults. It got Sam first, he's closest. It will get us, too, dude."

Nonsense. They'd poisoned him with *E. coli*.

I called Charlie Haynes when I got home and informed him: "Sam didn't die of a heart attack, he was murdered for refusing to sell his land. *E. coli* poisoning, Charlie. I just heard about it on the radio." A long silence on the far end, then Charlie said, "You know, Sharpe, you're loonier every time I talk to you. Do you realize it's one o'clock in the a.m.?"

I drove straight out Yucca Road to draw another water sample from Sam's well. The place was forlorn under its drapery of twinkling lights, spooky in the moonlight. I sensed ghost presences lurking about the trailer and watching me from the rusted-out cabs of vehicle cadavers as I got out of the pickup and walked to Sam's pump house, hoping no one would take a pot shot at me. No sign anyone had followed me. The desert silence was primordial, just the faint whock whock of water pumps in the distance, draining our aquifer to fill Infinity Sink and Cal's water tanks. I could make out a trio of them on the eastern horizon silhouetted against the night sky. Headlights pulled up alongside one and angled out across the yawning desertscape: close-set, fluorescent white LED lights, signature of that fleet of vans that had been trailing us—silent, ominous, hanging a hundred feet off the rear bumper. Big Brother out here in the middle of nowhere. How did they know I was here? I'd told no one I was coming. As I approached the pump house, a coyote snarled and fled into chaparral. The creak of hinges pierced the desert quiet when I opened the door. In my flashlight beam, Sam's well was sealed; no trace of white powder remained.

On New Year's Day, I walked through Tinkerspoon's trailer and caught him sitting in pajama tops (no bottoms) before a bank of computer monitors in his digital studio. "Take off your shoes, dude, and put on a hairnet," he ordered distractedly when I stuck my head in the door. I grabbed a plastic shower cap from a nail on the wall. "See that, dudeski, that's level 3. Nobody's ever been in this deep before." Pulsing lines marched across multiple computer screens, then retreated as Tinkerspoon did a finger jig on the keyboard and smirked. "Gotcha, bitch!" He had an erection. "For crissake, Andy, cover yourself." CPU towers rose five feet off the floor, monitors mounted atop monitors in that cramped space, a spaghetti tangle of cables, buzzing fire wire boxes; the room levitated on an ominous electronic hum. Made me nervous being in that electro-magnetic pulse haven.

"Shower and get dressed, Tinkerspoon. We need your vote at the DGLA tonight."

"How'm I gonna shower, dude? There's no freaking water."

On our way to the Noonans' place, Tinkerspoon told me he had hacked the Strategic Air Command, the most secure computer system on earth. "Jesus, Andy, don't do anything rash."

"Me?" Tapping his chest and smirking. "Hey, dude, I got world love in my heart."

"Yeah, I could see that earlier."

When we walked in the front door, Penny caught my arm and mewled, "Where've you been, Albert?" Wearing a silky, low-cut gown. Ches gripped my arm from the other side and got right up in my face. "Have you decided, Sharpe?"

"About what?" Half gagging on his putrid breath.

"What do you think?" Glancing at his wife. "Our master of ceremonies proposition."

"I already told you I'm not interested."

"Careful, Al—" he winked "—you wouldn't want to wind up on the losing team. By the way, there's a matter we need to discuss when we're through here today, the three of us."

"Discuss? With you and Penny?" I was aghast. It was true then: those two were in cahoots.

"That present a problem for you, does it?" Ches's courtly smile.

Before we drank too much eggnog, I stood up in the living room, tapped my glass, and proposed a vote on the Realty Roundup. "We don't want the valley filled with houses; we moved out here for peace and space." Glaring at Ches who reclined on his Barcalounger, sipping eggnog.

"You want to stop busting my balls, Al," he said softly. "The Roundup is a done deal; the board made its decision."

"Nonsense," cried Daph Thompson. "We never agreed to it."

We lost the membership vote when Clover Abernathy abstained and Esther voted with the Silk Set. Remarkably, Winky Hale voted with us. I looked daggers at Clover: after all I'd done for them, designing their new house for practically nothing. Maybe I was naive. Ches seized my elbow as I headed for the door after the meeting. "I thought you'd stay a minute—"

I jerked free. "Gotta run, Ches. If it's about my land, I'm not selling. And the water! Tell you what, could you leave us a little to wash our necks now and then?"

Ches touched a finger repeatedly to his upper lip. Warts bloomed over his nose and forehead, puffy as toadstools. He needed to have them looked at. "That's right! I'd forgotten you have a well, Sharpe. Yesss, I'd forgotten."

"Me, too, dude," Tinkerspoon volunteered as he exited.

"So you do, Andy. So you do. The Water Authority will need to look into it. We can't have illegal wells and folks pilfering groundwater that doesn't belong to them." He smiled pure evil.

"My family has drunk water out of the ground for a hundred-fifty years, dude."

"Is that why Cal killed Sam Jenson," I asked, "for water 'pilfering?'"

"That's not funny, Albert. Not funny at all." Punching my shoulder, not affectionately. The bruise would remain for days, like a melanoma, blue-black and foreboding. I fled the house, avoiding that mystery confab with the Noonans...for now, anyway.

11

ENTER TRINKLEY

(Or Birth of the Desert Liberation Front)

While weeding the winter garden, I heard a sucking sound from the well house. I put my ear to the well cover, sounded like water burping and gurgling down a half-clogged drain. I lowered a bolt down the well shaft at the end of a 180-foot cord and heard it clink against the submersible pump at bottom; the string bone dry when I pulled it up. Cal's wells had drained what remained of our aquifer. I called his office, hopping mad, but Cal was off in Hawaii. "What's he doing over there," I asked his secretary, "ripping off their beaches? Your employer is a cold-blooded killer, did you know that?"

Cal's megawells had drained the top aquifer to fill Infinity Sink and artificial lakes in the new subdivisions on Jack-o'-Lantern Road. He flat out stole our water. Cyclone fences topped with razor wire surrounded new well clusters across Angie Beach's former land and Doberman Pinschers patrolled inside them. Cal was sinking another dozen shafts down to 3,000 feet through the sand graben between the first and second aquifers, spending millions to water the desert. How had he financed such a huge operation? Though I'd been watching it coming for months, I refused to fully believe it, couldn't accept that anyone would steal the water from under our feet, especially one of our own. Didn't want to accept it, as Mona claimed. I thought about Rob Thompson's dynamite solution, but who knows what would happen if we blew Cal's wells. The Ancient Salt Sea might swallow us

My well recovered sluggishly after that initial draining, but the water was more brackish than ever. When Cal returned from Hawaii, I would demand he pump some of our water back into the ground from his lakes. I got busy on a mockup for a desalination plant, but soon realized that the highly refined filters needed for reverse osmosis were beyond my limited technological know-how and my budget. I would have to do without them.

My design involved hyper-heating saline water by running it over a solar panel grid, and then into a low pressure chamber where it was flash steamed; steam wound through copper cooling coils to condense out as fresh water. Flash distillation is an old technology, but I tweaked the solar and energy conservation elements: cold salt water trickled over copper condensation tubes as it moved towards the solar grid; solar panels seconded as an energy source to chill Freon in the refrigeration unit, tapping the hot/cold differential to lower air pressure in the decompression chamber through simple heat exchange technology. I liked the Rube Goldberg element of my plan and use of the sun as the sole energy source. Built it out of used water heaters, old refrigerators, and air conditioning units from the county dump. Patsy K Jones and Finley, home on an extended winter break, complained that the meadow below the treehouse looked like a "Legoland Junkyard," full of old appliances in various stages of disassembly. I wasn't sure it would work—or if it worked in miniature that it could be enlarged to process ten thousand gallons an hour.

One afternoon, Patsy K sauntered out and leaned elbows on my workbench. "Wachuupto, Dad?"

"Inventing fresh water."

"Ubercool!" Patsy K leaned over the table, displaying inches of cleavage in a loose-fitting halter top. She smiled knowingly when I tried looking elsewhere. The girls were doing field research for their senior project: *Sam's Coalition: Sociology in Action*. It wasn't long before I missed my solitude and peace of mind, even after the lonely Christmas. Finley taped a note to my refrigerator:

> dad,
>
> like I know why you hid the truth about mom. i can handle it. totally!
>
> finley

I dropped my own note in the wooden mailbox at base of her tree:

> Fin,
>
> Sorry I didn't get there sooner.

Dad

Sam's Coalition met regularly. Little Les set up a chalkboard and scrawled a crude map of Saint Angel Valley. "Here's how she breaks down, people: Hanover Brothers Investment Corp. in New York owns 5 percent of local land, Orange Development Corp. owns 6 percent, TexHome and SALCO combined hold 48 percent—Ches and Cal's bunch—and rumor has it they're uniting with Orange Corp. to form Super SALCO." Tapping the board emphatically with a stick of chalk. "That's 59 percent of local acreage in developers' pockets. John Q. Public owns 41 percent. They got us by the short hairs." Les began erasing small vacuoles within the amoebic protoplasm of Super SAL-CO. "This used to be Angie Beach's land. They wanted Devastation Acres down to Purgatory, but Big Al stiffed them. As you know, they got Sam's place at bank auction."

"After they murdered him," I said.

"No, Al, we can't prove that," Daph chided.

"We can't prove Kennedy was assassinated by the military-industrial complex either."

"They gonna cover every inch with low-cost-pop-up-staple-together houses and invite L.A. and Orange County out here to live in four-bedroom McMansions starting at 200 grand. And they'll come, people."

"No way, dudeski!" cried Tinkerspoon. "Isn't nothing out here but sage and creosote bush."

"Don't matter. Saint Angel Valley Water Authority is got our drinking water." Les jotted hatch marks around the amoeba. "This richere is the shit-out-of-luck line, people. Anyone outside it loses their water rights." Marking an X just beyond the amoeba's northeast perimeter: "That's you, Tink." He X'd out Second Chance Acres across the road. "Here's you, Al."

It was like taking a knife in the chest. But Les had left a wedge of Angie Beach's former land behind Tinkerspoon's blank. It intrigued me.

Patsy K Jones watched Les speculatively, her head tilted to one side, a tiny smile playing on her lips, while Finley sat stunned, her mouth open. "They can't just do that?—" looking at me "—like just steal our water, can they?"

"Who's to stop them?" Rob asked. "I overheard Jennifer Sorrentino at Planning brag that Saint Angel will have half-a-million-plus population in twenty years. She thinks that's just hunky-dory."

"Love it or leave it, people!" Les thumped his chest.

"Or burn it the fuck down." Rob didn't beg the Lord's forgiveness this time.

Les shot out a finger at him. "Watch out! There's forty thousand Marines over to Camp Pendleton in case the natives get restless." Pointing far off to the west of his map.

"We can fight this," Daph Thompson insisted, "form the Desert Liberation Front, a.k.a. Sam's Coalition, and shut it down."

Cheers all around, except for Matt Littlefeather who farted air through his lips.

We formed committees: Les and Rob would co-chair "Security," Daph and Sage "Environmental Issues," Tinkerspoon and me "Water Resources," Mona and Patsy K Jones "Public Relations," Finley and Matt Littlefeather "Direct Action." Matt thrust a fist in the air. "Whoooweee, little girlfriend, here we go." We mailed a stern protest to the DGLA (a copy to *The Saint Angel Clarion*): "Your mad lust for green grass and swimming pools contravenes your role as guardian of the high desert and makes you brokers of high desert density and environmental chaos." Tinkerspoon and I were to lodge a formal complaint with the Saint Angel Valley Water Authority.

#

Ches Noonan sat at front of the council chambers like a Chief Justice surrounded by his dark-robed colleagues. The misshapen warts on his forehead had grown with his ambitions, and his foul breath washed over us like an evil wind, causing Tinkerspoon's eyes to water. Ches declared that there was no relief the Authority could offer them, since only owners with 800+ acres could subscribe to Authority water. "We estimate the deep aquifer is already overdrafted and some pumping has to be curtailed." The new Water-master, a man named Hartley, projected a 36% overdraft of the primeval aquifer by 2020 at the current rate of usage. "Take an overdraft like that and dismal projections for future rainfall, we don't have a drop to spare."

"Much as we'd like to help out, Albert, I expect the Authority will seek a court order to close your wells as illegal infringements on the public do-

main," Ches said solemnly.

"My property is been in our family for one-hundred-fifty years, dude," Tinkerspoon protested. "We never had to ask no one's permission to pump water."

"Priority in time no longer guarantees priority in right in California," John Sylvester, SAVWA's attorney, told him.

Al Sharpe insisted, "We have 'overlying,' 'residual,' and 'correlative' rights to that water, same as you do. We've been pumping all along."

"I see you've done your homework," Sylvester said.

"Prescriptive, more like. Drawing water what don't rightly belong to you." Al didn't at first recognize Cal Hale, sitting at end of the long table, having never seen him in a suit. He looked like a troll banker, his long silver hair combed straight back Willie Nelson style. But Al recognized the gravel in Cal's voice. He was on his feet, approaching Cal with a finger outthrust. "There's the sunnuvabitch who murdered Sam Jenson. He should be locked up."

Cal leapt up, hands raised against Al, his eyes blinking rapidly. "Goddamn it all, Sam died of heart failure."

"E. coli poisoning, whatever sneaky way you did it. I suppose we're next."

The Tweedledee twins, Charlie Haynes's new deputies, approached Al, their mirroring sunglasses reflecting light.

"Leave it!" Cal cried. "Al's crazy, but he ain't much dangerous."

"I will be if you keep stealing our water. It's him you need to watch out for, Cal and his death water."

Ches pounded his gavel for order. John Sylvester informed Al and Tinkerspoon that they'd lost their water rights when SAVWA took prescription of them. Moreover, their rights—if they had any—applied only to the upper aquifer, not the deep one recently tapped.

"Cal and them already drained it, dudeski," Tinkerspoon protested.

Cal grinned. "Why in blazes would I want your water? I don't take much. I never drink the stuff."

"What about TexHome Development Corporation," Al demanded, "what right do they have to our water? They don't live here."

"Do we have a TexHome Development on the list, Tom?" Ches asked the Water-master, who flipped through a huge binder.

"Nope. Don't see any."

"They been developing wells on La Cienega Land," Tinkerspoon cried in exasperation.

"Cienega," the Water-master echoed. *"Nope, don't see it. We have a Cienfuego, Juan Carlos at Tennessee Valley Ranch."*

"They're drilling wells all over the valley," Al cried in disbelief, *"behind Sam's place, on Angie Beach's old land—TexHome Development and SALCO and Cal Hale Construction."*

"No, sir." The Water-master shook his head. *"No record of any new wells."*

"No new wells? Y'r fucking crazy, dude. You disappeared them or what?"

Those imperious patriarchs at the front table regarded Tinkerspoon with grim visages out of a turn-of-the-century Daguerreotype. They had indeed "disappeared" the wells, which were unsanctioned, unrecorded, undrilled, unowned, though fully functional. "You dudes will be hearing from us," Tinkerspoon warned, shuffling papers together like a lawyer, tossing back greasy black hair as they exited.

Going home, they passed a new development at the junction of Creosote Canyon and Jack-o'-Lantern Roads, houses lined up cheek by jowl. It didn't make any sense: people coming out to the wide-open spaces to live crowded together. "They won't come this far," Tinkerspoon said as they neared home, sounding desperate. Al remained silent, fearing the worst would soon be upon them.

Surveyors arrived bright and early next morning, as if Ches had called someone at three a.m. and told them to get moving. Trinkley and his string-bean assistant peered through theodolites, drove marker stakes in the ground, and trespassed indifferently on Al's property beyond the black slough. When he asked what they were doing on his place, a stocky, balding man said, "It won't be yours much longer, pal." He planted a yellow tripod on the ground and checked for level, then peered through what looked like a high-tech bombardier's scope; monitors mounted on the transit above key pads lit up with numbers.

#

Something snapped in me. I slogged through the shallow end of the slough, tarry muck sucking at my boots, and got my shotgun from the house. Finley and Patsy K Jones stood watching me from the treehouse deck in their underwear.

"What's going on, Dad?" Finley shouted.

"You girls get dressed." I charged the surveyors from a thicket of scrub oak near the slough. "Kiss your ass goodbye, pal," I shouted, "won't be yours much longer." I fired a round in the air; the baldy fuck yelped and lit out. I recognized him as the man Rob had cursed outside Mimi's Diner: Trinkley—Trinkling Dan, the Boss's Man! His white van was already peeling rubber before he got the door closed, leaving his assistant and gear behind. I gathered up the fancy the-odolite, bags of instruments, and chart books and heaved them in the slough. It puckered tarry black lips and swallowed them, releasing a foul burp. "Anything on my property belongs to me," I informed the skinny assistant, who crouched by the road, arms raised in the air. Fin-ley caught my arm from behind, perhaps fearing I would throw him in, too.

"Dad! Are you like totally losing it or what?"

"No, baby, I'm finally coming to my senses."

Tinkerspoon was whisper-shouting from across the road: "I'm in, dude."

Trinkley's white van and another returned an hour later in a cara-van with two Saint Angel cop cars and stopped by the mailboxes. They resembled the white vans with close-set headlights that had been trail-ing us. The Tweedledee twins leapt out of one police cruiser, guns drawn. I walked up the drive to meet them. Charlie Haynes stood with a foot on the running board of his SUV. "This fellow claims you threatened him, Sharpe. Is that correct?" Trinkley peered around the side of a van with a Cal Hale Construction logo on the door.

"You really think I'd do that, Charlie?"

'Someone got you mad enough you might."

"Stop right there!" one of the Tweedledees barked as I approached Charlie's car, drawing a bead on me with his service revolver.

"Whoa up!" I threw hands in the air. "Who are these clowns, Charlie? Jesus, are they going to shoot me?" I couldn't see their eyes behind mirrored sunglasses. Creepy. "Not to worry, fellahs," I told them, "nobody out here will steal your eyeballs—except old Aunt Ag-gie Lubo maybe. You never want to look directly at Aunt Aggie." They glanced at Charlie for a cue.

"Put those goldarned pea shooters away," he snapped. "This ain't Los Angeles yet. Albert may be different, but he ain't much danger-ous." Nodding towards Trinkley. "Those surveyors will want their equipment back, Sharpe."

I pointed at the slough, just visible behind a screen of willow and cattails. "They're welcome to it."

"He threw it in that swamp is what he did," Trinkley cried. He was beyond fury, his eyes seemed to spin in their sockets.

"You left it in an inconvenient place on my property, I had to move it."

"No way I'm going in there," the assistant cried. No doubt Wallers was nearby, scavenging birds and rodents stuck in the tar at slough's edge, careful not to venture in too far. La Brea Tar Pits II. No telling what was trapped in there. I nodded at the cruiser in my drive. "You'd be surprised how fast it could swallow a car that size." The Tweedledee Twins edgy, hands parked on their gun butts. Charlie eased down into a smile. "Calm down, Al. These boys are just doing their job."

"So was Adolf Eichmann. Did you know that surveyors were some of the first to join the NAZI party in Germany?" I asked Trinkley

"Albert talks," Charlie said. "He invents the damndest gizmos. One year he had a back scratcher at the county fair: you pressed a button, a cupboard opened, and out popped a mechanical hand on a telescoping arm to scratch your back. Damn clever."

Trinkley studied me charily. "I suppose you invented that slough."

"Mother Earth did. There's going to be lots more around here, like there were a century ago. The Indians called them *cienegas del diablo*— devil's swamps."

"Loony tune." Trinkley dismissed me with a wave of the hand. We struck a deal: they could go on working if they kept off my property. The Tweedledee Twins hung out to make sure I behaved myself, not straying far from their cruiser. They had some learning to do if they wished to stay in Saint Angel; they would soon be busting kids for borrowing quarters from our parking meters.

That night we roasted marshmallows over a campfire of surveyors' stakes the girls had pulled up. Trinkley was outraged when he returned next morning, shouting "white trash" from his van on the road. Charlie Haynes threatened to put me in lockup if it continued, so I called a tet-y-tet with the girls and Tinkerspoon. "Move those stakes if you want to but leave them in the ground." Tinkerspoon rubbed his hands together. "Fuck up the grid, dude."

#

I sat straight up in bed, hearing Sondra's voice call me from a dream, risen from death's slough. I made out her bald head stuck through the open window, glistening in moonlight, and watched in horror as she wriggled in through the window sash. "Wake up, Al."

"It's you," I cried, "Tinkerspoon! You shaved your head." His odor filled the tiny room—a mixture of dog chow, old sweat, and hot circuit boards. "You scared hell out of me; I thought you were my dead wife."

"Don't turn on the light," he pleaded. "Fuckers could be anywhere, dude."

"Which fuckers?"

Tinkerspoon sat cross-legged on the floor under the window, chuckling. "I tinkerzapped 'em, dude: TexHome, SALCO, Cal Hale Construction. Got into their accounts and diced the numbers. Piece of fuckin' cake. Dudes enter their codes and they'll get a fuckin' spoon dance." He gurgled laughter. "Fuck 'em! They take our water, we tinkerzap the bastards."

"Shhhh, take it easy, Andy."

He grabbed my arm in the dark, whispering avidly. "What Les says about Ches and them, it's all true, man. Ches is worth maybe ten figures, and I couldn't locate all his accounts. Those dudes own everything." Andy slithered back out the window and was gone just like that, a digital ghost. Outside, animals emerged from their burrows, tarantulas padded across open spaces, coyotes yarooed far off across Creosote Flats, the smell of pepperwood and sage lingered on a spicy breeze. I thought I heard a metallic rattling in the distance—likely Tinkerspoon opening his front gate.

I went out first thing next morning, on instinct, to check my pump house. The heavy-gauge padlock had been sheared off with bolt cutters, the air pressure valve on the storage tank was removed, and fine white powder was sprinkled over the valve seat and the dirt floor, just like at Sam's. *E. coli*, anthrax, cyanide powder, ricin...? For all I knew we were poisoned already. I took ladder rungs two at a time, climbing up to the treehouse, and shook Finley awake. "You okay, baby?" Touched lips to her cool forehead. "Patsy K, hon, you all right? Listen, girls, don't drink the water. Someone's tampered with it. They're out to poison us."

Finley sat up, gawking at me, eyes blinking off sleep. "What are you talking about, Dad? I was asleep. PC check, are you like losing it or what? So who would want to poison us?"

"Wallers!" I cried and fled down the ladder.

"Have you totally fried your marbles?" Finley called after me.

I found Wallers stalking a dark toad at verge of the slough, grunting contentedly, dropped to my knees and kissed his leathery forehead. Called Charlie Haynes and told him to get out and test my water for toxins. "Someone tampered with my well; they're trying to poison us."

"This another of your Sam Jenson deals? Because I'm warning you, Sharpe—"

"Didn't I tell you this would happen? He was on my place last night, I heard the bastard."

"Who was?"

"Can't say for sure: Cal Hale, maybe Trinkley. Whoever it was, he's been here before, snooping around."

"Why would Cal Hale poison you? You don't sound poisoned to me, Al, just loopy." He hung up. I called Tinkerspoon and asked if he'd noticed anything odd last night.

"*El Rapido* was barking blue meanies, but I didn't see nothing."

We bought bottled water at BuyRite and had our well water tested by AquaLab in Riverside for every toxic white substance we could think of. Thirteen hundred dollars for a water test.

Total Coliform:	*absent*
E. coli:	*absent*
Anthrax:	*absent*
Cyanide:	*absent*
Ricin:	*absent*
Caustic alkali:	*beneath Fed. accept. limit*
Heterotrophic plate count:	115 (*within Fed. accept. limit*)

<u>note</u>:   *Traces of a compound sugar detected, likely sucrose. Glass container holding the sample possibly contaminated.*

They'd poured powdered sugar in my water tank. A friendly warning from Cal, no doubt. I scrawled a sign on the pump house door: NO ONE DRINKS THIS WATER.

#

Lately, when she thought about her mother, which she did often, Finley remembered vague, whispering voices, and her father asking repeatedly, "Was she aboard or wasn't she?" People's awkward, agonized faces peering at him like rodents, shaking their heads, seeming to plead with him, making awkward umpire-like motions with their hands as if asking for time out. When/where? At the airport, waiting for her mother's plane that would never land? She recalled feeling, even way back then, that something was wrong with this picture. She couldn't understand why her father wasn't as devastated as she was. Rather, he seemed puzzled, lost; he walked about mumbling to himself. Recently, she told him flat out that she knew with a certainty that her mother and her traveling companion hadn't gotten on that plane. They disappeared. Her mother had abandoned her and run off with that Charlie person.

Now she worried that her dad was going widgety, always talking about Cal Hale and Ches Noonan's plans to control the valley. Just dumb. Cal was a lanky, goose-necked hick who swore a lot, and Ches couldn't control his own weight. At first, passing SALCO signs going up on empty tracts, Al bought into rumors that they were posted by the government on land deemed unfit for human habitation. He refused to believe that developers were buying up the valley. I can empathize with that. When the first white settlers arrived in the valley 150 years ago, I ignored old Grandfather Lubo's (and Tahquitz's) warnings about the white eyes, believing that the newcomers would take no more than the native peoples did. But the Anglos had grandiose plans; they killed our game, stole Indian lands, and filled in black cienegas. If Al couldn't accept the vision of our valley paved with houses, neither could I. "Open your eyes, bro," Rob Thompson chided him. Finley told Patsy K Jones that whenever her dad got nervous he did the ostrich number. "So why can't he just face things, like that my mom got a case of fuck fever and split, for instance? I can handle it, even if it was with a woman."

"PC check, everyone's got avoidance issues, even you. Dad and Penny Noonan, for instance." *Patsy K did a killer Penny Noonan imitation, right down to the way she shook her booty and wrinkled her nose.*

"My dad isn't fucking Penny Noonan, I don't believe it. Besides, she's married."

"PC check, what's that got to do with anything?"

"I know my dad, okay. He wouldn't do that."

"But he is doing that!"

Little did she know that her father had once crammed a pair of Penny's panties down the "Forget Hole" in an old live oak tree in the Bad Things Cemetery, where they were swallowed into the darkness along with other forgotten things.

Angie Beach called from the Cayman Islands to inform Tinkerspoon that she was listing the remainder of her La Cienega holdings.

"That's right behind my place, dude."

"Relax, Andy, we won't let her do that," Al promised him.

"How we gonna stop her?"

"I'll buy it," Al decided, recalling that empty space behind Tinkerspoon's on Lester's map.

Al was astonished to learn how much smoke-scrubber money remained in his equities portfolio—enough to make him wonder why he lived like a pauper. Not enough, however, to finance two million dollars worth of real estate: 340 acres at six thousand dollars per. Some royalties still trickled in, but not enough to keep up mortgage payments (if he could secure a loan). A plan came to him all of a piece, as his inventions often did.

"That's mighty steep for desert scrub," he told Symphony Thomas at Angel Realty.

"That will all go to homes," she said. "I thought Ches Noonan might be interested."

"I'd prefer you didn't call Ches. I'm going to buy it."

"It's a forty-thousand dollar, non-refundable deposit, Al."

"I'll write you a check right now."

"Why goodness!" Symphony wiggled in her chair like an excited child. "That's the easiest sale I've ever made."

Al told Colin Allsport, his attorney, that he just needed to hold the property long enough to discourage developers. "That's the plan. They're locusts: they come in, do their damage, and split. We might not be able to stop them, but we can slow them down."

"So you're buying with the intention to default? That could be considered fraud, you realize. I can't be party to that." When Al rose to leave, Colin batted his palms downward. "Sit, sit." Even after twenty years of North Hollywood attrition, he retained his British accent. "Ballocks! People borrow money every day knowing they can't make their payments. It's the American way." He smiled.

Al planned to establish "an itinerant's nature conservancy." He would purchase the land and find homeless folks to occupy it, and make payments until he exhausted his resources; the bank would then foreclose, but his goal would be accomplished. "No developer will buy land that comes *with squatters." Lines on Colin's brow migrated upward like a flock of geese. "What harm in it, really? You'll be preserving the natural habitat, providing a home for the homeless, and forcing a charitable heart on your bankers. It's win-win. But you'll be out a bundle, Sharpe"*

"It's only money."

Nonetheless, Al felt guilty talking to John Hobkins down at Western Enterprise Bank, knowing he was conning him. Hobkins was a good man. Al looked good on paper, given his portfolio and history of semi-annual royalties. He agreed to put down another $120,000 and make payments of $10,450 a month. He left the bank feeling giddily nauseous, knowing he would soon be bankrupt. But passing the Noonan place on Two Horse Flats Road on his way home, he planted his hand on the horn in celebration.

Mona's friend, RJH, Saint Angel's most successful Internet day trader, had years before convinced Al to "sex up" his portfolio by investing in Biotechs and cutting edge IT stocks to maximize earning potential (mentioning nothing of risk). So Al "sexed up" his equity holdings to the max—including Finley's college fund. What was about to happen shouldn't have surprised him; he knew the Second law of thermodynamics: what goes up in a closed system must come down. Everything we do comes back on us—although not quite yet.

One morning as Al worked on his desalination system, retreating water reversed course and barreled up his well shaft, blowing his pump and pump house high into branches of a sycamore tree, water geysering into the air as if he'd struck oil. It flooded his meadow and the canyon, and spilled across the road into Tinkerspoon's trailer. The girls splashed about in their swim suits, thinking it a lark, while Tinkerspoon frantically carted computer equipment to his roof, watching that Old Faithful spout rising from Al's well in awe. He believed Cal's water tanks were emptying through it, but Al surmised—from its virgin taste—that it was second aquifer water, fossil water, heretofore untested by the human tongue, rising under great pressure through holes Cal's drillers had punched in the shale confining it to flood the overlying aquifer and geyser out well shafts. He stood beneath that geyser, water crashing down on his head and shoulders. Delicious," he told Patsy K Jones, who danced around him in a string bikini. He and the girls linked arms and spun around in an impromptu hora. A smell of ozone tart as ginger filled the air. They lapped water and giggled, thousands of gallons of earth water falling down atop them. The ground gurgled underfoot. They kicked legs high in the air like a line of Las Vegas chorus girls.

Cal's pickup came sloshing up the drive, and he leapt out, shouting, "Damn it, Sharpe, you stole my water." Patsy K sat down in waist-deep water, smiling up at the sky. "Liquid sex," she mumbled. "Gawd...truly brackish." Cal's face went sunset red. "Bunch of damned perverts." Al Sharpe's own daughter, for crissake, and her half-naked girlfriend.

"Just sharing a drink of water together," Al said.

"My water!"

"Our water!" Finley was defiant.

Incredibly, Wallers was climbing a nearby oak, shinnying upwards on his stubby legs. Across the road, Tinkerspoon's dogs yipped and snapped at the current; Misty swam in frantic, marionette circles. Then came a great burp, a wheeze from the black swamp, and water rushed toward it with a roar, the undertow so strong they must grip hold of trees to keep from being swept away. The geyser folded in on itself and was gone. They watched water spiral clockwise into the slough, then regarded one another in amazement, touching their wet clothes to make sure it was real.

"Damndest thing I ever saw," Cal maundered

12

SAM CITY

I came upon Finley standing before her mother's memorial stone near The Bad Things Cemetery, her smoky breath hanging on the chill air. "I had a dream about Mom last night," she said, sensing my presence without turning around. "She wears her hair in a buzz cut now: super widgety. She kept calling my name, but I couldn't answer. I tried but no words came out." Turning around and looking hard at me: "She's alive, isn't she? We should like bury her so-called death in The Bad Things Cemetery."

"Listen, hon, sometimes we wish for something so much we convince ourselves it's true. I wanted to believe our marriage was still alive after it died, I convinced myself."

"I'm not you, Dad. Okay?"

"I'm saying we're good at fooling ourselves. You'll learn that some day."

"Don't patronize me. Being younger than you doesn't make me less perceptive."

"No, of course not. I'm just saying...." Her tone alarmed me, not like Finley. It was as if her mother had taken root in her—Sondra's bullishness. Maybe a mother who abandons her daughter, by whatever means, is bound to reappear in some guise.

"I know she's alive, I've talked to her," Finley said flatly.

"Talked to her? Now you're scaring me. That's crazy talk."

She shrugged. "So go ahead and call me crazy. I know what I know, even if you won't accept it." My daughter turned and walked away from me, something she'd never done, leaving me dumfounded and shaken. Everything was changing in our lives: the land we loved, the people we loved, our own personalities. We were caught up in an epidemic of rampant, senseless change.

At least we had water again. Something adjusted underground, and our water table rose to a new high, Pissing Springs gushed full on for the first time in decades, emitting the sickishly sweet odor of rotting lilacs. Our well water was vaguely green and left a residue on glasses. Wallers sloshed it out of his trough into mud puddles and lay beside it, chin on stubby forelegs, letting it stand a time before drinking. Pig smart. Tinkerspoon was convinced they were laying traps for him on the Internet. He'd seen anti-viral fingerprints the last time he'd hacked TexHome Development's site. "I wrote a new invasion program, dude. When they log on, all their numbers spiral down a virtual toilet." He punched a fist in the air. "Tinkerzap 'em, dude." Mona was steering clear of me. "I'm no masochist," she said, whatever that meant. Western Enterprise Bank kept pestering me with questions about my financials, wanting more documentation of my earnings and—especially— my outlays. They could not accept that I lived on five hundred dollars a month (all the rest went for Finley). "What would I spend money on? I don't eat out, don't date, don't buy clothes, don't go anywhere," I told John Hobkins. "There's groceries and gas, but I don't eat much, and I grow a big garden. I generate my own electricity, pump my own water, haven't been to a doctor in years, don't take drugs. Drink a little beer and cheap whiskey, sure, smoke a little weed I grow myself—maybe I shouldn't be telling you this." He nodded wistfully. "No luxuries, no liabilities. You're the ideal candidate for a loan, Al," he said. "I know this, but my underwriter doesn't buy it."

"Everyone is hiding something. That's a given in the banking business," Mona explained.

What was I hiding? I had no idea; maybe I was hiding it from myself. I told myself I no longer desired Penny Noonan. Why then did I keep having dreams of balling her while she laughed perversely and Ches sat at foot of the bed cheering us on?

Little Les rode out on his bicycle one gloomy day, did his over-the-handlebars dismount, doffed his leather cap and clutched it in both hands as he approached me at work under a canopy. Red long underwear visible under his regulation black leather vest. "I'd like to pay your little girl's girlfriend a visit if you don't mind, Al."

"Bit short of your age bracket, isn't she, Les?"

"That don't bother me. I never bought into the age crap, I believe in evolution."

"It's up to her, Les. I have nothing to say about it."

They went on hikes in the Juan Antonio Hills on drizzly February days—Finley often with them—Wallers following at their heels like a grunting dog; though he'd soon tire and return home. The best time of year for such treks: creeks alive in washes; fairy shrimp sprung mysteriously to life in vernal pools; spicy green of pepperwood, sage, and ceanothus on the air; precocious wildflower bloom on the hillsides—Indian paint brush and early poppies—clumps of mistletoe adorning oak trees; ground squirrels hightailing it for their burrows at hikers' approach. One day they returned shortly after setting out. "They're coming!" Les shouted from afar, "cutting a road behind Tink's. Fuckers are right here at your doorstep." Tinkerspoon and I went to see for ourselves. A huge yellow dozer carved a swath across the flats extending back to the Juan Antonio Hills, a Brobdingnagian rock-crushing machine clanked away, conveyor belts spewing fresh gravel onto a huge mound. We'd been hearing it for weeks, I realized, but had convinced ourselves it was distant thunder. Tinkerspoon sank to his knees as if shot. "Nothing to panic about," I assured him, "it could be years." Although my own heart clattered like a loose piston.

"They're Tinkerzapping us, dude," he whispered.

I went down to County Planning and learned SALCO planned to build 1,300 housing units on *La Cienega* land behind Tinkerspoon's. I laughed, incredulous. "That's five thousand people. Saint Angel was smaller than that when I moved here eleven years ago."

"Marvelous isn't it?" the clerk said.

"I thought they were required to hold a public hearing."

"They have. Several hearings."

"We never heard about them."

She made a dismissive face. "Announcements don't always get into the paper. They were posted on our website."

"We've been monitoring your website; it's been down for two months."

"Oh, yes. They're working on it." She smiled and told me that TexHome was building another 4,000 units out Infinity Canyon Road. "Five years from now you won't recognize this place anymore."

I backed out of the office waving hands before my face.

#

No denying it anymore: housing tracts sprang up like brush fires along Jack-o'-Lantern Road, like seeds blown on a vagrant wind, or an algal bloom reddening the sea, or basal cells forming scaly patches over the skin, or Ches's epidemic of warts. No metaphor will hold before such trespass.

The rumble of earth-moving machines hung on the air twelve hours a day from deep back on Angie Beach's former land. They scraped away chaparral, scooped out ponds, pushed up berms, and cut in cul-de-sacs, headlights tunneling through dusty air. Coyote Canyon, where the Los Coyotes band of Cahuilla led by Chief Chapuli made a last desperate stand against white encroachment in 1851, was obliterated overnight, along with a village site Littlefeather's people had occupied for a thousand years. Al Sharpe had long since stopped trying to convince himself it was the sound of golf course construction carried over the mountain from Palm Springs on freak Santa Anas. But when Finley pointed out terraces fresh cut in Little Ramona Mountain to the east, Al threw up a hand and muttered, "heat waves." "So who's in denial now, Dad?"

He tried to convince himself that the machine gun percussion of hammering was Indians target practicing up on the plateau; he would have to speak to Sage Littlefeather about it. They put up billboards on both sides of Creosote Canyon Road announcing:

CANYONLANDS RANCHO ESTATES

They must be shooting a movie, Al decided, while housing tracts moved inexorably closer across the flatlands. Al Sharpe was skilled at negative capability, both accepting and denying things at once. Chaos reigns, entropy rules. He knew this to be true in the natural world, but could not accept it in his life.

*Then suddenly they were upon them: a line of houses where once had been open chaparral, orange wooden skeletons two-stepping westward from Jack-o'-Lantern Road in a danse macabre. Hearing the staccato rapping of framers' hammers, Al sank to his knees and scrubbed his face with dirt. How had they built them so fucking fast? How many would there be? When the Littlefeathers took Finley up to Singing Springs under winter's last full moon, she looked out over the once dark valley and saw grids of incandescence, the roving headlights of earth-moving machines. They had stolen the night. The springs themselves, which once moaned like a gourd flute, were dead quiet. "They stole the power," Sage grumbled. On the way home, they passed real estate placards: **Singing Springs: 3-8 Bedroom Luxury Homes, From the 130s**. Matt flew out of the truck and kicked them down.*

Once his loan was approved, Al sought occupants for his La Cienega land. Mona Sahlstrom accompanied him to Hemet, dressed in thrift store chic. *They walked a warren of unpaved streets, a rural slum in Valle Vista which Mona termed "a white-trash theme park." Tiny bungalows were crowded cheek by jowl in a desiccated forest of dead eucalyptus and scrappy pepperwood trees, filthy urchins screamed in dusty yards, and pit bulls charged chain-link fences as they passed, snarling and biting the wire. It was an updated version of Charles Dickens' blighted London, where poverty was passed down from generation to generation, but with a soundtrack of rock-a-billy and salsa music blending in an itchy mix. Dust rose spontaneously into the parched air as if by magnetic force: no rain in ten months. Quixotically, amidst the rubble, gleaming Cigarette boats and 4x4 pickups, obscenely elevated on tractor-trailer tires, occupied driveways—homage to credit card culture. They sensed people watching them from behind dark windows. A teenage boy whizzed past on a quad, spraying them with filthy water from a puddle, leering back with a Darth Vader grin from behind the face guard of his helmet. Mona seized Al's arm. "Could we leave? This place gives me the willies." They had stopped before a rundown trailer, where a heavyset woman with rooster-red hair stood in the open doorway. "You from over to Sulkey's?" she asked.*

"I don't know any Sulkey," Al replied.

"My husband says you's probably from over to Sulkey's, come to collect rent."

They stood at the low fence beyond which a toddler was sprawled naked in the muddy water of a wading pool. "Actually, we're looking for people who want to live rent free," Al said. A burly, black-bearded man with a shaved head stepped out of the trailer.

"Free rent? Now that's some bullshit right there." He shook hands with Al over the fence. "I'm Mike, this here's my wife Melie. People call us M&M." Mike looked Mona up and down and patted his belly in mute approval.

"I'd invite you in, but I ain't got to cleaning yet today," Melie said.

"She ain't cleaned shit since Easter. It's a fucking pig sty."

"Go fuck y'rself, M." The woman cuffed the side of his head.

Al explained his scheme: people could live on Sam Jenson Acres rent free so long as they kept it tidy and fire safe. He'd supply some building materials. "I can't guarantee how long you can stay; I hope indefinitely."

Mike said they might be interested. "So whadyou get out of it, brother?"

"I need people to occupy my land, pure and simple."

"We can do that, oh yeah! My wife's fat ass...oh yeah. Hell yes."

Soon there were twenty neighbors gathered in M&M's yard, drinking beer and discussing Al's proposal, shouting at new arrivals: "Free rent, hell yeah." An impromptu party.

Mona was dubious going home, telling Al this was his most harebrained scheme yet. Little Les agreed. "You can't just invite any old somebody onto your land. You're gonna have grief, bro. I might move out there myself if the neighbors was good people." There would be one dwelling per twenty acres, Al decided, seventeen in all. With Rob, Sage, and Little Les, he built three small model cabins, using wood salvaged from Sam Jenson's barn, but settlers who arrived in clunker cars like dust-bowl refugees, dozens of them, ignored his plan and built crude shacks and lean-tos in a scraggly mesquite thicket at the east end of the property fronting SALCO land, creating a rural slum at once christened "Sam City," finding comfort in proximity. More of them than Al bargained for, but it gratified him that they considered him Robin Hood.

Townsfolk talked of dope addicts, lowlifes, and criminals camped out in "Shit City." Harvey Suarez believed they were a fanatical suicide cult. Cal Hale claimed an Arab sheik bought the land for a terrorist training camp (he'd seen men wearing rags on their heads out there); Mrs. Sylvester spoke of hippies. Al took out a second mortgage on Second Chance Acres, determined to forestall bankruptcy as long as possible. His plan looked good in the abstract, but was thorny in practice, as most revolutionary social schemes are.

#

You learn a lot about people when you start a revolution. Daph Thompson had a gift for organizing, while firebrand Rob—who, at DGLA get-togethers, would drop his trunks and moon Silk Setters sipping wine coolers across Ches's pool—was suddenly a reluctant naysayer: "Yo! You think they're gonna roll over and play dead? If God wants houses, there's gonna be houses." Patsy K Jones, rage queen and propagandist, called him "brackishly stupid." "Your brain is totally God-washed." Finley played mediator, Little Les was strategist, honest Mona was our furtive spy at the bank, Tinkerspoon was, of course, our techie, Matt Littlefeather beat a low drum of fury, and Sage was just sage: "You can't never stop them, but sometimes you gotta slow them down." Me, I was jack of all trades and resident dreamer. It was agreed we would return to the DGLA and volunteer to help with the Realty Roundup, then sabotage it. I would do the master of ceremonies thing to keep tabs on what they were up to. We clinked beer bottles together to seal the deal.

Some days later, while planting new seedlings in the front garden, I looked up to see Trinkley's white SUV parked out by the mailbox. I hid behind a bush near the road, watching Trinkley study surveyor's stakes, his head cocked, swatches of rusty hair spilling from his cap, jeans rolled meticulously up his ankles ("toad people," Finley calls his kind). Just then a fleet of flatbed trucks rolled up Creosote Canyon Road, ferrying bulldozers. Trinkley pointed where they should unload: on my property! I ran to grab the fire extinguisher from the pump house and approached Trinkley like he was a blaze that needed dousing. He raised a prohibitive hand, his face salmon pink and oily.

"Stay back, fella."

"No-no-nobody told me about this," I stuttered in outrage.

"No-nobody told you? T.S.F. Hey—" shouting at a trucker "—by the boulder, asshole."

"That's my property."

"Not today." Trinkley pointed at stakes which the girls had moved twenty feet back onto my place—in the wrong direction. "You want to get out of the way and let us work here, fella."

"No...fella, I want you the hell off. Now!" I advanced on a truck backing onto my land, its moronic back-up beeper nagging, waving my arms and shouting. I heaved the fire extinguisher, which hit the cab with a metallic clang and bounced off. Air breaks squealed, men shouted, and I ran to fetch Wallers from the canyon, caught the bandana around his neck and charged Trinkley and his minions, whooping to fire Wallers up. He snorted fury, thinking I'd cornered a ground squirrel, and crashed through the brush on his stubby legs, tugging me along, taking Trinkley for an over-sized rodent. "Sic him, Wallers. Eat his baloney." I never saw a short, ungainly man run so fast. He leapt up on a truck's running board and banged on the door for the driver to haul ass. Trucks retreated down the road, Wallers squealing and nipping at their heels. I moved those stakes thirty feet back off my place.

Trinkley returned with Charlie Haynes and demanded he arrest me and shoot my "devil pig." I got a rope around Wallers and tied him to the front bumper of Charlie's squad car for safe keeping. Charlie up in my face: "I've had about enough, Sharpe. Like it or no, they are going to build houses. You just as well get used to it."

"By whose permission or consent? Not mine, not Tinkerspoon's.

The Planning Commission never held public meetings to solicit our response; that's not legal."

Trinkley snorted a laugh. "No one needs your consent, fella. Tex-Home intends to subdivide right up to your doorstep and maximize their investment. This is America, shit for brains."

"Take it easy," Charlie chided him. "No reason to throw fuel on the fire."

Trinkley doesn't talk, he launches words at you like missiles, leaning forward to see how hard they strike. "T.S.F." (*Tough Shit, Fella*) is his pet phrase. I stared at the bald fuck, thinking Rob was right: someone should shoot that fat-assed prick. A housing development next door to Second Chance Acres, unacceptable. Impossible.

"Besides," Trinkley was saying, "isn't anybody owns that land. It's scattered among stockholders all over the world. There isn't anyone to complain to."

"I'm saying we should have a say in the matter, Charlie, those of us who live here."

"T.S.F.," Trinkley said. "Get used to it."

I wanted to strangle the smug turd, but Wallers had pulled the bumper off Charlie's squad car and lit out down the road with it clanging and leaping behind him, squealing like the devil was after him. Charlie Haynes nearly in tears. "Goddamn it all, Al. You're going to pay for that bumper."

So it began. Giant yellow dozers, wheel loaders, graders and balloon-wheeled dump trucks, backhoes, and hydraulic shovels rumbled day and night, tearing up land east of my place. I'd arrived in hell without going anywhere. I heaved stones at the behemoths, managed to crack a few windshields. A one-man Intifada. Operators tried to run me down. I spiked their water coolers with fetid Pissing Springs water, gratified when Trinkley hightailed it for the bushes, clutching his belly. I began tampering with pipe bombs (hate to admit it). Anger had swallowed me whole.

Les said they were required by law to notify all property owners within two hundred yards of a proposed development. The clerk at County Planning insisted they'd mailed notices to me "and a Mr. Sanchez. Our records show three attempts: *attempted/unsuccessful*." "We've been here," I insisted. "Is this anything like your website problems, a convenient failure to communicate?"

"You plan to accuse me of killing anyone tonight?" Cal Hale

asked me as we filed into the Noonan living room to discuss the Realty Roundup, his cheeks patchy red from broken blood vessels, hokey string tie, and pale, water-thieving eyes. A canny rogue playing country rube. I saw dozers moving across Cal and Ches's eyes, the gleam of money. It got the wiring glowing red hot in my brain, but I managed a tepid smile. "We're back, Cal, that's all."

"Delighted to have you," Ches said. "Bygones be bygones." He squeezed a purple growth on his neck. Dis-fuckin-gusting. Daph said that at heart we really did believe in greening the desert. "But given the heat and Santa Anas, you know, your faith wavers sometimes." Sounded half convincing.

"Oh, gracious, yes," Clover Abernathy cried, honestly delighted to see us, as was Winky Hale. Even the Houstons and Philadelphias seemed pleased by our return. Ches toasted us with a glass of champagne. "God bless America, God bless the DGLA, keep Saint Angel green, by God."

"Hear hear!" John Sylvester said.

"For the children's sake," Mrs. Houston added.

Penny Noonan's vulpine eyes tore me slowly to pieces and devoured me. She wore the red silk kimono she always wore at our trysts, black bikini underneath, no doubt, or nothing.

At one point, Ches pinched my elbow. "We need to talk, Albert." His breath worse than Wallers' after feeding in the black slough. "There's something you want from me and something I want from you." He winked.

"No, Ches, nothing...really. Nothing I can think of."

"I know what's going on in my own home, boy."

I stared at him, stunned, recalling Mona's warning. "That's over, Ches. I promise you."

"Nonsense. We'll talk, Albert." He winked again. "Now get busy, Penny's waiting."

Couldn't believe my ears, nor fathom what was going on when Penny hooked a finger under my chin and led me toward the guest room. I knew Mona was watching, though didn't turn to look. Penny's nylons swished liquidly together as we walked arm in arm down the dim hallway, like a hallway in a sleazy hotel, lit by blue bulbs in clam shell sconces high on the walls. I nearly collided with John Sylvester stepping out of the john, silver hair aglow. His broad face rotated toward Penny then back to me, a puzzled moon. "That you, Al?" I mumbled about needing to use the john, then followed Penny towards the back of the house like a skittish teenage boy. Crazy horny given the illicitness of it. Plump cupids grinned at us from guest room wallpaper, but when I grabbed her ass, Penny shoved me off. "Have you taken leave of y'r senses, Albert? Ah have guests." Kneading my cheek between her fingers, she unknotted the belt of her robe and let it slip back off her shoulders, buck naked but for nylons and garter belt. Straddled me on the guest bed, while her "guests" gathered around the pool beyond tinted windows. They kept their faces modestly averted; I didn't give a damn, I was lust drunk on violation.

Afterwards, Penny went for a dip in the pool. I stole into Ches's work room across the hall. A plat book lay open on a huge table, displaying Saint Angel Township Sections 246-62, including a stretch of Creosote Canyon Road and Second Chance Acres, outlined in red. My canyon, twisting into rez land, was hatched in blue pencil, words snaking along it: "Fill in." Others were jotted faintly across my property: "Completes Canyonlands Acquisition," as if the bastards already owned my place. Ches's battle plan left there for me to find. Penny stood in the doorway, dripping wet in her string bikini.

"Happy now, you little shit? You can't help y'rself, can you, Albert?"

"You planned this, didn't you, you two? Left it here for me to find?"

"Don't be a simp. Now skedaddle before Daddy finds you in here."

"Why," I continued, "would Ches want me to know? Maybe you left the book open to inform me what Chester has in mind—to warn me. Did you?"

"Git!" she said.

I slipped out the back door and went over the wall, making sure no one saw me, feeling like a sneak thief, a mendacious rat, or a nascent subversive.

I drove the back way, past the junction of Jack-o'-Lantern and Creosote Canyon Roads for the first time in weeks, past a full-blown suburb: stucco perimeter walls, sidewalks, traffic lights, instant pop-up landscaping. Even the air felt tamed. I blew right through a red light, anomalous out here in the middle of nowhere, and past a strip mall. Believe it! High-desert fast food. They'd put up ranch-style McMansions every five hundred feet along the Katydid Road shortcut: **Rancho Nuevo Luxury Living.** When I turned on the radio, a maudlin voice updated the *E. coli* death toll in Nova Scotia to "ninety-six souls." I rested my forehead a moment against the wheel, startled alert by an air horn. A loaded lumber truck approached half into my lane, a close call.

A black slough miasma overrode the fresh smell of new turf. The feet of a dog or coyote stuck out of a bog just beyond the road ditch, a boy's jockey shorts spewed to one side. Jesus! Awful foul smell. I stopped the truck and fashioned a sign from one of the real estate placards that I was constantly pulling up and tossing in the pickup's bed, using red lipstick Mona had left in my glove compartment:

EXTREME DANGER

STAY BACK!

Hundreds of small toads, bruise purple in color, covered the slough banks, stalk eyes turning towards me in unison as if controlled by a single brain; they hopped forward en masse. I dashed for the truck and sped away, tires spinning over their slimy, popping bodies as if over a crunchy oil slick. Sage Littlefeather says the land feels pain and expresses it in earthquakes and droughts, and, seemingly, in black bogs and dark toads. I arrived home to find placards lined up along the road in front of my place:

YOU'RE HERE!

CANYONLAND ESTATES

Trinkley's van was parked by the mailbox. I swerved in behind and slammed into it. Patsy K Jones caught my sleeve as I exited the truck. "Let it go, Dad," Finley insisted, sensing my fury. She had watched me pace along the road like a caged beast, while belly scrapers scalped the earth to raw red flesh east of us, shoved earth and brush into hillocks which giant trucks hauled away, scraping up the desert and discarding it. A red fog of anger enveloped me.

"Where's your damned pig?" Trinkley asked, approaching us.

"You can never be sure."

Watching me, the surveyor patted the butt of a pistol in a braided holster on his hip. "Your problem, fella, you're anti-progress, you and that devil pig."

"PC check," Patsy K said. "Your problem, Mr. Widget Wonk, you're fat and butt ugly."

Trinkley's eyes widened comically, he aimed his hammer handle at her. "Watch your mouth, young lady." He hammered in another placard on a wooden stake.

"You can't put those in front of my place," I told him.

"Sure I can, that's county property six feet either side of the pavement. T.S.F." He walked over and started to drive in a stake dead center of my driveway, winked at me. "Maybe not." I yanked a sign out of the ground and broke the stake over my knee. "They're coming down."

"Don't you touch those signs, fella, that's vandalism."

"This is vandalism." Gesturing at monstrous machines working both sides of the road to the east of us.

"Land rape," Patsy K said, yanking out another sign.

"You know like your problem, mister?" Finley up in Trinkley's face. "You aren't happy unless you're making other people miserable. You need help. Seriously."

Trinkley giggled nervously and backed off. "You bet, little girl." The girls began pulling out signs in earnest, stomping on them. When Trinkley reached for his gun, I stepped between them. "Take that out of its holster and I'll rip your fucking head off."

He leapt back. "Get off me, you maniac!" Spittle showered my face. His hands wiped frantically at his chest as if I'd smeared him with shit.

"Truly brackish, Dad," Finley said as he drove off. "Totally." The girls regarded me in admixed alarm and wonder.

Later, we learned that Tinkerspoon had been hiding in a junk pile out front of his trailer, holding Trinkley in the sights of his 30.06 while he was putting up signs. "If the dude stepped across the road, I would'a offed him." Things were getting serious.

13

THE REALTY REVENGE

Little Les scooted into the booth at the diner and traded five with Sage. "Whassup, chief? I hear ol' Ches is buying himself a rez and putting you lazy Indians to work."

Matt gave me a deadpan look. "He think that's funny or something?"

Les grinned, the polished teeth of a sunbelt biker, blue bandana tied pirate fashion around his head. "I'm just saying, bro. There's rumors you're selling us out, people are talking."

Matt and Sage exchanged a look. "That's Cahuilla Nation business, Anglos got shit all to say about it."

"We opposed it, okay," Sage interrupted his brother. "We lost her in tribal council. The tribe leased it for ninety-nine years to SALCO and them."

"Jesus fucking Christ," Rob groaned. "Forgive my French, Lord."

"That's Indian jobs and shit over there. We got to eat same as you." Matt looked away.

"So Ches is right: everybody sells out in the end."

"Isn't nobody sold out." Sage slammed a fist on the table, silverware jumped.

"We have to stop them," I said quietly. "That's all I'm saying."

Sage regarded me sullenly: broad, pock-marked face, flattened nose, eyes hot embers. He nodded, I nodded. Years back, when Finley had pneumonia and I sat at her bedside at hospital day and night, Sage appeared at two a.m. one morning and touched my shoulder as I snoozed. "My watch, brother. Go home and get you some sleep." He walked right in past the night nurse like a ghost without her seeing him.

The Crispleys passed our booth, Jack's hand on Meg's back, both looking straight ahead. Rob stood to block their path. "Whassup, Jack and Meg?" Grinning. They gimped him smiles.

"How you fellas?" Jack asked.

"We'd be cool if you people stopped trashing the valley," Rob said.

A tide of red flooded Jack's forehead into the roots of his sandy hair, freckles popped out on his forehead. "Some of us work for a living. That's premium houses we're building."

"That's staple-together particle-board shacks thrown up by Tex-Mex rent-a-dick labor is what it is. You won't hire local anymore." He thumped a finger against Crispley's chest.

"Okay, Rob, let it go," I said. "Isn't Jack's doing."

"Yeah it is. Crispley would eat his mother's lunch." Rob's nose nearly touched the shorter man's forehead in cartoon-like confrontation. Sage hooked elbows with the men and walked them outside. Lately, Rob spoke of little besides blowing up housing developments.

#

Matt Littlefeather's group—the La Cienega del Diablo Indians who opposed leasing reservation land to Ches Noonan—collected scorpions, rattlers, and tarantulas, milked venom from the snakes, and fixed tiny plastic sheaths over scorpions' tails, while Sage organized his Indian friends, Sam City folks, and Les's Devastation Acres pals for the "uprising": The Desert Folks Liberation Society's Realty Revenge. Daphne, Mona, and the girls bought matching powder blue hostess skirts and blazers to wear when guiding tours of model homes, in keeping with the Roundup's theme: "Back in the day." Mrs. Sylvester clapped her hands upon seeing the outfits. "They're just so darling...so Fifties!" The Roundup's brochure read: "Raise your children under the cheery high desert sun in friendly Saint Angel." Secretly, in what was to be their own surprise addition to the Realty Revenge, Finley and Patsy K Jones enlisted their Carlsbad High friends and rehearsed nightly, lilting out welcoming phrases in a digital sing-song like futuristic call girls. Rob and Tinkerspoon amassed red dye and incendiaries, working furtively with Little Les on "special projects." "No bombings," the others insisted. "No structures," the men promised. Sage's wife, Wynona, made kachina dolls, "black poppets," Mona called them. God knows what she planned to do with them. Al polished the speech Mona helped him write for the kick-off barbecue. Ches fit him out in a western casual suit.

He called Al the weekend before the Roundup/Revenge. "Say, Albert, why don't you get me a copy of your speech." It was the first they'd spoken since Ches told him he knew about Al's affair with his wife. "You plan to manage me, Ches?" Al said after a pause. Ches chuckled. "I'll leave that to my wife." Al felt like he was leaping out of the water with a steel hook through his cheek, caught. They'd been playing him all along: Ches arriving home while they were balling, leaving that plat book open for him to find. But why? To make him an unwitting accomplice?

"*You wouldn't know anything about that lot of winos and human trash living over on the old La Cienega land behind Tinkerspoon's, would you?*" Ches asked.

"*I've seen them,*" Al dissembled.

"*They are defecating in our model homes. I won't tolerate it.*"

"*I hear they lack sanitary facilities.*"

"*That's your problem, Albert, it's your land. I understand you provide them well water when your well is illegal to begin with. The Water Authority intends to look into it.*"

"*Nobody touches my well, Ches. That's something I won't tolerate.*"

"*We'll see.*"

#

Finley returned home in a sullen funk after two days on the coast. While we washed dinner dishes together, she asked me if I thought dreams are a form of longing. "Sometimes." I wiped soap suds from her chin. She stepped away. "Just stay off, Dad." She went out the back door towards the canyon. Her anger astounded me.

"What's troubling Finley?" I asked Patsy K, who was painting signs recycled from real estate placards we'd harvested with Little Les in my living room.

"Some brackish dream she had about her mom where Sondra is locked up in a cage and Fin can't find the key. What's really wack, she's Facebooking some Internet troller who knows all sorts of shit about her mom. Right? I told her, schnay, like PC check, you can't trust the Zuckernet. It could be some perv…anybody! She won't listen, she's super into it." Glancing sidelong at me. "Schnay, maybe I shouldn't be telling you this."

"What person on Facebook?" I was alarmed. "Who knows about Sondra? What are you saying? Someone is stalking Finley on the Net?"

Just then, Finley burst in, panting hard, trying to catch her breath. "Gawd, it's awful," she cried. "Ugly's ugly!" We ran out with her to see. SALCO had clandestinely brought cement trucks in the back way, across *La Cienega* land, and was pouring foundations a hundred feet from my property line. In the ongoing racket of heavy equipment, we hadn't noticed them. We stood on a raised pad staring in disbelief. "No roads, no sewers, no power, they don't do it that way, people," Les said. "Infrastructure goes in first."

"So they want to occupy territory as fast as they can," Finley said.

I clutched my forehead. "I thought we had a good three months."

Little Les nodded. "Should've. They've ramped it up big time, people."

I sat on a perimeter wall until long after dark, watching concrete housing pads take on an ancient patina in the sunset before melting into night and earth. The land scraped to bare bone in feverish moonlight. I made out a necklace of lights at base of the Juan Antonio Hills, where once had been darkness. They'd stolen our solitude. "Invasion of the life snatchers," Finley called it. *Faux* prosperity mocking the land's parsimony. Nature colonized. I watched ragged hills go black, a rind of fragile robin's-egg blue lingering on their crests before being sucked into night's oblivion. Peaceful again, no inkling of hideous two-story houses looming up around me. Can we lose peace and quiet forever? Is it an endangered species? "You were lucky to leave when you did, Sam," I muttered. "You couldn't stomach this, old friend." Ironic that the man who had so valued water had died drinking it. Fury turned in me. This was like arriving home to discover thieves had made off not just with your belongings but with your entire life. I couldn't bear to lose Second Chance Acres.

Finley was changing, too. Troubled. Now this peculiar business about a mystery woman she'd met on the Internet. Who could it be, one of Sondra's former colleagues, a shamster freak, some hideous human parasite? I tried talking to her about it; she became furious, told me I shouldn't be prying into her personal life.

Headlights crawled along Creosote Canyon Road, stopped at my drive, then moved slowly on: one of Cal's goons in a white van no doubt. Tinkerspoon had dug a tiny sleeping chamber under his trailer, convinced they would blow it up over his head. All of us holding our collective breath, waiting for the appointed moment.

#

The future arrived all at once, with spring's stingy rain and flocks of raiding starlings. Rental cars and airport shuttles from Ontario Airport poured down Lancaster Road, ferrying in Realtors from Portland, Oregon and Sandusky, Ohio, who gawked in puzzlement at coins stacked beside parking meters and Indians in native dress (including aging hippies from Devastation Acres and Sam City) who stood in silent witness before Mimi's Diner and Dave's Auto Parts, staring menace at them. ATM machines in front of Saint Angel Federal, which hadn't functioned in years, now dispensed cash—but in the wrong denominations; Mona Sahlstrom saw to that. Locals, watching Realtors from Minnesota and Texas doled out five dollar bills instead of the five hundreds they'd requested, told them, "You get used to it. Welcome to Saint Angel." "Things will change," Realtors told each other. Many had survived the real estate collapse of the Eighties. It was really quite beautiful here, though they hadn't expected so many Native Americans, nor the dreadfully bitter coffee (not a Starbucks in sight), nor the awful accommodations. Those who had taken rooms in private homes were fortunate.

Realtors from the Michigan contingent were chased from their rooms at the Valle Vista Motel that first night by scorpions that darted across bathroom floors and clung precariously to ceilings over their beds (Matt Littlefeather's girlfriend supervised the maid staff there). I.T. Rawlings from Cobbs Corner, Wyoming said it was dreadful. "When I moved my eyes right, the little beast scampered right, when I moved them left, it went left, about to drop on my nose." John Snodgrass from Flint, Michigan had felt something hairy dart up his leg "making straight for the family jewels. I pulled back covers and there's the ugliest goldarned tarantula you ever did see. Thazzit! I'm outta here. Later for Saint Angel of the spiders." Others were willing to give it a go. J.Q. Dusquinex from Baton Rouge said she'd be darned if a few "bugs" chased her from her room. "I'll buy some Raid and go for the little shits." She laughed gaily. "We have gators and water moccasins back home."

Over at the new Holiday Inn, Matt Littlefeather's crew had smuggled a seven-foot defanged diamondback into the lobby, but the Texans and Arizonans staying there merely counted its rattles and got to arguing about which state had the most deadly reptiles, agreeing that California snakes were wusses. "Hell, the state's Democrat!" However, early risers were not amused to find snakes weaving sinuous wakes across the motel pool next morning. "We'd want to play down the rattlesnakes in our advertising," one said. Another, drinking a bloody Mary at seven a.m., said he was put off by the DGLA's claim that a river ran through town. "The Colorado River is fifty miles east." While an Oregon Realtor clasped hands behind his head and smiled. "Hey, mountains, palm trees, sitting by the pool before Easter is okay by me. Besides, they have one of the largest deep aquifers in the state." He smiled up at the San Jacintos, unaware of Tahquitz glowering back at him.

Rob and Little Lester barged into his house and rousted Al out of bed early, whispering something about blood. Believing at first that they were Ches's goons, Al reached for the baseball bat beside his bed. He looked back and forth between them. "Blood?"

"We got the main feeder valve shut down, but we got arguing about which one is the primary tank. We need a third opinion, brother," Les said. "We need you to give her a look see."

"Can't do it. I'm part of the welcoming committee this morning."

"Why are we whispering?" Rob asked.

The men looked at windows aglow in the first tepid light of dawn.

"It's gonna be a real beaut." Les grinned.

Sage and Wynona Littlefeather were sleeping off a night spent hanging kachina dolls from power lines and tree limbs. Wynona had delivered a hearty serving of her famous carnitas tamales—with beavertail cactus, Serrano pepper, and tequila—to Harvey Suarez at the Saint Angel police department that evening, knowing Harvey would eat gluttonously then fall asleep at his desk, giving them time to hang the dolls. A woman who cooked that good had to be a good lay, Harvey thought before drifting off. Finally, getting out on patrol at dawn, he noted spooky little dolls hung like old tennis shoes from power lines. He managed to fish one down and whispered into his radio, "It's some weird mothers: black legs and a white skull face. There's signs of Satanism all over town right now." He'd read an article about Satanism being on the rise among teenage kids, who learned about it on the Internet. Lifting the doll's stiff burlap dress, exposing gnarled root legs beneath it, Harvey got an erection. The doll reminded him of Mona Sahlstrom, whom he'd had a hard-on for since she moved to town. He'd once dreamt of her pitching to him buck naked while he squatted behind home plate in catcher's mask and knee pads, playing ball in high school.

Sage scoffed at the dolls at first, but seeing them hung from high places like an army of mute aliens, he considered the kachinas a stroke of genius. If he was a white Realtor, he would take one look at those weird Native-American voodoo dolls and decide there were better places to make money. Realtors disagreed that morning whether the dolls had been there the night before. J.Q. Dusquinex from Baton Rouge said sure they had. "It's proba'ly their way of saying, 'Howdy! Y'all come.'" A man from Fort Worth rubbed stick legs between his fingers and brought them to his nose, smelling sage and urine. *"Funny kind of welcome."*

That morning, when the "hostesses" in matching powder-blue skirts and blazers drove van loads of Realtors past the model development at the junction of Dead Creek Canyon and Lancaster Roads, they found perimeter walls graffitied with hieroglyphic stick figures in pornographic poses, backward swastikas, and spray-painted slogans:

> *BROWN POWER*
> *PROPERTY OF LA CIENEGA NATION*
> *DIE REALTY SCUM*

Seeing passengers' startled expressions, Patsy K Jones smiled slyly. *"It's just the brackish natives. Sometimes they get pissed off."* A Houston executive said he didn't realize they had an "Indian problem." *"PC check,"* Patsy K said, *"mostly it's a white people problem."* J.Q. Dusquinex from Baton Rouge threw back honey-blond hair and laughed throatily. *"Ah guess we'll just have to grow on them."* She was all right, Patsy K thought. The Houston executive wondered how he'd gotten stuck in a van with J.Q. and this nutty gal, though he had to admit they both had great tits.

Realtors found the bloody hand prints on walls and front doors of model homes even more unnerving. A nervous woman from Wichita asked Mona Sahlstrom what they meant. *"Exactly what you think they mean,"* Mona answered.

Little Les climbed the ladder at back of an eighty-foot-high water tank on a butte behind Sam Jenson's Place that the three men had decided was primary. Concealed from the eyes of construction workers arriving on the flats below, he removed hex bolts securing the metal hatch atop the tank and dumped in fifty pounds of red food coloring and gelatin he'd brought up in a backpack, then lay atop the tank grinning up at a bice blue sky and out across the valley and chaparral-covered hills to the north. Once there was nothing out here but Sam's place; now they had terraced the hill behind Sam's and scraped the earth bare of vegetation on all sides of his trailer and tumbledown barn, which they left standing for the moment, nervous about rousing the ire of local citizens. They were building houses on the hillsides, a sprawling outlet store mall on the flats. Les thumped on the tank with a fist; the hollow base thrumming brought workers' heads up below. *"We're going to help you out here, old buddy,"* Les promised Sam. Seeing a pickup heading up the winding road toward water tanks, Les threw his pack down *and abseiled more than climbed down the ladder, feet slipping over the rungs. "Time to hit it, people. Cavalry's coming."*

That afternoon, hostesses led tours of model homes and drove Realtors out Lancaster and Tourmaline Roads to show off artificial lakes and nascent golf courses—Cat tractors towing spiked drum harrows to flatten and aerate the soil in preparation for seeding. The girls delivered their lines in a practiced sing-song: Sixty percent fescue grass, thirty percent Bermuda, ten percent rye, and blue, and Zoysia, too, for water conservation.

They guided groups through furnished models, turning on taps in kitchens and marble-tiled bathrooms, as Cal had urged them to do: "We want water running, gurgling, and spraying all over, ladies. Hell! We want the desert flooded with gawddamned water." Daphne, Finley, Mona, and Patsy K Jones pretended alarm along with their guests when water poured out blood red from the spigots. "Oh goodness," they cried, "we thought that was cleared up."

"Is it rust?" asked the Oregon Realtor.

"Unh-uh. There's a whole lots of Native American and Mexican blood floating atop our reservoirs from the bad old days. You need to let the tap run a few minutes."

"Blood!" Realtors stared aghast at red water swirling around toilet bowls.

Patsy K Jones and Finley conducted impromptu tours through Sam City, walking guests past dilapidated shacks and drunks and junkies sprawled in the ashen dregs of fires. Gaunt pit bulls lay in the dirt, eyeing them with black, menacing stares. Gnawed chicken bones and broken glass littered the ground, clothes were hung to dry on dry bushes, and the place reeked of raw sewage. "These are your nearest neighbors," the girls chimed. "Very nice people once you get to know them—when they're not wasted." Realtors had begun deserting en masse.

Those remaining were seated at long tables covered with butcher paper in the Spanish courtyard of the new Saint Angel Links clubhouse, with pulsing drumbeats and the chants of Sage's tribe drifting over the walls. Al tapped his beer bottle for quiet and looked out over two hundred upturned faces—out-of-town Realtors and local officials. He dropped the prepared speech that Ches Noonan and Imogene Sylvester had signed off on over his shoulder into a fountain behind him and spoke extemporaneously:

"Most of us out here are what you'd call 'losers.' We gave up on the American dream long ago and found a haven in Saint Angel.

Little Les got his ass shot in Nam, and when he came home people pretended not to know him; I lost my wife in a plane crash; Mona escaped a bullying husband. This place isn't much, but it suits us. But by the time you folks are done with it, it will be like everywhere else. Nowhere, America! No place we want to live. We don't want your damn houses and SUVs and big box shopping and road rage and fucked-up kids. (The whistles from Sam's Coalition inside were redoubled by those from outside the clubhouse.) Littlefeathers' people, the original Saint Angelinos, were not even invited to sit at table with us tonight. You plan to make them trespassers on their own ancestral lands. Don't deny it. You people don't even realize what you're doing. We've prayed to Tahquitz on the mountain to bring a plague of dark toads and bad water down on your heads. And he's answered our prayers."

At that instant, purple toads (released by Tinkerspoon's crew) hopped underfoot or landed splay-footed on dinner plates. Realtors' faces were horror-struck, Silk Setters were aghast, but Penny Noonan clapped her hands in delight. Ches leapt up beside Al and clapped with her. "Great stuff, Al. True, home-grown Saint Angel after-dinner humor. Don't you love it?" Grinning like a badger. Ches could turn anything to his advantage. Outside the clubhouse, chants and drumming rose to a crescendo. There was a ruckus of shoving and shouting as Realtors fled. Old Timothy Leary O'Toole from Devastation Acres, in a full headdress of multi-colored eagle feathers, heaved his huge gut against Trinkley; they belly-bumped like rutting bull moose. Stone-faced Indians shook their fists at departing Realtors and warned them not to come back, while Charlie Haynes, Harvey Suarez, and the Tweedledee Twins, plus sheriff's deputies from Tourmaline, looked on helplessly. Men with grim, shadowed faces, who had been stalking us for weeks in their white vans, stood watching like thugs from The Sopranos, hands clasped in front of them, while Matt Littlefeather's bouncer pals from the casino, huge hatchet-faced men, watched them back.

Just then, there were detonations from the east and north. All froze in stunned silence. Then Indians and Sam City folks cheered and threw hats and war bonnets in the air like graduating cadets. Rob breezed past, whispering, "Pinyon Dam, praise the Lord!" "Damn it, Rob," Al cried. Penny linked arms with him. "I do love it." She wore a western shirt and jeans, a flashy silver belt buckle. "Ah see eggsactly what you kids are up to. Whose idea was the blood? That was about brilliant. Ches is fit to burst a boil."

"He'd better get used to it. Chester doesn't need the whole damned valley."

"Sure he does, darlin'. Daddy needs it all. He's negotiatin' with Mother Nature to lease the moon."

Mrs. Philadelphia passed with her small-headed friend in tow. "Have you heard about our toads? They're in the commodes: dark, ugly, squirmy little beasts." Al told how an army of them came out of a black slough and chased him to his car the other day. "I thought I was done for." Penny tightened her grip on his arm and whispered, "Tell your pals I will help out any way ah can. Ah do love it."

Later, the Realty Revenge crew would argue about which tactic had been most devastating to the Roundup: bleeding spigots, or kachina dolls, or Al's speech at the welcome barbecue, or bedraggled hippies and Indians in DayGlo war paint amassed around the clubhouse, waving tomahawks and beating drums, or Patsy K Jones' and Finley's bawdy surprise, which no one expected, least of all Al Sharpe.

#

When we emerged from the clubhouse, hookers in fishnet tights and hot yellow short-shorts leaned against cars in the parking lot, hands perched wantonly on hips, cheeks outlandishly rouged. I didn't at first recognize Patsy K Jones—white bra and thong showing through sheer pink baby doll PJs—or Finley in a leopard print leotard and black knee-highs, her spiky hair dyed yellow. Penny burst out laughing. "Brilliant, girls, brilliant!" "Tops or tails, pops? Same price," Patsy K propositioned me. Finley clucked her tongue. Black and white hookers surrounded a realty executive from St. Louis. "What kind of place is this?" he cried. "We're Saint Angel's angels," Finley purred. Imogene Sylvester shook her head in dismay. "Honestly, I don't recognize this town anymore."

After Finley's angels invaded the Holiday Inn lobby, I had to go to city hall to bail the girls out of jail. Charlie Haynes was furious. "I've had all I'm going to take of this nonsense. I suppose that's your bunch blowing things up, Sharpe."

"I don't know anything about that, didn't even know about this." Gesturing at Finley's Carlsbad High pals, who sat on wooden benches doing their best to look contrite, barely suppressing giggles. Black and Latino girls favored platinum wigs and white girls glossy black falls.

Charlie thumped a finger against my chest. "Destruction of property. Someone will pull jail time for that stunt. What in hell's got into you people?"

Finley interrupted. "PC check, Charlie, what's got into all of you?"

Charlie turned on her, sputtering mad. "Get those tramps outta here."

Never thought I'd see the day Charlie Haynes was pissed off at Finley.

Penny called me next morning. "You get your butt over here, Albert." Staking claim to me as surely as her husband had claimed the valley. I no longer understood the rules. I knew Penny was taken and Mona was the better match. Maybe I was hooked on suspense, turned on by the excitement: explosions, shouting Indians, high school hookers, the whole madcap Mardi Gras of it. Penny had straddled me in the front seat of her big caddy in the clubhouse parking lot the night before, jeans down around her ankles, while Realtors from the Midwest streamed past us in the gathering dark. Charlie Haynes was right: we'd crossed the line. I was about to come when she planted the heel of a hand against my forehead. "Fun's over, Albert. No one stiffs Daddy; take his money and go. Don't be a simp. I'm speaking as a friend. It's a cruddy hole in the wall, anyways."

"It's home. I built it with my own two hands." I'd gone instantly flaccid.

"Sounds about pathetic." She rolled off me and yanked up her panties. "Daddy won't stand for it, y'hear?"

I sat there exposed and foolish. "I thought we weren't doing this anymore."

"We aren't."

Penny ran out to the pickup next day, one eyelid swollen shut, eyelid the glossy plum purple of dark toads' hides. "Are you crazy, comin' here?"

"You asked me to come. What happened? Did Ches do that?"

She firmed a hand over my mouth. "Listen, I smell blood on Daddy's breath. If he caught you here...Listen!"

"Wife beating bastard." I tried to exit the pickup, but Penny leveraged her weight against the door. "You don't stand a chance, Albert. Listen—" pushing "—he isn't here. Daddy isn't here, damn you to hell." Leaping on my back as I started for the house. We staggered into the cactus garden, her bony knees clutching my waist. "It wasn't

Daddy, okay! Not Chester."

"Who then?" I shook her off. "Cal Hale?" Because I'd heard rumors.

"Hmmph!" Penny planted a hand over my mouth and shook her head, told me how they planned to take the few remaining Realtors out to Wild Horse Mesa that afternoon, onto rez land. "Daddy wants to show them the potential. Listen, Albert, he's onto you. He knows."

As I drove away, shaken, Harvey Suarez's pea-green cruiser fell in behind me and followed me to the Thompsons', where we held an emergency meeting of Sam's Coalition. I told them about the clandestine assemblage at Wild Horse Mesa. Rob proposed we blow a water tank. "Show the bastards our teeth." On his way out, Tinkerspoon called, "I'll handle it, dudes. Call it 'Flight Plan A.'" Grinning back at us. I dreaded to think what he had in mind.

Half an hour later, jumbo jets began buzzing town at maybe two thousand feet before lifting again, engines backing off, then accelerating with window-shattering roars. Tinkerspoon had hacked into air control computers at Ontario Airport and LAX and rerouted planes over Saint Angel. Rob and I hightailed it out to Wild Horse Mesa. Never saw anything like that scene: 747 "heavies" gliding down slopes of the San Jacintos on air currents, engines screeching, solid granite quaking underfoot and mountains rattling like loose teeth, one plane every couple of minutes. Realtors from across America hid behind vans, hands over their ears, faces contorted in pain, kneeling on that desolate plateau as if suspended at the end of an existential runway, planes skimming so low that you could count windows. "Good Lord, but you folks get a lot of air traffic out here," someone shouted. "I'm going back home to Chicago for some peace and quiet." Rob and I traded high fives. Ches came strutting towards my pickup, a finger outthrust. "This your stunt, Albert? I might have guessed."

"Wife-beating coward." Anger hit me in an adrenaline rush; I tried to get out of the pickup and go for him, but Ches's halitosis threw me back against the seat.

"You leave my wife out of this. You're on thin ice, boy."

I hung a wide U-ey around him on the flat and headed for Wild Horse Road.

Tinkerspoon was frantic when we entered his dark computer room, eyes bugging at monitors that had become radar screens, blips and dotted trajectories moving across them. Sweat dripped off his chin and soaked his shirt. He leaned forward into a mike. "Five-Eight-O heavy, bear twenty degrees north, adjust altitude to 9,000 feet. Pronto, dude! Jeez...that was close."

"Control, for goodness sake! We nearly scraped paint off that Pan Am," a scratchy voice protested.

"Control—" another crackly voice "—are you drunk or what?"

Tinkerspoon leaned into the mike, static electricity hovered in a phosphorescent halo around him. "Bad hair day, dude."

"Tower, this is American Four-Five-Three. You want us to hold steady at 18K? Request change of altitude. There's just all kinds of turbulence up here."

"Attention all units, this is Control," Tinkerspoon shouted. "Return to previously designated altitudes and stand by for instructions from LAX tower. They'll get you down safe and sound."

"You're not LAX tower?" voices chorused.

"Not really, dude." Tinkerspoon slumped in his chair, while outraged voices squabbled all sides. He closed out screens, relinquishing air control back to the towers. Grinning mightily.

"Christ on a tollhouse cookie," Rob chortled. "Forgive my language, Lord."

"What are you doing, Andy? You could have killed people."

"I took them the scenic route, dude."

TV news was full of it: a lunatic hacker had seized control of flight control towers at Ontario and LAX, a major FAA investigation. Meanwhile, ATF agents in navy blue windbreakers crawled over the bomb site at Pinyon Dam, collecting fragments. The dam was intact, but there was a large crater in the ground nearby. We held a Realty Revenge barbecue and toasted ourselves. All but Tinkerspoon, who hid out in the secret room under his carport, like a pyromaniac kid who delights in starting fires then suffers paranoid paralysis in their ashes. Our festivities were interrupted by Ches Noonan driving at head of a convoy of cement trucks. His crew cab squealed into the drive and crashed through the front gate towards picnic tables, sent us scattering. Ches leapt out and came for me, like a cartoon superhero of environmental disaster, the landscape warping around him. He stopped inches from my nose, forefinger tapping my chest. "You think you've won, Sharpe? You think you drove off my national sales force? You and your pals defeated Saint Angel Land Company? You think you can screw my wife with impunity? Hah!" I stumbled back. Remarkably, he emitted no trace of halitosis, merely a vague hint of peppermint.

They got right to it: building forms and pouring foundations right up to my property line and Tinkerspoon's. I imagined Andy huddled in his concrete paranoia bunker, teeth gritted at the sound of clanking machinery and men's shouts. Workers erected a tent city and went on double shifts, working around the clock under klieg lights so bright you could sit in Finley's meadow and read the newspaper. Wallers retreated under the cottage, owls vamoosed. We encamped at the mouth of the canyon and sat dejectedly around a campfire, Les's face seemingly chiseled from tawny marble in the firelight, an arm draped around Patsy K's neck. Sometimes I found them curled up together beside dead embers of the fire early in the a.m. and covered their naked bodies with a blanket. Patsy was of legal age, after all. No harm, no foul. Near midnight, Tinkerspoon emerged from his hidey hole to join us, eyes darting wildly about. "Look at all the equipment, dudeski." He gestured at a phalanx of machines along my property line. "Hey, a single low belly runs you eight hundred grand; they have a couple hundred out here. We're talking serious money: Koch Brothers or Warren Buffet or maybe the Chinese." Little Les chuckled at Tinkerspoon's paranoia. Poor guy was antsy as a tweaker. "You better get you on over and stay in my cubby cave, Tink. Isn't nobody going to find you there." But Tinkerspoon had already vanished wraith-like into the darkness. Little Les shook his head. "I dunno if he reminds me more of Peter Pan or that fruity fairy with the stardust he hangs out with."

"Tinkerbell, you widget." Patsy K pinched his cheeks.

They'd framed a palisade of two story monstrosities east side of my place; dark insect eyes peered unblinkingly down on the garden and black slough—on us. Creosote Canyon Road had become an L.A. suburb. Coyotes disappeared with the owls, their yipping serenades silenced. Then one spring night, shortly after they made their debut for the season, crickets fell silent. Gone. Imagine summer nights without crickets. It's like they sold the night to a hedge fund.

Orange Douglas fir skeletons marched toward Tinkerspoon's strip of land extending far back off the road. He paced across his narrow yard kicking at junk, stood mid-road shouting obscenities at construction crews, chased off health inspectors Ches sicced on him with a shotgun. They wouldn't give up: mouse-turd inspectors, mind-health inspectors. Tinkerspoon stood naked in his carport, a can of gas in one hand, cigarette lighter in the other, and threatened to immolate himself like a Buddhist monk if they didn't leave. Where else could Tinker-spoon possibly live besides Saint Angel? There has to be some place for the ne'er-do-wells and misfits to go.

Finley, Patsy K, and Little Les stood at roadside one early morning as construction workers arrived for work. Finley lifted her arms toward passing trucks, fingers outstretched, chanting:

> *I curse you with leukemia*
> *I curse you with bad corpse breath*
> *I curse you to midnight hell*
> *I curse you to evil death*
> *Developer men, destroyer men*
> *Men who break the desert's heart*
> *Anyone who builds here*
> *I curse you straight to hell*

Repeated ritually in all directions. "Those are some strong words," I said.

"They're killing the land, Dad. I want to stop them. Where are the owls and snakes supposed to live? I'm conjuring Tahquitz to help us."

"Where are we suppose to live?" Les added.

"Can I join you?"

We were out every day at dawn, chanting as construction workers' rigs rolled past. Word got around. Daph and Rob, Sage, Matt, and Mona came out. Incredibly, Clover Abernathy and Esther Johnson came, even Mrs. Philadelphia's small-headed friend ("It's getting to be a bit much, don't you think?"), and Sam City folks. We stood in a row at roadside as workers left the site in the afternoon, our chants reaching out to them, Rob's among the most ardent—furious that they'd brought in Texas crews and wouldn't hire local. Rigs moved slowly past, men growled: "Motherfucking white trash." Even Sam Jenson joined us—looked like Sam anyhow. He added nuances:

> *All them grass-grow swimming-pool guzzlers*
> *Water wasters and all them others....*

He asked Finley to help him work in "scab," but she said, "We don't curse the workers. It's not their fault." I realized it wasn't Sam but one of the cadaverous evangelicals, Death or Pestilence.

One day Penny Noonan came out and slipped in between Finley and me, linking arms, a breast brushing my elbow. "I heard you kids were having just loads of fun." Mona was flat pee-o'd about it. "I didn't invite her out here," I insisted, "she just came."

"That's what you keep saying. You wait, Al Sharpe. Just you wait."

I promised her it was over between us, but of course I couldn't be sure.

Trucks slowed as they passed, and construction workers became antagonistic and heaved beer bottles at us. Still, our line grew longer as townsfolk joined in; maybe fifty of us out there each day for the evening chant. Helen Woo brought her tai chi class. Sonny, the skinniest old man in California, ran past each afternoon, his wattled arms raised in a victory salute. Around a bend in Creosote Canyon Road, Harvey Suarez kept watch in his squad car, concealed behind a salt pine. Mona confronted him. "What are you doing here, Harvey? We're exercising our first amendment rights. It's not illegal."

"Should be," he said. "So should you."

Workmen stopped jeering and rushed past us, eyes forward. Anger and guilt are a toxic combination, no telling where they will lead. Two crew cabs stopped one evening when our ranks were thin, men leapt out with crow bars and nail guns, and a bald man with a sunburnt head hissed, "Dirty sonsabitches." Little Les pulled out the Glock 10mm he kept tucked under his belt; Sage stepped in front of the bald man. "You planning to murder us, brother?"

"Fuck no," cried a Latino plasterer. "We ain't gonna kill nobody."

Patsy K pointed at his crowbar. "PC check, just crack our heads open?"

I recognized the bald man as Trinkley: slack-bellied, pant cuffs rolled up above penny loafers, ears stuck out like handles on a beer stein. He aimed a nail gun directly at my forehead and grinned. "Get off my road, Sharpe."

"I'm standing on my own property here."

"T.S.F. It was your property, pal, not anymore."

"Haven't we been through this?" Anger was a red balloon expanding rapidly in my head, pushing against temples. I stood watching him, holding the turd's eyes. My calm gave him pause; the hand holding the nail gun trembled. Tinkerspoon stepped between us, holding the nail gun up to his own head. "Go ahead, dude, fire. You people already fuckin' killed me."

"Your place stinks to shit, man," a worker said.

"Yeah, dude, but it's my shit."

That silenced them, except Trinkley, who placed the nail gun against Tinkerspoon's forehead. "T.S.F.! Go ahead, doood, make my day."

"No, pal, you make mine." Little Les ground the muzzle of his Glock into Trinkley's ear, left arm strapped across his chest, left hand gripping his right biceps.

"Now wait a...just a...you maniac—" Trinkley let the nail gun fall to his side. "Are you people crazy?"

Les grinned, a gold incisor gleaming in sunlight. "You never can tell." Pulling aside the leather vest to display a faded tattoo across his collarbone: BORN TO KILL/READY TO DIE. He popped out the clip and shoved the gun back under his trouser band.

"Anyways," Finley said, "it isn't you guys we're cursing, it's your bosses."

"Crispley!" one of them said.

"Dickhead Shortbread," said a huge bearded man behind Trinkley.

"Fuckin' Trinkley," another grumbled. "Asshole."

"Me?" Trinkley cried, incredulous.

"I'm down with that." The big man cuffed Trinkley's shoulder. A Latino man with cut-away shirt sleeves squared off with him. "You docked me two days pay cause I short cut two cheat rafters, man. Two fuckin' cheat rafters, man. Wha's that shit?"

"Shortbread docked me a week for doing a magnum at lunch. I told him I could drink a kegger and still give him a day's work." The huge bearded man had the deepest voice I'd ever heard, as if all the dark toads from our black sloughs had taken up residence in his larynx.

They joined us, stood there after work and cursed their own livelihood. Big John Anderson shared his dream of moving to Oregon, "somewheres you can stretch out your arms." "That's where we used to live before they started building houses here," Tinkerspoon said. They weren't much different from us, really. If not excessed yet, they would be once the construction juggernaut was spent. They added "the hammerers' song" to our chant (though they rarely used hammers anymore):

All them bossmen shortbrain fuckers
Larry Short and Charlie Duckers
Old Tom Friend who signs our checks
Lame B.I.s who inspect our decks
Trinkley-dink who docks your pay
And chases all the chicks away
Developer men, Destroyer men
Men who break the desert's heart
We curse you with bad corpse breath
We curse you with evil death

We all took it up, until the day Jesus Diaz came squealing up in his pickup and leapt out waving his arms. "Hey, man, that shit's working too good. Short had him a heart attack. He fell down fuckin' dead, man." We went silent. It wasn't Short we wanted but Cal and Ches and those far off greedsters whose faces you never see.

Sam City people sent a delegation to complain to me that they could no longer use bathrooms in Ches's model homes; he'd brought in guard dogs. They complained about the constant hammering when I'd promised them peace and quiet. "Hey, it's not like you have a God-given right to quiet and free toilets," I said. Melie eyed me woefully. "I'm disappointed in you, Al. I thought you was a straight shooter." Her husband Mike nodded. "Same old same old."

"Tell you what, I can't make my payments much longer, anyway. I'd like to deed the property over to you folks before I default."

"Deed it to us? So we pay the mortgage?" Mike eyed me suspiciously.

"No, the loan's in my name. Chances are you can stay for years. They lack resources to evict you."

Mike's eyes darted cannily from me to Melie. "So we could sell it?"

"Afraid not, the bank will repossess. I hoped you folks would stay on until then; that was the plan."

"Whose plan?" Melie asked.

I received warnings from county planning and the health department about illegal dwellings and unsanitary conditions on my *La Cienega* property. Les told me Sam City folks were Mary Jane farming next door on SALCO land. "Scrappy crew you got there." Colin Allsport suggested I use the squatters as a pretext for defaulting on my loan, citing a relic California law which permits a buyer to quit deed without penalty if hostile aboriginals occupy his land. "Not specifically Native Americans, you understand. They could be indigenous hippies and tweakers."

"I just want to stop Ches from building more houses."

Colin shrugged. "Suburbanites won't fancy living next door to hostile aboriginals."

Things were spinning out of control: too many people dependent on my well. I used Sam Jensen's old John Deere tractor to haul a water tank on a trailer back and forth to Sam City in the dead of night, supplying squatters with water. They complained it tasted like duck piss. Meanwhile, my relationship with Mona had progressed from strained to grossly peculiar. She often slept over on my living room couch, while Patsy K and Little Les took the floor. Middle of the night, Mona would come in and tap my shoulder. "Scoot over, buster. I can't sleep with those two screwing like rabbits all night. God, she's a groaner." Crazy irony: Mona crawling into bed with me to escape sex. "Don't start poking my ass again, Al," she warned. "I'm not a pin cushion."

"That wasn't me, I was asleep."

"It was your dick."

"Maybe, but I had nothing to do with it."

She was soon snoring softly; tiny hairs tingled erect along the side of my body facing hers.

Meanwhile, Finley was haunted by some trouble she wouldn't discuss. She spent hours holed up in the treehouse on her laptop and strolled the property speaking sotto voce to someone on her cell, sat on her mother's flat memorial stone outside the Bad Things Cemetery, legs crossed under her, laughing and making dramatic gestures with her hands, whispering into the cell like she had whispered secrets into her hand as a girl. She threw me dark looks when I approached. I asked if there was something she wanted to talk about. "What for? You won't tell me the truth, anyways."

"Who are you talking to? Do you have a new boyfriend?"

"It's really none of your business, Al."

"Al?" I asked. "So I'm not 'Dad' anymore?" Her anger baffled me.

#

The spring was unseasonably hot, tokening a hellish summer. "Hot days in May, you'll die in July," as the saying goes. We held our collective breath, sensing things coming to a head. Ches Noonan learned from John Hobkins down at Western Enterprise Bank that Al Sharpe was behind the Sam City fiasco, buying land from under his nose and peopling it with squatters. The man was blatantly screwing both his wife and his business prospects. The first he could tolerate, not the second. Ches's breath blanketed the valley in an evil haze. "Can't the man use Altoids?" Old Mrs. Carmichael carped. Pastor Schwartzkopf at The Church of God's Final Truth preached about "sulfurous emanations rising up from hell," mentioned in The Book of Revelations. "Behold, the end of days!"

Chester might forgive Albert and his dirtbag crew for their hijinks during the Realty Round-up—some of them half clever—but defrauding Saint Angel Land Co. of $57 million in profits, according to Ches's calculations, was perverse. He stomped into an emergency session of the Water Authority demanding Al Sharpe's well and rez wells be condemned. "I don't believe we can do that," SAVWA's attorney, John Sylvester, advised. "You damn betcha we can, it's our water." But the La Cienega Tribal Council had brought suit against the Water Authority and SALCO for taking water they claimed rightfully belonged to them under The Mission Indians Relief Act of 1891. New wells had polluted "the ancient and holy groundwater supply with saltwater from deep earth." Moreover, new developments violated the Reclamation Act of 1902. They graffitied developments' perimeter walls with blood-red warnings and crude profiles of Crazy Horse.

Chester had decided that the squatters' haven of dilapidated shacks and makeshift tents, peopled by naked hippies smoking devil weed and exposing their genitals to the sun (and crapping in his model homes), could no longer be tolerated. Nor could this nonsense with his wife. The final evening of the Realty Roundup, Ches leaned forward to sniff Penny's hair and tapped his wife's forehead with a finger. "I catch scent of that SOB around here again, I'm warning you, Penny—" Unwilling to say what he would do. She shrank away from her husband's carnivorous breath.

The morning after Al Sharpe defaulted on his loan, Ches sent Trinkley in with a crew of dozers to scrape Sam City off the face of the earth and burn its remains. Trinkley told how occupants fled screaming every which way, wrapped in blankets or stark raving nude. The few who threatened resistance were held at bay with shotguns. However, Big John Anderson turned his dozer around and drove it through the perimeter wall of a nearby development on into the master bedroom of a model home before climbing calmly down from the high dozer seat and flipping Trinkley off. He'd joined the opposition.

After Al defaulted, after Hobkins was fired for approving his loan, the bank made noises about seizing Second Chance Acres, on which Al had taken a second mortgage. Ches Noonan approached bank officers about acquiring his loan. Al's garden was devoured by a plague of grasshoppers, which birds refused to eat, and black toads emerged by the thousand from the black slough and turned the ground liquid and slippery underfoot; Wallers sniffed them but left them alone. Those grim evangelicals, Death and Pestilence, said the toads tokened the end of days. The windows of new houses glowed pink at sunset, and a first scent of barbecued meat wafted in from the suburbs, but suburban lanes, flanked by sere patches of lawn and anemic palmettos, were shrouded in deathly stillness. New 4X4 pickups were parked in drives, and garage doors stood open, displaying shelves packed floor to ceiling with household goods, each garage a mini big box store, but houses already showed signs of dereliction: stucco walls were cracked and discolored, roof tiles were slipping off. They had aged instantly as if afflicted by a rare hormonal ailment. Rob called them "ghettos for The New World Order." They seemed to Al Sharpe a mortgage on alienation: inhabitants leading sterile, anonymous lives, captive, paranoid, isolated from the outside world. The burbs were like ominous sets in a David Lynch film, their tepid and soulless sterility concealing clandestine depravity and despair.

Mysterious white vans disappeared for a time after the Realty Roundup, then Mona reported one following her home from the bank, holding her in its halogen headlights. Daphne Thompson glimpsed two men watching her from a van as she walked to her car after school. She asked a posse of boys in her fifth period, who fancied themselves Saint Angel's Badass Crew, if they could get a good look at them. "Rag heads," one of them reported. "Naw, they're white dudes, Mrs. T.," another said. "Skinheads. I got me a good look at them." A third boy reported seeing no one at all. "That van was flat empty, Misses." Al warned Finley not to venture out on hikes alone.

"What do they want from us?" Mona asked in an emergency Coalition meeting.

"They want me," Al said. "First Sam, now me, then Tinkerspoon. They want our water."

"Who they working for, people? Cal, or Ches, TexHome, or Mile High?"

"Saint Angel Land Company," Rob Thompson insisted.

"PC check, if they wanted to hurt someone, they would have done it by now," Patsy K reasoned. "They're trying to scare us."

Finley talked about returning to the coast. "What about your chant?" Al asked her. "Right now," she said, "I have other priorities."

15

THE DEVIL'S GRIN

We'd had warm springs, but never 105 in early May, 68% humidity. Even the weather conspired against us. I spent a few days on the coast to escape the heat. My pickup's temperature gauge flirted with disaster by the time I got home and pulled down the drive past a wall of new houses that had been bare frames when I left. M&M's Ford pickup was parked in front of my cottage—bed half rusted out, green peace symbols painted on the doors. M&M were sprawled in my living room, Mike in boxer shorts, Melie in bra and white cotton panties as big as flour sacks. "Just walk right in why doncha," she chided me.

"Why shouldn't I, it's my house. I don't recall inviting you two in."

Mike shot out a finger. "Correction! *Was* your house. We've taken possession."

"Of my house?"

"There you go again. Isn't your house no more. You what you might call 'forfeited.'" Melie's fists posted below her love handles, neck and huge belly bright pink, blood-flushed. Some sobering vision: Melie standing half-naked in my living room. I couldn't help but stare in disbelief.

"Isn't my house?"

"He don't catch on real quick, does he? Your bed sucks, I about sagged off last night."

"Bed suits me fine." I dropped my rucksack on a chair.

Melie threw it out the door and motioned for me to follow. "Y'r outta here, Albert."

Mike grinned. "Mel gets bitchy when she don't get her proper bed rest."

"All right, you're welcome to stay until we build you a new place in Sam City."

Melie shook her head. "We don't got no toilets or running water over there."

"Well, I realize it's crude."

"This is crude, that's crudulous."

"Why you still talking about Sam City? That shit's over," Mike said. "We got boosted out, end of story. Mel says you likely arranged it y'rself."

"You were kicked out, evicted by the bank, you're saying?" First I'd heard of it.

"M, tell him would he stop staring at my tits, please. I can't stand comfortable in my own living room."

"*My* living room!"

"Get over yourself, Albert."

Mike belly-bumped me out the door, and stood in the doorway, arms folded, prohibiting re-entry, twin skulls tattooed on his elbows. "Hey, you got any more beer, Al?"

I left them to it, not sure how to deal with this. I needed a plan. When Finley and Patsy K and Lester got back from their camping trip, they'd be outraged. I should have been myself, but I felt a little guilty that they'd been evicted from Sam City. That wasn't in the original plan...or maybe it was. I climbed up to the treehouse, hoping to hang out there, but Finley had padlocked the door. Another first. Who was she trying to keep out? We never locked doors on Second Chance Acres; my cottage door didn't even have a lock. I slept that night in my pickup bed, while my tortured bed springs squawked inside. Awoke next morning to Mona standing beside her car in the drive, frowning at a pair of oversized underwear hung to dry from a tree limb. "I have company," I told her.

Her chin bunched. "The candy couple, M&M?" She waved her hands, looking past me, shouting, "Would you stop that, it's disgusting." Mike stood pissing off my front porch in his underwear, grinning at her.

"They have laid claim to my house."

"Nonsense!" Mona crossed the yard in a fury. "You two get out of Albert's house this minute." Wallers fell in behind her, squealing menace. Mike retreated inside, Mona and Wallers followed. Some ruckus: shouting and squealing, Melie's white ass floating like a fulgent moon across a darkened window, Mike squealing back at Wallers. "Get y'r fucking pig off me." Mona heaved M&M's clothes out a window. When I entered, Mel's face was nearly touching Mona's, red as a baboon's ass. "Donchou dare touch my clothes, bitch." Bare breasted, twice Mona's size, but Mona held her ground, impassive as stone. She picked up a bra—huge ballooning cups—shrugged, and tossed it out the door. "Get dressed," she barked. "You're embarrassing Al." Melie yammered back at her incomprehensibly.

"It's all right," I said, "they can stay. We'll figure something out. We shouldn't be squabbling among ourselves. We need to prepare for what's coming."

"What's coming?" They all asked in unison.

#

It was a monsoonal sky, thunderheads piling up on the forward ambitions of tropical storm Juan, making its way north from Baja with California on its mind. Cumulus stratofortresses piled up over the mountains, and lightning flashes reached down to dance atop peaks like incandescent spider legs. Air at 81% humidity pasted shirts to our backs. We could see rain falling in sheets from the clouds but not a drop touched ground. "Takeetz is big thirsty," Sage said, "laps it up before it reaches us." Weather forecasts had gone gothic, as if written by one of the Bronte sisters:

> *"A brooding onshore flow will bring sultry, insufferable heat to the southland today. Dead air will cloak the land, fostering a supernatural quiet wherein nothing is heard but the chirr of dying insects suffocated under toxic humidity...."*

Angry viewers called to complain, preferring cheery weathermen with their lame jokes and bad hair pieces to loony poets. Some blamed the forecasters for their misery; the messenger is never held blameless. Brownouts limited air conditioning and left Palm Springs a ghost town, tarantulas staggered out of their burrows punch drunk in the midday heat, and coyotes wandered the roads, tongues lolling out of their mouths; they scaled fences and drank water from swimming pools, occasionally took a dip or snatched a family pet and slipped slyly back over the fence. New arrivals from L.A. stood stunned and dismayed, looking out clerestory windows of new houses at a parched landscape gone deviously liquid under heat waves. Out here, nothing was as it seemed; rather, what was unnatural seemed friendly, while the natural seemed hostile. Matt Littlefeather laughed derisively. "They gonna wilt or turn all to liver spots." New graffiti appeared on development walls, proclaiming: "Saint Angel for the sun people."

After the water was shut off in their end of town, Rob and Daphne Thompson pitched a tent on Second Chance Acres (Al still had water). The Saint Angel Valley Water Authority had imposed draconian quotas to punish the town for its complicity in the Realty Revenge. Lawns dried up and trees died; while in new suburbs, water gurgled and sang from fountains, lapped at the shores of artificial lakes, watered golf courses, and was used liberally to hose down driveways. Melie shrugged. "The gots get lots and the nots get squat, that's your New World Order." She strolled Second Chance Acres stark-raving naked below the second story windows of overlooking McMansions, ignoring Mona's admonitions. Moms rushed their kids away from the windows. When Daphne gleefully shed her clothes, Mona shrugged and joined them. Rob recited Paul's warnings to the Corinthians about ills of the flesh, then shed his own clothes and walked in the shadow of new developments, shaking a fist like Prophet Samuel, warning of the coming destruction.

When Finley returned from her camping trip with Les and Patsy K, she insisted that M&M leave her father's house at once. It was quite a sight: willowy, mild-mannered Finley confronting those—for lack of a more flattering analogy—human walruses, her 100 pounds versus their 600, and backing them into a corner. They had been defiant before everyone else who confronted them, but were apologetic to her, saying they'd be out tomorrow, they didn't want to upset anyone. "You can stay back in the canyon with the others," Finley said. But when Les came in and started throwing their things outside, M&M became intransigent, sitting on the floor and refusing to budge. Not even Lester was strong enough to move them. Al arrived and said it was all right. "Let them stay. They need it more than I do."

"What are you talking about, Dad? It's your house."

When Harvey Suarez drove out to say they'd had complaints from the neighbors, the entire crew met him naked at the front gate. Poor Harvey backed off, waving hands before his face and mumbling about families with children next door, alarmed and provoked not so much by M&M as by Mona's dark bush; he'd always imagined her shaved.

That night, Al asked Patsy K Jones what she thought was troubling Finley. "She's not herself lately; she seems angry at me about something."

"Listen, Dad, PC check, I promised not to tell you."

"Tell me what?"

"It's getting weird, right! So I'll say this much: there's this brackish woman she met on the Internet who claims to be her mom. Finley believes it."

"*That's preposterous. Her mother is dead. What woman?*"

"*Schnay, just forget I said anything.*"

He would have preferred to. It was too bizarre to take seriously, but then what wasn't lately? No holds barred. Some nights, as they slept under stars at the canyon's mouth, Mona stirred beside him, and Al placed a hand on her thigh to calm her. Both of them were keenly aware of the earth's malaise, which mirrored their own. He told her about this mystery con mom that Patsy K had mentioned. Mona insisted Finley was too smart to be taken in by some Internet troller.

At last, they had surrendered the pretense of separation and become a couple (which Finley had long wanted them to do), forgiving one another their shortcomings and indiscretions. Isn't that what love is about, accepting another's shortcomings, maybe even celebrating them? Al marveled at life's irony. It took his daughter's alienation to unite them, just as his bond with Finley was enhanced by her mother's disappearance. While Mona attributed her new clarity to the Gingko-biloba-Echinacea-green-tea infusion she'd been using. In the social confines of what had become a commune, they experienced something of the erotic inhibitions of the Victorians, who longed for one another without consummation, so sexual tension became delicious. Given all that naked flesh, Al was permanently erect.

Meanwhile, Ches's men cut a road across Sam City behind Tinkerspoon's. Labeling him the "Alan Greenspan of the New World Order," Tinkerspoon claimed that Ches secretly controlled The Fed, WTO, and the World Bank, and had close ties to the White House. The fact that none of this could be proven confirmed it. No one doubted that Ches was supreme leader of Saint Angel development and the DGLA. The well water that sustained them had become increasingly brackish as Ches and Cal's deep wells pulled sweet water from the aquifer and replaced it with water from The Ancient Salt Sea. One day soon, there would be a crumping explosion nearby, pickups would race past, and men shout, "They blew Pinyon Dam—for real this time. Developments are flooding." Not yet.

Al received an unexpected phone call from Mona's former lover, RJH, his unofficial stock advisor, who warned him the Biotech bubble had burst and Al was about to lose his shirt on the stocks RJH had advised him to buy. "You could have warned me," Al yelled into the phone. "I couldn't, actually," RJH said, "that would be insider trading."

#

NASDAQ had shed 2,000 points in the meltdown; my Biotech stocks lost 90% of their value overnight as shareholders abandoned ship en masse. I hadn't been paying attention, distracted as I was by homegrown troubles. I had invested Finley's entire nest egg—her college fund—in Biotechs, had bought in high, believing the boom had long legs and would yield great returns. But we were wiped out. Barely enough remained to cover a year of college. My own portfolio was nearly exhausted on Sam's Acres, which the bank had repossessed. Fools rush in and all.

Then Tinkerspoon disappeared. No trace of him in his carport hidey hole. Flat gone. Rob speculated that dark toads and black swamps were swallowing everyone up. Mike boasted, "No, sir, isn't nothing could swallow Melie." Metaphorically, anyway, Rob was right.

They send in earth-moving machines to mangle the landscape, do a leveraged buy-out of peace, quiet, and pursuit of happiness; boxy multi-story monoliths rise around us like apartment blocks in the Czech Republic; multiple glass eyes peer down, making us feel like microbes under a microscope; small, grinning faces crowd windows when I stumble out of the canyon mornings to piss—the back of beyond become a Glendora suburb. *Saint Angel de las Afureas.* Black sloughs migrate eastward towards the development's perimeter wall and west towards my cottage.

Sitting over coffee at Mimi's, I told Matt Littlefeather's girlfriend, who waitresses there, that she and Matt should move out to my place. "We all run around like naked hippies." Luella whacked my forehead with the heel of her hand. "You got a dirty mind, Al Sharpe." Thin as a reed, maybe 110 pounds to Matt's three hundred. Matt and Sage slipped into the booth; Sage slapped a copy of *The Saint Angel Clarion* down on the table. "Check it out."

SAINT ANGEL MAN ARRESTED
FOR COMPUTER CRIMES

Andy Sanchez (A.K.A. Tinkerspoon) was arrested by Federal Mar-shals last night at his home on Creosote Canyon Road. Authorities have charged Sanchez with hacking into computer systems at the Pen-tagon and the Strategic Air Command (SAC) and attempting to disarm the nation's nuclear arsenal.

A spokesperson for the U.S. Attorney's office in Los Angeles told the *Saint Angel Clarion* that Mr. Sanchez has been charged with numer-ous crimes, including high treason. In a statement issued through his court appointed attorney, Sanchez claims the charge is unfair. He says he intended to disarm the Russian and Chinese nuclear arsenals after disarming U.S. missiles, but was still learning those languages. "If you don't know how people speak, you can't figure out how they think, dude. And if you can't get into their head, you can't get into their sys-tem," Sanchez said.

Further charges against Sanchez are expected to be forthcoming in connection with an incident last month in which LAX and Ontario Airport flight control tower computers were invaded by a hacker and several incoming flights rerouted. "Right about now, we consider Andy Sanchez to be public enemy number one," a spokesperson for the U.S. Attorney's office in Los Angeles told the *Clarion*.

"Arrested? Last night? I would have seen them," I insisted. "No one was out there last night." Then I remembered that Tinkerspoon's dog, *El Rapido*, was hanging around my cabin this morning. I thought it odd since that dog flat hates me and Wallers hates him.

"That isn't only half of it," Sage said. They drove me solemnly out Yucca Road past Sam's place, past the huge new Singing Springs De-velopment and the earthen dam retaining Yucca Reservoir, which was filled with fossil water; a damp fetor lingered on the air. Huge signs at road side announced the DESERT AIR MALL—windowless concrete boxes surrounded by acres of parking lot. New suburbanites would need places to work and shop, after all.

\#

Sam Jenson had lived out Yucca Road happy lonesome, considering any neighbor or passing car a rude invasion of his privacy. *No explaining Sam to the new breed of exurban minivan drivers on their cell phones or the rednecks who built their houses, how he sat out in the desert scrub on his battered aluminum lawn chair reinforced with duct tape on cool evenings after scorching hot days, listening to the first yarooing of coyotes in the hills. Just pleasuring. He had no use for iPhones or iPads or the interconnected world they facilitated. Sam knew connection to be a myth; he knew we are all alone in the end. Our only sure connection is with nature. Sam could identify a granite spiny lizard by the sound of its scurry, he could identify every desert bird by its call, his companions were the animal tribes of the desert.*

They'd already begun terracing The Coyote Hills behind his place before he died. From his front porch, Sam could hear the remorseless whump-a-ty-whump of well drilling rigs on flats behind Indian Springs Hill, the hiss of welders' torches at work on storage tanks atop it. He walked out evenings with his .30-30 and target practiced on a billboard across the road—FUTURE HOME OF THE DESERT AIR SUPERMALL—then would aim straight up and fire off a round at God, his mouth distorted in a snarl. "What inna hell is a supermall, Sharpe?" he asked Al, who hadn't heart to tell him. No way Sam and a shopping mall could coexist. Sam scorned Cal and Ches's offer for his land, though they were offering enough for him to buy ten thousand acres in Montana. Sam was Saint Angel every inch, our very soul. You can't relocate a place or transplant its soul. You might as well kill it.

After his death, Sam's place remained a nature preserve within prog-ress's devastation—two forlorn palms at top of the drive, great clumps of prickly pear and old car chassis strung with Christmas lights surround-ing the trailer, a wind-tattered banner on the chain-link fence fronting the road: DON'T DRINK THE WATER! JOIN SAM'S COALITION NOW. A notice scrawled in chalk on Sam's water tank read: **Warning! This well contaminated with E. Coli.** *Cat tracks cut the earth raw to the north, graders larger than Sam's trailer tore up sage. Each evening, heavy-equipment operators parked their machines in phalanxes, with their glistening blades aimed at Sam's place.*

#

Sage reached back and gripped my shoulder as we rounded the long bend in Yucca Road. "There's your white man's future, brother." Sam's place was reduced to rubble: vestiges of his flattened Airstream, barn, and car chassis pushed into a huge mound; palm tree trunks stuck out forlornly. They had scraped Sam's Acres off the face of the earth. A billboard in his drive proclaimed: *COMING SOON: JENSON AIRS LUXURY MANORS.* It might have been funny if it wasn't such a befuddling non sequitur. Across Yucca Road, a row of glass, steel, and concrete buildings was going in—columns, architraves, roof lines like alpine ski jumps, logos of American super-merchandising out here mid desert. DESERT AIR SUPERMALL. I cried out as if wounded; Sage gripped my shoulder. "It's done, brother, finished. Nothing you can do about it."

When I arrived home, a white Saint Angel Valley Water Authority van blocked my drive, and a dump truck filled with dirt idled in the meadow by my cottage. They'd removed the pump house and posted a notice: *Well condemned by order of The Saint Angel Valley Water Authority.* They had pulled up the steel plate covering the well shaft and were about to start lifting out pipe lengths with a backhoe, but that's as far as they got. Melie squatted naked over the well shaft as if seated on a toilet, gripping a galvanized pipe between her legs. Mike stood beside her, arms folded, confronting the Tweedledee Twins, whose silver sunglasses mirrored the scene. An M&M standoff.

"I told them they ain't touching this well, Albert. No way."

"God bless you, Melie." Anger rising in me like molten lava.

Tom Hartley, the SAVWA Water-master, rattled papers in his fist. "I have a court order to fill in this well. The lady don't get up, officers will have to remove her."

I whistled through my teeth. "I wouldn't advise it, boys, you don't want to get Melie mad."

"She'll eat your lunch." Mike nodded, grinning at the Tweedledees, who bunched chins to chests and studied Melie gravely.

"So Ches wants my water? I guess a fat man doesn't know when to stop eating." Hearing Melie clear her throat, I added, "Wasn't referring to you, Mel. You're a plump angel."

"She better gawddamn move," Hartley said. "I got orders to fill this well."

"Tell you what, Tom, I'll let you fill it in on condition you use dirt from here on my place." Winking at M&M.

Hartley lifted his cap and settled it back on his head. "We might could do her, I don't see why not. What you think, Roy?"

I guided Roy back through brush on the backhoe towards the black slough. No one caught on until it was too late. When balloon tires came within reach, the ground collapsed into a sinkhole under the backhoe, and it went straight down into the muck. Quick as a cat, Roy was standing on the seat, panicked, watching that tarry black amoeba engulf the machine under him, multiple tongues lapping at metal. He leapt for shore at the last instant; it took all of us—linked hands to ankles in a daisy chain—to pull him out of the slough onto solid ground. Roy stripped naked and scrubbed furiously at his pale skin, while I sprayed him down with the garden hose. "What inna hell you got in there? It smells like shit and burns like fire ants."

"That's earth bile. Sorry, Roy, I thought you'd have time to get off. The slough must be creeping under solid ground." One of the Tweedledees threatened to arrest me. "On what charge," I asked, "feeding a backhoe to a slough?"

"Reckless endangerment and willful destruction of property."

"Roy drove it in there himself, you saw him."

"Now that's a crock," said the other Tweedledee. They promised to return once they'd discussed it with Charlie Haynes, not daring to call and disturb him at his weekly golf game. Tom Hartley promised to be back with more equipment to fill my well. Just then, Little Les careened up on his bike and did his over-the-handlebars dismount, stood panting, glaring at the intruders. "You never gave us a fair hearing," he growled. "That violates due process." Sweeping a hand towards the mountains. "The land never got a fair hearing either. That violates the due process of natural law. There'll be grief to pay, people."

As if to punctuate his words, Tahquitz Peak lit with what appeared to be a lightning flash, followed by a thunderous blast from the vicinity of Yucca Road. Cops drew their guns and sprinted for their cruisers, heads ducked—forgetting me, as would the Water Authority for weeks to come. Things had taken a radical turn. Little Les was lathered up like a thoroughbred; Patsy K rubbed his shoulders and cooed endearments; a smell lingered about him, the sweetly mordant smell of high-nitrogen fertilizer. Developers had fired at us and we'd fired back. We drove sixteen-penny nails through bottle caps and sank them in the driveway, posted a sign on the gate: DANGER MINE FIELD. Les went into hiding. Blowing Yucca Dam had flooded the Singing Springs Development, and Ches wanted blood.

Walking that evening along Creosote Canyon Road, I passed a dark

SUV parked in front of Tinkerspoon's: FBI, Ches's people? I walked tensely past, not able to see through tinted windows. They would have their revenge; SAVWA thugs would be back to fill my well. Once authorities have you in their sights they hold you there, as does Fate, that ultimate authority figure.

The SUV fell in behind me as I walked, keeping pace; when I stopped, it stopped. Didn't Ches realize (if it was Ches) that we'd won a pyrrhic victory in the Realty Revenge, that my affair with his wife was over? I saw a huge set of teeth poised on the horizon, ready to chomp down, a prominent gold incisor in the top row, Ches's sewage breath poured over me. I gagged and sank to a knee. The car's bumper rudely clipped my legs, brakes squealed. I turned and slammed a fist on the car's hood and walked around to the driver's side, ready to thrust my hands through glass and grip the bastard's throat. The window rolled down and Penny's face tipped up toward me like a piebald moon, glowing feral red in fading light, as raw as my anger.

"You? I thought you were Chester or Harvey Suarez."

"Hmmmph, you do have pee-cool-yar fantasies, Albert. Since when did mah husband worry you at all? Ah assure you, Daddy intends to nail your greasy hide to the barn. Now get y'r little weenie in this car." She'd gone goth: hair spiked stiffly upward, more indigo than black in the diffuse light; she wore tiny gold earrings shaped like skulls, a choker necklace with a glistening blood stone clutched in its silver fingers, blouse unbuttoned to her navel, small breasts glowing white as candled eggs. A hand shot out the window snake quick and clamped my scrotum; I shouted alarm, my knees went weak. "You used me, you little prick," she snarled.

"Jesus, Penny, that hurts!" She let go. I staggered away from the car on wobbly legs. "Maybe, yes, maybe I used you. But no more than you used me."

"You used me to take revenge on mah husband. That's revoltin.'"

"It's nothing to do with Ches—" I got control of my breathing "—I was crazy attracted to you, I fell hard, lost track of myself for a time. Don't you know that?"

She gripped my chin in her fingers and pulled my face close, looked hard into my eyes, tiny pinpricks of light like dying embers deep back in her pupils. She didn't speak. After a long awkward silence, I broached what I knew was a dicey subject, especially at this moment, but it was weighing on me. "Do you think...is Ches's offer to buy my place still open? D'you think?"

"You want to sell Second Chance Acres to Daddy?" She laughed derisively.

"Just my acreage along the road. Not much choice if I hope to save the rest. I took a big hit in the Biotech crash, about wiped us out."

Penny's eyes glowed in the fading light. She seemed amused, seemed to be quaking with laughter inside. "Al Sharpe selling out, ah can't b'lieve it. Shame on you, Albert."

"What choice? I'm ruined, I blew my daughter's future. I'm just wondering if Ches's offer remains open."

"You best talk to Chester. Ah don't pry into his bizness affairs." She caressed my cheek with the back of a hand, lips stiffened into a grim white line. "Daddy intends to have it all, evrah inch, y'know." She swept a hand toward the horizon. "They'll build to the max. Chester figures his share at ten thousand dollars a head." Laughing caustically. "Daddy won't tolerate some little prickweed standin' in his way. You best sell, Albert; you best move before it's too late. You wouldn't want to be run over, you and your little girl." Patting my cheek like you might a stray dog.

"Doesn't he have enough already?"

She sighed hard. "The more Daddy has, the more he's missing. Truly, he frightens me, Albert. Sometimes mah husband looks at me like he intends to fit me for a new hide. It's got to where ah can't go skinny-dippin' in mah own pool."

"A pity. You love that. So you planning to enter the real estate business, too?"

"That's about the silliest thing ah ever heard. Why would I want to do that? Ah don't need the money and ah don't much like houses." Patting my cheek again. "You're sweet, Albert, but clueless. Ah could never get serious about you."

Dense darkness had congealed around the car, interwoven with the croaks of dark toads from the verges of black sloughs that were percolating up across the landscape, their moldy, vegetable breath intertwining with Ches's.

"You'd best get gone now, Albert. Daddy will be in touch." Sounded like a threat. She threw the gear shift into reverse and nearly ran over my foot as she squealed away, pelting me with gravel, then pulled a wide, shrieking U-ey and came back gunning for me, headlights spearing wildly. I somersaulted down the road verge, my cheek coming to rest in cold tar. I lay there a time wondering if Ches had sent her, if she'd been there at all, if you could trust anything anymore. A taint of roofer's tar engulfed me, ooze tugged coyly at an arm, inviting me down through cracks in the earth's crust into that primordial black muck which, according to Sage Littlefeather, forms the earth's volatile, festering core. Once fiery and alive, it had died and decomposed. My arm stank of compost when I extracted it. Walking back home—alert for Penny's predatory car—I passed from freak spring heat into an equinoctial gale, lashed by cold rain and wind, shivering by the time I reached home. Harvey Suarez's patrol car was parked out by my mailbox.

"You go swimming in a swamp?" Melie asked when I entered the cottage. "Wheeewy, smells like it."

"It's nothing, Mel. Ghosts."

#

"I have to get away for a while," Finley said. "It's getting weird." She planned to drive Patsy K's Volvo to the coast. "My parents will be there," Patsy K assured me. "It's cool."

"So Patsy K will be living with me and you will be living with her parents? You want to tell me what's going on, hon?"

"No *problema*, Al. So I just need some fresh air, right? I'll be okay."

"We could use your help. They want to take our place, they want our well."

"You've had my help, Dad. What good has it done?"

"Is this about your mother? The mystery woman you've been chatting with on Facebook who claims to be Sondra?" I glanced at Patsy K, realizing I'd betrayed her trust. Finley gave her a chiding look. I barged on, "You're too trusting, hon. That woman is obviously a con. You're too smart to fall for something like that."

Melie came out in her blue terry robe and stood listening beside Patsy K, arms folded.

"So Mom's like dead, remember. I warned you to stop patronizing me, Al. I can take care of myself. I just don't want to stay out here right now, okay. It's creepy. I don't even know who's living here anymore." She slid Melie a dirty look and slammed the trunk closed.

"You're talking crazy. This is your home: the treehouse, Wallers." I followed her around the car. "Is this about losing your college money?

I'm sorry, honey, I was an idiot, okay, I blew it; but I'm going to put it right, I promise. I'll sell the front acres."

"What are you even talking about? I really don't care what you do, Albert, I'm outta here."

"She's got a mouth, I'll give her. I wouldn't of expected it from your kid."

"Leave it, Melie." However, I was puzzled, too. Finley hadn't done adolescent rebellion. Maybe she was making up for it. "What about your chant?" I implored her. "We need your chant. I always look forward to it."

"Find something else to look forward to. I'm not your look-for-ward-to doll."

"Wheeewwwyy," Melie whistled.

"Mouth check!" Patsy K said. "Seriously."

"Shuddup, okay, everybody shut the fuck up."

We stood stunned, not recognizing this new Finley. Maybe it was true: some Internet witch had sunk talons into my daughter. She shook her head in the curt way she did when she was angry, pony tail bobbing. "I'm going, okay." Patsy K took her aside, speaking emphatically. "Schnay," Finley keep saying, ardently shaking her head. "PC check, I need to do this, Patsy K." Voice rising. "It's just something I need to do." She walked around to where I stood watching and took my hands, struggling to soften her expression. "It's going to work out, Dad. Trust me." Three straight lines puzzled her brow. "I still care, okay, but there's stuff I need to do. Second Chance Acres may be your whole life, but it isn't mine."

"I never intended it to be, hon." Realizing that perhaps, unwittingly, I did. Can't be helped: wanting our children to find what we've found. It's part of parenting. She went limp when I hugged her. I couldn't fathom this change in her, couldn't imagine how I'd failed her and alienated her affections, but I had. Surely, she blamed me for her mom's disappearance. Maybe I was to blame. Once I thought I could be father and mother to her both, but I'd failed in both roles.

We watched the Volvo drive away, warping a little in heat waves that snaked off the asphalt, Patsy K shaking her head. "PC check, I'm sworn to secrecy on the details, Dad, but I don't like it."

16

IT WAS HOT

Baked sage brush, grit-in-the-teeth hot. Sam Jenson-style hot. Santa Ana winds dried brush to tinder and rattled insect carcasses in orb spider webs—*Yavi* winds, the Indians call them, devil winds. Dust devils scurried across fields, tumbleweeds swirling inside them like clothes in a dryer. Clouds darkened the sky but produced no rain, merely got us itchy under the skin. Eyeballs scraped dry in their sockets. Mona claimed to smell Sam's corpse decomposing in the heat, but it was just Ches's breath—a haze of putrefied anger that smothered the valley. All the worse since we were sleeping outside. M&M had abandoned the cottage, since its adobe walls trapped heat during the day and released it at night. They were like two blubbery beluga whales beached naked atop sleeping bags, a startling epiphany in morning sunlight.

I drove out to the building fields to find Ches, past shirtless brown men in orange hard hats crawling over rafters and huge D9 cats pushing up house pads. Pulling back onto Creosote Canyon Road, I glimpsed a white blur bounding cross country after me, trailing a plume of brown dust. Ches's Chevy crew cab leapt the ditch and squirreled onto the tarmac, swerving side to side on my ass like a teenage punk in a game of freeway grab ass, horn blaring, Ches's huge face stretched banner-like across my rearview. Crazy SOB! I waved at him to back off. When he tried to pass, I cut him off. He bumper thumped me, jolting me forward. My right front tire whumped as if over speed bumps: gone flat! I thought of Sam lying dead in his trailer and slammed the brakes. *Damn you to hell, Chester.* My pickup fishtailed, Ches's crew cab slammed into it, and I went nearly back through the seat, my head slamming against the head rest. I saw in the rearview Ches thrown forward against his shoulder harness, mouth gagging open. His crew cab remained in place while my pickup caromed ahead as a marble does when struck by a steely. I leapt out, shouting.

Ches staggered a few steps from his rig and slumped to his knees, hand clutched to chest. I went back to help him up. "You all right, Ches?" Judging from the dead weight of him, he wasn't. He gripped my arm. "Is it your heart?"

"So that's how it is?" he managed. "You screw my wife, fuck my business plans, then you try to kill me?"

"I thought you were trying to kill me."

"Rib's broken." He groaned.

"Sorry, Ches...real sorry."

"The hell you are." He looked up at me, eyes sun-scorched, the color of faded denim. "Don't deny it; I have video footage of you two screwing like bunnies." He laughed and gripped his chest, gasping for air. "Uhhh...Penny says you dumped her flat. I won't tolerate it, Albert. The gal's my wife!"

"Of course she is. Good Lord, Ches, should I call an ambulance?"

"Uhhh...We'll get to me, we were discussing my wife."

My eyes took refuge in the epidemic of warts that had invaded his hair line. Thinning silver hair combed straight back over a scalp tanned mahogany brown, not unlike the dark, freckled dome of Penny's mons through pubic hair. A disturbing but unavoidable analogy.

"Listen, Ches—" not sure what he wanted me to confess or deny "—I didn't dump her exactly. Isn't that simple. I just thought, you know, it had gone too far. She's your wife." I smiled awkwardly.

"Of course it's simple," he snapped. "Dumb simple. You broke her heart...uhhhh...." He trailed off in a coughing spasm.

"I think you'd better sit down, Ches."

A thick forefinger thumped my chest. "Don't tell me what to do. Uhhhh...there's a proper way to treat a mistress, Sharpe. Show some respect. Penny's my wife, for crissake. I don't want her whining to me about that...uhhh...'little prick, Al Sharpe.' I won't have it."

"But...certainly...of course not. I don't know what you're saying. I don't know what you want from me. Are you....You want me to keep balling your wife?"

"Damn you! I don't want to know about it. What do you take me for...uhhh?" He leaned against the pickup, coughing harshly, gasping for breath. "Penny likes fucking down...uhhhh. Some kind of dominatrix thing. I can't...I can't...uhhh...do that for her—" holding up a hand, calling for time out "—Not into it...uhhhh. Tells me she never felt so superior as when she's screwing you, Sharpe."

"Penny said that?"

He remained silent a time, catching his breath. "I'm a busy man, Sharpe, I don't have time to hump around the countryside like a witless jack rabbit screwin' other men's wives. I have businesses to run and money to make."

"It's over, *finito*, I promise. God's honor."

He gripped my shirt collar in beefy hands, his breath gone evil again, washing my face like a foul tongue. "Like hell it is, boy. I want Penny happy, you understand me? I won't share the house with a mopey woman. If Penelope wants Al Sharpe, by God she'll have Al Sharp…uhhhh. You're her meat pure and simple, boy."

I stared at him, dumbfounded. "And I have nothing to say about it?"

"You forfeited your say when you climbed into my wife's drawers. You're a smart man; you ought to know that." Finger thumping my forehead. "I'll be watching you."

"Is that your men following me in the van?"

"Cal's, mine, TexHome's…doesn't matter. We aren't the fools you take us for, you and your damn squatters and loony bird friends. Some hullabaloo. Leave it to Al Sharpe to reinvent real estate." Ches chuckled, then moaned and clutched his ribs.

"You better sit down, Ches."

"Penny tells me you want to…uhhh…reconsider my offer."

"Don't want to, have to. It's why I came out here today. I blew Finley's college fund."

He chuckled. "Doesn't surprise me much. Happy to help out. I'll want your place and the plot behind Tinkerspoon's, the whole shebang…uhhhh. Eighty-four-hundred per acre, take it or leave it. That would give you a nice piece of change, let you put your little gal through college and start over. You can keep your damned canyon. Isn't any use to me. Take it or lose it, Al."

"I told you, Second Chance Acres isn't for sale, only my acreage along Creosote Canyon Road. The bank's already got Sam City."

"Not interested. All or nothing, Albert, that's how it is. I want what's mine—every inch—and I mean to have it." Sweeping a hand over the landscape. "You're way out of your league here, boy."

"Not my place and not Tinkerspoon's either. *I'm warning you,* Chester, back off."

His eyes blinked at my raised fist. Astonished me to see it, too. He sighed. "If it was up to me, I'd call the whole thing off. I don't covet your land, Al. But there's investors to consider, fiduciary responsibilities, progress—"

"You call destroying our Saint Angel way of life 'progress'?"

"Always a price to pay for progress, Albert."

"You think I'll betray my friends and Sam's Coalition and everything we've fought for?"

"Sure you will, once you get your price. What's the use of all your fine principles? They don't eat and shit. Your pals would sell in a heartbeat if the shoe was on the other foot."

"I've made some bad choices," I admitted, "awful fucking choices—"

"It's me or TexHome. They want to build a 500-acre tract, houses packed cheek by jowl. I will do ranchettes, one-acre parcels, maintain the spirit of the place. I can't hardly bring myself to run you out, Albert, but there's no choice. I'm talking to the bank about purchasing your loan."

"You can't do that…they can't."

"Sure we can, if you won't make your payments. The bank wants out from under. Better to sell your loan than repossess. Sell directly to me and you'll come out ahead. We can go down to my office right now and draw up the papers. Glad to help out."

"Is this about Penny? The Realty Revenge? Payback time?"

Ches groaned. "Could you help me into my truck? I'd…uhhh… appreciate it."

I stooped over for him to lean on me. "What about my well?"

"Can't be helped; you have no water rights. No time to dillydally, Albert." His head came up, nostrils worked in alarm. "We've got leaking gas!" He shoved me aside and sprinted for my pickup, no trace of sore ribs. Steam hissed from under the hood, gas puddled under the cab, and I could hear an electrical wire spitting sparks as I approached. Ches swept hands low over the ground. I seized his arm and leapt for the ditch just before the pickup blew. Like a Hollywood detonation: great fireball and the hood spinning into the air in slow motion. Lying on our backs in the ditch, we watched it drop nearly atop us, Ches panting, nostrils working, our feet in the tarry verge of a black slough. Flames leapt impishly from the pickup to a clump of dry mesquite, and the chaparral burst into flame—creosote bush and Ceanothus—embers curled off and spun away into *La Cienega* land, grinning red devils on Santa Ana gusts.

Sirens soon screamed in from all directions, CDF planes dropped orange retardant, Sam City trolls emerged from their burrows to fight the flames with shovels and axes. No use. It was a hot fire with ample fuel. Might've wasted the whole valley, but Tahquitz had other plans. As smoke billowed up into piling thunderheads that afternoon, clouds burst open and poured down four inches of rain, leaving a haze of steam and smell of damp ashes on the air, a spice of ozone and sage. However, it was black sloughs as much as rain that saved us, vacuuming up flames, which thrashed in their death throes, strangled in the clutches of amoebic muck. Skeletons of framed houses along Creosote Canyon Road glowed like red hot coals in the gloom. Ghost houses. Nature rules, happenstance reigns.

#

Soon, houses began creeping back from my property line, some folding in on themselves like gate-legged tables, upper stories tucking into lower, or the black slough swallowed them whole—pools, SUVs and all—growing ever larger as it gorged. Advancing on us one side, retreating on the other, keeping us off guard. Tinkerspoon heard great blooping sounds middle of the night. He'd escaped a week after the Feds nabbed him. He convinced his jailors that he was Mexican—did his chameleon thing, spoke Spanish, went dusky—then woke up one morning fully Anglo and walked right out past guards who thought him someone's lawyer. "There's a powerful psychology behind prejudice, dude."

A dozen of us were living on Second Chance Acres now, including Matt Littlefeather and Luella. More indigenous than Indians, Matt said. Sam City folks more still: barefoot in rabbit skin loincloths, subsisting on snared rabbits and cactus fruit, hiding in underground burrows from the rent-a-cops hired to patrol the land. We heard their drumbeats from afar as they danced under the moon, yipping like coyotes. Through sweltering May and June, Little Les and Patsy K lived in his naturally air-conditioned culvert in the wash. The rest of us moved deep into the canyon, finding cool serenity back where walls narrowed and rose vertically. Looking up past them at a strip of night sky stippled with stars, we could believe we were back in Saint Angel again.

Curiously, builders started leaving houses unfinished. Jack Crispley's crews framed one, then hurried on to the next, leaving bare frames behind. They poured foundations around the clock, as if they sensed the earth's malaise and wanted to occupy as much territory as possible before the economy, foul weather, or common sense shut them down. Acres of skeletal stud walls were left to bleach in the sun. Sage said old Tahquitz was flat pissed off, belching and farting, so angry that he yanked the arrow out of his head and stabbed it in his belly. Once, so the story goes, the God of Water stole his young bride and shot an arrow into his head. Now Anglos wanted to steal his land.

Then it got stranger. One morning, I walked out of the canyon to the front gate. But wasn't any gate, no Creosote Canyon Road, no Tinkerspoon's trailer. In their place was the ragged L.A. skyline, towering buildings sporting obscene wall-length ads for movies and ass-hugging jeans. I nearly stepped onto a freeway—I-10 perhaps—bordering my property; a semi sent me reeling back with a blast of its air horn. All the hubbub of city life sprang up around me. It seemed I was standing on a precipice overlooking that urban scene, like Jesus overlooking his spectral desert kingdom in the book of Luke. I expected the devil to pop up and make me a proposition. Homeless men in knit caps pushed shopping carts through skid row alleys, and my black slough revealed itself as the La Brea Tar Pits, swallower of mastodons. Where had once been Finley's treehouse was now wall-to-wall ranch styles. The canyon had closed up; I made out a zippered scar like a Cesarean up its belly. Upscale houses sat atop the mesa above it. I shrieked and fled back into what had been my place, climbing fences, running through yards pursued by pit bulls, dashing through houses and out the front door, on through the next house, sprinting through a scene out of *Boogie Nights*: four couples making love on a roiling water bed, which I crossed in two woozy strides, a used condom stuck between my toes. To my relief, the canyon's stitched incision dissolved as I approached and admitted me. Lewis Carroll never imagined such oddities.

Melie asked, "You sure it's Los Angeles and not St. Louis somewheres?" Mona had to see for herself, but no trace of L.A. when we exited the canyon, no trace of Ches's developments either. "Those houses were here," Mona insisted, "I'm sure of that."

"Maybe the earth has joined our rebellion; maybe it shed them off."

"Houses coming and going, cities, it's not natural."

"What's natural anymore? We've passed over into post-natural."

We heard a clattering on the road: Death and Pestilence pushing shopping carts full of their scavengings, wearing blue knit caps like the homeless on L.A. streets. I asked them if, by chance, they'd seen a city around. Death's thin shoulders trembled. They leaned on their carts in the drenching heat. "Sodom and Gomorrah," Pestilence spat. "Evil is near abouts wore the preacher out, carnal sin and lechery," he said in a piping high voice.

"So you saw it, too, those couples on the water bed?"

Death glowered at me, gray crosses branding his eyeballs. "Them who can, let them see."

"You fellahs may just as well join us. You could use the rest, and we could use your help."

From then on, the city appeared and retreated at irregular intervals. Some never saw it. Little Les said it was like ghost cities he'd seen in Nam: buildings were props flipped up from underground and retracted by the Viet Cong. But I saw encroaching urbanity as a Tsunami, as much metaphysical as physical. "PC check, like the whole country is going coast-to-coast city," Patsy K said. "Get used to it."

I called Western Enterprise Bank to discuss my mortgages; I'd stopped receiving mortgage notices. A recorded message informed me that Western Enterprise had merged with World Wide Financial Corp. A nasal voice kept repeating that they valued my call and a customer representative would be with me shortly. Finally, a digital voice asked me to state my name and account number, then an actual human with a thick Indian accent said, "I'm sorry, Mr. Sharpe, I'm showing that account 'flagged,' sir."

"What does 'flagged' mean?"

"I am sorry, sir, this is not my department. I can patch you through to Accounts Delinquent, sir."

"Delinquent?" I demanded.

"I show ninety days delinquent, Mr. Sharpe. So sorry. I can patch you through to our Account Resolution Service, sir."

"Could you patch me through to your Saint Angel, California branch?"

"I am sorry, sir, that won't be possible. We have eliminated the inconvenience of walk-in banking, sir. World Wide Financial has streamlined its services to provide customers with *Instant 1-800 One Stop Online Banking* in 74 countries."

"You've closed your local branches?"

"Certainly not, sir. Our goal is to save you the inconvenience of antiquated banking services. We wish to liberate your banking experi-

.ess on L.A. streets. I asked them if, by chance, they'd seen a city
.ind. Death's thin shoulders trembled. They leaned on their carts
.n the drenching heat. "Sodom and Gomorrah," Pestilence spat. "Evil
is near abouts wore the preacher out, carnal sin and lechery," he said in
a piping high voice.

"So you saw it, too, those couples on the water bed?"

Death glowered at me, gray crosses branding his eyeballs. "Them
who can, let them see."

"You fellahs may just as well join us. You could use the rest, and
we could use your help."

From then on, the city appeared and retreated at irregular intervals.
Some never saw it. Little Les said it was like ghost cities he'd seen in
Nam: buildings were props flipped up from underground and retracted
by the Viet Cong. But I saw encroaching urbanity as a Tsunami, as
much metaphysical as physical. "PC check, like the whole country is
going coast-to-coast city," Patsy K said. "Get used to it."

I called Western Enterprise Bank to discuss my mortgages; I'd
stopped receiving mortgage notices. A recorded message informed me
that Western Enterprise had merged with World Wide Financial Corp.
A nasal voice kept repeating that they valued my call and a customer
representative would be with me shortly. Finally, a digital voice asked
me to state my name and account number, then an actual human with
a thick Indian accent said, "I'm sorry, Mr. Sharpe, I'm showing that
account 'flagged,' sir."

"What does 'flagged' mean?"

"I am sorry, sir, this is not my department. I can patch you through
to Accounts Delinquent, sir."

"Delinquent?" I demanded.

"I show ninety days delinquent, Mr. Sharpe. So sorry. I can patch
you through to our Account Resolution Service, sir."

"Could you patch me through to your Saint Angel, California
branch?"

"I am sorry, sir, that won't be possible. We have eliminated the
inconvenience of walk-in banking, sir. World Wide Financial has
streamlined its services to provide customers with *Instant 1-800 One
Stop Online Banking* in 74 countries."

"You've closed your local branches?"

"Certainly not, sir. Our goal is to save you the inconvenience of
antiquated banking services. We wish to liberate your banking experi-

ence and save you time with premier *Instant One-Stop Service,* sir."

"What use is my local branch if I can't contact it?"

"I can patch you through to our Customer Suggestion Box, sir."

"Would you fucking patch me through to someone I can talk to about my loans?"

"I understand, sir. I can patch you through to our International Banking Service at 1-800-INT-BANK. Please follow the key pad instructions for loan and mortgage inquiries or click us up at WWF.com for 24/7 instant banking satisfaction."

"Does John Hobkins still work for you people? I heard he was fired."

"I am sorry, sir. World Wide Financial prohibits its employees from discussing personnel."

"Tell me, are you human?"

"Very sorry, sir, I can't discuss this. Have a prosperous World Wide day, sir. Goodbye."

I was account-flagged and lost in World Wide limbo, but I had other worries. We had gone into siege mode, anxious and careworn—except for Mona who thrives on tension. She says, "Calm makes me edgy; you never know what it's concealing." There were shortages in local stores. One day there was milk but no eggs, the next day eggs but no TP. We had daily brownouts. Not a problem since we were off the grid, anyway. But gasoline shortages worried us; we needed gas to run a generator to pump water and burn strings of Christmas lights Matt had salvaged from Sam Jenson's place and strung up in the canyon. The lot of us huddled troll-like under strings of blinking, multi-colored lights that illuminated canyon walls overhead, befuddling cliff swallows and bats that zigzagged crazily through the unnatural twilight, clutching woolly moths in their teeth.

Folks made themselves comfortable, anyhow, back in my canyon, built lean-to shelters of palm fronds, as Soboba Indians once had, under rustling Washingtonia Fan Palms migrated over the mountain from Palm Springs, crowns reaching the tops of canyon walls. Folks lay around half naked. We hid the well under long-needled cholla cactus. Wynona Littlefeather taught us how to rub spines off tender young beavertail cactus joints and roast them over the fire, along with yucca stalks that tasted like sweet potatoes, and how to leach acorn meal to make *wewish*—steaming, insipid Indian porridge. "Now you see why we eat store-bought." Sage grinned. But Wynona's Navajo fry bread and Coachella tortillas were to die for. We planted corn, beans and tomatoes, which prospered in the hothouse atmosphere. Wallers hung out deep in canyon narrows near Pissing Springs, where mud had dried alkali white and made him look like an albino. He grunted contentedly, with so many fingers to scratch between his ears. Pig happy. The canyon was our Desert of Eden. I'd always known it would come in handy one day. Matt and Les lashed together a rope ladder to reach a crow's nest lookout atop the mesa.

Sitting by the campfire evenings, my friends' faces bathed in firelight all sides, I'd go taciturn, turning Ches's offer over in my mind along with Finley's future, knowing fate affords us no *second* second chances. But Judas was no role I envisioned for myself. "Sharpe's chewing worry biscuits over there," Matt Littlefeather said one evening. "Whazzup, Al?"

"I'm thinking that this won't be any kind of place to live soon."

Sage laughed. "You just figured that out? Nowhere won't be any place to live, brother. The earth is gonna close down circuit by circuit: Sub-Saharan Africa first, then the Middle East, then Asia. Over here, people won't see trouble coming until it's too late; white men have a genius for denial."

One night, Tinkerspoon sidled up beside me. "I had a dream last night," he whispered. "Pop told me, 'It's over, Andy. You best leave.' I'm outta here, dudeski, I'm gonna sell."

"Me, too!" I decided right then. "Going down to sign papers with Ches tomorrow. Get her done. They will hate us for it, you know, even Finley will hate us," I whispered

Wynona Littlefeather's eye whites held us from the shadows. "What meanness are you two plotting over there?"

I held my tongue, but Tinkerspoon said, "We're plotting to sell to Ches and fuck everybody over, dudeski."

Rob laughed, but Wynona clucked her tongue in disapproval.

"Fuck it! Not my choice, dudeski; the bastards ripped off our choices."

"You selling us out?" Matt asked. "You, too, Sharpe? Your pop wouldn't never of sold, Andy, not old man Sanchez."

Tinkerspoon looked away, stung. "Pop? I dunno. In my dream he sold. Yeh...he prob'ly wouldn't."

"You ain't your old man," Sage said. "You don't fill half his shadow."

Tinkerspoon looked wounded.

"Maybe I won't either," I blurted. "Maybe neither of us should sell."

"No way, dude. You said you're selling." Tinkerspoon's eyes lingered on Sage.

"I've changed my mind."

"What about Finley's college money and all, dude?"

"I've got two hands, I'll work, start a maintenance service. Come in with me, Andy. You can do computer repair."

We watched Tinkerspoon's face reconfigure for one hopeful moment in the firelight, then go slack again, or come to pieces, rather, like a cubist portrait, features disjunct.

I called Finley on her cell just before we turned in for the night. No answer. "She won't take my calls," I told Mona. "I think she blames me for losing her mother."

"What did you have to do with it? Sondra died in a plane crash."

"I'm not saying it's rational. She feels cheated. I think she believes I've been lying about Sondra all these years. Claims she's been talking to her mother on the phone."

Mona blew air out of her lips. "Talking to her dead mother, that'd be a trick." Rubbing the back of my neck with strong fingers. "All adolescents feel cheated. They resent life for stealing their innocence. Finley skipped all that turmoil and rebellion; I never knew a happier girl. It worried me, I knew it couldn't last. She's doing adolescent rebellion now. Of course she feels cheated, she lost her mother. She needs room to figure it out and assert her independence, she needs to rebel. It's healthy."

I shook my head. "I have no idea what you're talking about. What's healthy, what isn't, how can you know?" Glancing sheepishly back at her, a slice of her face visible in moonlight. "Why didn't we get married? Finley always wanted us to. Maybe it would have been healthy."

"Because we didn't want to. I can't be her mother, Albert, if that's what you mean. I can't do that for her."

"There's this irrational hunger in her that needs filling. She thinks I don't give a damn."

She threw a hand and lay back. I could see her looking up at the sky, her face relaxing in a smile. Then we heard Wallers trotting along, grunting plaintively. He sniffed us over from head to toe like a dog might, then lay heavily down beside me with a grunt. Mona no longer tensed up when he poked her with his rubbery snout. She'd grown half fond of him. "I can't decide," she said, "whether your pig no longer stinks or if I've grown accustomed to it."

"Oh, he stinks all right, but he keeps the snakes and scorpions away."

#

"I know I have been ducking your calls, Dad," Finley admitted. "I've been really busy."

"You have a job?" I asked.

"Just the old one at Starbucks. They wanted me back."

"Everyone wants you back."

"Schnay, Dad. Listen, I just wanted to let you know I'm okay. Not to worry. I just needed to get away, right, I needed time out."

"That's what Mona's been telling me."

"You lied to me, Albert. That totally pisses me off, okay. I thought you hated lying."

"What did I lie about?"

"You know. Listen, Al, give it up, okay. So I know what's going on, I know you wanted to protect me from the truth. I can handle it, really. I know Mom's alive, I know she never got on that plane with Charlie, she never died in any plane crash. That's bullshit, okay. I know Mom abandoned us, I know you tried to hide the truth from me. Maybe I understand that instinct, but it's time to give it up and come clean. I want you to, I need you to, Albert."

"When did I stop being 'Dad'? Of all this crazy talk, that's craziest."

"Mom disappeared into thin air, lost in the clouds or whatever, but she didn't die."

"You can't really believe that. Her body wasn't recovered, no. Not many were."

"Listen, Al, I like talk to her on the phone every day."

It took me a moment to collect my wits. "Yes, Patsy K told me some nutjob in New Mexico claims to be your mom. You know how crazy that is, Fin? You can't possibly believe it; you're not that gullible...I hope."

"Widget bitch! She promised not to tell you. I can't trust anyone anymore. It's like an epidemic or something. You lied to me, Al, you totally disappoint me. Like how could you do that? How could you steal my mother from me? So you wouldn't have any competition?"

"You really believe that?" I said hoarsely. "You believe I'm capable of that?"

"I don't know what to believe anymore. I plan to find out. I'll be out to get my stuff. So Rob blew up the dam, right?"

"Shhhh! For crissake, hon, my phone could be bugged. What are you even talking about?"

"You're getting really weird, Al, totally brackish. All of you. So I'm not your 'hon' anymore, okay?"

"I've never lied to you, Fin, but there is something I haven't told you. We have a problem."

"Totally. I know, Dad, okay, like I know it all."

"How could you? I never told you I invested in Biotechs. They've tanked, the bottom fell out of the Biotech boom. Your college fund, is gone. We lost it all."

"Good going, Al," she said indifferently.

"I'm sorry, baby. I thought it was a good idea at the time. I'm just sick about it. We may lose Second Chance Acres, too. I took out a second mortgage to cover payments on Sam City land. Maybe stupid, but I did. I intended to sell some stocks to cover the next few months' mortgage, but there's nothing left to sell."

"Second Chance is mine, too, you know. And Mom's. You can't just lose it."

"Sorry, honey. I'm doing all I can—"

She hung up on me. The dial tone sounded like existential tinnitus.

#

They posted signs out front:

WARNING DRIVEWAY MINED
RABID PIG LOOSE ON PREMISES

On the slough side:

DANGER QUICKMUD!

Because "strange" is always your best defense against authority. The black slough belched up that backhoe, which lay corroded and forlorn on its side at muck's edge. They'd be back: water Authority functionaries, World Wide Financial goons in dark suits, SALCO thugs in white vans. "Gonna have Alcohol, Tobacco and Firearms over here, like over to Wounded Knee," Matt said. He thought of himself as an indigenous activist, one of the Alcatraz 89 or Geronimo's followers.

"Why's that, Matt?" Daphne Thompson asked. "We don't have explosives...as far as I know." Sliding eyes at Rob and Little Les.

"Don't matter shit what we got, people. It's what they think we got."

Ches's anger poured over us in foul exhalations, supplanting the ancient smell of creosote and sage, the sweet smell of orange blossoms in groves north of town, the malty stench of dairy farms out by Mystic Lake. In the morning, fly spume drifted on the air, landed on everything organic, and hatched maggots. The black slough festered and glistened with a restless, roiling black carpet of them. Mona couldn't sleep for their writhing. Once they metamorphosed, flies would blot out the sun. They say Ches's skin glowed green from bacteria at work in his gut—both devouring and sustaining his innards at once. The mother wart on his forehead had elongated and calcified into a rhinoceros horn. Oddly, his developer buddies and DGLA loyalists didn't notice, but Penny did. He prowled the perimeter of Second Chance Acres like a panting dog, the sweat of his tongue dripping down on them from the mesa above. Builders parked D9 cats along Creosote Canyon Road, and The Tweedledee Twins camped at top of Al's drive in their patrol car. M&M believed they were spies from the Scientology headquarters in San Jacinto, who wanted to seize the land and build a compound on it.

They were awakened early one morning by the sound of breaking glass out on the road: windows smashed out of cars parked there, a message scratched into Al's mailbox with a wood chisel: "Your next Sharpe." "Now it gets interesting, people," Les said. Daphne thought it was fear of change that inspired such hostility. "Nah," Wynona Littlefeather said, "people just like to be mean, y'know."

Death and Pestilence formed an Armageddon contingent with Larry The Lion from Sam City. They sat each evening in a niche carved in soft stone back by Pissing Springs and read aloud from the book of Revelations. The post-apocalyptic glow of a campfire projected their grotesque silhouettes two stories high against a canyon wall. Others mulled over their own mesquite blazes, and the pops of burning wood ricocheted like gunshots down the canyon. They hid their cars under brush on La Cienega land

and traded off sentry duty in Les's crow's nest atop the mesa. Tinkerspoon smeared his face with slough muck, covered his head with datura leaves, and stole through adjacent suburbs. He smelled so bad that dogs whined and cowered away from him. "They're mostly abandoned, dude," he reported. "We should move in over there." "We should burn the fuckers down," Rob said. "Sorry, Lord!" The more Rob got into religion, the more he obsessed about destruction.

Little Lester mimeographed an edition of Saint Angel's Dirty Underwear—"The Filthiest Yet"—which he and Patsy K Jones distributed door to door in town, outlining crimes against Saint Angel: SALCO and TexHome stealing our water and our valley, making obscene profits off our misery, their goons trailing and intimidating us, breaking car windows, murdering Sam Jenson in cold blood. Cal Hale demanded an apology. "Else you'll be sorry, Lester, and Al Sharpe, too." When Al asked if Cal planned to add them to his "kill list," Cal merely laughed at him.

We got temblors almost daily and saw what looked like puffs of smoke high up in the mountains. Dislodged boulders careened down ravines, sounding like tumbling bowling pins. Tahquitz was furious. Al had begun digging a cavern in mudstone walls of a shallow side canyon, the entrance concealed by spiny mesquite. It was something to do while he waited for whatever was coming. He felt sick about Finley but decided it was best to keep his distance. She would eventually come to her senses.

Just as they'd accommodated to chafing dry heat on Second Chance Acres, the sky darkened and hid the mountains, the temperature plummeted, cool air collided with hot in a calamitous confrontation, Tahquitz beat his chest, and volleys of thunder shook the mountains. The sky opened and rain came down in sheets. M&M stood naked in the meadow, grinning upward; rain pelted their slick heads and cascaded off their bellies. All joined them, laughing, wallowing in the mud, their dry skin soaking up moisture.

But what started out joyful became misery. From insufferable summer heat to bone-aching chill. Water sloshed in shoes and soaked sleeping bags. Campers retreated under canyon ledges and sat before the drowned bones of their campfires like shivering elves, glowering at the ceaseless rain. Pissing Springs swelled from a trickling stream to a muddy, churning river that stretched between canyon walls. Death and Pestilence moaned Bible verses at the sky. We were dripping miserable. Rising water emptied into the black slough, where it spun clockwise in a hissing dark vortex and was swallowed like water spiraling down a drain. Bivouacked in the mud,

Sam's Coalition approached despair. Sick of eating cold beans from a can and wringing out sleeping bags after sleepless nights spent huddled under tarps, listening to water tap dance on plastic sheeting, they crowded into the cottage and Finley's treehouse. Folks started to mutter about going home.

#

My footsteps crunched over frozen mud. Hard freeze in late June, unheard of. Moonlight glowed on snowcapped San Jacintos, the air frigid crisp, aluminum bird-scare strips rattled in a chill wind. An owl moved across the moon, hooting low. Dogs barked and a smattering of lights popped on in top floors of houses looking down on Second Chance Acres; floodlights lit yards. I cursed them and knew with a certainty I wouldn't sell, would forfeit my front acres if need be and do whatever it took to save the rest, would remain on the place like a puncture-weed thorn in development's shoe. Life, as Gabriel Garcia Marquez tells us, offers constant opportunities for survival.

As if to footnote this, I became aware of white vans parked out front, headlights spearing into darkness. Men, huddled near my front gate, went quiet as I approached, mud crunching underfoot. "Something I can do for you fellows?"

"It's Al Sharpe," a voice called, "it's him!"

Intuition said to flee but I approached the gate. "You fellahs want to step off my property? You're trespassing." Arms seized me from behind and hoisted me over the gate; hands gripped my legs and armpits and toted me out to the road, stood me up in headlight beams like a road show minstrel. I made out grim, beefy, vaguely familiar faces; Cal dodged behind a van door. "You plan to kill me, too, you old bastard?" I shouted. A rough hand clamped my mouth shut. I bit into gristle and my mouth filled with metallic blood. "Damn!" A fist slammed the side of my head and sent sparks flying behind my eyes. "Shitty little cowards," I moaned.

So it started. One man threw punches while others pinned my arms behind me. I recognized Trinkley's bald, round pate. He cocked back a two-by-four like a baseball bat, square edges forming straight lines in surreal brightness, his teeth jigged rodent-like against his lower lip. "T.S.F." A blur of movement.

I came to on my knees surrounded by plaster-spattered jeans and work boots, the right side of my face numb, but I could feel blood curling over my chin. A "Cal Hale Construction" logo was concealed by a thin glaze of spray paint on a van door. Not smart, sending thugs out in a company car. I recalled Les's warning: *Don't never let them get you on the ground.*

"Enough," someone said, but a high-pitched, furious voice insisted, "Around here we fight back, chickenshit."

"Dickhead," I managed. "Cowards!"

He kicked me in the chest, I keeled backwards, eyes fixed on that two-by-four poised like a blurred executioner's sword above me. No end I ever imagined for myself: beaten to death by the hirelings of a string-tie-wearing yokel in front of my own place. I spat blood onto Trinkley's shiny black surveyor's boots laced military fashion up the ankles.

#

How staged it looks: crew cab pickups and white vans parked helter skelter, blocking the road, headlights spoked toward the white hub of action. Al's head slumps against his chest. A fist connects in a red explosion of light against an eye socket, and another jerks his jaw aside. Someone raises a two-by-four. His assailants are stiff, posturing kabuki figures, one stepping forward, then another in a vicious round, torsos starkly silhouetted in headlights, but faces blurred, unrecognizable, bones cracking under the impact of anonymous fists. Al is defiantly indifferent to the pain. A blow sends numbness up his nose and deep into his brain stem, another releases fireworks, red rage, yet he keeps arms locked at his sides and barks "cowards" at his assailants, further enraging them.

"Give up," someone pleads. Al laughs feebly and raises his middle finger.

"Give it up, pal, say 'uncle.'"

He makes out Cal Hale's face cowering behind a dark van window. "Murderer," he mumbles, "chickenshit murderer," before a blow from a huge man closes his mouth for good. He collapses face forward onto asphalt, permitting the real work to begin: hammering boot toes, broken ribs, bruised kidneys. Ches's words echo in his head: "Everyone sells in the end."

A blast from Little Lester's shotgun ends it. Figures charge from the bushes, shouting like berserkers, brandishing clubs and shovels. Matt Littlefeather's fist whumps a construction worker atop the head and he deflates in slow motion. Rob Thompson butts a balding head with mutton chop sideburns with his forehead; Tinkerspoon hears the crack from where he is hiding in the bushes one-hundred feet away. Kawhock! Like Derek Jeter connecting with a fast ball. Sage Littlefeather watches consciousness escape from Trinkley's ears like smoke and fears it is the man's soul; Rob has killed him. Melie sits atop one of the mutts who had been kicking Al and slaps him silly. Battle-savvy Lester, knowing when the day is won, shouts, "Hold her right there, people." He motions the intruders to their vans with a shotgun. "Get the fuck gone." They do, peeling rubber, and he fires a farewell shotgun blast into the rear of a retreating van.

Les kneels over Al and places fingers against his carotid artery, firms a hand over his mouth and pinches his nose. Al sits up, coughing for air. Les nods. "They landed a few, tell you what, brother!" Al's left eye is swollen shut, the other watches fleeing taillights. For a moment, he isn't sure whether the figures towering over him are friend or foe, but he makes out Sage Littlefeather's quixotic bowling shoes in a flashlight beam and starts to giggle. Lester stands mid-road. "They'll be back, people. Trust me."

#

Mona bathed my wounds with warm water, wincing as she cleaned the gash in my scalp. It burned something fierce. Looking at her bold black eyebrows and troubled gray eyes with my one good eye, I realized I was fond enough of her to call it "love." I swooned again, woke to Wynona Littlefeather binding a poultice of evil-smelling leaves over my swollen eye. "You're hard headed, Al Sharpe, I'll give you that. And a good thing, too. Your eye looks like a eggplant. This should pucker it back." My tongue found a gap in my mouth where should have been a tooth.

I woke hours later to Finley peering down at me, her face pale and riven; she'd lost weight. They had me in bed in the cottage. She fussed at my wounds with a daughter's healing fingers. I seized them. "Where have you been, hon? I've been calling you."

"Doing something stupid," I heard her whisper.

"I lost your college fund, baby."

"I know, I don't care, I don't even know if I'm going to college."

I held her hand. "We'll work it out, always do."

"I want to kill the assholes who did this to you," she hissed. "Remember that lady I told you about?"

"The one who claims to be your mother?"

"So I went to see her...."

Between my good and bum eyes, her image blurred, then doubled, before resolving to a single self. Not Finley but Mona—her face inches from mine—saying they needed to get me to hospital. "He's babbling nonsense." I seized her hands. "Where's Finley? Where'd she go?" Rising on my elbows and looking imploringly about the room. "She was just here."

"You see what I mean," Mona said to the others. "He has a concussion."

#

Tinkerspoon, wandering the neighborhood that night as he often did, watched from the bushes as three vans pulled up. He expected they had come to torch his trailer, having sussed him out. His computer room was lined with asbestos insulation panels he had salvaged when they were removed from Saint Angel High School. He believed that lungs which had thrived on desert air full of wind-borne silicates would be impervious to asbestos fibers, but he couldn't be sure his computer lab would survive a serious blaze. Seeing beefy men drag Al out to the road and start to work him over, Tinkerspoon fled over frozen ground to wake the others. Little Les took charge; Matt, Rob and the others seized makeshift weapons, Rob promising he'd send the bastards straight to hell. Daphne stood barefooted on frozen ground, feet wide apart, a sleeping bag draped over her shoulders, and touched the men as they passed, giving them her blessing.

An hour later, several men checked into Saint Angel General to have buckshot removed from their rear ends (Dan Trinkley among them). They told a story about a hunting accident. Esther Johnson, the night duty nurse, called Charlie Haynes at three a.m. "We have a situation, Chief. Gunshot wounds, five at once, all in their heinies."

"Any fatalities?" Charlie sat up in bed. He dreaded such late night calls.

"It's not a gang war, Chief. More like serious mischief."

Pulling into the hospital lot, Charlie noted buckshot holes peppering the rear of a white van. It was out of season for hunting any game he knew of with a shotgun. "Looks more like it was hunting you," he told the men who sat in a row on molded plastic chairs, looking foolish in white hospital gowns, shifting eyes at each other and squirming from buttock to buttock, repeating a cockamamie story about shooting rats at the county dump. "We know it's frowned upon," Trinkley said, "but everyone does it."

"I never heard of rats that shot back," Charlie said. When Trinkley tried to explain, Charlie held up a hand. "I've heard enough. Just haven't decided what to charge you boys with yet." He took fingerprints and photos of their red, wounded rear ends and let them go. Thence the rumor mill got busy: talk of odd doings out at Second Chance Acres and five men killed in a shootout between construction workers and Sam's Coalition, who were holed up in Al Sharpe's canyon preparing to make a last stand. People spoke of Waco and the Alamo. Folks from Devastation Acres wanted to volunteer; they had an army surplus howitzer. Townspeople considered Al Sharpe a homegrown folk hero.

Some days later, mail carrier Angie walked back through the ersatz mine field into the canyon with a registered letter from World Wide Financial. Al stared at block lettering: FORECLOSURE. FINAL NOTICE. He had a week to come up with $76,000 or they would repossess Second Chance Acres. "What final notice? This is the first I've received."

Angie shrugged. "I've been trying to deliver."

"They're going to take my place," he told her.

"They can't do that, you're our most famous citizen."

"And one of the poorest."

#

I called Patsy K's parents to ask about Finley, since she wouldn't answer her phone. "Hello there, Albert," her father cried cheerfully. "How's life down on the farm?" Chuckling.

"Listen, Peter, I've been trying to reach Finley but she doesn't answer her phone. I just want to know if she is all right—if she needs anything. I don't have to talk to her if she doesn't want to."

"I'm afraid she isn't here. She left a couple of days ago. We thought she'd gone home. That was the impression she gave us."

"She said she was coming home, you're sure?"

"No...no, I said that was our impression. She didn't say where she was going precisely. I would tell you if I knew, Albert."

"Sure you would. Sorry, I'm concerned is all. There's a woman she met on the Internet—"

"We did think it odd that she didn't take Patsy K's car. You'd think she would drive out to Saint Angel."

"Call me if you hear anything."

"Certainly, Al. I wouldn't lose any sleep over it. She's likely off on an adventure with a friend. She's a spirited girl, a special kid."

Nonetheless, I had a sinking feeling. Something was wrong. The needle on my intuitive compass, which had long been frozen where people were concerned, was quivering crazily. Mona assured me that Finley had good instincts, wherever she was. "Maybe not so good where her mother is concerned," I said.

We huddled dejectedly around a fire far back in the canyon that evening, freezing rain hissing at wood that smoldered rather than burned. M&M had developed a wet bronchial cough; we bundled them into bed in the cottage. Wynona placed a pan of steaming jimson weed leaves (*kikisu-lem*) on the bed table to ease their congestion. As we spoke, Death and Pestilence's doomsday chant mixed ominously with thunderous rain pelting plastic sheeting overhead. "Maybe it's time to arm ourselves," Les suggested, his breath lingering ghostly on damp air. What would once have brought furious protest had us nodding, except for Mona, who said, "Could we get real here, please!"

"This is real as it gets, people."

17

DOOMSDAY

"Do you know where she's gone?" I asked Patsy K.

Les replied for her. It had already gotten that way between them—one completing the other's thoughts. "Your wife died in a plane crash, didn't she, Al?"

"Yes, eleven years ago."

"You know I don't like prying into other people's business, but I'm worried about young Finley."

"PC check, Sondra absolutely died, *verdad*? You're certain, Dad?"

"Of course I'm certain. What's this all about, you two?"

"Finley doesn't think so, I guess you know. I told you she chats with some lady on Facebook, this widget person she thinks is her mother, anyways. Like a total no proofer, okay!"

Finley, she said, had posted messages on social media and on a site called *ParentFind.com*, saying she was looking for her theoretically dead mother, Sondra Millers Sharpe, who had taught at UCSD and supposedly died in the crash of Flight 452 off of Coronado Island eleven years ago. But Finley had reason to believe she didn't. "So like did anyone know her or know where she was? Some troll friended her, claiming to be Sondra, some widget freak from New Mexico. Finley totally bought into it. So they are like bosom buddies, exchanging photos and all kinds of totally not cool personal data—even about you, Dad—for-your-ears-only-nit-grit stuff you should never share on line, with anybody! Definitely not with some Internet stalker. PC check, they were like always on the phone before she went to my parents' place."

"That's who she was talking to? She wouldn't tell me."

"Listen, Albert—" glancing at Les "—it's not like she thinks you offed her mom or anything, but she believes you wanted her dead. You drove her into lesbo limbo or something. I don't know what this wack job wants, okay. I don't think it's money. I think she wants Finley," whispering this last, "brackishly weird as it sounds. It's gotten seriously scary."

"Maybe it's an online pen pal kind of thing, a girlish fantasy. Finley's not as mature as you are, Patsy K." Sounding Pollyanna-ish, even to myself.

"If it walks like bullshit and talks like bullshit, it is bullshit," Les said. "It's all these predators out there trolling social media and the whole freaking Internet, sexual predators, and money moles from North Africa, and terrorist recruiters from Yemen and Algeristan—some fucking place—trying to get into young people's heads and old folks' bank accounts, Neo-Nazis and Muhammad freaks sending death threats on twitter-tweet, sex prowlers seeking young girls, even fucking Tink hacking Ches and them's sites—for the righteous cause, maybe, but disrespecting their privacy, nonetheless. I got zero use for that shit. I'd no more go on the Freaknet than volunteer to walk point in Nam."

"You widget." Patsy K slugged his arm. "So this brackish bitch wants Fin to visit her in Albuquerque. Schnay, bad idea, brackishly stupid. But she won't listen, she's desperate behind believing this nutjob is her mom returned from the dead."

Les made a clucking sound with his tongue. "Now she's gone missing."

I was shaking my head in denial. "Doesn't sound like my Finley. She's not that vulnerable." But thinking of her laughing gaily on the phone, I wasn't so sure.

"Believe it," Les said, "she's got it worked out in her head: you're in denial, you can't accept your wife left you for a woman, so you make up the plane crash story and buy Second Chance off a patent you sold, not Sondra's death benefit. You've been lying to her all along. I hate to be the bearer of bad news, especially where your daughter is concerned. I know you'd take a bullet for her. But you gotta know. She wants it to be true so bad that she'll believe a stranger over her own father. It's gone hard serious."

"Reality check, Dad. It could be some human trafficking thing. It's the way they swing. And this woman is with some guy now; she's no longer lesbian. PC check, it doesn't work like that. It's not flavor-of-the-month club, right. My friends who like girls like girls. Period. They don't all of a sudden get the cock gospel."

I was trying to take it all in: clandestine phone calls, Finley's anger, the padlocked treehouse, her life padlocked where I was concerned, her disappearance, some strange woman in New Mexico. Some deep hole in Fin that needed filling. Why hadn't I seen it? Scared hell out of me.

I called Charlie Haynes. "She's disappeared, Charlie. Didn't tell me a thing. I think she's in Albuquerque with a woman she believes to be her mother."

"I thought her mother passed away years ago."

"She refuses to believe it."

"Kidnapped, you think? I don't believe she'd run away. You think...?"

"Some woman she met on the Internet, according to Patsy K, some con artist who claims to be her mother for God only knows what reason."

"Oh, for the love of God, Finley has more sense than that. You'd better file a missing person's report," Charlie said disconsolately. "I'll put out an APB. Damn it, Al. Here lately it seems like we're living in a TV drama. Do you know anything about those boys who came to Saint Angel General with their asses full of buckshot? I'm guessing you do."

"Can't tell you a thing, Charlie. Nothing you'd want to hear."

Mona threw the Tarot and drew a card she called "Eternal Bliss." "No worries," she said, "Finley has things she has to do. It's about rebalancing." She believed all things are connected in a delicate web, like the ancient Taoists did. The tiniest breath sends ripples across the entire fabric of being. A child sleeps in Baltimore and her dreams lap a far shore in Borneo. I blow a kiss toward mountains half hidden behind an awkward clutter of roof angles, and it touches feather soft against Finley's cheek—wherever she might be.

#

Finley stood at the door of the adobe cottage trying to summon courage to knock. The scene was right out of a movie: Spanish-tiled roof and a cactus garden out front, two huge saguaro cactuses, rust-red earth and sandstone boulders, a dirt road winding into the hills past other whitewashed adobe cottages. A dry wind rattled cottonwood leaves. She imagined toe-headed rattlers napping in the midday sun. Her hand hovered at the knocker. Funny how you can want a thing, but when the time comes to take it you lose courage. She punched the door chime and heard a carillon of chapel bells in diminuendo inside. The great oak door opened and her mother stood in the doorway, smiling shyly, outlined in a corona of white light against the inner darkness, half spectral, seeming in the rush of sun-

light as if she had indeed emerged from death. She was older than Finley had expected, her face haggard, mouth obscenely painted with pink lipstick that leaked beyond the contours of her lips. In photos, her mom's face was long and narrow with high cheekbones and a broad, thoughtful, patrician forehead. Her brow had narrowed, cheekbones had slid down her face, and eyes crowded the spine of her nose. Was that even possible: physiognomy changing so radically after little over a decade? Her eyes had paled from the slate blue of those imperious eyes on Mom's Memorial page to a faded, sketchy robin's egg blue, half spooky. Finley stood studying this face she hadn't seen since girlhood, trying to reconcile it with memory. Sondra's hair, at least, was closely cropped in a brush cut, as she'd seen it in a dream, gone salt and pepper above the ears.

"Here's my Finley," Sondra cried in a voice familiar from phone calls. "Let me hug my baby." She clung to Finley and rocked her back and forth, reeking of beer. Finley went instantly limp. "Mom?" she managed, trying to puzzle out how her mother could look so unlike the photos in her scrapbook, how time could wreak such havoc. She was no longer the tall, regal woman warrior they had painted in Dad's mural.

A gruff male voice rescued her from her quandary. "Cat got your tongue, gal? Give your mother a proper hello after all these years. Don't stand there letting the heat leak in. C'mon in and take a load off." He thrust a cold beer bottle at her, beaded with drops of condensation. "Have a brewski." He winked and bottoms-upped his own, expecting her to follow suit.

"I don't like beer," she said shortly.

"Will you look at the girl, Patsy. Isn't she something to look at? Like her mother back in the day."

Finley turned to Sondra. "Who's he? I thought it would just be the two of us."

"It's just Pete. I told you about him on the phone. Peter, will you carry Finley's bag back to her bedroom, please, dear?"

He snatched up the bag. He was what Mona Sahlstrom would call "a runt," head too big for his body. But strong in that sinewy way small men can be, all long muscle. Not bald, as she'd first thought. His head was covered in blond fuzz through which his sunburned scalp glowed incandescent red like the skin of a hot pot-bellied stove. Faded tattoos such as an old sailor might wear twined over his forearms: she imagined big-busted women and anchors away, maybe a faded swastika. His orange T-shirt bore the logo of "Baby Boomer's Bar and Hell Hole" beneath a hollow-eyed skull with a tongue sticking out through gaping white teeth. He was all squirrely menace cloaked in grinning affability. How could her mother hang out with such a person? Sondra kept touching her arm in a pesky way, prattling on about how beautiful she'd once been, so that girls in her classes were jealous of her and the boys made passes at her.

"You taught college, right?" Finley asked curtly.

"Sure I did. You knew that." Her eyes closed repeatedly in a nervous tic. "Sociology and psychology and what not. I have always been interested in people; they fascinate me."

"At UCSD, right? You have a doctorate in anthropology?"

"That's correct." Her mother's eyes remained closed for a moment, then opened as if in flight. Nothing fit: she lacked the didactic stature and thoughtful reticence of a college professor or even a high school teacher. On the phone, her voice had sounded far off and surreal, like the voice of Marlene Dietrich on a tinny recording. She insisted that if Finley wanted to meet her she must come alone and tell no one where she was going. "That's absolutely necessary. Not your father or anyone." When Finley asked why, Sondra said merely, "Insurance fraud. You wouldn't want Albert getting in trouble…me neither for all that."

Light motes streamed in the tiny windows and were swallowed in the interior gloom. It was like a cave: dark, heavy wooden furniture seemingly chiseled of stone, papers scattered over the coffee table, beer bottles left willy nilly on deep window sills and fireplace mantel, like they'd had an impromptu party the night before and hadn't cleaned up. There was a plate of tiny cocktail sandwiches on the oak dining table, beer in a plastic cooler. "You must be hungry, sweetheart. I've made lunch." Sondra gestured at the table.

"I'm fine." Finley sat on the leather couch, directing her gaze slowly, unapologetically around the room. "So you really are my mom?"

"I really am, sweetheart. I always have been."

"Well, I for one am starved." The man scooped up two mini sandwiches in his right hand and stuffed a third into his mouth with the left, chewing and grinning: all white teeth and bread.

"My dad insists you died in a plane crash eleven years ago, you and your girlfriend, Charlie," Finley said. "He swears you did, he absolutely believes it. So what's that? My dad like never lies to me."

"He can believe what he likes. I'm sure he has his reasons. But, as you can see, I didn't." Her eyes closed tight again. "I'm alive. Not saying he's a liar or anything."

"So whatever happened to Charlie? I thought you two were like an item."

Her mother seemed taken aback. "Charlie? Ohhh, yes. Listen, I will explain all that to you after we get to know each other a little better. It's complicated."

"Makes for quite a story," the man said with the trace of a southern accent, chewing with his mouth open. What was he doing here? Like Sondra's pit bull or something?

"So I really need to hear it, okay. Totally. I want to know what you've been doing all this time, like where you have been." On the phone, Sondra had said something vague about Australia.

"I realize this is…unexpected. Me appearing out of the blue and all."

"Right! Like I'm your dead mother returned from the grave. That's way up there on the weirdness scale. Totally blew my mind."

"It happens," the man said, "more often than you think."

Sondra laughed and closed her eyes again. "It was the only way I knew how to do it, honey. I was so thrilled to reconnect with you. I was ecstatic, wasn't I, Peter?"

"Over the moon."

"Me, too," Finley said, betrayed by a sudden flush of emotion, not altogether trusting it.

"To hell with me, anyways. I want to know about my little girl." Sondra clapped her hands. "How's your father, how's Al?"

"He lied to me, okay. He says you died in a plane crash."

"And likely believes it. He didn't expect me back, anyways. I wouldn't of myself, but when I saw your Facebook posting, I just knew you were my little girl. I recognized you right off." She sat down beside Finley on the couch in tight black cycling shorts and hugged a bare knee to her chest, toes splayed on the leather cushion: purple nail polish which she couldn't imagine her mother wearing. Her cheeks were sallow and her shoulders stooped. Finley sensed invisible fingers of the woman's greed reaching out for her and wondered if it had been a mistake to come.

"So how could you recognize me? You don't know anything about me, really."

"I just knew. A mother's intuition." Her eyes shuttering.

"Do you remember what you used to say when you tucked me in bed?" It came to Finley as an inspiration, a sudden, imperative memory.

Sondra tapped her head and made a face. "It's all in there somewhere."

"Memory's a bitch," the man said, "excuse my French."

"How could you forget something like that? You said it every single night."

"Sleep tight, don't let the bed bugs bite," Pete suggested, his mouth full of sandwich. They were a tag team, those two, covering for each other.

"So remember the snow globe you gave me for Christmas with snow drifting down? It's still like my most valued possession."

"Well, of course I do," Sondra said primly, eyelids shuttering again. "There's a little white church and a path winding through the woods. Sure, I remember."

"Schnay, there's a farmhouse and a snowman, no church. How could you forget that?"

"Yes, I remember now." Tapping her head again. "Dummy me."

"Another brewski?" the man cried. "King of beers!" He had one ready for her, although she hadn't touched the first.

Something was wrong here, something terribly wrong. "You left. How could you do that to me? How could you abandon your little girl like that? How could you walk away and leave us hanging, thinking you were dead? I hated you for that, okay."

"Lighten up," the man barked. "Just take it easy. There'll be time to explain everything, like Lindy says."

"Lindy?" Finley demanded.

The woman threw a dismissive hand. "Oh, he does that. Lindy's his ex; he confuses us sometimes. I hate that." She glared at him.

"Everyone just lighten up," the man repeated.

"I don't have to lighten up, okay. PC check, you like abandoned me."

Pete opened his hands in a conciliatory gesture and screwed up his mouth.

Sondra said, "I've suffered for it every moment since. Ask Pete. I can't sleep, I have stomach cramps. I am delighted you are giving me a second chance, sweetheart. It means the world to me. I'll make it up to you, I promise."

"Second chances are a really big deal in our family. I believe in them, so does my dad." Finley felt a touch relieved.

The woman took her hand. "You are close to your father, aren't you? I'm glad of it. Al is a special man. So what have you told him about me?"

"Nothing. He doesn't even know I'm here, doesn't know you exist. It's not his business, really. He wanted you out of our lives. I honestly think he like wanted you dead."

"It hurts me to hear you say that. Doesn't it, Peter? I'm so awfully sorry *he feels that way. I suppose he was angry with me; he felt abandoned. I don't blame him."*

"Perfectly understandable," the man said. "It happens."

"I used to hate you for dying, you know. I can't see hating you for being alive. So like was it me? You didn't want to raise a kid? Or my Dad? Or your girlfriend? Why'd you leave?"

"All of the above." The man nodded pensively. "Hey, it happens."

"I won't deny I've failed you, honey. I've failed us both." She closed her eyes again for a long moment. "I want to get reacquainted. I want you to spend some quality time with us. Isn't that so, Pete? We're in agreement there."

Finley looked back and forth between them: the woman perched predatorily on the couch as if ready to pounce, the man leaning forward, elbows on his knees, slowly rubbing his hands together.

"You left me, so now you want me to leave my dad. How's that supposed to work?"

"Nah, now that's not what Lindy...your mother is saying, little gal. She's only suggesting—"

"Shush up!" the woman barked. "I admit I wasn't much of a mom, I wasn't any good at it. Your dad was a better mother to you than I was; I couldn't compete. I confess it, and I'm sorry. Of course you'd visit him. I wouldn't ever want to deny you your father."

"The thing is, Mom, are you reliable? Are you at all?"

The woman appeared stunned, swilling beer around at bottom of a bottle, studying it with a woeful smile, eyes closing tight, then opening wide as if seeing something unsettling there. She looked abruptly sideways at the man, perspiration beaded her brow. "Am I reliable, Peter? I understand your concern. Of course I do. I'll tell you what, sweetheart, let's take it one day at a time. Can we do that? You be the judge."

At that moment everything clicked—the nervous tic and bad answers, the inconsistencies: Finley knew this woman, whoever she might be, was not her mother. Dad once told her that Sondra didn't perspire, due to malfunctioning sweat glands or something which made her super susceptible to heat. But this woman—Lindy!—glistened and wilted with sweat. Finley recalled Patsy K Jones' and Lester's warnings about Internet trolls, how you arrived at the appointed meeting place and nothing was right: people weren't who they claimed to be, strange men were present. This woman, with the tinny voice and purple toenail polish and sweaty brow, was an impostor. Finley struggled to ward off a panic attack and stay in control, but she felt nauseous. She looked into the man's wily eyes, trying to ascertain whether the wolf intuited her fear. The woman placed a hand on her shoulder. When you sensed yourself in trouble, her father had advised her, you must let fear work for you and throw yourself wholly into the moment, seeking a way out. She leapt up and before even knowing what she was going to say said she needed to go to the bathroom.

The bathroom window offered no escape: a mere slit set deep in thick adobe walls. She was cornered. Through the cracked bathroom door, she heard them whisper-arguing in the front room, the woman saying, "I never agreed to this at all," the man insisting, "It has to be today. People will get suspicious." "We need to gain her trust first," the woman rejoined. What did they want from her? She had no money. What did they plan to do to her? She dreaded to imagine it: human trafficking and girls locked in cellars.

She dashed through the living room, saying she had left her backpack outside. It is through action, her father often said, that you learn what you need to do.

She fled blindly across the road and up a butte through chaparral, dodging cactus. Glancing back, she saw Pete emerge from the house behind her. She cut across a golf course on the far side of the hill; the desert scape abruptly ended and she was on an artificial carpet of thick green turf, like the Noonans' lawn. The little man came tripping full speed down the ragged slope behind her, nearly plunging headlong. Finley realized she had left her cell phone back with her belongings and had no way to call for help; all the 9-1-1 numbers in her life—Dad's, Mona's, Daphne's, Patsy K Jones'—were stored in her cell. Monster Mom had it. Her whole life in there. Her heart beat high in her chest, her sides ached, her lungs bellowed. Pete was gaining on her, his arms pumping fiercely. She waved both arms at a foursome of gray-haired golfers gathered at the tee on a fairway ahead and shouted. The men stood indifferently watching the chase, seemingly discussing it, while the little man gained on her; and she veered hard left into a stand of trees, seized control of her breathing and her pace, holding him at bay. She hadn't run cross country in high school for nothing.

She didn't know that her father, Mona, Little Lester, and Patsy K Jones were nearby, searching for her. They had driven all night to Albuquerque at Al's urging. They checked the bus station, motels, and restaurants, talked to the police, and filed a missing person's report, with nothing more to go on than Patsy K's recollection that the mystery woman on the Internet said she lived in Albuquerque. Little Les and Patsy K Jones asked people on the street if they'd seen the girl in a flyer they'd made up. No one had. If only they had checked the golf course a mile out of town, they might have encountered a foursome of gray-haired men who could have told them about the girl they saw dashing across a fairway, pursued by a small, ragged man, how they delayed teeing off, fearing the two were in range, and watched her disappear into a stand of cottonwoods. Her pursuer stopped mid fairway, resting hands on his knees and panting. "Get the hell outta-the-way," one of the golfers shouted at him. "Hold your horses," said another. "There's something fishy going on. Maybe we should call the cops." "It's none of our business," said a third. "For all we know, she's a druggie who robbed the guy's house." "For all we know he's out to rape her," said the fourth. They stared at him as if he'd made a wet fart.

Al was heartsick when they couldn't find her. His intuitive sensors told him they were close. Although the sense of alarm he was feeling could have been about Second Chance Acres rather than his daughter. He wanted to stay a few days and keep looking, but the others convinced him it was pointless, predicated on thin conjecture. "Fin said something about calling a number in Albuquerque," Patsy K Jones said. "PC check, that doesn't mean she's here. Not to worry, Al, she'll be okay; she has a good compass." Secretly, however, she was worried. She kept calling Finley's cell to no avail. Although once someone picked up; she could hear them listening, but they didn't speak.

"We need to get back home," Mona told Al, "and stop the hemorrhaging."

#

Harvey Suarez nailed the eviction order next to the last one posted on Al Sharpe's front gate. Charlie instructed him to put it in Al's hands, but there was no way he was walking back in there, given that demented pig, the naked fat lady, and Little Les who had been crazy ever since crawling into VC tunnels in Nam clutching a knife in his teeth. All of them were crazy. Moreover, that malicious black slough had swollen with the rain and extended its fat fingers across the property. No way in hell. Besides, he felt sorry for Al. It was his place, after all, not the bank's. He wasn't carrying water for any damn bank.

Al sat huddled at the mouth of the cavern he had carved in the mudstone wall of a side canyon, deep enough to keep a fire smoldering at its mouth, spluttering against the ceaseless downpour. He clutched his knees, *peering out through a vitreous sheet of water cascading down over the cave's mouth, thick as plate glass, nearly as solid, imagining Finley's face suspended midair beyond the waterfall, trying to tell him where she was. His ribs were still bruised from the beating he'd taken. Death, Pestilence, and Larry the Lion were bivouacked in their own cave nearby. Tinkerspoon would appear lizard-like, water beading on his plastic rain slicker. Giant slugs navigated damp cavern walls, their digestive tracts working under transparent skin. "Mass extinction, dudeski," Tinkerspoon said, the first words he'd spoken in days. "Then we'll get a Cambrian explosion of natural freaks."*

"Go to the cottage and dry out, Andy," Al insisted. "You'll catch your death."

"Dark toads, dude, rain in June, transparent slugs, and stink bugs in our sleeping bags. It ain't natural." Tinkerspoon licked up water pooled in a crevice of his slicker. It occurred to Al that Tink would flourish in a saner world that knew how to make use of him.

They slept in the cave that night, though Tinkerspoon smelled like a bog creature, their own Caliban, and were awakened early by the militant clatter of tank treads on the mesa above. Rocks and mud cascaded down canyon walls. At first, Al thought it a rain-induced mud slide, but the rain had stopped. Tinkerspoon seized his arm. "It's happening, dude, they come to fill your canyon." Al saw a gleaming blade atop the far wall and a dump truck load of dirt cascading over the ledge, cracking the branches of mesquite trees far below. The men slid down a breccia of mud and gravel and scrambled over heaps of rubble on the canyon floor, walls sloughing off all sides. A pumpkin-sized rock landed with a pock in soft mud not two feet from Al. He ran shouting into the main canyon. "Wake up! It's doomsday."

#

Clanking blades, creaking treads, shouting voices, Trinkley grinning down at us like a paunchy middle-aged kid, with his cap on backwards. I wanted to drive a stake through the fat fuck's heart. The preacher stood mid-canyon shaking a fist and cursing him in full-on Biblical rage, while gravel clattered down canyon walls. Little Les and Patsy K were interrupted mid orgasm on my living room floor. Les so angry he tried climbing straight up cliff walls to reach them through a hail of falling dirt. They had already buried Pissing Springs by the time I reached my lawyer Colin Allsport. He told me we might obtain a temporary restraining order, but he doubted it.

"Why temporary? It's my fucking property."

"Correction: it was your property." He reminded me of my missed mortgage payments. "You ignored eviction notices. They're going to respond, Al. You have to expect that."

"Not like this! Can't be legal. They switched banks on me, I didn't receive their notices."

"It won't fly, Al. You pay your mortgage every month like everyone else."

"I'm broke, I asked for an extension. I've got rocks falling on my head and Cal's goons kicking the shit out of me. My daughter is missing...."

"Slow down, Al. You need to know when you're beaten. You can't take on the whole bloody world."

"We can't let it keep spinning out of control either. Get that restraining order."

I heard shouts up on the mesa. Rob, Les, and Matt Littlefeather had climbed up rope ladders to reach Les's crows nest on top and were motioning men off D9 cats at gunpoint, wearing neckerchiefs over their faces like wild west outlaws. But no disguising Matt, biggest man in the valley, a tuft of unruly black hair sticking up off his head in a Mohawk. Operators climbed awkwardly down from excavating machines with their arms raised. A dump truck escaped along a dirt track back into the rez. Les fired a slug at it from his shotgun, which left an impressive hole. He wheeled and fired off a round at Trinkley's feet. "Didn't I warn you not to come back?" Trinkley slumped to his knees beside a low belly, mumbling, "Damned lunatic, you'll regret this." Matt Littlefeather yanked his chin up. "You're trespassing on Indian land over here, dipshit."

Trinkley's eyes looked panicked, but he couldn't help himself. "T.S.F., it's not yours any longer, chief. You're trespassing on the property of TexHome Mesa Manors." Floating a hand parallel to the mesas.

"This has been Indian land for 5,000 years," Sage shouted. His brother spooled out detonation wire from a knapsack and planted a charge under the huge wheel of a low belly. Rob motioned with his rifle for construction workers to "Git! Before I waste your sorry ass." They ran flat out for their pickups. Les advised us to clear the mesa; he was about to convert that low belly to a shit storm of shrapnel.

He grinned at Trinkley. "Except for you, you stay put. T.S.F." But Matt dragged him on his ass to the rope ladder and ordered Trinkley to climb down. "You're our insurance policy, fat man." Preacher Death stood below, calling down Sodom and Gomorrah hellfire on the violators of God's green earth. I realized we had just declared war.

The blast merely blew off two wheels. A low belly loaded with dirt makes for an impressive bunker. Men took up positions along the canyon rim like Geronimo's rebel warriors; women fled for town. I spent the night in Death and Pestilence's cave, huddled over the fire with Tinkerspoon and Patsy K Jones, who stared ahead, besot. "PC check, you can't just blow things up. People get righteously pissed off when you blow things up. I've got a brackish bad feeling about this." "Me, too," I said, "very brackish." I was worried sick about Finley and couldn't sleep. I should have stayed in Albuquerque. But Patsy K and Les were right: we couldn't be sure she was in Albuquerque; she could be anywhere.

Maybe five a.m. it began. A cool blue mist bathed the valley, coaxing up earthy scents of sage and creosote bush. What I'd taken for the throaty cooing of doves resolved to rumbling engines on Creosote Canyon Road. I heard a voice cry, "It's a dummy!"

#

Coming awake in the crow's nest, Matt Littlefeather heard someone call him a "dummy" and was about to fire back a volley of obscenities, but scrambled to his knees and peeked over a palisade of rocks at a small army of uniformed men on Creosote Canyon Road below: CHP crouched behind squad cars, FBI in blue wind breakers, and helmeted men in flack jackets and cammo gear swarming out of armored personnel carriers, .50 caliber M2 machine guns panning the ridge. "What the fucking fuck's fuck!" Matt dropped to his belly and covered his head with his hands. "It's a dummy," repeated a man who was sweeping Al's driveway for mines. "Fakes." He looked like the Pillsbury dough boy on TV in puffy layers of protective padding. Matt made out the balding pates of the Tweedledee Twins and considered firing a warning shot at them. A distant rumble came from beyond serried roofs of new houses to the east, as if Tahquitz had a belly ache, and an enormous armored bulldozer rounded the long curve in Creosote Canyon Road, its treads tearing up pavement, the biggest machine Matt had ever seen. His comrades snoozed on in their hideaways behind the rocks, while Little Les's 12 gauge leaned against a boulder. Matt made out a line of green Federal Marshal's cars approaching on a dirt track leading up onto the mesa.

"Wake the fuck up!" he shouted.

Binoculars and gun sights zeroed in on him. Little Les leapt to his feet and peered over the rock rim, immediately dropping to a crouch, while Rob Thompson stood like a scarecrow in his underwear, grinning and shaking a fist at the army below. "Whoopee, Lord! They called out the special forces." He stood out in the open shouting curses at them; Little Les tackled him. Matt rolled down a decline, away from the canyon rim, and crawled into a gap between jumbled boulders barely big enough to accommodate him, relieved to discover the crypt widened inside. It smelled of old bones. Sage had warned him not to go up top with "those loony birds." "There's a time to stand tall and a time to run, brother." Matt heard water dripping back in the cool damp darkness and hoped that Luella had gotten away safely. He grinned to think he'd nearly gotten his ass shot off for that obstinate SOB Al Sharpe.

Car doors slammed, footsteps came clattering past his hidey hole, and then it went dead quiet. Sam's Coalition had surrendered without firing a shot. It was hours before the K-9 squad arrived, dogs pawing and growling at the mouth of his hideout. Matt made out gleaming fangs and feared the dogs would come in after him. He crawled out on his belly and was surrounded by men who made ugly jokes about large Indians in small holes. They cuffed hands behind his back and shoved him, weak and bedraggled, into the backseat of a Federal Marshall's car. Rob Thompson sat in a car nearby looking defiant. No uprising is ever won in the first battle, Matt thought. There would be martyrs.

Meanwhile, police stood up behind squad cars on the road below, watching Little Les descend the west canyon wall on his dirt bike, leaping boulder to boulder and doing switchbacks midair, skidding sideways down a rough granite slope, making a 360-degree turn, and crash landing in a breccia of decaying granite and sandstone at the foot of the escarpment, rocks sliding down with him into Finley's meadow. Charlie Haynes applauded, but a CHP lieutenant shouted at his men to lock and load. Charlie ran along the firing line, waving his arms and commanding officers to hold their fire. Lines of command were blurred: four separate police agencies were involved in the raid, each with its own chain of command. FBI agents charged onto Second Chance Acres in pursuit of Les, past a sign warning DANGER QUICKMUD, thinking it another bogus warning like the land mines, until one of the agents sank in the muck. Another nearly stepped on Al Sharpe hidden in cattails at the slough's verge. Little Les released a piercing whistle, and Patsy K Jones materialized from the canyon.

Miraculously, they dodged agents and skirted the black slough, emerging onto the road with Patsy K perched on the handlebars, kicking at Les's ribs as if he were a horse. Les heard motorcycles revving behind them, radios crackling; he would have tried an ascent of the east wall of the mesa but knew it was hopeless with Patsy K Jones aboard. Motorcycles closed on them; he was about to lose hope when a wooden gate swung open in the stucco wall enclosing a development, admitting them and quickly closing again. Two grinning boys in backwards baseball caps—unlikely allies—waved them in, and they made good their escape through a maze of houses, zipped back across Creosote Canyon Road hidden by the behemoth dozer, and fled into La Cienega wilds. Gone.

18

FLIGHT

Al Sharpe lay concealed in rushes and salt grass at the edge of the black slough which affectionately suckled his toes like Wallers sometimes did. A dark toad, perched on a broad stink cabbage leaf inches from his nose, regarded him dispassionately. Beyond, in Finley's meadow, police were ransacking his cottage and the treehouse. Al watched Harvey Suarez string yellow don't-cross tape around the slough's perimeter not ten feet from where he lay. He could feel the gelatinous ground gurgle under his belly and knew it was just a matter of time before the slough swallowed him. Tinkerspoon's trailer groaned and snapped to pieces under the treads of a giant dozer, which backed up over the wreckage making loud beeping sounds like a computer in distress. Al hoped it hadn't crushed Tinkerspoon, hidden in the bunker beneath the trailer. Then the earth turned to jelly as the largest dozer Al had ever seen—treads and operator's cab shielded by armor plating—crashed through the brush, its great gleaming blade snipping up his work shed and leveling his cottage, adobe walls pulled under treads as if into the wringers of an old-fashioned washing machine. Remnants of his life popped out through shattered wood and pulverized adobe, including a segment of the living room mural: Sondra with a hand shielding her forehead, looking Amazonian. The Cat backed and filled atop ruins, completing the job, then pivoted toward Finley's treehouse, gentled high in the limbs of a giant black oak. Charlie Haynes blocked its path, shouting, "Stop! You people are in my jurisdiction."

The gleaming blade turned toward the slough, Al's hiding place. Cops applauded as the machine scraped up pepper trees and the Bad Things Cemetery and pushed them into bubbling muck. Al was trapped between the slough on one side and that huge blade approaching him on the other, with no hope of escape. It seemed a fitting end: Second Chance Acres, and he himself, sinking into the Ancient Salt Sea at center of the earth, the vortex of extinction. Although it seemed just as likely that he would be crushed under tractor treads. At the last moment, he watched a dark toad leap onto the concave metal blade as it loomed over them and spring away to safety *on the adjacent slough bank, much as skateboarders leap off a half pipe. More awkwardly, Al scrambled up onto the recurving steel just as it was scooping him up, rode the blade out over the slough, and sprang off onto the far bank, concealed from watching police by the huge machine—until it abruptly disappeared, swallowed by the black slough. Harvey Suarez said it went straight down "like a rock dropped in a mud puddle. We didn't have no chance to pull the operator out. Just down!" Men shouted, pointing at Al Sharpe who had managed to slap free of the muck and zig-zag away into the brush. Shots were fired. Cops lit out in pursuit. Some would blame him for the operator's death.*

As for Tinkerspoon, he wiggled up through the trap door of his bunker, pushing aside scraps of metal, wood, and insulation. He had heard the Cat treads rumbling overhead, causing the concrete walls of his bunker to quiver and crack with loud pops, and feared it would collapse atop him. It held. He drifted away like an electron, moving in and out of substantive form, excessed from a state of corporeal being.

Finley, too, at that moment, seemed fleeting and incorporeal. The sin-ewy little man (whom she called "Popeye") would have her clearly in his line of vision, chasing her down a fairway, and she would disappear over the lip of a green, melding Ariel-like into the landscape. Once, she headed straight for a golfing cart with two women aboard, waving her hands and calling urgently to them. They stopped and conferenced with her, throw-ing Popeye wary glances while he paced in circles a hundred feet off, like a hound that has pursued its prey up a tree. Then charged forward with renewed fury, yelling that the girl had stolen his wallet. She, trusting no one now, fled toward a water trap, a small lake, really. Behind her, she heard the women say something about calling 9-1-1, but that didn't deter Popeye Pete. He came at her full sprint, intending what? To drag her back to the adobe cottage, rape her, spill her blood? What did he want? No time to ponder; her mind was full of panic.

#

I don't run fast but I run far. I dove into a thicket of creosote bush and prickly pear, slid on my belly like a baseball player into dust and dried cactus husks. Men ran right past both sides. Pin-cushioned when I emerged, palms and belly full of thorns. Couldn't get across the road into *La Cienega* land: squad cars patrolled it, shotguns stuck out windows. Somewhere the yolky baying of hounds. Panic coursed through me. I scampered back to the slough, which belched diesel oil and Cat parts, and covered myself head to foot with handfuls of black muck roiling with maggots to hide my scent, expected it to smart something awful in cactus wounds. Instead, it neutralized their sting. I hung out all day near the slough, knowing they believed I'd gone on. High-strung bloodhounds, noses skimming the ground, dodged away from the slough as if electric shocked. Dried muck pulled at my skin; cactus thorns formed angry pustules. By nightfall, I was thirsty miserable and ready for a new hide. I scooped up handfuls of water from a puddle pulsing with mosquito nymphs, guessing it would make me sick. And considered my options:

1. Make my way to the rez.
2. Surrender to Charlie Haynes.
3. Set off cross country for Tahquitz's stronghold in the mountains.

Three seemed my best bet. But plans are futile for a fugitive. Opportunity dictates the plan. I crossed under the road via a culvert, sloshing through rank water on hands and knees, was running across *La Cienega* land at a good pace in the twilight when a helicopter sprang over a ridge and caught me in its spotlight as if sensing me there. I ran in that beam, loudspeakers commanding me to hit dirt; hairs on my arms and the back of my neck bristled in the glare. I imagined how it would feel to be shot: a stunning blow, then darkness. Or did pain come on gradually like a bee sting? Something snared my foot, and I slid down the sides of a pit which had opened abruptly beneath me, landing hard on my ass and blinking up into the yellow light of a kerosene lantern.

"Gotcha!"

A grinning hag face peered into mine in the dim light: crooked teeth, chapped lips, scraggly silver hair, nose a pocked, tuberous vegetable. I scampered away into a corner. Surely one of the "Mud People" Grandfather Lubo spoke of—Tahquitz's castoff wives, thousands of years old. Her breath earthy and sour, how I imagined gopher breath would smell. She reminded me of the trap door spiders Finley and I once collected, which lure their victims into underground lairs, pounce, and suck out their blood. Outside, I heard the chopper buzzing in furious circles high above the hatch that concealed the burrow. She cackled a laugh: "Now y' see 'em, now y' don't. Drives them little fuckers crazy."

"DayGlo," I cried. "Damn! I thought I was done for."

She whistled into a length of PVC pipe protruding from a dirt wall. "Get him, DayGlo?" a tiny, distant voice inquired. "Affirmative," she shouted reply through that underground intercom. "We been monitoring y'r progress, Alberto. Ugh, you smell like swamp shit." She ordered me to strip, dribbled water onto a rag from a Mason jar and sponged me down like a baby, nipping out cactus thorns with bony fingernails; I huddled naked, cupping a hand over my genitals. She brought me up to date: M&M had escaped into the mountains, as had Les and Patsy K, Matt and Rob were busted, Mona and Daph Thompson were off to town with Luella, Sage, and Wynona Littlefeather, and Tinkerspoon was anybody's guess. An earthquake had cracked the water main leading down from SAVWA's storage tanks and half flooded new developments.

"Earthquake?" I asked.

"There's been dozens. Ain't you noticed? The fault is come to life again. Mother Nature's on our side." Her grin was missing teeth. "They say stores in town is running low on food, together with half the country. Ches Noonan's breath is got so bad you can't hardly go up top without a rag over y'r mouth."

"Guess I stopped smelling it."

"They won't dare to speak the truth. People know but won't dare speak it. Like the Kennedys' assassination. It's blistering hot at the North Pole and raining cats and dogs in the Sahara. We're done for. Them builders is gone back to Texas, anyways. There's some Sam City folks talking about taking theirselves a new house, but I prefer my hidey hole to them morgues. Y'r thorny as a porcupine, Alberto. Tell you what! You want to wash your back side, you got to do that y'rself."

"Do you think copter cops saw me come down here?"

She patted my bare ass, holding me with her right eye while the left wandered. "Get dressed, Alberto. Y'll catch y'r death. People needs you and nature needs you. Y'r our last hope."

"Me? I am?"

There came a warning whistle through the intercom. DayGlo supplied me with water and rabbit jerky in a cloth bag and instructed me to rub myself down with sage to blend into the scent of the landscape, clapped my cheeks and told me to "git," cops were headed our way. "Don't worry none about me," she said. "I'll give 'em such a scare they won't pee for a month." She was a good witch dressed in rabbit skins.

Thus began my circuitous escape across *La Cienega* wastes. Doubling back to confuse the dogs, caking my shoe soles with coyote scat, holing up under bushes, often no more than fifty feet from my pursuers. I fled up dead-end canyons and doubled back over rock rubble, watching the cop posse pass below me from behind boulders, excited dogs howling. The third day, I saw that Geronimo Ortiz had joined the chase. Bad news. He could discern footprints on bare rock, would smell me through coyote scat. Fortunately, Geronimo was old and slow. I made my way from hideout to hideout, leading my pursuers in devious circles, harbored by Sam City fugitives who passed on sightings of Tinkerspoon or Les and Patsy K, but knew nothing of Finley. Couldn't say why or what I was fleeing exactly. SALCO and TexHome had trashed my life, not me theirs. But fleeing has its own logic. I would awaken from a mid-day cat nap and scurry out of a hidey hole just ahead of the posse. Sometimes I rested high in branches of a black oak tree, until a chopper buzzed low overhead. Sam City folks told me that half of them belonged to news organizations.

#

We were glued to our TV sets for news about Albert's flight. Bloggers who called themselves "Al's Allies" charted his route, while Saint Angelinos filled in the gaps with trickles of gossip from former Sam City people and local cops. I hung close by Al's side and did what I could for him. Mostly, I cheered him on. We all did.

Back in town, Mona's and Daphne's phones kept ringing. Caller ID said the calls were from Finley Sharpe, but the caller hung up when they answered. Not a good sign. "Run!" Mona shouted into the phone.

Popeye nearly caught Finley as she went over the chain-link fence separating the golf course from Route 85. He had her cornered. She leapt up onto the fence as high as she could, fingers snagging steel mesh, feet frantically seeking a toehold. He slammed against the chain-links beneath her, nearly knocking her off, and caught hold of her foot. She smashed his hand against chain-links with the other foot just as her fingertips were about to lose their grip on the wire. He cursed and let go. She clawed up the fence and went over, screaming at him, her face against the wire mesh on the far side mere inches from his. "What do you want? You going to kill me?" He coddled his injured fingers. "Now I might, little gal."

As a girl, Finley had loved playing capture the flag in the canyon lands with her father and the Littlefeather brothers. They taught her how to elude a pursuer, how you threw yourself behind a bush or rock and holed up, dead quiet, letting your pursuer pass. She knew Popeye would be over the fence quick as a cat once feeling returned to his fingers. She fled across the freeway through swerving traffic and blaring horns, tucked and rolled down the embankment and hid in a ragged, garbage-strewn saltbush thicket. Sixty seconds later, Popeye came sliding down the embankment in pursuit, not fifty feet away; he glanced both ways along the highway verge, then moved on into a motel parking lot, dodging between parked cars, looking for her. Finley crawled through a culvert back under the road, over muck and stagnant water. Another principle of escape: backtrack to your starting point. No one expected you to return to the place from which you had fled.

Time and again, when police had him cornered, her father ducked behind a clump of sagebrush and disappeared. CNN filmed one such episode. "He's there, then he isn't!" the commentator cried in amazement. Al Sharpe was a You-Tube sensation; people followed him on mobile devices and discussed him with strangers. He was an escape artist super-hero who could vanish at will in broad daylight, climb straight up ravine walls like Spiderman, subsist without water, food, or rest like El Coyote. Some claimed he could make himself invisible. "The guy's better than Houdini," one cop told a reporter. "It's an honor to pursue him." When murder was added to other charges against Sharpe, we muttered collective protest, recalling that authorities had charged him with manslaughter for the death of a heavy-equipment operator before learning the huge Cat tractor was remote controlled. A bookie in Las Vegas started a betting pool, wagering how long Al could evade capture. In various MFA writing programs across the country, young writers started novels about him. A Fox News commentator suggested that he captured the American spirit like no one since Davy Crockett: "Freedom and resistance to tyranny."

But the old hunting guide Geronimo Ortiz deflated the myth of Al's disappearing powers, noting seams in the ground where his footprints abruptly ended. Police used dogs to ferret earth squatters out of their underground cubby holes where Al was finding shelter and sustenance. A right wing talk radio host compared "Al's army of underground trolls" to "the commie underground back in the day."

Al was forced to escape across the Juan Antonio Hills into the Badlands, a wasteland of wind-sculpted dunes and mudstone hills rifted by dry arroyos, where nothing survived but cholla cactus, and there was thought to be no water source in the summer. It had turned beastly hot. Al holed up during the day and traveled at night, hoping to reach the San Jacinto Wilderness. To elude canny old Geronimo Ortiz, he entered ravines and climbed part way up walls at canyons' terminus, clawing toeholds in rotting sandstone, then backed out of the canyon, covering his tracks with fine sand, or traversing a breccia of gravel and stone at the base of a wall, which didn't readily reveal his passage. He jogged all one afternoon over the northwest corner of the Badlands, flattening himself against the ground when choppers passed over (he had strapped a thatch of tumbleweeds to his back so that, lying prone, he blended seamlessly into the desert-scape). He'd begun to think he had a certain flair for escape. After all, he'd been escaping his entire life.

Standing on a mesa before dusk, looking down on a blighted Badlands moonscape, Al despaired. His footsteps would expand in the sand so any novice could track him. Wind-borne sand might cover his tracks, but it could also blind him. Temperatures reached 160 degrees on the desert floor. He considered giving himself up. The air, once so clear and sweet in the high places, was gagging foul. Ches's breath had infected pullulating sloughs in the valley with a festering turmoil of maggots; the air had spoiled. But things can always get worse. He saw a horse posse traversing a saddle in the hills from the La Cienega side. Though his legs ached, he set off at a run: kin to Jesse James, Billy the Kid, and Willie Boy, an outlaw son of the wild west.

Finley re-passed that foursome of golfers in polo shirts and Arnold Palmer visors standing on a green pointing their putter handles at her. She waved, refusing to look back to see if Popeye was following. Her father made that a first principle: never look back. It was a philosophy she often discussed with Patsy K Jones, who repudiated it. "PC check, you can't know where you're going if you don't know where you've been."

That night, Patsy K watched headlights disappear into dips behind them on Dead Creek Canyon road and reappear again atop rises. "Evasion check," she shouted over her shoulder at Les and gripped the handlebars she was perched on, expecting him to veer off road down the loose gravel of the embankment. But Les held steady. Defiant, she wondered, or spacing out? The van gained on them along the straightaway: cops, or construction dickwipes, or Cal's loonies? She squinted back into blinding headlights. "I think we better bail, Lester." He pedaled blithely on, humming that phrase he loved from "A Whiter Shade of Pale." Sixties check! Lester could play it safe or perilous, you never knew which.

Early that morning, hidden in chaparral on a hill top overlooking what had been Sam City—dwellings crushed and pushed into berms—they had been awakened by a chopper skimming over a nearby ridge. Les shouted "Dust-off" and rolled onto his stomach, hands shielding his head, lost in a Vietnam flashback. They didn't imagine all the fuss was over Al Sharpe.

The van's headlights, she could swear, went on high alert just behind them. "It's a free country," Lester said, defiant, flipping off the van, which swerved over and slammed into them as it passed: a strident clang of metal on metal. At the last instant, Patsy K Jones made out the driver's clenched teeth, then was launched forward off the handlebars (Les's hands against her back) and ran midair as long jumpers do, landing on her feet half way down the embankment, pausing a moment before tucking and rolling. She landed hard at the bottom. When she opened her eyes, she thought for a moment that her back was broken. Her hand found a beer bottle in the road ditch. She stood up, gripping the bottle, watching figures pantomime through dust motes in headlight beams on the road above. A bald head glowed minaciously red, arms flailed. There were shouts—whether they at her or she at them she wasn't sure—as she charged uphill at them, brandishing the bottle overhead, numb and fearless.

"I wouldn't of thought Al Sharpe capable of crushing a man's skull," Charlie Haynes was saying, "but I never knew this running side of him either." The posse had split in two when Al's path diverged into two distinct tracks a short way into the Badlands. Seemingly, he was circling back in his tracks, and the two groups, approaching from opposite directions, would surely close in on him. But they had gone far enough that this logic was breaking down. No man could run fast enough to circle back repeatedly on himself without being overtaken. They were aware of the legend growing around him and exchanged wild theories of their own, camped as they were that night at Willie Boy Rock. Some believed there were more than one of him. "There's times I swear he's watching us," Harvey Suarez said.

"Is this like those cockamamie stories that he can disappear into thin air," Charlie Haynes admonished him.

"I seen him twice, only it wasn't him." Harvey stared into a fire of crackling cactus joints, knowing his boss would disapprove of such talk.

Geronimo Ortiz nodded gravely. "I seen him, too."

"Maybe it was the horse's ass in front of you." Charlie nodded at Cal Hale.

A rancher named Alvarez from Purgatory told the story of Willie Boy, a Paiute Indian in the early 1900s who killed his girlfriend's father in a fit of drunken rage, then lit out across the Conchilla Desert near Palm Springs pursued by fifty men. Willie Boy covered forty miles of desert a day, barefoot, without water or food. He kept doubling back, outsmarting his pursuers with his superior knowledge of the terrain, sometimes lying not twenty feet from where they camped. The men threw wary glances beyond the meager circle of their campfire. "It only ended when he shot himself," Alvarez said. *"Papers back east was full of it. Maybe this Sharpe fellow is got some Willie Boy in him. You want my opinion, he's lying out there belly up somewheres. Vulture bait."*

"I hope not," Charlie said. "I'd like him to have a chance to clear himself."

"Not a snowball's chance in hell," snapped a Riverside deputy. "We got two murders over to Ironwood where victims were clubbed to death, like your man over here on Dead Creek Canyon Road."

"We're still waiting for lab reports on that," Charlie said. "I'd like to know how a man could travel on foot from Juan Antonio Hills to the murder site on Dead Creek Canyon Road and back again in two days with a hundred men on his tail. It must be eighty miles."

"Maybe they got him rigged up bionic or something. They say his pal is a computer whiz."

"Now that's a load of horseshit. Al Sharpe's different, but he's no freak." Charlie feared to think what the second posse, composed entirely of Riverside deputies, would do if they found Sharpe first. Or what Cal Hale would do. He kept an eye on him.

Al Sharpe lay atop a granite boulder behind their camp listening to the men's speculations. Under different circumstances, he might have been amused, but he was dehydrated and hungry, his feet swollen, lips so badly chapped it was agony to open his mouth. His left leg spasmed; he massaged it, terrified of making a sound. His ribs were still sore from the beating Cal Hale's men had given him. Once the lawmen were asleep, he would set off again. By day he must shelter from the fierce sun. It was their routine: he ran by night, they trailed by day, since Geronimo's night vision was poor. He tried to stay just ahead of them to keep track of their progress, an unorthodox form of flight.

That afternoon, seeing riders approach closer than he'd expected them to be, Al rolled to the bottom of a sand dune and burrowed into sand so hot it scalded his skin. Horses came sloshing down the slope, hooves knifing into sand around him in confused circles. Incredibly, they didn't step on him. Riders shouted that he had backtracked on them again and rode *off.* Al rose from his sandy grave, spitting out grit, and crawled to the top of the next dune from which he made out a far off ridge above shimmering heat waves, the boundary of the San Jacinto Wilderness. Freedom. His more immediate goal was Harkin's Tank, a natural basin where rain water collected at base of a rocky reef. He was suffering severe dehydration. He had awakened from indifferent sleep some hours earlier to find, lying beside him, a mysterious map sketched in charcoal on a rabbit skin, guiding him to the tank. Sometimes they left him bottles of water, or dried fruit, or vivid dreams of The Ancient Ones. He caught fleeting glimpses of them at times, what Sage Littlefeather called "the old ones." Once, when he collapsed face down in the sand, DayGlo and an Ancient who resembled Sage helped him to his feet. The landscape he traversed was becoming less wasteland than state of delirium. Lizards stood on their hind legs and cheered him on like onlookers along a marathon route, whistling hawks floated high overhead, pointing the way with their wings. At times, fatigued beyond endurance, he sat on a wind-blown shelf, lacking strength to shield his eyes from the abrasive sand blast, and awaited his pursuers, ready to surrender. What in hell was taking them so long? Finally, he gave up and trudged on.

Finding the granite basin brim full, Al lay on his belly and lapped up water with his tongue as coyotes and lizards do. It tasted vaguely of alkaline but blessedly wet. Ten minutes later the posse arrived; Charlie Haynes had surmised that Al would make his way to the tank. Al listened from behind a rock to Cal telling how Ches Noonan had caught Sharpe swimming bare-assed naked with Penny Noonan in his pool twice in the past week. "That's ridiculous," Charlie scoffed. "Who in hell have we been chasing then?" Al drifted off into a dream so vivid that it cast a spell on him for days to come.

#

I'd moved into the Noonan place with Mona and Penny. We lounged naked about the pool, the gals rubbed soothing lotions into my skin, while Ches looked on, frozen in a block of ice, hot breath forming a bubble around his head.

I woke to the dying glow of their campfire which painted sandstone boulders orange; surrounding dunes glowed like glistening mounds of snow in the moonlight. Harvey Suarez had nodded off on guard duty near the tethered horses, which snorted and pawed the ground when I fled past towards the San Jacintos and safety. Willie Boy watched me from atop a dune. I crossed a wash at dawn and went in among mesquite, heard horse hooves clopping over hard clay. A horse crashed through the brush and clattered to a stop in gravel. Cal Hale raised his rifle, a watery blue eye poised in the gun sight, the sky behind him blood red. "Hell, you could shoot a man out here and wouldn't nobody know but the buzzards."

"And the Indians." Sage Littlefeather materialized behind Cal, his lasso snaring and toppling him from his horse. Shadowy others emerged from the rocks, bare-chested, hair braided Comanche style. I thanked them for leaving me food and water, mounted Cal's horse and galloped off into the mountains.

When I actually did awaken, the sun was high overhead, my pursuers gone. I'd had my first real sleep in days. Scooping up handfuls of water from Harkin's Tank, I heard a hoarse cough from a rock ledge above. A mountain lion guarding its water hole. I stood slowly up and backed away step by step, hands raised in surrender, hoping the cat craved only water, not red meat. I could see its tail flicking atop the ledge. I set off in the direction from which I'd come—away from mountains, and cougars, and the posse that was pursuing me—back toward the Juan Antonio Hills, knowing my best chance of escape was returning to where I'd started. Occasionally, I heard a far off chopper, but saw nothing of my pursuers besides their tracks. I reached the Juan Antonio Hills just before dark, crossed over a saddle, and followed Weeping Springs Canyon down towards Saint Angel. Incredible what vigor resolve brings even to the wasted.

Hours later, I slipped over the perimeter wall and through the Noonans' guest room window, wondering if Penny had left it unlatched for me. Ches's pickup wasn't in the drive, though the air was foul and caustic. A reptile peered back at me from mirrored closet doors: skin scaly, eyes swollen closed. Surely not me. I lapped water from the bathroom spigot until my belly ached and capillaries swelled in my head and washed my face, leaving a white towel soiled with grime. Occurred to me I might lay down to sleep on the guest room bed and not be discovered for days. What better hideout than your enemy's house? But I had another agenda—offspring of delirium perhaps.

Stepping out of the guest room, I heard Penny on her cell—in the master bedroom? I tiptoed down the dark hallway, heart in my throat. Penny stepped around a corner and nearly collided with me in the darkness. She screamed; I caught a hand over her mouth. She trembled in my arms and stumbled away when I released her. "My God! You smell something dreadful, Albert."

"Yeah, I could use a shower."

"Hmmmph. Ah sah-pose you came to murder us, like poor what's-'is-name."

"I didn't murder anybody. Jesus, Penny, what do you take me for?"

"Ah couldn't say anymore. They found a body in your swamp, your tattooed soldier pal."

"Little Lester? Little Les was murdered?" I remembered the posse talking of murder that night in the desert.

"Mah husband is next, ah sah-pose. Why else would you come here of all places?"

"I hoped you...hoped I could hole up in the guest room a few days."

"And ah should bring you table scraps? Slip back and screw you once Daddy goes to bed?" She howled laughter.

"Listen, Penny, I'm in deep shit here. Deep deep shit."

"You want to hide in mah home? That's about pathetic, Albert. That's hilarious...if it wasn't pure lunacy. Ah'm dialing 9-1-1." She had her cell. "You best run. Ah b'lieve you lack the moral fortitude to hurt me. Daddy would crush you like a grape."

"Damn it, Penny, why would I hurt you?" I grabbed her keys off the entryway hutch and fled in her Caddy. How could I have imagined that Penny Noonan would offer me refuge?

#

She backtracked nearly in her own footsteps, crossing the golf course, and going back up over the hill toward the adobe cottage. Never looking back. As she crested the rise, she heard scuffling behind her and threw up her hands. "You are a scuzzy coward, okay." Turning to face him, she saw a jackrabbit bound away through the scrub, leaping high in the air, as lean and sinewy as Popeye. She picked up a heavy granite stone from a road ditch and knocked on the cottage door. The woman, Lindy, stood in the doorway staring at her and the rock she was holding, her face befuddled with fear. "I want my stuff," Finley insisted. "My phone. Now!" When the woman brought them, Finley asked what they had wanted from her.

"Friendship," Lindy said. "We just wanted your friendship, sweetheart. I couldn't have children of my own."

#

I ditched Penny's caddy near Bautista Wash and walked west along the wash channel towards Tourmaline, leaving footprints in soft mud, then backtracked east through ankle-deep water to conceal my passage. Police would think I'd fled in the opposite direction. I followed a stream of water coursing along the paved channel between sloping concrete walls that glowed chalk white in the moonlight, occasionally making out a dark circle low on a wall—iron hatches covering storm sewer culverts that fed the wash. Bog breath had lifted from the land, the air crisp and clear, vivid stars overhead. Reaching the spot where creepers covered canal walls and half concealed one of the hatches—just as Les had described it—I found the iron bar he said would be there and rapped on the hatch. Muffled gongs hung on still air. No response. The hatch let out an agonized squeal when I opened it, thin yellow light spilled out into darkness. "Lester? Anyone home?" Nothing. I ducked inside and closed the hatch behind me. "So you're alive, old buddy? Thank God." Nothing. Candles burned atop wooden crates, arching walls of the huge culvert held the ancient patina of a medieval castle, glazed with wood smoke. Cloth bunting and Sixties rock posters decorated walls, along with papier-mâché figures in bas relief: bare-breasted Indian goddesses that appeared to have broken through concrete. Feathered fetishes. Spooky-hip coziness. A bed stretched wall to wall in shadows at the back. Water dripped somewhere in the darkness. I made out a figure huddled on the bed, watching me, eyes aglow in the darkness.

"Patsy K, is that you, hon?"

Nothing.

"Are you all right, hon? It's Al. I never quite believed this place existed. Where's Les?"

"Lester is dead," she said in a monotone. "They killed him."

"Who did?"

"The people who beat you up, that baldy fuck and Cal's goons."

She was scratched up, full of cactus thorns. For two days, she said, she'd been trying to work up courage to go out and call her parents. No trace of the brazen Patsy K Jones in this cringing girl. I sat on the bed and held her. She traced fingers over my face. "Is it really you, Dad? I thought they killed everybody."

"Yes, it's really me."

Patsy K told how they were run down. Les went down hard on the pavement. Trinkley and his men kicked and clubbed him with tire irons. "Fucking animals. I came up the embankment and hit one with a bottle. Another knocked me down and straddled me. He ripped off my shorts, he was going to rape me, but I butted him in the face when he unzipped his pants, like Les taught me to do. I slid down the embankment into a cactus patch. It saved my life, they didn't follow. I didn't feel the thorns until later. They're everywhere: my hands, my ass, my knees, the soles of my feet." She touched my hand. "I know they killed him—all that blood."

I told her the police had found his body near the black slough.

I pulled out what thorns I could with my teeth. Pitiful, her skin puffy and festering. I washed her and cleansed her wounds, got her properly to bed. "Tomorrow we'll go after the men who did this." I lay awake, past exhaustion, beyond despair. Lester dead, Finley missing, Second Chance Acres destroyed—our homes and lives.

I woke Patsy K before dawn. She smiled and reached to stroke my cheek, then her face fell under the weight of recollection. "Dad...it's you. I thought..." I touched a finger to her lips.

"Listen, Patsy K, do you think you can make it to Mona's place in town?"

She limped painfully around the dirt floor. "I think so."

"Go with her to Charlie Haynes and tell him what happened, just what you told me." It didn't occur to me until after she'd left that Charlie was likely still out hunting me.

#

Second Chance Acres was scoured bare by dozer blades, but for brush around the black slough and large oaks and sycamores at the canyon's mouth. The remnants of Al's cottage and shattered fruit trees were pushed into windrows for burning. Incredibly, Finley's treehouse remained intact, a note pinned to a ladder rung:

> **are you okay, dad? please call me. i want to kill
> the whole fucking world. love you, finley**

Al couldn't imagine how it had gotten there. It appeared to be her handwriting. Had she returned from wherever she'd gotten off to? He had no phone to call her.

Heat and humidity were already intolerable at seven a.m.. A hurricane in Mexico had brought monsoonal soupiness, but no rain. Al heard a tractor engine up on the mesa. By the time he pulled boards off windows and entered the treehouse, dump trucks moved sluggishly past, carrying dirt to fill his canyon. They would knock down the mountains and fill the oceans; there would be one endless city covering all the continents and Oceania between. They would name it New Atlantis or Globetown. The "excessed" might take refuge in the Ancient Salt Sea, ferrying pairs of the earth's creatures down with them on submersible arks. But where to find trees enough to build them?

Police arrived shortly. Al staggered out onto the treehouse deck to greet them: an army of CHP troopers, Feds, and sheriff's deputies, a SWAT team from Riverside. Men advanced in formation like British Redcoats, shoulder to shoulder, automatic weapons at port arms, trailed by an army of journalists (vans with dish antennas parked on the road), and behind them demonstrators: Devastation Acres folks, townspeople, fist-waving college students who considered Al Sharpe a Green hero. All those gun barrels fixed on him. A cop with a bullhorn ordered Al to strip to his skivvies and climb down. Protestors shouted at him to stay put. Al did as he was ordered, standing stiffly on the ground while cops circled behind him. They kept their distance, posed in wide-legged stances like German storm troopers. He was Sitting Bull, rumored to have supernatural powers, able to catch bullets in his teeth. Tinkerspoon appeared out of nowhere and joined him, his arms raised high. "Hope they don't shoot us in the back, dude." Police probed the bushes for others. The crowd was becoming surly; naked Sam City people emerged from bushes and surrounded the cops. The deputy with the bullhorn shouted, "Disperse! At once!" Larry the Lion, with his shaggy mane of orange hair, defied him, pointing imperiously toward the black slough, shouting, "That way, Al. Run for it!"

He could skirt the slough and make his way up onto rez land. The crowd would provide all the cover he needed until he reached the thicket of sedge and cattails surrounding the amoebic muck, but Al told himself he was done running. His feet, however, had their own agenda. He burst through Sam City people and ran straight at the police line, a CHP officer's twin shotgun barrels aimed at his stomach. He could dodge the cop, but, locking eyes with him, Al felt anger balloon in his head and burst in full-on mind rage. He would carry the complicitous bastard with him into tarry death or run right over the SOB. Al grit his teeth, as the officer did, and leapt into the air just as the man squeezed the trigger. He felt the double blast of shot rush between his legs, his knees slammed the officer's shoulders, and Al rode him to the ground, then scrambled forward on hands and knees through salt grass. He was up and running, propelled forward by the surge of shouts behind him:

RUN ALBERT   *TAKE HIM DOWN*

*   He ran straight ahead over the slough's glazed surface. Incredulous witnesses would talk of Jesus striding atop Galilee's waters. However, the slough's surface was nothing like water, rather like the hard crust that forms atop drying cow paddies: soft/hard at once, seductive in the devious way of black cienegas. It gave under his weight; he sank a bit farther in with each step and could feel amoebic muck tugging at his shoes. It sounded like someone was shooting off firecrackers, which popped in the air near his ears. Gunshots, he realized. It amused him that cops were such poor shots, though maybe these were warning shots. Then a bullet nipped his shoulder, taking cloth and flesh. Hearing the erratic percussions from the firing line behind, Al realized he wouldn't hear the shot that killed him. He was pondering that existential irony when his left foot sank into elastic pudding, his right foot just kicking forward when Al's intestines exploded through skin below his navel and tore away a swatch of T-shirt. Transported with wonder through that distended, slow-motion moment, he watched the bullet burst rudely out from inside his belly, carrying white, coiled, spasming guts in tow. His cupped hands attempted to catch blood jetting outward in a graceful arc and hanging in a mist on the air. Such a pity to lose all this: life, Finley, Second Chance Acres, Saint Angel, his own puny self. He might have been devastated, finished right then, but there were practicalities to consider: should he try to reach the slough's far verge before collapsing, belly-down, atop dark toads, his fingers clawing for a hold in Second Chance mud? Or relinquish all to mother earth and plunge straight down into the slough's grumbling maw, leaving no body for Finley and his friends to dispose of, no paltry, broken trace of self? He was, after all, a firm believer in recycling, all things returned to the whole. Eventually, he would wend his way down through fissures in the earth's crust to reach the Ancient Salt Sea, or the slough's acidic chemicals—tannic acid and formic acid—would preserve him intact like a bog man, or he would merge with that dense organic soup and become slough muck himself. An odd, insistent buzzing*

filled the air. Maggots, which had formed a pelt over the black slough and wriggled into the crevices of tree bark, had completed their metamorphosis and launched forth in a skirling black flight of flies, a darting, susurrant cloud that darkened the sun, flew into mouths and ears, and whirled over the ground in evil, opportunistic dust devils.

#

I lie on my back on solid land, my legs in roiling slough muck. Looking down at the wound in my belly, I am relieved to see it is off to one side, a clean shot, blood welling out of it, but no trace of eviscerated intestines. Incredible. Seemingly, I'd imagined that. Flies swarm over my face and form a restless, scheming pellicle over the wound. I hear men's voices approaching: Charlie Haynes with a small contingent of police and EMTs carrying a stretcher. He hitches up his belt and casts an angry eye about the place. "What have those sons of bitches done? Looks like they shot you, Al."

They carry me out through a haze and shift of swarming flies. I am aware of Tinkerspoon emerging from the bushes to turn himself in. "I can't live like this no more, dude." He smells so bad that Harvey Suarez refuses to put him in his squad car unless they wrap him in a blanket. All around us, birds are gorging on flies, catching them midair or pecking them off the ground. A regular love feast.

Paramedics work me over on the way to the hospital, applying compresses, fixing an oxygen mask over my mouth. Charlie rides with us, telling me they checked Patsy K Jones into Saint Angel General. "I promised her we'd get the bastards. I told those damn fools you weren't capable of a thing like that. But what do I know? I'm just a small town cop. One question, Al, would you have surrendered if it was just me come out to bring you in? None of this running nonsense?" I nod at him. "I thought so. We've got a big surprise waiting for you at the hospital," he says.

I wake to Finley leaning over my bed. "I missed you, Dad. I missed Second Chance Acres. They've like totally trashed it." Her voice convulses in a sob. Mona is there, too, rubbing fingers through my hair. "Wheeewy, one big tangle." Leaning her forehead against mine.

"Where have you been?" I ask my daughter. "I've been worried sick about you."

"Doing something stupid, okay, brackishly stupid. I'm over that now."

I take her hand. "We haven't spent all our chances yet. Not by nearly."

Mona tells me developers have cleared out, like locusts she'd seen in Iowa as a girl. "They came in, devoured everything, and left." Her vague gray eyes hold mine. Charlie Haynes says, "Someone else can charge you with evading arrest, Sharpe, I won't. I'll tell you what, you're a free man." He tells how they chased a Mexican illegal half way up Tahquitz Mountain, believing it was me. "Scared hell out of the poor man. You want my opinion, every time old Geronimo got a whiff of you he led us off somewheres else. Him and Sage. That's the way we are, we hang together. We'll get those murdering bastards yet. I guarantee it."

EPILOGUE

So it ends. *Almost. Wallers emerged from the canyon with Death and Pestilence. It was rumored that they survived on a mash of maggots and honey mesquite beans. As things sorted out, charges were dropped against Rob Thompson and Matt Littlefeather. Trinkley and three companions were arrested the day of Little Lester's funeral and charged with aggravated assault and first degree murder. The memorial service was held down in the wash channel at Patsy K Jones's behest, and Little Les's ashes were sprinkled into the stream of water meandering westward. Most of St. Angel was there. People sat atop channel walls, feet dangling, or milled about, peering wondrously into Les's culvert home. They resolved to rename the channel "The Lester Edwards Memorial Wash." It was a funeral, everyone understood, not just for Les but for the troubled time he was martyred to and the death of a town no one wanted ours to become. Even DGLA Silk Setters paid their respects. "I didn't really know him," Mrs. Philadelphia said, "but I truly wish I had." The first stirring of a Desert Green Lawn Association revival on the wind. "Like it used to be," Imogene Sylvester said, "before we lost our sense of perspective."*

Matt Littlefeather and Luella married in September. Al and Mona decided not to marry and spoil a good thing. A sheriff's deputy from Riverside was suspended pending an internal investigation of his role in shooting Al Sharpe, a fleeing, unarmed man. Irate over the manner in which TexHome, World Wide Financial Corp., SALCO, and law enforcement agencies violated Al Sharpe's property rights and civil liberties, a Riverside Superior Court Judge dismissed charges against him. "A man's home is his castle," he reprimanded corporate counsel in the civil suit that followed. "We lose sight of that principle and we lose everything." He ordered plaintiffs to restore Al Sharpe's and Tinkerspoon's property to them in its previous condition. When lawyers complained in chambers that Sharpe and his people had damaged their clients' heavy equipment, the judge snapped, "I'd have blown it to hell if it trespassed on my place."

Al's attorney, Colin Allsport, struck a deal with developers and the bank to forgive Al's debts if he agreed to drop his suit against them. The black slough made his land worthless anyway. The court found Tinkerspoon's antics so amusing that the presiding judge gave him a light sentence and wondered aloud why the Pentagon didn't make use of such a valuable national resource.

Newcomers mostly moved back to Orange County. The few who remained soon learned our ways and are welcome additions to Saint Angel. A few locals moved in to the abandoned suburbs, though, by and large, houses out Creosote Canyon Road and elsewhere disappeared board by board, supplying the Tri-Cities' renovation needs for years to come. Only bare concrete slabs remain, overgrown with sage and desert creepers like tributes to a lost civilization: Ozymandias Saint Angel style.

Perhaps the most significant event was what became known as "the Millennial Earthquake," which cracked the vast pluton dam of solid granite thousands of feet down at west end of Saint Angel Valley. Water stored in the second aquifer whooshed along subterranean fissures toward the sea. In places along the fault line, the ground subsided and black sloughs bubbled up. Without water, the land in our valley became worthless again, refuge for the excessed, the unwanted, the ex-convict, and ne'r-do-well. No place for lovers of green lawns and blue pools. Suburban lakes dried up, golf courses turned brown, and sand crept over the greens again. Everywhere, the bleached bones of houses stood as monuments to greed and human folly.

#

We were right back to where we started. Not much water. Never had been. I got to work in earnest on my desalination plant. My new cabin lacked the charm of the adobe cottage, but it had better plumbing. I'd asked TexHome to spread fill dirt they'd dumped back in my canyon evenly over the canyon floor, and Sam City people farmed it, growing corn and squash as the Anasazi did for centuries in Canyon de Chelly. Regular Garden of Eden. Some took up permanent residence in Sam City, claiming the land by right of occupancy in the face of conflicting title claims. Tinkerspoon bought vintage cars on his settlement earnings and began restoring them. "I need to get away from electrons, dude," he said. "I need to get my hands dirty." Poor Patsy K grieved Little Les's death for years; she'd fallen brackishly hard for him. You can't replace a soul mate.

I ran into Ches Noonan downtown one day some months after it ended. He looked much as he had in the old DGLA days: spiffy, crisp new shirt and polyester slacks, hairline restored (new rug, I guessed). A hint of peppermint on his breath. He said he'd been forced to put their house on the market, shaking his head incredulously. "I've taken big losses. Suppose I got a bit overextended. Dreams, that's my problem."

"They can get ahead of you," I agreed. "Be careful what you wish for and all."

Ches nodded. "Dreams are dreams," he said. "There's no containing them."

"I understand Cal's been implicated in Sam Jenson's death."

"You always said he was guilty. Doesn't surprise me. Cal is uncouth; he always left the toilet seat up." Ches clapped my shoulder. "You know, I used to take you for an example of what I didn't wish to be, Sharpe. No offense. A certain lack of—" a smile played over his lips "—ambition. Your lawn, for example." A whiff of the old halitosis returning.

"The desert is no place for lawns, Ches. Seems you would have learned that by now. I came to believe you controlled the whole works: SAVWA, SALCO, the DGLA. Now it appears you didn't."

Ches laughed hugely. "One hell of a load of acronyms, isn't it? Nobody controls, Albert. I'd think you would have learned that. It's like a stone rolling downhill. We try to keep up with it, that's all we can do. No one controls. It turned a bit unpleasant there at the end."

"Little Lester." I nodded.

"Terrible thing, terrible." Ches shook his head. "Violence!" Spitting the word out of his mouth. "Incredible what you learn about people. We have to try to live together, after all."

"Amen. Let's do that."

We shook hands there on the street and went our separate ways. However, I looked back to catch Ches watching me as he got into his car parked at the curb. "You should come visit, Albert," he called. "We would like that. Penny would love to see you."

I froze right up, convoluted feelings rushing me all in a jumble. But I waved and nodded. "I'll do that." Plucked two quarters from a little pile at curbside to feed my meter and made a mental note to repay them. No doubt he'd tell Penny he had seen me. I remembered how we'd flirted innocently by the pool. Maybe Ches was right: it's like a stone rolling downhill, we can't control it.

When finally we did see each other—the Noonans invited us all over for the traditional Thanksgiving feed—Penny and I were amiable, mutually deciding that nothing had happened between us. Just a vivid fantasy. Maybe it all was. You'd think so, the way we gorged and laughed and celebrated the Noonans' new mortgage and Finley's acceptance at Berkeley. Mr. Philadelphia said, "She takes after her old man." We toasted the resurrection of the Desert Green Lawn Association, and Mrs. Philadelphia and Imogene Sylvester, Daphne Thompson, and Mona stripped to their skivvies and leapt in the pool. Cal Hale, who was found not guilty of manslaughter, toasted Sam Jenson, tears pooling in his eyes. "Dammit I miss the old son of a bitch." Ches announced solemnly that he was donating Sam's former land for the establishment of the:

SAM JENSON HIGH DESERT PARK AND MEMORIAL MUSEUM

The DGLA's first project would be to restore the place to its original condition—junker cars, Christmas lights and all. Sage Littlefeather raised his beer bottle to second the motion. We would put Tinkerspoon's old computers on display, Sam's baseball cap and folding aluminum lawn chair, a bust of Wallers (who'd died in his sleep that fall), flyers from the Realty Roundup and Revenge, copies of *Saint Angel's Dirty Underwear*, Wynona Littlefeather's kachina dolls, Les's crushed bicycle, and Winky Hale's swan-feathered angel. The moment we started work out at Sam's place, black sloughs began to subside, dark toads disappeared, and the mountain stopped grumbling. Old Tahquitz was appeased.

So we are back to normal again here in the Kingdom of The Excessed. Waiting, Rob Thompson says, for the next onslaught. I disagree with him. Disaster is never inevitable. We go about life in our separate ways which tangle together in a single ravel, one strand inextricably linked with the others. We are never isolated, never fully alone. So I believe I speak for all of us when I say, If you ever pass Saint Angel way and think of visiting, you'd be more than welcome.

# # #

THE CHARACTERS

Al Sharpe: **The novel's protagonist and co-narrator, "Master Inventor," DGLA member and anti-development activist, Finley's dad**

Saint Angel: **Common name for the town and valley of Santa Rosa de Los Angeles, the novel's co-narrator**

Finley Sharpe: Al's daughter, high school student, anti-development activist

Sondra: Sociology professor, Al's former wife & Finley's mom (deceased)

Charlie: Sondra's lover (deceased)

Mona Sahlstrom: Al Sharpe's girlfriend, loan officer at Saint Angel Federal Bank, DGLA member & anti-development activist

Matt Littlefeather: Soboba Indian native son, casino bouncer, DGLA member & anti-development activist

Sage Littlefeather: Soboba Indian native son on tribal council, DGLA member & anti-development activist, Wynona's husband

Wynona Littlefeather: Soboba Indian anti-development activist & Sage's wife

Sam Jenson: Desert rat & survivalist, cranky DGLA member & the inspiration for "Sam's Coalition"

Rob Thompson: Carpenter & angry Jesus freak, DGLA member & anti-development activist, Daphne's husband

Daphne Thompson: Schoolteacher, DGLA member & anti-development activist, Rob's wife

Tinkerspoon: Computer hacker & descendent of early Mexican-American settlers, DGLA member & anti-development activist (a,k.a. Andy Sanchez)

Little Lester: Vietnam Vet, publisher of *Saint Angel's Dirty Underwear*, anti-development activist

Ches Noonan: Wealthy real estate developer, pro-development President of the Desert Green Lawn Association, Penny's husband

Penny Noonan: Ches's wife, Al's lover, & novel's sexiest character, pro-development member of the DGLA

Cal Hale: Owner of Cal Hale Construction Co. & drought denier, pro-development member of the DGLA, Winky's husband

Winky Hale: Dedicated collector & Silk Set member of the DGLA, Cal's wife

Silk Set Faction of the Desert Green Lawn Association (DGLA):

John Sylvester: SAVWA's attorney, Imogene's husband
Imogene Sylvester: John's wife
Mr. Philadelphia: A banker & SAVWA board member, Mrs. P's husband
Mrs. Philadelphia: Mr. P's wife
Mrs. Philadelphia's small-headed friend
Mrs. Houston: Child advocate, Jake Houston's wife
Jake Houston: Pro-development county planning commissioner

Esther Johnson: Nurse at Saint Angel General Hospital, neutral member of the DGLA

Clover Abernathy: Neutral member of the DGLA

Pablo Ortiz: Ches & Penny Noonan's gardener

Angie Beach: Owner of much of the original *Rancho La Cienega* Spanish Land Grant, Tinkerspoon's girlfriend

Charlie Haynes: Saint Angel Chief of Police

Harvey Suarez: Saint Angel cop

Tweedledee Twins: Saint Angel cops

Dan Trinkley: Cal Hale Construction's head surveyor (a.k.a. Tripod Trinkley, Trinkling Dan The Boss's Man)

Mike & Melie: Early occupants of Sam City (a.k.a. M&M)

Lindy: Claims to be Finley's mother

Pete: Lindy's boyfriend (a.k.a. Popeye)

Tahquitz: Demon living in a cave in the San Jacinto Mountains who eats men's souls in Soboba Indian mythology (a.k.a. Takeetz)

MINOR CHARACTERS:

Timothy Leary O'toole: Leader of the Devastation Acres community in Purgatory

RJH (Richard John Henry): Merchant & Mona Sahlstrom's occasional lover

Tom Hartley: Saint Angel Valley Water Authority

	Water-master
Tom Hernshaw:	County supervisor and ally of Ches Noonan & other developers
Sonny:	Skinniest old man in California
Jack Crispley:	Ches Noonan's construction foreman, Meg's husband
Meg Crispley:	Jack's wife
Loretta Sims:	Owner of a lesbian dude ranch
Father Flannagan:	Catholic priest
Grandfather Lubo:	Littlefeather brothers' grandfather, expert on native customs
Leon DeValoir:	Ches Noonan's lawyer
Lon Studenmire:	Well driller
Symphony Thomas:	Agent at Saint Angel Realty
Colin Allsport:	Al Sharpe's lawyer
John Hobkins:	Loan officer at Western Enterprise Bank
J.Q. Dusquinex:	Realtor from Baton Rouge, Louisiana
Angie:	Mail carrier
Geronimo Ortiz:	Native-American hunting guide & tracker
John Anderson:	Heavy-equipment operator
DayGlo:	One of the "underground trolls" who helps Al escape

DGLA: **Desert Green Lawn Association:** a social & community- improvement club in Saint Angel

SALCO: **Saint Angel Land Company**, Ches Noonan's investment company

SAVWA: **Saint Angel Valley Water Authority**

TexHome: Large international real-estate developer

Dirt Faction: Anti-development members of the DGLA who form Sam's Coalition & The Realty Revenge (a.k.a. Dirtbaggers, Dirtbag Crew)

Silk Set: Wealthy, pro-development members of the DGLA

Second Chance Acres: Al and Finley Sharpe's beloved canyon home in Saint Angel Valley

Rancho La Cienega   Large early Spanish land grant in Saint Angel
***del Diablo*:**   Valley

Sam City: Property that Al Sharpe buys to save from development & occupies with squatters

OTHER
ANAPHORA LITERARY
PRESS TITLES

PLJ: Interviews with Gene Ambaum and Corban Addison: VII:3, Fall 2015
Editor: Anna Faktorovich

Architecture of Being
By: Bruce Colbert

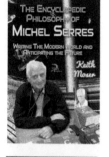

The Encyclopedic Philosophy of Michel Serres
By: Keith Moser

Forever Gentleman
By: Roland Colton

Janet Yellen
By: Marie Bussing-Burks

Diseases, Disorders, and Diagnoses of Historical Individuals
By: William J. Maloney

Armageddon at Maidan
By: Vasyl Baziv

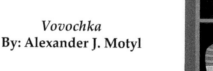

Vovochka
By: Alexander J. Motyl

CPSIA information can be obtained
at www.ICGtesting.com
Printed in the USA
FSHW012030051218
54278FS

9 781681 143200